QUENNELL HOUSE

The Cousins – Part 3

by

Elizabeth Riding

Text copyright © 2016 Susan Elizabeth Mayer

All rights reserved

ISBN: 978-1539133179

This is a work of fiction. Names, characters, businesses, places, events and incidents are either a product of the author's imagination or used in a fictitious manner. Any resemblance to actual persons, living or dead, is purely coincidental.

Printed by Create Space, an Amazon.com company

Contents

List of characters   iv
Preface   v

PART I: THE SWING RIOTS

Chapter 1   November - December 1830   *7*
Chapter 2   The new Earl of Morna   *15*
Chapter 3   The Wests   *27*
Chapter 4   Morna is introduced to Larkhill   *35*
Chapter 5   The Conversazione   *61*
Chapter 6   Jacob causes trouble   *75*
Chapter 7   Escape!   *84*
Chapter 8   Sebastian   *100*
Chapter 9   Christmas at Larkhill Manor   *109*
Chapter 10   Boxing Day and beyond   *120*

PART II: THE MURDER

Chapter 11   New Year 1831   *132*
Chapter 12   The late Mr Horace West   *146*
Chapter 13   The Inquest   *159*
Chapter 14   The Funeral   *169*
Chapter 15   Rupert in confusion   *182*

PART III: RESOLUTION

Chapter 16   Rumours   *192*
Chapter 17   Good Deeds   *203*
Chapter 18   Another attack   *215*
Chapter 19   Alibis   *227*
Chapter 20   Explanations   *244*
Chapter 21   Denouement   *252*

Epilogue   *267*

Characters

The Hon. Rupert Darville, aged 40, of Quennell House
Harriet Darville, his wife, aged 31, of Larkhill Manor
Henry, aged 8, and Lizzie, aged 6, the Darvilles' children
Young Clem, Rupert Darville's ward, aged 14
Ralph Darville, the 5th Earl of Morna, aged 50
Sophia and Rosa, twin daughters aged 9, of the deceased 4th Earl of Morna
Sebastian Romero, aged 22, the 5th earl's friend and secretary

Horace West of Bourne Park
Euphemia West, his laudanum-addicted wife
Frank West, their dissolute son
Letitia (Letty) Learoyd, their daughter
Archdeacon Learoyd, their son-in-law

William McAllister, K.C., Harriet's 'cousin'

Sir Charles & Lady Durrington, friends of the Darvilles
George Durrington, their son, a magistrate
Juliana, George's wife
Will and Catherine Hinton, friends of the Darvilles
Colonel and Mrs Talbot, friends of the Darvilles
Sir Archibald Walcot, coroner for the county

Dr Makepeace and his wife
Reverend Butterworth, Rector of Larkhill
Bernard Butterworth, his son, Rupert Darville's secretary
Lydia Butterworth, the Rector's schoolteacher daughter
Miss Humble, Harriet Darville's former governess
Mr Brownrigg, the Darvilles' land agent
Jacob Ombay, aged 23, Rupert Darville's native valet
Mrs O'Leary, nursemaid to Sophia and Rosa
Delilah, Horace West's former slave and paramour
Jem Davies, the Darvilles' coachman
The Trottmans, tenants of Larkhill Manor's Home Farm
The Haycocks, a farm labourer's family

Preface

Quennell House, the third book of *The Cousins* opens in November 1830. Since July, England had been terrorised by an agricultural uprising, known as the Swing riots, that raged across the southern counties. Farm labourers rioted for a better minimum daily wage. Tenant farmers claimed they could not afford any increase because of the high rents charged by their landlords plus the drain of paying tithes to the clergy and high local taxes. The result was an outbreak of rick burning, arson, machine-wrecking and general criminal behaviour. Mobs roamed the lanes, sent threatening letters to magistrates, clergy and landowners and demanded a hearing of their grievances. Two bad harvests, widespread unemployment and village radicals prompted local panic and a national political crisis. Although the rioting would move on to Dorset and the eastern counties by the end of December, the inhabitants of Larkhill were not to know this.

Against this background I have written a domestic story and a mysterious murder. The tone of the book is slightly darker than the previous two. Rupert must come to terms with his brother's lifestyle and emerge from his ivory tower to protect his family. Harriet struggles to retain her independence within the marriage. I have tried to give the Darvilles the values and attitudes of their time and class; they are traditional paternalistic landed gentry. I have made no attempt to make them politically correct in twenty-first century terms.

I have altered dates only once; the craze of 'animal magnetism' did not reach England until about 1840 but all aspects of mesmerism swept through society like wildfire when it arrived. I have no idea where Mrs West found Dr Mazzotta.

Most of the information regarding the Swing riots came from *Captain Swing* by E.J.Hobsbawm and George Rudé (Lawrence and Wishart, 1969) and from *Swing Unmasked: the agricultural riots of 1830 to 1832 and their wider implications*, edited by Michael Holland (FACHRS publications, 2005). I would like to thank Muriel Goddard for her image of 'the beautiful boy' and I am grateful to Robin Clegg for his word on astronomy. As ever, all mistakes are my own.

November 2016   Elizabeth Riding

Other books by this author:
Larkhill Manor, part 1 of The Cousins
Hibiscus Lodge, part 2 of The Cousins
are available on Amazon Kindle or CreateSpace

Part 4 of The Cousins – *'Esmé McAllister'* is in preparation, set in 1851 against the backdrop of the Great Exhibition

PART I: THE SWING RIOTS

Chapter 1   November - December 1830

'Mistress, mistress! Wake up, do! For the Lord's sake! There's a fire!'

Harriet was already half awake; she always slept lightly when Rupert was away. Her maid's flurried entry and the rattle of the bed curtains woke her completely.

'A fire? Where?' She struggled out of bed. 'Are the children safe?'

'It looks to be at Home Farm, madam, so Mr Dunch says.'

Through the diamond panes of the window Harriet saw a flicker of flame where none should be. Clouds of dark smoke mingled with the grey dawn making her stomach shrink in fear; the rioters had come to Larkhill. At that moment someone banged frantically on the front door of the manor and then swung on the clanging bell.

'Jenny, help me dress at once. Find something warm and serviceable. I must go down there.'

'Oh, no, ma'am; 'tis too dangerous. You don't want to be going near that mob; they be murdering devils.' Harriet ignored her young maid and hurried into her clothes.

Since July, England had been gripped by an agricultural uprising which had swept through the southern counties like a contagion. The whole country was in a panic. Farm labourers rioted for a better minimum daily wage but the tenant farmers claimed they could not afford to make any increase because of the high rents charged by their landlords, the drain of paying tithes to the clergy and high local taxes. The result was that Wiltshire had been terrorised for most of November by rick-burning, machine wrecking and roaming mobs demanding money with menaces.

By the time Harriet, dressed in her winter cloak and bonnet, reached the vestibule, Dunch had ascertained from young Mattie Trottman that a gang of about fifty men had set light to a hay rick and besieged the Home Farm. Mattie's elder brothers were holding them off with a fowling piece. The child was white-faced and spent with running.

'Thank goodness all the wheat is in the barns. Did your father set guards?'

'Only me, mum. 'E said no guard could hold off they gangs. I was only a lookout, to warn like.'

'They are after the threshing machine of course.'

'Yes'm but they didn't take no mind when Michael told 'em it was yourn.'

'Then I had better come and protect my property. Dunch, rouse Jem from the gatehouse; you may send him for Mr West, he's the nearest magistrate.' She looked around. 'Mattie, stay here. Cook will give you breakfast. I shall collect Mr Brownrigg on the way; he will be my escort. I'll need a lantern and the gig.'

'Will you take the master's new rifle, madam?' asked Dunch very much alarmed but not surprised by his mistress's actions.

Harriet hesitated. 'I should but Mr Darville always locks the gun cupboard. Beside I have no idea how to use it. I would not want to make the situation worse.'

Twenty minutes later Harriet drove down the lane towards Home Farm, her land agent by her side. The acrid smell of smoke from the burning hay clogged her nostrils before she saw the blaze of the rick in a nearby field. Rough men gathered round the fire for warmth, jugs of cider in their hands. Silhouetted figures capered against the yellow flames and rising sun like a scene from Dante's Inferno. Harriet loudly bemoaned the loss of good winter fodder. From a distance she could hear the shouts of the rest of the mob in the yard.

'They're drunk,' said Brownrigg. 'You really should not approach them, ma'am. Mr Darville would see me hang if any harm came to you.'

'Mr Darville is in Ireland and I know you have a pistol in your pocket, but I would much prefer if you did not use it. There is nothing we can do about the hay rick but I must help the Trottmans.'

As the gig clattered to a halt at the back of the crowd, several men turned round. In the morning half-light with their faces blackened or covered up they were terrifying. Many wielded pitchforks, flails or cudgels. Too many men carried flaming torches. Some were making a concerted effort to break into the barn where the threshing machine was kept. Harriet had a moment's panic and Brownrigg put his hand to his coat.

Over the heads of the crowd Harriet could see the Trottman brothers, Michael grasping an ancient flintlock and Mark with blood trickling from his head. Two farm servants were keeping well back. Upstairs, Old Abel Trottman hung out of the bedroom window cursing the mob to kingdom come. The women huddled in another bedroom, white faces pressed against the glass.

''Tis 'er, 'Tis 'er!' someone yelled, waving a fist. ''Tis Mrs Darville. Make 'er lower the rents so's we don't starve!' The crowd turned to mill around the gig. Gnarled hands grasped the bridle of the nervous horse. Brownrigg drew his pistol from his coat causing several of the rioters to drop back into the shadows and make for home.

'Mr Brownrigg, would you stand next to me and hold the lantern high, so they can all see me.'

'Is this wise ma'am?' whispered Brownrigg.

'I must say something; I cannot sit here and do nothing.'

'Quiet!' barked the land agent. 'Silence, Mrs Darville wishes to address you.'

Harriet stood up and smiled down into the upturned hostile faces. Her knees felt like blancmange. She was inspired to remove her bonnet so that no shadows obscured her face. This feminine gesture, something they had seen their own wives do a thousand times, disarmed the mob into attention.

Harriet licked her dry lips and began: 'You all know me, at least those from this parish do. The rest of you are strangers who have no business in Larkhill,' she called out.

'It is the business of every man to resist starvation and penury! Remember what the French have done! We've got our rights!'

'Is that you Mr Sharpe? Forgive me, I did not recognise you under your mask. I'm surprised you can find time away from your last; you are usually so busy before Christmas making all those dancing pumps. Have you shut your shop today? Can you afford to do so? If you think your rent is too high, then I advise you to approach Lord Lydiard. He is your landlord, not I. And I cannot think why you need to be here.'

Sharpe was Larkhill's cobbler, a known Ranter and suspected of inflaming the labourers with radical pamphlets. His literacy drew followers to his revolutionary ideas but he was not popular. The crowd sniggered and looked askance at the shoemaker. Harriet continued serenely, hoping her voice did not tremble.

'Those cottagers on my land know that the rent is fair and that Mr Darville and I are generous landlords. However, I concede that the failure of the harvest again has brought hardship this winter. I understand that the parish Poor Relief is not entirely adequate-'

'What about the tithes?' someone shouted. 'Trottman says he has to give a tenth of what he grows to parson so he can't afford to pay us no more wages.'

'I have no control over the Rector's tithes.'

'You 'usband has,' said a voice well-oiled with beer. Joe Ponting, she thought.

'I regret I have no control over my husband.'

The crowd laughed and Harriet allowed herself to relax a little but she knew they were a long way from safety. If her efforts failed, more blood would be shed and the farm and its outbuildings fired.

'If I promise that you'll be paid two shillings a day from now on, will you disperse like good people?' In the flickering torchlight, she saw the Trottman brothers exchange glances.

'But ma'am, we ain't got the money,' Michael Trottman loudly protested over the heads of the rioters. The crowd turned menacingly back to the young farmer.

'The estate will cover the difference in the wages-.'

'Mrs Darville! I beg you,' hissed Browrigg. 'The estate cannot sustain such a drain on its income.'

'We will decide how it will be managed later, Mr Brownrigg.' She turned a smiling face to the crowd. 'You have my word it will be done.'

'What about them as 'as no work? Yon damned machine of the devil 'as robbed us all of our livins.' She thought she recognised the protester as one of Home Farm's casual shepherds.

'Is that Nathaniel Haycock? I trust your wife is recovered from her fever? Should you not be with her?'

'Yes'm. She do bravely now,' he said before thinking. 'But I still ain't got no bread for my little'uns.'

The crowd grew truculent again and turned towards the barns. By now three men had managed to lever a door open with crowbars. it would only take a moment for a sledgehammer to crash into the machinery and destroy it forever. Harriet's palms began to sweat and Brownrigg cocked his pistol.

'If you stop those men,' she called clearly, 'then I promise I will have the thresher dismantled. If it is damaged in any way, when the yeomanry arrive – and I have sent for them – then I will name the ringleaders.'

At this news several more men slunk off into the pale dawn. A babble broke out among the dozen or so rioters who were left.

'How do we know we can trust her? She be rollin' in luxury and wealth while we live like 'ogs!'

'How dare you speak of a lady in that manner!' protested Brownrigg to the anonymous voice.

'If any of you remember my uncle, Sir John Larkhill, and his son Clement who died a hero at Waterloo, then I swear by their memory that the thresher will be dismantled and I will not lay information against you.'

The men murmured among themselves until Harriet put things plainly: 'That means that each of the Darville farms will be forced to employ many more men to thresh by hand. The old ways will be restored.'

'Aye, aye! The old ways is best! We got our ancient rights! Let's take un apart.' A general shout of agreement greeted this pronouncement.

'Ere John Tongs, you got the tools,' called a labourer in a smock frock. 'Get 'im took down before the soljers come!'

A mass movement towards the barn was followed by the Trottmans and the gig. Both doors were flung wide so all could see the sloping wooden frame with its iron cogs and wheels. It was a modest construction which took four labourers to operate but it threshed the corn a dozen times faster than by hand.

Larkhill's blacksmith knew that eventually Mrs Darville would need him to reassemble her thresher. With a guilty look and grunt of apology he unscrewed the riddle and sieves until the machine lay in pieces like a jigsaw. 'I'll have to break the frame, Mrs Darville, unless you want to wait for a carpenter.'

'No, break it if you must,' said Harriet stoically. She had hoped the thresher could be easily reassembled. She could not claim the insurance on her property after her actions. The blacksmith began to lever out the nails from the beams, trying not to splinter the wood.

'I still say we burn it!' cried one recalcitrant worker. 'Who's to say she won't put it together again as soon as we've gone?' Murmurs of agreement grew louder.

'I would say that's the least of your worries,' announced Brownrigg loudly. 'Mr West, the magistrate, will have sent for the yeomanry who must be almost at Larkhill by now. You've got what you came for, now be off with you!' The land agent thought this shameful situation had gone on quite long enough.

'Go home to your wives and families, and be thankful you are not on the way to the Assizes,' encouraged Harriet.

The men slouched reluctantly out of the barn under the Trottmans' wrathful gaze. Harriet momentarily gripped Brownrigg's arm for support. 'Forgive me, for a moment I thought we were in desperate trouble there,' she said breathing hard.

'I admire your courage Mrs Darville, though what Mr Darville will say when he returns-'

'I beg you will tell him nothing, Mr Brownrigg. I will explain everything that is necessary when the time is suitable. He should not be worried with business at a time of family bereavement.'

'Very well, ma'am,' replied Browrigg, not the least bit satisfied. 'Will you have a word with Mr Trottman?'

For the next hour the Trottmans re-lived the shocking events of the dawn. Mr Brownrigg's son, now his assistant, appeared. The men discussed with polite uncertainty the wisdom of Mrs Darville's actions. The Trottmans demanded repeated assurances from Harriet which she gave.

Brownrigg looked on with pursed lips. Old Abel was alternatively indignant and then jubilant; he was astute enough not to refuse his landlord's offer of supplementing the wages of his workers. The farm servants beat out the last of the flames in the smouldering hay rick and rounded up the comatose drunks to await the soldiers. Jem arrived to say the yeomanry was on its way, and to take Mrs Darville home. She insisted on staying to speak to the captain of the troop.

It was midmorning before the Salisbury regiment clopped along the lane. They dismounted and were welcomed at the farm house. As ever, they were too late, but the Trottmans had no hesitation in producing the incendiaries and naming those whom they had recognised. Mark Trottman admitted that in the dark and the mêlée in the yard, he could not identify who had thrown a rock at him, but Horace West had been thorough in drawing up a warrant to cover riotous assembly as well as arson.

When it came to the matter of the threshing machine, Harriet was forced to admit that she had ordered the men to take it apart and that she would be bringing no charges. She ignored the captain's pleas to reconsider. After an exasperated shake of the head he wasted no more time on a foolish woman; he was anxious to deposit his prisoners in various lock-ups. Her husband would doubtless take the matter more seriously when he came home and lay charges against the Swing rioters.

****

A few weeks later, Horace West sat in the study of Bourne Park and stared out of the window towards the river. The southern elevation of his house gave on to an ornate parterre, singularly colourless at this season. Bourne Park was a gentlemen's residence of the William and Mary period: solid, square, red-bricked with seven bays and a hipped roof. There was something of the Dutch about it. Despite the tall and spacious rooms the winter gloom was exacerbated by the ebony furniture of the study.

A path to the boat house ran under the French window. Beyond that came the ha-ha and a rough field dotted with piles of winter fodder for the park deer; the whole sloped down to the river Bourne.

Mr West belched, kneaded his stomach and discovered another reason to feel hard done by. Euphemia, for all her delicate constitution, never kept a cook who understood his digestion and Christmas would soon be upon them with all its suet puddings and rich sauces. He took another sip of sweet sherry.

He hated Christmas and knew he would particularly hate this one; there were bound to be scenes. His wife had insisted on inviting the neighbourhood to some soirée to be entertained by a mountebank.

Letty and that prosy-faced husband of hers would come. Without grandchildren there would not even be the pretence of jollity, a mixed blessing. Frank would be bound to make an appearance to keep his mother happy and to touch him for more money. Everyone took advantage of him. Did they not know how his shares had suffered in the crash of '25? But it was something he had not noised abroad. He had been quietly selling his investments for a while now.

The dull sky and monochrome landscape made him shiver. He hated the cold, he hated the drabness of England in winter; he would give his soul to be back in Jamaica. He should never have left. He glanced at the luminous landscape above the fireplace and yearned to be in Westerholm. Even his effort to bring a little piece of Jamaica back with him from his last visit had failed; Delilah was sullen and unresponsive, something he hoped she would overcome in time. He was becoming increasingly impatient with her the more she rejected him. He had chosen her because she was young and clean and in a moment of madness he had brought her to England as a servant. If he had known Euphemia would kick-up such a fuss he would have never have installed Delilah in the house.

Mr West had made his fortune in the West Indies. The threat of the abolition of slavery in British colonies had come at the worst possible time for him. Over-production of rum and sugar had led to a fall in prices and now the abolition movement was gaining strength. He resented the proposed legislation that would ruin many planters including himself. His heart had gone out of the business and because he did not trust any government to provide adequate compensation for the enforced freedom of his slaves, he considered selling Westerholm at a loss. But now he found he needed the little profits he made from his cane fields and molasses factory to sweeten Lord Lydiard, the patron of Larkhill's electors.

He badly wanted the nomination for the vacant parliamentary seat of Larkhill in order to enhance his reputation in the county. It was not enough to be a magistrate with that fool George Durrington undermining every decision he made on the bench. He wanted something more: status, respect, an entrée into the corridors of power and inside access to the financial markets. His most recent litigation had almost crippled him. He was afraid the seat may be offered to Rupert Darville whom he secretly envied and feared. And now there was this letter threatening his life. He read it again.

"Sir, Your name is down amongst the Black Hearts in the Black Book and this is to advise you and the like of you who are Parsons and Justices to make your Wills. You have been the Blackguard enemies of the People on all occasions. Ye have not done as ye aught. Captain Swing"

He knew he was not the only magistrate to have received a "Captain Swing" letter. The small farm of one of his own tenants had been attacked and now that interferring Mrs Darville had given way to the mob and dismantled her thresher. That's what comes of allowing women to run things, though Darville himself could not be trusted to come down heavily on the rioters. All West could do was issue an arrest warrant and send the insurgents to Salisbury to await the January Assizes. He wished magistrates could try capital crimes; he would see the rogues turned off with no compunction.

West was not a physical coward and would face down any mob of cottagers who challenged him but to receive a death threat on paper was something more unsettling. The style was of a literate man, not a peasant labourer and Larkhill had its share of radical shopkeepers and dissenting sects. He was conscious of the hostility directed at him whenever he rode into the town. He resolved to let his bull-mastiff roam the gardens at night to see off any intruders.

Nevertheless he wished he could get away. He wanted to be lying in a hammock on his veranda at Westerholm. He wanted the scent of bougainvillea to fill the air, a rum and lime at his elbow, and to watch the iridescent humming birds drink from flame-coloured hibiscus. Instead he was threatened by common labourers, saddled with an ailing wife who would not die, an unresponsive mistress, a ninny for a daughter and a libertine for a son. He could not bring himself to fix an epithet to his son-in-law.

He would take the next ship from Bristol bound for the West Indies except that no ship would sail at this season. Yet the dream took root and by the end of the hour Horace West had decided that if Lord Lydiard were not to give him the parliamentary nomination he would return to Kingston as soon as he could book passage. Certain arrangements would have to be put in hand; he would visit lawyer Askew and ask him to draw up the necessary papers. If Westerholm failed him, old friends in the colony would offer him an opening or he could always sell his experience to the American cotton planters of the southern states.

Now that his mind was made up he did not need to be hasty. He took another mouthful of sweet sherry. He felt better and would wait to see what the next week or two would bring. But in his heart he knew he wanted to leave all this behind.

He had his wish; within the month he was dead.

Chapter 2 The new Earl of Morna

The grey stones of the manor glowed with light, warmth and hospitality. Every hearth crackled with coal, beds were aired and food simmered in the kitchen. The old house bustled with extra servants hired from Larkhill. This time Harriet was well prepared.

For all his feigned indifference to the arrival of guests, Young Clement McAllister Larkhill hung out of an upstairs casement peering through the winter dusk in hopes of hearing the rumble of carriages. Just as the first flakes of snow drifted from the pewter sky, Young Clem gave a shout of warning and scampered down the Grand Staircase to greet his guardian and their visitors. Two hired coaches loaded with huddled figures and assorted boxes rolled up the drive to the manor, followed by a lumbering baggage wagon driven by the Larkhill carrier.

Dunch flung the oak wide. The horses steamed and stamped on the gravel. Grooms and servants scurried forward but not before Mr Rupert Darville had stiffly descended and caught his wife in a surprisingly enthusiastic embrace.

'By God, I'm glad to be home. Is everything well with you and the children?'

'Perfectly.' She smiled up into his almond eyes, which were now almost slits of exhaustion. 'Clem is home. I begged a few days off school for him for your return. I received your letter and the children are agog to see their new cousins. You met no trouble on the road?' The Swing riots of the previous months were uppermost in everyone's mind. Only a week before, a coach had been held up on the Salisbury road and its occupants robbed by starving labourers.

'No, none. I was more concerned for you.'

A red setter, a much-crossed lurcher and a black pointer with tongues lolling tore round the corner of the house at the sound of their master's voice. Their jubilance was overwhelming. Rupert rubbed their ears absently and pushed them away. 'Down Beauty, Peterkin. Hush, Lucky. Quiet! Yes, I'm back. Jem, shut these dogs to the stables. I presume you don't want them in the kitchen, Harriet, and our guests are not canine lovers.'

Rupert turned to assist his brother who was descending gingerly from the carriage. Lord Ralph Darville, the new Earl of Morna was fifty, tall, broad with a fleshy face and an air of attractive indolence. Harriet thought the fifth earl had a look of his uncle, Lord Patrick.

The cast of his cheekbones and a wisp of dark curls under his beaver proclaimed him a Darville. A fur collar pulled up against his face could not alleviate the blue tinge in his sensuous lips.

Harriet broke away from Rupert and stepped forward. 'Welcome to Larkhill Manor, my lord. You must be frozen from your journey. Won't you come inside directly? How delighted I am to meet you but, alas, under such unhappy circumstances.'

'My dear sister-in-law, let there be no ceremony, I insist.' He shook hands and smiled with such geniality that Harriet warmed to him at once. 'How glad I am to be here. What a magnificent old house. Such a journey we have had! Everything is so changed with mills and great machine-houses everywhere. I had also forgotten how cold England was. I knew there was a reason I had not graced its shores in twenty years.'

'Then I trust your visit with us will tempt you to venture home again more often. You must come and warm yourself by the fire. Your rooms are prepared for you. There are hot pigs in the beds.'

'What temptation,' he murmured.

She indicated the vestibule when out of the carriage stepped a young man who took Harriet's breath away. He was as beautiful as a Renaissance angel with bee-stung lips and lashes to hang pearls on. His chin was cleft and only the red tip of his perfectly straight nose dimmed his classical beauty.

'Allow me to introduce Sebastian Romero to you, my friend who has offered to accompany me as my secretary when in England,' said the earl. Despite his heavy coat, the young man exuded a faint scent of mimosa.

'How d'you do, ma'am?' the young god said above his muffler.

'You're an American!' said Harriet caught off guard. 'I beg your pardon. I thought you would be Italian with such a lovely name.' Rupert, as usual, had been less than explanatory in his letter.

'My father was Italian but my mother hails from New England.'

Harriet ushered her guests into the Great Hall. She beckoned Young Clem forward and introduced him. A footman offered glasses of warm brandy and water.

'Is this genuine?' asked the young man, released from his wrappings and staring up at the minstrels' gallery. 'It's like being in some old fairy castle.'

'Most certainly it is genuine,' Harriet laughed. 'Clement's ancestors built the house after the dissolution of the monasteries. He is the Young Squire here. Subsequent members of the Larkhill family have made various improvements over the years so I trust you will be comfortable while you are with us.'

Turkey carpets, a sofa and several wing chairs had been brought from Quennell House to make the Great Hall habitable. An intricately embroidered runner in jewel colours ran the length of the highly polished refectory table; a present from Elspeth McAllister. A cluster of oranges from Bristol glowed in a pewter bowl. The shutters were still open to let the last of the light in through the lancet casements and the hall was ablaze with candles.

'Do you have ghosts?' asked the young American. 'I'd surely love a ghost.'

'Sadly, no. But we do have priory ruins and an old fish pond which the children skate on when it is frozen. Do you skate, Mr Romero?'

'Sure do, but it's been a while since I've had the chance. We don't get much snow in Naples, do we – my lord?'

Harriet thought nothing of the secretary's hesitation; Ralph had inherited his brother Gerald's title only a few week earlier. 'If this cold weather continues then I'm certain the children will welcome your company on the ice.'

The earl looked on indulgently. 'You'll see many more fine houses while you're in England, Sebastian. There will be plenty of opportunities to enlarge your portfolio. Sebastian is a student of architecture,' he explained. 'We were introduced in Florence when he was studying there.'

Harriet smiled politely. 'When you are ready, my lord, my nephew will show you to your rooms and we trust you will join us in the green drawing room before dinner. However, if you would prefer to have a tray in your rooms after such an arduous journey then that can easily be arranged.' She hoped Clem had remembered to shut the upstairs window against the icy December air. Tongue-tied with sudden shyness, Clem led the gentlemen up the Grand Staircase, the young American marvelling vociferously at everything he saw. Harriet hurried outside to see what had become of her other guests.

Jacob was standing on the gravel amid an assortment of rugs, boxes and portmanteaux. He was now a stocky young man of twenty-three, dressed smartly and much admired by the maids but always holding himself aloof as Mr Darville's man. Dunch was directing the grooms and paying off the hired coach. Harriet saw Rupert standing by the second carriage, his hand firmly in the door.

'Come down, Mrs O'Leary, and bring your charges. We are home.' He wrenched open the door and a footman sprang forward to let down the steps.

Two little girls of about nine years of age were unceremoniously pushed out onto the gravel.

Rupert gave his hand to a bundle of worsteds and shawls that squeezed itself through the carriage door after them, to half fall, half bob in front of Harriet.

'Is it here we are at last, God save us? My ol' bones are shaken to smithereens. Tank the Lord we're safe. Ah, m'lady mam, how glad I am to have somewhere these poor orphaned angels can lay their weary heads and by the grace of God they'll always have me to take care of them.' A pair of sharp blue eyes darted about under a green satin bonnet decked with three bedraggled yellow feathers. The figure leaned precariously on a battered umbrella.

Harriet was amused at the appearance of this rotund body and outrageous hat. The straggling false curls at the front gave her the look of a wet Leicester sheep.

'You are the young ladies' nursemaid?'

'That I am, m'lady mam. Deidre O'Leary at your service.' The nursemaid bobbed again. 'I've had the care of the little angels since their sainted mother, God-rest-her-soul, was took from us.' Mrs O'Leary crossed herself. She reminded Harriet of wobbly toy.

Harriet bent down to the children. For twins, they were easily told apart. Sophia, the elder by a quarter of an hour, looked wooden. Rosa had a softer face but was equally as withdrawn. Both girls wore the shabbiest of clothes and threadbare cloaks, only their boots looked new. Their mousy brown hair hung lank over their thin shoulders.

'How do you do? I am your Aunt Harriet and we are so happy that you have come to live with us.' There was no response.

'Shame on you, Miss Sophia, Miss Rosa! Where is your manners?' scolded the nursemaid. 'Tank your aunt for her Christian charity.' The two little girls bobbed a curtsey but remained silent.

Harriet straightened up. 'Come inside and let Miss Humble take you to the nursery. Your cousins are wild to meet you. They're a little younger than you are. I'm sure your Uncle Rupert has told you all about them. Come along, Mrs O'Leary, before these children expire with cold.'

From behind the nursemaid a gentleman's gentleman climbed down with difficulty and accosted Harriet without hesitation. 'My master? Forgive me, Madame, but I must go to my master this instant.'

'You will find the earl in the Chinese bedroom,' said Harriet guessing this was Ralph's valet. 'One of the maids will direct you.'

'But I need his luggage, his trunks. Me'lor cannot appear in his travelling dress. He will need his liniment and a foot bath at once. You have the English mustard, yes?'

'You will have to wait until the carter unloads the waggon,' said Rupert tersely. 'Meanwhile I advise you to speak softly to the cook.' Rupert slipped an arm around his wife's waist and left Gaston fussing over his master's belongings with the carrier.

After seeing to her guests' needs, Harriet joined Rupert in his room.

'I'm sorry to impose the girls on you,' he said, peeling off his neck-cloth. 'We need not keep them long.'

'It is of no matter. We agreed this was the most likely outcome. You could not abandon them in Morna and the earl cannot have them in a bachelor household. They look poor little things, half starved. And who is the colourful Mrs O'Leary?'

'She was their wet nurse, who does herself well as far as I could tell. I suspect she drinks. I doubt if there ever was a Mr O'Leary. I could not shake her off and was glad enough to leave the children to her care on the journey. The girls were allowed to run wild after my mother died. Ralph and I discovered them playing barefoot around the stables. Gerald was fond enough of them and they of him, I believe, but no effort was made to give them any kind of decent upbringing or education.'

'And how long is the earl to stay with us?'

'I have no notion but he wants to do the Season and talks of going to London in the spring. Could you bear to have him for so long? I find him quite a pleasant fellow.'

'I'm sure he's delightful and this is just the opportunity for you to get to know your brother. Mr Romero will set hearts fluttering in the neighbourhood,' she added provocatively.

Rupert made no response.

'Ah, here is Jacob with your hot water,' Harriet smiled as the servant came in carrying a steaming can and towels. She exchanged a few friendly remarks with the young man whom the family considered a favourite. 'I will leave you to dress for dinner, Rupert, and I must change too, though I have not gone into blacks while you were away.'

'Neither has Ralph. Apart from ordering a mourning ring and three superbly cut dark coats when he was in Paris he refuses to be hypocritical about Gerald. I rather admire that. The secretary of course is a peacock.'

'Ah, so that is why the little girls were not in mourning.'

'I thought it best to leave all that sort of thing to you,' said Rupert with masculine indifference.

A knock distracted them and Young Clem's tow head came round the door.

'There you are Aunt Harriet. Forgive me for interrupting, sir, but Uncle Ralph sends his apologies and begs to be excused this evening. He would "like to take advantage or your kind offer and have dinner sent up to his room" – and for the secretary.'

'Uncle Ralph?' said Rupert in surprise.

'He said I may call him that. He said that if you were my uncle then he must be too. He's not stuffy at all, for an earl,' said Clem coming fully into the room.

'And you have met so many, have you not?'

'Well, no, but I thought he'd be quite top-lofty and he isn't at all. He has a yacht!'

'Such a valuable asset in the middle of Wiltshire,' said Rupert dryly, knowing how his ward's mind worked.

'Rupert, don't tease the boy. I suppose I must tell Dunch at once. At least we can have a quiet supper here together, my dear.' Harriet was not altogether displeased. Rupert in a weakened condition could so easily succumb to another bout of malaria; she welcomed the postponement of a formal evening until he was rested.

She looked up at Clem who was standing awkwardly inside the door. 'How disappointing for you Clem, to miss your first grown-up dinner. You were so looking forward to the occasion.' There was a flyaway coat with too many brass buttons waiting in the closet for its first wearing. 'Miss Humble is busy in the nursery-'

'You won't make me have dinner there, will you?' interrupted Clem, horrified at the thought of an evening with a parcel of children, fond though he was of his young cousins.

She thought for a moment for some way to compensate him. 'Why not act the host and invite Jacob to eat with you in your room. When your uncle dismisses him he may join you, that is, if you so wish it, Jacob.'

Jacob paused from tugging at his master's boots. 'Thank you, Mrs Darville, I would be most grateful, if Master Clem is agreeable.' His English was impeccable, thanks to Miss Humble, though he retained the speech rhythms of his native archipelago.

Clem grinned at his old playmate. 'By jingo, what a splendid idea. And may we have wine, and port afterwards?'

'One bottle of Rhenish,' said Rupert. 'And that is all.' The boots thudded to the carpet.

'And cigars?' asked Clem hopefully.

'Certainly not,' Harriet interposed. 'I do not allow smoking in the bedrooms, as you well know.'

Young Clem had the grace to grin. The previous summer there had been an unfortunate episode involving a stolen cigar and burnt sheets.

Harriet rose. 'The kitchen can prepare trays for us all, even if Cook does give warning tomorrow. Jacob can tell you all about Ireland and you can tell him all about school. Now I must inform Dunch and then go to the nursery to see how Miss Humble is managing.' She turned to her husband. 'I will return in an hour my dear and we can have that cosy talk together.'

****

The visitors slept late. Young Clem rode out early to exercise his palomino, leaving his aunt and uncle to a leisurely breakfast alone. Harriet hoped he would be safe, but did not want to frighten the boy with her anxieties. She trusted that his popularity in the district would protect him.

Nine years of marriage and motherhood had dealt kindly with Harriet. She was a little more womanly and at past thirty she had long considered herself to be a sensible matron. Her dark hair was parted in the middle and her beloved plaits were curved in front of her ears and drawn up into an elaborate knot at the back of her head. It was the fashion and she could not bear ringlets bouncing against the side of her face. Like all married women, Harriet wore a pretty lace cap at home even though Rupert hated to see her in one. The wide-shouldered gowns and huge top sleeves made her seem broader than she would like. In compensation she wore only one starched petticoat, chose gowns with low necks or adopted the modish wide lace collars she had seen when last in London. She refused to lower her hems to the floor saying she had no intention of trailing her skirts in the dust when she went about her daily business.

Rupert folded his newspaper. 'I will be very busy today my dear. Can you ensure I am not disturbed? I shall be in the library with Bernard.'

At forty, Rupert had fared as well as his wife; marriage to Harriet suited him. There were flecks of grey in the dark curls around his temples and when reading he resorted to spectacles but for a tall and studious man he carried himself well. These days he wore his hair swept back from his domed forehead and his sharp cheekbones and slanting eyes gave him an austere presence. Harriet wished he were a little heartier in health to inure himself against the ravages of the fevers that attacked him when he was low in spirits or exhausted. But, as Young Clem assured her, 'Uncle Rupert is wiry and very strong. Look how hard he rides with no fatigue at all.'

Harriet did not enquire how she was expected to entertain the earl and his friend when at the same time she had his nieces to settle in; she had long ago learnt that Rupert's work took precedence over domestic matters.

Harriet sorted her letters, rang for the cook to discuss the day's menus and made her way up to the nursery. She entered to be greeted by cries of delight from her children. Henry and Elizabeth looked up from the table where the four youngsters were tucking into hot porridge. The Darville children had their father's dark curls but little of his high cheek bones and only a slight cast of his almond eyes. Larkhill blood showed strongly in their small but solid frames.

'Mama! Mama! May we go out and play in the snow; it's all white everywhere!'

'Of course you may, Lizzie, in the afternoon but I fear there is only a sprinkling. You won't be able to make a snowman.'

'The snow will be gone by then! Oh Mama!'

Harriet relented. 'Then you may have a half day holiday; there is no harm if you miss lessons on the first day your cousins are here. I'm sure Miss Humble won't object.' Miss Humble, grey-haired now but still with a modicum of authority over her charges, looked relieved. She had already had difficulty with the two young Irish ladies.

Harriet looked smilingly at the little girls. 'Good morning, Sophia, Rosa. Did you sleep well?' They stared back at her with troubled eyes. Harriet had put the two children in the blue bedroom, with Mrs O'Leary on a truckle bed. She agreed with Rupert; it was too soon to separate them from their nurse, however undesirable the woman may be.

'Oh, indeed, indeed. Tis a sweet night's sleep we all had in that lovely room, so. And now this fine breakfast, with just a little piece of bacon and a few collops to keep a body going on this bitter mornin'.' Mrs O'Leary had risen from a chair by the nursery fire at Harriet's entrance and was bobbing like a fishing float. One of the housemaids, deputed to be nursery maid, rolled her eyes. Mrs O'Leary would make extra work and the Irish brats were savages.

Harriet's eyes rested on Sophia and Rosa who had said nothing but gripped their spoons with intensity and looked wary.

'I think it would be best if you came into Larkhill with me this morning. We'll buy you some pretty things to wear.' She smiled encouragingly. 'Would you like that?'

The girls stared at her as though she were speaking in a foreign language.

'Tank your aunt for her Christian kindness,' huffed Mrs O'Leary. 'An' to be sure 'tis no fault of mine, m'lady mam—

'Mrs O'Leary, please ensure that the young ladies are ready and bring them down to the vestibule in half an hour. You will accompany us.'

'Oh Mama, may I come?' wheedled six-year-old Lizzie. Shopping for finery was one of her greatest pleasures.

'No, Lizzie. You must stay and be introduced to your Uncle Ralph. Remember to curtsey and address him as "my lord", unless he tells you otherwise.'

'My father was a lord,' Sophia said fiercely. Everyone looked at her.

Harriet spoke: 'Indeed he was. And you and your sister are ladies. However, your papa's brother is now the Earl of Morna and we must pay him all due respect as you did to your papa.'

Rosa burst into tears and Harriet went to put an arm around her. 'There, there. Your papa loved you very much and is looking down from heaven to take care of you. He would want you to have some nice warm clothes and some pretty things, too.'

'I want to go home,' the child wailed, dropping salt tears into her porridge.

'This is your home now,' said Lizzie with the cruel accuracy of children.

Harriet attempted to soften her daughter's veracity. 'You have Lizzie and Henry to play with, and Mrs O'Leary is here. It will be Christmas soon and there'll be lots of good things to eat and presents.' She wiped Rosa's cheeks with the corner of the child's untouched napkin.

'I'll let you play with my doll's house,' said the soft-hearted Lizzie looking anxious. But Rosa was not so easily appeased and howled all the more.

'We don't want your old doll's house. We've got one of our own, in Ireland,' said Sophia. This was evidently news to Rosa who stopped sobbing in surprise and stared at her sister.

Mrs O'Leary lunged forward with a raised hand, 'May God forgive you, Miss Sophia for such lies and you with not a brass farden' to your name let alone a fine dolls-house like Miss Lizzie's here.'

Harriet quelled the nursemaid with a look. 'That will do, Mrs O'Leary. In this house, only Mr Darville or I will raise a hand to any of the children.'

'May we take the sledges out, Mama? I could show Sophia and Rosa Athena's temple,' asked Henry, bringing his own priorities to the fore.

'Perhaps this afternoon. We must find warm clothes for our guests first.'

Lizzie looked at her cousins' garments for the first time and wrinkled her nose. 'Did you come away in a hurry? Have you no other dresses? Where are your shoes?'

Harriet chose to ignore the bare feet kicking under the table.

'Miss Elizabeth, sit down and finish your breakfast. It is not ladylike to jump up from the table that way.' Miss Humble steered Lizzie back to her place. She knew Henry would not be disturbed from his porridge.

****

Rupert entered the library to find a rotund young man hovering by the desk with a sheaf of papers and a portfolio in his hand.

'Good morning Bernard. I'm pleased to see you so early this morning. You had no difficulties getting here?' Rupert took his seat and looked at the orderly piles of documents.

'No, sir, the snow has almost melted in Larkhill, though they predict more to come. I trust all the arrangements in Ireland were satisfactory, sir?'

Rupert allowed his young secretary a certain amount of licence. Bernard Butterworth was the youngest son of the Rector who had carved a niche as Rupert's quiet amanuensis and researcher. When Rupert did not need his services the secretary coached Clem when necessary and gave Henry and Lizzie extra tuition. His self-effacing habits and sombre brown garb made him almost invisible in the wood-panelled library amid the leather-bound volumes.

Rupert rifled among a pile of papers in front of him without looking up. 'Thank you, Bernard. We entombed the earl with his ancestors, now it's long live the earl. I see you have been your usual thorough self. Has anything urgent transpired while I've been away?'

'Nothing that cannot wait, sir. I gave any letters of condolence to Mrs Darville.'

'Very good. Have there been any more disturbances? We passed a set of ill-looking fellows on the road.'

'Another rick was burnt over at Cherton last week, the owner was forced to pay a sovereign to the mob to prevent further damage.' Bernard assumed that his employer knew all about the attack on Home Farm.

Rupert grunted. 'The yeomanry will have to be called out again if this continues. Have we heard from the Royal Society?'

'Oh, yes,' said Bernard leaning over to open another portfolio marked "Correspondence". 'Your article on the Transit of Venus will be published in the *Transactions* in January. The editor of the *Encyclopaedia Britannica* wishes you to write an article on "prisms" and you have been invited by the Bath Astronomical Society to give a lecture on the rings of Saturn.'

'Find my appointment book, would you; it seems we have a lot to do.'

****

Harriet bought sombre, ready-made clothes for her nieces from the new modiste that had opened in Larkhill. Sophia remained dumb and unhappy throughout the proceedings. Only Rosa started to respond shyly to Harriet's sartorial suggestions after a nervous glance at her sister.

'You will have to make some minor adjustments to the pantalettes, Mrs O'Leary, but you can do that in daylight when we get home.'

'Oh m'lady, mam. It's terrible I am with a needle. Cookin' an' cleanin' now that's my favourite ting. I could do it all day. But I could no more set a stitch than save me life.'

Which explained why the nursemaid was peacocking about in her late mistress's old finery, thought Harriet.

'I'm sure you will make an effort, Mrs O'Leary, or you and your charges will of necessity be confined to the blue bedroom for the remainder of your stay. We cannot have Lady Sophia and Lady Rosa appearing in such shabby garments as they have now.'

Sophia baulked at the milliners, refusing to try on the oversized and heavily decked wide-brimmed hats. 'I hate all of them,' Sophia muttered as Harriet tied a cream confection under her chin. 'I don't want a hat. The ribbon chokes me,' she said tearing at the huge bow.

The milliner cast a worried look at her client. 'I can assure you they are the latest styles, Mrs Darville, copied from the Paris modes.'

'I like the flowers,' whispered Rose looking longingly at a gorgeous creation of pink ribbons and roses high on a shelf.

'It is most unsuitable for winter wear-' began Miss Parsons, her professional integrity aroused.

'Then the roses you shall have,' said Harriet. 'And the smallest, plainest bonnet in stock for Lady Sophia, if you please.'

The girls' boots were barely worn which meant that only new cloth slippers would have to be purchased from the haberdasher. Harriet was relieved not to have to visit Mr Sharpe the cobbler after her confrontation with him during the riot. She would go to a tailor in Salisbury for the children's winter coats but Miss Williams could produce two simple but warm cloaks. An hour at the draper's and haberdasher's satisfied Harriet's needs and the younger Miss Williams, now alone in the world, was pathetically grateful for the commission. All the while Mrs O'Leary hassled her charges, demanding extravagant praise for their benefactress. Sophia glowered and ignored her. Rosa looked miserable. Harriet turned for home with relief. What should have been a pleasurable morning had proved to be a trial.

In the barouche, driven by a well-armed Jem, amid their parcels and boxes, Harriet said: 'If you cannot sew, can you knit, Mrs O'Leary?'

'Now there's a crying shame, m'lady mam. Me poor hands is crippled with the rheumatiz, so they are,' she said releasing her umbrella for a moment and displaying plump if grubby fingers in half-mittens. 'I couldn't hold a knitting needle to poke a pig wit.'

'I have no desire for you to poke a pig, but knit a beret for Lady Sophia.'

'Ah, an' t'would be the greatest wish of me heart to be able to do such a service for the sainted angel, but tis no use tryin'. For sure Miss Humble could whip one up in an instant.'

The woman would have to go, thought Harriet.

On her return, Harriet found Mr Romero reading in the oak parlour. This room was tacitly reserved for the ladies of the house but the young American did not seem at all out of place. He looked like a beautiful Meissen ornament with his crossed legs and languid white hands.

'Good morning, ma'am. I knew you would not mind my being here. I did not like to sit in the drawing room alone and the earl has not yet risen. This is such a pretty chamber, the oak panelling reminds me of the houses in New England.'

'Have you seen Mr Darville this morning?' she said sitting down with a smile.

'Your butler tells me he is in the library with his secretary and does not care to be disturbed.'

'My husband is a dedicated man of letters. I know he has a considerable amount of work to catch up on. You must not be offended if he seems a little abstracted at times.'

'No, ma'am. I understand he is a famous world traveller and astronomer of great renown. I would not intrude on such an important man.'

'He will be flattered you think so. But won't you tell me a little of yourself, Mr Romero?'

She took a good look at him in daylight. The classic features were topped by tousled brown waves. His boyish face was clean shaven and glowed with a light tan. Pale poets might be in vogue but Harriet approved of this sign of health. The soft collar and a floppy bow at his throat gave him a rakish air. She guessed that his coat, of the most gorgeous cerulean blue, was made in Italy. His yellow satin waistcoat, in the latest low cut, sported fantastically embroidered dragonflies. The trousers were of the modern style with a fly fastening. On his feet he wore square-toed shoes and on his little finger an onyx cameo signet ring. Again she smelt a heavy hint of mimosa.

'You are like a ray of summer, Mr Romero. Have you lived in Italy long?'

Chapter 3   The Wests

A tread on the stair. A board creaked. Delilah huddled under the bedclothes wishing she had not heard. It had been three days since his last visit and this was inevitable. She began to pray, clutching her talisman until her knuckles whitened. She heard the door latch being lifted. West had deliberately put her in an attic room which had once confined a poor lunatic, and kept the key with him. Although he did not lock her in every night, he felt more in control with the ability to do so.

She heard his slippered feet cross the room and squeezed her eyes tight shut, muttering in prayer. Horace West put his candle down on the night stand. There was a soft slither as he let his robe fall to the boards. Then West lowered himself slowly onto the bed. She felt the horsehair mattress sag under his weight and almost rolled against him.

'Wake up there, girl. Stop all that heathen muttering; Obeah don't work on Christians. I need you to keep me warm.' He pulled the blankets from her grasp and swung into the bed beside her. She could smell him; a sickly waft of sherry on his breath, a hint of frowsty sweat. He pulled her over to face him and heaved a hairy leg across hers. With his arm he trapped her into lying flat.

'There, you like this, don't you?' he said roaming his hands over her body, squeezing and pummelling.

Delilah knew she had to get this over with as soon as possible and made no struggle. His hands were tugging at her nightdress, pulling it above her waist and exploring her thighs. She flinched and tried in vain to relax. He raised himself to lick her face like a dog and moved down to suckle her breasts. Delilah stared into the darkness making no sound, her fingers gripping the rough sheet beneath her.

'Goddammit!' West broke off. 'It's like coupling with a cod fish! You could be a little nicer to me, if you know what's good for you. I would give anything for a little kindness.'

Delilah did not move. 'I am your slave, massa.'

He grunted and heaved himself on top of her. 'And don't you forget that. Open up now, my little black flower and you'll see how happy I'll make you.'

He was a brutal lover and she cried out in pain. When he had finished he rolled over and promptly fell sleep. Delilah fumbled for a rag under her pillow and put it between her legs. She dragged her nightdress around her, got out of bed and went to her wash stand.

She broke the ice in the jug and washed herself as best she could. The freezing water on her skin seemed like a penance; she hoped it was enough to purify her. The thought of falling pregnant was her constant terror; West would throw her out. How would she survive in this cold, hard country where everyone shunned her? And what if she caught the pox; she was permanently sore.

West woke, conscious of the empty space by his side. 'Come back to bed sweetheart; it's cold. What are you doing sitting by the window?'

'I have never seen dis white stuff falling from de sky before.' She stared through the black bars on to the whitening landscape.

'Snowing is it? You'll see a lot of that around here before the winter's out. Come back and keep me warm now.'

Delilah did as she was bid. West put his arm round her and they lay like spoons. He was soon snoring. Great tears slid down Delilah's cheeks and into the pillow. She was a branded slave and there was no escape in this hostile, freezing country; West had made sure to impress that upon her. Death was the only salvation..

****

It became accepted that the earl would not appear before ten in the morning but Young Clem had begged the loan of Harriet's mare so that Mr Romero could join him in his daily exercise of Minstrel Boy.

'By all means. Juno is eating her head off in the stables; it would do her good to have more exercise,' said his aunt. She was also pleased that he would have company in these precarious days. 'Do take the dogs with you, but don't let them stray near any sheep, or on anyone else's land.'

Clem said in a rush: 'Do you think I should give up my stock, Aunt? I would not want to be out of fashion.' It had taken him quite a half an hour to wind it into a grubby fall.

'And replace it with a bow like Mr Romero? I think while you are at home you may dress how you wish. Mr Romero wears formal dress at dinner which would be expected wherever you dine.'

Clem immediately started tugging at his stock and then asked. 'Do we have another cheval glass? Mr Romero does not like to always intrude on Uncle Ralph and use his.' Harriet had moved Rupert's full-length mirror into the Chinese bedroom for her guest; Rupert never used it.

Harriet was surprised. 'Apart from my own, there is no other in the house, but I believe one of the bedrooms in Quennell House has a long glass. Hobson can send it across if your uncle agrees.'

Over breakfast, Harriet told Rupert of the proposed arrangements.

'A cheval glass?' cried Rupert in astonishment. 'Did he ask you for it himself?'

'No, Clement did.'

Rupert did not look happy. 'And your Juno? I would not have you deprive yourself of your mount, my dear. I'm only surprised the young man is ready to untidy himself on a horse. Can he ride?'

'I assume so or he would not wish to accompany Clem. Juno is very docile; he will come to no harm if they keep to the lanes. Surely Mr Romero rode in Ireland?' asked Harriet, sensing her husband's displeasure.

'I have no idea. I did not notice. He spent all his time sketching the interior of the castle.'

As Harriet thought this was a reasonable pastime for a student of architecture she could surmise nothing further and returned to the perusal of her correspondence.

'We have a letter from Philippa. They are to spend Christmas with the Beaumonts in Paris. She hopes to see us in Town in the spring.'

'I have to give a paper at the Royal Society in April. You could come with me.'

'Good Heavens,' she exclaimed, picking up another note. 'Mrs West has invited us to a conversazione.'

'I cannot think what either of the Wests would have to say that would interest me,' replied Rupert not looking up from his own letter.

'Euphemia is very eloquent on paper. We are invited to meet a Dr Mazzotta, lately of Turin, proponent of the art of "animal magnetism".' Her voice gurgled with humour. 'Mrs West adds that "knowing Mr Darville to be a man of science and interested in magnetism, she begs leave to believe that the demonstration would be of interest to you and our noble guest." So it is not to be of the arts but of natural philosophy that we must converse.'

Rupert snorted and turned over his letter. Harriet looked at her husband with raised eyebrows. 'I wonder if she is to be the subject of the demonstration. Goodness knows she has tried every cure known to medical science and some which bordered on witchery. Poor woman, she is deluding herself; only release from Mr West will provide any cure.'

'Who else has been invited?'

Harriet re-examined the letter. 'She does not specify apart from Lord Lydiard who will be their guest for the night on his way down to Taunton.'

'West is angling for the Larkhill nomination in earnest, then. I heard as much from William when I was last in Town.'

'If you would refuse the nomination yourself, you cannot blame Mr West for trying to further his own interests.'

'He may be disappointed. I hear there's young relative just returned from Cape Town that Lydiard could put in place.'

Harriet dropped the Wests' invitation onto a pile of other correspondence knowing that to tackle Rupert on anything domestic before ten in the morning was a wasted effort. A conversazione would be the ideal diversion for the earl, she felt. The proprieties of mourning would not be breached by an afternoon's intelligent conversation on matters of the mind. Her own ever-lively curiosity was stirred.

An hour later the earl appeared pomaded, wide-shouldered and wasp-waisted on the Grand Staircase. He was clutching a cat.

'Oh dear, I see you have found one of the kitchen tabbies,' said Harriet crossing the vestibule. 'We do try to keep the animals under control but the children, especially Lizzie, will entice the cats up to the nursery. They make such good pretend babies, she says.' Harriet held out her arms for the creature.

Morna scratched the cat expertly behind its ear and was rewarded by a blissful purr. 'I think your daughter shows great insight. I regard cats as a delight and have my own spoilt creature at Villa Mimosa.'

'Then by all means adopt this one if you wish, my lord. I take it you are not fond of dogs?' She led the way into the Great Hall.

'Morna, I beg. May I usurp a brother's privilege and call you Harriet?'

'As you wish, my lord.'

He followed her into the Great Hall, still stroking the cat, waited for her to take a seat opposite the crackling fire and joined her, chatting amiably. 'We have an excess of dogs roaming round our village at home; wild and untrustworthy curs. One is forever on alert for rabies. I am sure your creatures are superbly trained and gentle as doves,' he said, eyeing the Irish setter dozing before the fire. Beauty raised her head from the Turkey carpet, stared at the cat on the earl's knees and went back to sleep unmoved by the encomium.

'I own a preference for the feline; so soothing to have a cat in one's lap, don't you agree?' said Morna.

'They certainly are warming on a winter's night. I have read that the Chinese use them as hot water bottles.'

'Better than pigs?' he asked with a twinkle.

She laughed. 'Notwithstanding pigs or cats, I trust you slept well last night despite the cold and that breakfast was to your liking?' She had scraped a film of frost from the inside of her window that morning.

'I slept like a top. My man brought me thin toast and conserve, made from your own apricots I'm told. They are such difficult things to grow, especially in this climate.'

Harriet made a mental note to check her supplies in the still room. Without the hot houses of Quennell House, the family was dependent on their own walled garden and one glass house to furnish the manor with any luxuries.

'My lord – Morna – I have been perplexing myself as to how we can entertain you and Mr Romero while you are with us.' Harriet believed in being direct. 'Christmas will naturally be a modest affair in the light of the family's bereavement: church, the waits and then our Christmas Day feast. I would not want to deprive the children entirely.'

'Bless my soul, of course not. Let's have a little jollity after all this gloom. Ireland was wretched: cold, wet, incomprehensible, a barbaric country.' He almost shuddered and the cat mewed in sympathy.

Harriet was taken aback but carried on. 'Certain of our neighbours have invited us to their houses. I know it is their dearest wish to meet you,' she said honestly. 'There will be few evening parties and no dancing of course, but afternoons of cards and conversation.'

The earl looked politely interested.

Harriet continued: 'If you care to come to church with me on Sunday you may meet some of them first and decide if they are to your liking. They are not fashionable people but have good hearts.'

'You attend church?' queried Ralph.

'Yes, I take the children regularly. Why do you look so surprised?'

'You say no evening prayers with your household and, according to Lord Patrick and my late mother and my own observation, Rupert has long been an atheist.'

'What my husband thinks does not necessarily always chime with my own understanding.'

'Nor mine,' said the earl casually. The cat jumped off his lap.

'Oh, I beg your pardon, my – I am all the while assuming you are of the Anglican faith. Do forgive me. If you prefer, you must take the chaise into Salisbury to the Roman Catholic church there. I daresay someone will give you directions.' Harriet felt flustered at her faux pas. 'I wonder if Mrs O'Leary will want to go?' she said looking at him, horrified.

'The woman's a pagan for all her protestations. However, I will take Sophia and Rosa to your Anglican service. I shall take possession of the Darville family pew; I have a whim to sit where my grandfather snored. Mrs O'Leary will have to attend to keep the girls in order. Now I take it that Sebastian has gone riding with that delightful nephew of ours? What a charming boy, don't you think? He has all the enthusiasm of youth and none of the self-consciousness, I find.'

Harriet would not have described Clem in such terms but said loyally: 'He has a kind heart and an honest disposition, and is very much the boy.'

'Yes, even at twenty-two Sebastian has a most child-like nature and something of the colonial outspokenness. He is quite refreshing, you must agree.'

****

Like Mr West, his son-in-law was not looking forward to Christmas. Archdeacon Learoyd had no problem with leaving his Winchester clergy unsupported at one of the Church's busiest seasons if it procured his own advancement. The Bishop of Winchester held a seat in the House of Lords; one did not argue with one's superior, especially if he were one of the Lords Spiritual. However, Dr Learoyd did not relish the thought of long diocesan meetings with the Bishop of Salisbury or the suggestion that he should offer to assist in some of the Advent services in Salisbury cathedral. To add to his irritation, in an unguarded moment he had acquiesced to his wife's desire to spend the holidays with his in-laws in Larkhill. He regretted his weakness but took comfort in the thought that his special ecclesiastical duties would give him a reason to escape Bourne Park.

It was always the same. His brute of a father-in-law sneered at him as though he were privy to some disreputable secret. Mrs West would be like a grey ghost flitting from room to room, plunging between euphoria and depression. And if his scapegrace brother-in-law were to appear there was certain to be yet another unseemly row over money. To cap it all, these visits brought out the worst in Letty. Instead of pouring oil on troubled waters, her incessant chatter, which the Archdeacon could usually block out, took on a more strident tone as she attempted to fill the silences in the house.

'Mama and Papa so look forward to our visits. It would be foolish not to take advantage of them being so close when you have to be in Salisbury just now, though why my lord bishop should want to send you away from Winchester at this time of year I cannot think. He has no concern for our safety but imagine how hurt Mama and Papa would be if we didn't come. No one should be by themselves at Christmas, not even Frank and he is sure to turn up like bad penny for he is forever in want of money though that of course is not why one should neglect one's filial duty even if the journey is so tiresome and uncomfortable--'

'You delude yourself, Letty. Your parents do not want us any more than we – or should I say "I" – wish to go. As for Francis, he would be happy to spend a week with anyone that would house him, provide him with liberal quantities of brandy and take him ratting. We would have been much better served accepting Dr Newman's invitation'.

Dr Learoyd was a small, neat man with a shock of pale, springy hair. He had a weakness for fobs and rings and knew his calves looked well in black silk stockings. Around his neck hung a particularly fine pectoral cross. In matters of personal appearance there were advantages in wearing clerical black though he luxuriated in the rich vestments of his office. The clergy under his pastoral care referred to him as "the Dandelion", not always with affection; several had cause to remember his bite. He pulled his shovel hat over his forehead and shut his ears against his wife's commentary on the snowy landscape beyond the carriage window. His attempt to rest his heels on the opposite seat was thwarted by the shortness of his legs.

'But it is such a long way to Oxford and in such weather as this, you could not have travelled back and forward to Salisbury and you know my lord bishop would not approve; Larkhill is quite far enough,' said his wife as the carriage jolted through another pot hole. 'And I am certain the carriage has something at fault; I have never been so shaken about. What if the carriage breaks down and we are trapped here for any mob of labourers to attack us.'

Letty Learoyd was a soft and vacant-looking woman, half afraid of her husband, but incapable of thinking beyond the rosy clichés of life unless in a stream of gentle complaint. His silence prompted her to speak again.

'How can you be so uncharitable when Mama is ill and Papa has promised us a generous legacy; it is the least we can do to give them our company. It's not as though we have had the blessing of offspring to brighten their old age, not that Papa was ever very fond of children, goodness knows he couldn't wait to pack Frank and I off to boarding school when they went to Jamaica, of course if Mama's babies had survived in Kingston just think how many brothers and sisters there would have been, so perhaps Frank and I are better off as we are.'

Learoyd spoke without opening his eyes. 'I would not depend on your father for any money. If he has promised us anything it is only to spite Frank. You know he alters his will as often as his mind.'

'But he always comes to his senses in the end, Mama says so. At this holy time of year I'm sure you would wish us to keep the fifth commandment in our hearts.'

He lifted the brim of his hat to stare at her. 'Thou Shalt Not Kill?'

'No, no, what a silly you are! "Honour thy Father and thy Mother"! Goodness, for a clergyman you are wonderfully ignorant.' She gave a nervous titter.

'I see you are quoting from Exodus not Deuteronomy.' His own preference was for the Catholic catechism. 'My mother and father are dead; I will leave you and Frank to do any "honouring" that may be required.' He pulled his hat back down over his eyes, folded his arms and let his chin sink onto his chest. He longed for a cigar.

Letty Learoyd shrank back. Dear Martin would never allow her to speak when she had so many interesting observations to impart. Her husband was a poor companion at the best of times and she had been looking forward to having him to herself on the journey. She studied his thin lips and shaven chin, the only visible features under the wide curly brim of his hat. She sighed, knowing that when he awoke at the next turnpike she should inform him of her mother's other guest, Dr Mazzotta.

She could not be certain how her husband would react and had been putting off the news ever since Mrs West's letter of invitation had arrived. Euphemia had begged her daughter to come and support her during the conversazione. It was to be in the way of a medical experimentation, her mother had written. Unfortunately, Dr Mazzotta insisted on having an audience and Mrs West could not rely on the attendance of her neighbours. When Euphemia had explained her son-in-law's High Church Anglicanism to Dr Mazzotta, the Italian "magnetiser" had calmed her with the assurance that Roman Catholics believed in miracles and matters of faith and were not the High Anglicans almost the same?

Chapter 4   Morna is introduced to Larkhill

At the same time that the Learoyds were approaching Bourne Park, Rupert and the Earl of Morna, well wrapped up in greatcoats and mufflers, were slowly riding the mile and a quarter from Larkhill Manor to Quennell House. Their horses ambled up the drive, whitened by a dusting of snow. An occasional rook cawed its warning in the leafless branches above them.

'Our grandfather had these elms planted. If you're here in the spring you'll see them at their best,' said Rupert.

'I had not realised England could be beautiful even in this appalling weather.' The earl would much rather have been lazing in front of a fire with a book but on reflection he was glad he had agreed to accompany his brother. Morna looked about him at the rhododendron bushes and laurels that provided a welcome touch of greenery in the bleached landscape. 'Is there much timber on the property?'

'Not enough according to Harriet and Brownrigg. They have schemes for planting more spruce and selling timber for pit-props to the mines.'

'How astute. You do not take an interest in the estate?'

'I have never been particularly interested in agriculture, arboreal or otherwise and I have no sentimental attachment to the place, if that is what you mean.'

'But it was your childhood home; where our mother ran off to, with you in her arms.' There was a tinge of acid in Ralph's voice.

'I believe she stayed with maternal relatives until matters were settled with our father. I was two years of age when we came here.'

They turned the bend in the drive. The boxy white house came into view, looking grey against the snow-whitened background.

'Ah,' said Morna. 'Palladian, with amendments.'

Rupert swung himself from the saddle. 'I knew your purist eye would condemn the parapet on the roof.'

'On the contrary,' said Morna, dismounting to join his brother. 'Shall we consider it as an English embellishment, rapidly becoming the vernacular style, I understand. Sebastian would be most interested to see this.'

Hobson was waiting for them. 'Good afternoon, sir, my lord.' He bent his head. 'Mrs Hobson asks if you would care to partake of refreshment after you have seen over the house.'

'By all means. Please thank your wife. We shouldn't be above half an hour. I take it all is well since General Harper's departure?'

'Yes, sir. We have had no trouble with the pipes freezing this year thanks to the new lagging and we're lighting a fire once a week in each of the principal rooms according to Mrs Darville's orders. I trust the cheval glass arrived safely at the manor?'

Rupert nodded absently. He had been primed by Harriet who knew Mrs Hobson would wish to accommodate her old master. He shed his long benjamin and hat but Morna, finding the marble entrance hall chilly, declined to be relieved of his greatcoat.

'Come into the Italian salon. They may have lit a fire there. I am between tenants but have hopes of letting the place in the spring and Harriet insists on keeping the rooms aired.'

A fire did burn in the grate but it gave off a paltry heat. Morna immediately went over to the hearth and stood with his back to it to survey the room. Most of the furniture was shrouded in Holland covers. The earl raised his eyes to the huge, gaudy glass chandelier.

'You should cover that thing to avoid offending the eye as well as preventing dust. I cannot think why Mama was forever pleading poverty; that Murano monstrosity would have paid for a few seasons' hunting.'

'You know perfectly well it is the ruinous expense of Castle Morna coupled with our father's profligate habits that drained the family fortunes.' Rupert did not refer to Morna's own demands on the estate. 'Mama was happy enough living in Leicestershire until Gerald needed her in Ireland. She sold Haydonlea, as you know.' This was in direct consequence of Morna's gambling debts.

'Poor Gerald did nothing to rectify matters.' Ralph continued to scrutinise the room, furnished in the somewhat dated rococo style.

'And what will you do, now you've come into the inheritance?' Away from Larkhill Manor and the family and literally on his own ground, Rupert felt it was time to tackle his brother alone; they would not be disturbed here.

'It's too soon to say,' replied Ralph. He wandered over to scrutinise the Titian; the Canaletto had long been sold. 'Oh, I doubt I will live in Ireland and, as the estate is not entailed, perhaps I should dispose of the castle? Would you object?'

Rupert was half expecting this bombshell. Harriet in her practical way had said outright that, considering Ralph's distaste for Wexford, this should be considered as a possible option, but he could not like it.

'Who would have it? Two thousand acres of waterlogged bog. If you wanted to run sheep on it you would have to displace the tenants and spend money to drain the land.'

'For someone who is not interested in agriculture, you have a reassuring grasp of the situation.' Ralph moved away from the painting. The amount of money necessary to bring the Morna estate back to solvency did not bear thinking about, let alone the settlement of his own debts. 'However, I do not entirely despair; the castle may attract one of your new-made men from the north or even an American looking for somewhere to flaunt his wealth.'

'Romero is not rich then?'

'Alas no, his attractions lie in other directions.'

There was silence for a moment. 'It's pointless to ask whether you intend to marry, I suppose?' asked Rupert stiffly.

'Quite pointless. Who knows? I might meet my heart's desire in London and produce a brood of little Darvilles. If they are as charming as your children I should enjoy that. But then Gerald's girls rather sour the prospect.'

'Talking of Gerald's girls. If they don't settle then school is the only answer. Harriet went to a very good establishment in Poole.' He waited to see whether Ralph raised any objections.

'Poor little things, to be sent around the country like parcels.' The earl paused for a moment. 'I suppose as head of the family I have an obligation to educate my nieces, therefore if you do take that path then you may send the bills to me. They may as well reap something from the estate as I gather they have not got the emeralds.'

Rupert ignored the barb.

'Incidentally, why haven't you sent Henry to school?' continued Ralph as though he had not spoken of the family heirlooms.

'We would not wish to separate him from Lizzie at the moment. You and I may not be close as brothers but they seem to have some extra bond; I see it between them every day.'

'Surely you have a tutor for him? He seems a studious boy.'

'My secretary, Bernard Butterworth, coaches him in Latin and Greek.'

'And you teach the boy mathematics and natural philosophy?'

'Of course.'

'But nothing of the beaux arts or history?'

'He gleans that from his study of the classics. Miss Humble still gives both the children lessons.'

The earl raised his eyebrows in faint surprise. 'A somewhat sterile education. What of Art and Music and Beauty?'

'We seem to have strayed from the subject,' said Rupert.

'I would wish to know what your intentions are towards the Wexford estate. I know Castle Morna only as a recent visitor, and that only for funerals. I received nothing from our father when he died except a seal ring and feel I owe him nothing. However, I would be loath to lose the family property entirely.' Rupert was very serious. 'We have a duty as landowners to our dependents.'

'Oh, I daresay I shall keep an acre or two so that you can come over and hunt. Or do you think your wife would enjoy being chatelaine of a castle after my demise? She could certainly fulfil the role with the utmost competence.'

'Don't be ridiculous. I ask only that you look thoroughly into all aspects of any transaction before you make any final decision. May I recommend another family connection? Sir Hamish McAllister, a lawyer of great reputation in government circles. He will have time on his hands now the Whigs are in government and he is a man of influence in many spheres. His advice would be invaluable. You must look him up when you go to London.'

'Will he put me in the way of a buyer for the castle? Would he be interested himself?'

'He already has one,' said Rupert laconically. 'In Aberdeen.'

'Ah, a canny Scot' said Ralph with a mock sigh, examining and discarding a delicately painted grisaille snuff box. 'Sebastian would adore this pretty thing – if he took snuff.'

Rupert realised he would get nothing sensible out of his brother at this juncture and suggested they continue their tour.

'Mama left the house to you, I understand,' said Ralph as they passed from room to room. He admired the modernisations that Harriet's money had provided.

'Yes, our father left it to her in perpetuity and then Gerald gave it to me. I'll live in it again one day. When Clem comes of age or marries I shall bring Harriet and the children here.'

'What an enviable prospect. And meanwhile you have the income from the tenants, when you have any.'

They climbed the stairs, Ralph stopping every now and then to examine the family portraits. There were not many and they were inferior to those in Castle Morna.

'Mama is the only one to have any hint of character in her face.' He paused to examine a vivid Reynolds. Sophia Darville at thirty had been striking: tall with a mass of tight dark curls, slanting eyes and the bearing of a duchess.

'The Darvilles are a dull lot,' he said examining a small family group. 'But how angelic I looked with all those long curls. Even Gerald looks saintly, or was it just his natural stupidity? You, of course, had not yet been born.' He turned away quickly, looked about him and peered over the balustrade to the black and white chequered floor below.

'The entrance hall is a perfect cube,' said Rupert the mathematician. 'I used to play marbles on those black and white squares.'

'And so this is where you spent your childhood. I often wondered what had become of you and Mama and tried to visualise what you were up to. Father would never speak of you, naturally, and I was packed off to Harrow when the scandal broke.'

'I was never sent to school and had the occasional governess or tutor.'

'A cossetted child,' murmured Ralph.

'On the contrary, Harriet tells me I was neglected. I know I was not strong. The only family I had were the Larkhills. Our mother was never here.'

'Well, I cannot say I was entirely happy at boarding school, though it had its compensations as I grew older.'

After admiring the new billiard room and three other salons Ralph's said: 'It is a delightful house and I am quite envious but I have seen enough to satisfy my curiosity and was something said about refreshment?'

Rupert led the way to his favourite room. The library looked forlorn but Rupert felt more comfortable there despite the cold. One wall was devoted to the volumes of the *Nautical Almanac* to which Rupert regularly contributed. Many gaps on the shelves testified to where he had long ago removed books to Larkhill Manor.

Ralph strolled to the windows. 'What a light, bright room.' The snow brought a glare to the windows and bounced off the whitewashed barrelled ceiling. 'And what is that edifice on the hill?'

'Athena's Temple. Our grandfather had a fancy to build his own ruins. The ladies like it; one former tenant held tea parties in it.' Rupert had a plan to turn the folly into an observatory but would not waste this on the earl. At the moment his telescope was on the roof of Larkhill Manor.

'Ah, the ladies; one must not criticise their whims, though I much prefer your priory ruins, which are at least authentic.'

'They are not my priory ruins, they are Young Clem's. We tend to take them for granted.'

Mrs Hobson entered carrying a tray of Dr Johnson's punch, apologising for the lack of fire, saying they had lit one the previous day to get rid of the damp.

She tried not to stare at the earl; despite the ten-year age difference the likeness between the two brothers was unmistakeable.

'Thank you Mrs Hobson. Is all well below stairs?' The housekeeper turned her eyes from the earl.

'Yes, sir. Except that Mr West sent over a message yesterday, about the gypsies.'

'Gypsies?'

'Camped down by the little stream, sir. He wanted General Harper to see them off, not knowing that the General had already left.'

'I will look into it Mrs Hobson. As long as they are not obstructing the old cart track or straying onto our land there is no need to worry.'

When she had gone the earl took a seat but Rupert paced the room, examining the shelves with some anxiety. 'Dammit, some of these books are getting foxed.' He flipped open a Morocco-bound volume.

'Who is this nervous Mr West?' asked Morna.

'A neighbour. His land abuts ours and borders on the river.' Rupert did not look up from his task.

'And the gypsies?' asked Morna, blowing gently on his punch to cool it.

'West is a magistrate. If the gypsies were trespassing he has the authority to see them off himself, therefore I assume they have camped on common land. It's typical of the man to whip up contention and try to involve others.'

After another silence Morna observed: 'And this is where you wrote your famous opus?'

'No.'

'Oh?'

Rupert relented. 'I wrote *A Narrative Account of a Voyage Around the World* while I was in London and Cambridge.' His voice carried a hint of impatience. 'There have been other works since then which I wrote in Sir John's library at Larkhill. They would not interest you.'

'I stand corrected. I have written a book, too, did you know? Of course not, how could you? Not such a learned tome as yours but I flatter myself it found favour with the cognoscenti. It was on shell cameos,' he added as Rupert had not asked.

'You have an interest in such things?' said Rupert with a shade of surprise.

'I hold them to be exquisite little gems of history. The Contessa de Rimini considers I have an unerring eye for a genuine Renaissance piece.'

'And this is what you do – in Italy?'

'I do many things. There is a vineyard and olive grove attached to the Villa Mimosa. I take an interest in the harvest. In the spring I travel; I have many friends in Rome, Florence and Genoa and they in turn visit me. The villa is rarely without some guest. In the summer I sail. I keep a yacht on Capri. It has been such a boon to have Sebastian staying with me; he's proved himself to be a most adaptable crew.'

Rupert's lips thinned. 'I can see why removing to Ireland does not appeal to you,' he said replacing a book on a shelf.

'I'm so glad you understand, though I have not yet decided what I shall do. But I feel a loyalty to my people at Mimosa far more than I could to Gerald's Irish tenants.'

****

The appearance of the Earl of Morna, his friend and the two little girls in the Darville pew on Sunday caused a sensation among the townsfolk. The emancipation of Roman Catholics the year before had failed to rid most English Protestants of their prejudices, and the newcomers were stared at as if they were giraffes.

Mrs O'Leary's conscience was appeased by a half-sovereign and to Harriet's delight Rupert said he would come and sit with her and their children in the Larkhill family pew. This was an event in itself and the town felt doubly honoured by the appearance of both brothers. Despite the bitter wind, people lingered outside St Saviour's in the hope of being introduced. The drawback was the high box pews that prevented the congregation from staring at their betters and the gentry from talking to their neighbours. Morna wrapped a rug around his knees and opened his missal. The young American took in the whitewashed walls and naked beams above him and felt very much at home.

The balcony was empty, the local musicians having been replaced by Mrs Butterworth at the harmonium, which was all to the good as there was no one to peer down into the pews and see Lady Sophia and Lady Rosa pinching and nudging and playing pat-a-cake throughout the service. Mrs O'Leary did nothing but cross herself ostentatiously at every response.

The church was lit with Advent candles but nothing could alleviate the cold rising from the stones. This was the season of austerity before the feast. The Reverend Butterworth, blessing his clerical wig for warmth, gave a sermon with verve, stressing the values of one's allotted place in society. The recent unrest among the farm workers had made the gentry close ranks.

Over the years the Reverend Butterworth's congregation had diminished; so many of his flock had defected to the Methodists. A new chapel at the other end of the town drew away much needed income from the plate. Tithes were becoming harder to collect; either no one had any spare coin or donations in kind were growing scarcer as hardship gripped the small property holders.

Rupert Darville, as his patron, was most generous. Apart from the increased stipend there were regular gifts of game from the manor and Rupert had lent his name to the Rector's book *Coleoptera of the Wiltshire Downs* which had sold very well in the first few years of publication. Bernard, the youngest boy was settled in the post of secretary to Mr Darville and the Rector had hopes that his daughter Lydia would flourish in her teaching career. Nevertheless, the Butterworths were anxious and the sight of a titled gentleman in the pew gave the Rector hopes of gold in the collection plate.

After the service Rupert did his duty and introduced his guests to his neighbours. George Durrington had escorted his mother-in-law and two of his children to church. Sir Charles Durrington was confined to his bed with a broken ankle and Juliana was also at home indisposed. Harriet's heart sank as she guessed the reason; Juliana was perpetually pregnant and had only just weaned her youngest.

Lady Durrington plunged her hands into her old-fashioned muff. 'Harriet, do you come to us on the fourteenth as usual? If you dare brave the roads. But then you have faced down the mob already, I know. We saw no one this morning but one cannot be certain that the unrest is over. The earl and his friend are most welcome to join us but I understand if the obligations of mourning preclude it.'

'The children would not miss the party for the world. I cannot speak for the earl but will send a note, whatever is decided. Do give Sir Charles our good wishes, broken bones can be uncertain things. I would stay and talk longer but our guests are not used such a cold wind.'

The agreement among the townsfolk was that the earl and his friend could not be papists and were fine gentlemen. Ralph's engaging manners endeared him to all. His friend set several female hearts racing even if the men were wary of the young popinjay. The little girls were pronounced disappointing despite their new clothes but it was agreed that Mrs Darville would soon put all to rights. The Rector found fault with nothing as he and his wife had been invited to midday dinner, a rarity since Mr Darville had moved into the manor on his marriage.

'I have not heard a sermon like that since I was at Harrow,' said the earl, dividing his creamed sole with a thick slice of bread. His tone could be interpreted in any number of ways.

The Rector beamed. 'I'm pleased you approve, my lord. I try to instil proper principles into my flock. In these troublesome times it behoves a man of the cloth to remind his congregation of their blessings. You will have heard about the Swing riots which have ravaged the county? Many farm machines have been smashed to pieces and Mrs Darville's tenants, the Trottmans, have been forced to revert to hand threshing under threats from the rioters.'

'Harriet? What's this? You did not tell me of any disturbance.' Rupert said sharply.

'There was little to tell,' said Harriet mildly. 'I did not wish to worry you with the matter so soon after your return. We will speak of it at another time.' She turned to her brother-in-law. 'We keep the thresher at Home Farm so all our tenants might avail themselves of it. However, I cannot deny that its use puts many field labourers out of work and I believe the more prosperous farmers can afford to pay those they do employ a much better rate. But the farmers are forever pleading poverty and the burden of tithes-' She broke off, conscious of her clerical guest. 'The misery is that the last two harvests have been a disaster for everyone. There is much poverty among the cottagers, as you know, Mrs Butterworth.'

Mrs Butterworth nodded vigorously. She and the doctor's wife were mainstays of the parish ladies' sewing circle, the fount of some charity and much gossip in Larkhill.

'Where does the word "Swing" come from?' asked Sebastian. Clem was astounded at the American's boldness in initiating a conversation. The Rector was frankly uncomfortable sitting opposite this beautiful young man in his dazzling brocade waistcoat and did not know what to make of him. At least the earl wore a dark coat and a waistcoat of superfine; he was an English gentleman, for all his bonhomie.

Everyone waited for Rupert to reply but it was left to Bernard to say: 'I believe it is a reference to the flexible part of the flail, or the "swingle", used in hand threshing.'

'I take it Enclosures are at the root of the problem?' asked the earl, accepting another glass of wine. 'I have some distant memory of civil unrest arising from the movement when I was a boy.'

'I cannot see it as a valid excuse for the recent uprisings; the labourers lost their own plots of land thirty years ago,' replied Rupert. 'Larkhill has one of the last remaining commons in the district; it's much reduced and now only fit as rough grazing for a few hogs.'

'Is this the common where the gypsies are camped?' asked Sebastian, oblivious to his solecism. Rupert was surprised that the young man knew of the gypsies. Only Morna could have mentioned it. Instead of replying, Rupert chose to ask Mrs Butterworth how her daughter had fared in her pupil-teacher training.

'But, forgive me, what then is the cause of these awful riots?' persisted Morna unwisely. He had not yet encountered Rupert in full flow.

His brother put down his knife and fork. 'I'm inclined to think the unrest is a culmination of many things, including short-term cash contracts. It is a melancholy fact that the agricultural workers are worse off than before the French wars. Appallingly low wages, bad conditions and incredibly long hours of work have all contributed to the unrest. Wellington would have called out the army but now the Whigs are in power, we hope for a more enlightened approach.' There were times when Rupert thought that his own class treated dogs and horses with more decency.

Harriet continued sorrowfully. 'The failure of spinning work for their women and children has almost put it out of the power of the village poor to live by their own industry. All the mills hereabouts have robbed the cottagers of their livelihood. And now the agricultural machines have replaced their income from winter hand-threshing.'

'You cannot stop scientific progress,' said her husband sharply.

'I cannot prevent poverty and hunger, either, more to my shame,' she retorted.

She turned to her brother-in-law. 'The labourer is no longer regarded as part of the farmer's family; many are thrown onto parish relief as a result.'

'How perverse that they should destroy the very corn that would provide work or feed them,' said Morna.

'Indeed my lord, there's no accounting for such wicked actions with wheat at sixty shillings a bushel. But wages in Wiltshire are low, only eight shillings a week compared with ten or twelve in the rest of the country,' said the Rector, with no intention of commuting his tithes in compensation. 'Thank the Lord we have been spared the worst of the terrible rioting which has spread from Kent and Sussex. That dangerous radical William Cobbett predicted long ago that there would be major unrest from the working classes and now we have it. The sooner the man is jailed the better! I myself have had my wood pile burned, with no redress. In retaliation I have written a tract on *Rick-burning, Rioting and Tithes,* a well-argued rebuttal, if I say so myself, but I fear nothing will stop these incendiaries.'

'Dear me, what a barbarous country. Sebastian, we'll be safer in London,' said the earl. 'Remind me to take my pistols when next we venture out.'

Harriet said: 'I assure you, my lord, we have had very few gangs roaming the roads in this neighbourhood, and those that do demand only money for beer or food. Our friend, George Durrington is a magistrate; you met him this morning. He has been to several meetings with the ringleaders and says that their demands are quite sensible.' Harriet sounded no more convincing to her guests than she did to herself.

When the Butterworths had left, carrying a welcome brace of pheasants, Clement took Sebastian down to Home Farm to meet the Trottmans. Miss Humble tactfully withdrew to the nursery. The remainder of the family retired to the green drawing room. Rupert occupied himself by playing a Beethoven sonata on the piano. Harriet wondered if he were worried about something or just considering his next scientific monograph. She was not looking forward to their inevitable *tête-a-tête*.

'We will have a light supper tonight to allow the servants time to go to Evensong,' she explained to her brother-in-law.

'How delightful. I am used to having only one meal of the day, the rest a little fruit or salami. There is nothing as satisfying as a plate of fresh figs.'

She laughed. 'I regret we cannot accommodate you in such exotic dishes. But take comfort from the fact that you need our English puddings and tarts to fortify you against the freezing weather. Larkhill is an unsophisticated society.'

'I like your friends, Harriet. They are most unpretentious people. The despised Mr West was not among them, I noticed.'

'Oh dear, no. Mr West quarrelled with the Rector many years ago over some matter of property, I believe. Mr West is not the most tolerant of men. He and his wife attend St Mary's in Hunniford.'

'Then I am never to meet this ogre?'

Rupert struck a discordant note and rose from the piano. 'Unfortunately, yes. My wife has seen fit to accept an invitation to a conversazione at Bourne Park. Don't feel you have to attend, Morna, though your presence is the transparent reason for this unprecedented honour.'

'Then do not let us disappoint anyone. I would not deprive the gentleman of my presence,' replied the earl and asked whether Sebastian was to be included.

'As our guest he would naturally make up one of our party,' replied Harriet, diplomatically. She knew Mr West would take an earl on any terms. 'I do hope you won't be too bored. The subjects will be medical or political. The Wests are not very artistic people.'

To Harriet's surprise Rupert broke in: 'I would like you to meet the Hintons. They are more our sort. Will you come with us to Hinton Parva for the New Year's Day hunt?'

'Not on Boxing Day? Or does my memory of the English at play betray me?' Morna stroked the cat on his knee absently.

'Not at all. The Larkhill hunt always meets on New Year's Day, though other packs favour Boxing Day.'

'Sebastian would appreciate a good run with the hounds. He hunted in Virginia, he tells me. He's such a dashing young chevalier, so *sportif*. Could you lend him a horse? I regret that I would disgrace you in the field but I would happily be a follower in a carriage.'

Harriet quickly broke in over her husband's frown. 'Of course, my lord. I will be taking the children in the barouche if you care to join us. Otherwise there is always the chaise. Mrs Hinton usually asks us for the day before, for her son's birthday party. We shall see the New Year in at the Hall and you will meet more of the county. We will not be attending the ball, naturally.'

Morna allowed a shade of disappointment to cross his fleshy features. 'I shall come in the barouche with the children and keep those nieces of mine in check. Were you aware that they are almost heathens?' he said in amusement. 'Sophia informed me this morning that they rarely attended church, either Protestant or Roman. One would have thought the servants would have taken them even if Gerald had lapsed. They can barely read the prayer book.'

'Were they baptised Catholic?' asked Harriet in some anxiety.

'It seems so. Patrick once told me that it was the only occasion when Gerald defied Mama. He may not have cared for his wife but he cared deeply for his daughters. I understand they were an *idée fixe* with him; he doubtless felt remorse over marrying the barmaid.'

Harriet looked at her husband in dismay. 'What should we do?'

'Nothing,' said Rupert. 'You may take them to church with you Harriet and Butterworth may confirm them in a year or two, if you feel it is important.'

He had long ago accepted that Harriet would attend St Saviour's regularly despite his absenteeism. He believed she attended more for social reasons but recognised that Young Clem and the Darvilles needed to be accepted by the neighbourhood. He felt no concern for Gerald's children and hoped to pack them off to boarding school as soon as he could now that Ralph had raised no objections.

****

Rupert asked his wife to attend him in the library. 'Sit down Harriet. What's all this about the threshing machine?'

Harriet took her seat by the fire and folded her hands. She felt a little apprehensive and schooled herself into calmness. 'The merest nothing. A small hay rick was burnt. Mr Brownrigg and I decided to temporarily take the thresher out of service. In the interest of the safety of all our people,' she said easily.

'Have you been threatened?' A frown creased his brow.

'No, not at all. It was a decision I came to myself.'

'And how do your tenants take to this preposterous idea? Smith won't want to reduce his profit and the Shaws can't afford to.' He sounded exasperated. 'The Trottmans cannot be happy about this backward step.'

'I admit, there were some difficulties when I first proposed it, but now everyone's machinery and ricks are safe until all this disturbance is over. Did you know that the rioters destroyed a seed-drill belonging to one of Mr West's tenants a fortnight ago? I would not have that happen here. You have been away for more than a month and have no notion of what damage the rioters have done. However, it is now known in the parish that the manor is not using the thresher and we have a surplus of labour who are grateful for the work.'

'And do your tenants intend to pay the threshers any increase in their wages?'

'No,' she said evenly. 'The farmers feel it is enough to offer employment.' This was a disingenuous reply. As well as getting the corn to market later than usual and hence losing the best price, she could not expect her tenant farmers to find an increase in day-wages for their workers.

'Then I assume it is the estate which is acceding to their demands? What does Clem say to all this? I am his guardian. You should have done nothing without my approval.'['

'You know the labourers' wages are subsidised by the Poor Rate,' prevaricated Harriet.

'I do not like this, Harriet. You have given in to threats whether spoken or not. Goodness knows what they will demand next. Such leniency will be construed as weakness. Look what happened in Kent.' Rupert had spent a profitable afternoon catching up on a month's worth of *The Times*. 'A magistrate gave the rioters only a three-day prison sentence and the same night another threshing machine was torched. You see what trouble leniency can bring.' He was pacing now. 'I am surprised at Brownrigg allowing you to take this course. You should have waited until I came home to consult with me on the matter.'

Brownrigg had continued to deplore her generosity but had conceded that others were taking the same action.

'You do not normally concern yourself with the manor's affairs. I explained it all to Clem and he was perfectly satisfied with my actions as long as the Trottmans were safe.' She sounded defensive.

'Clem is not yet fifteen and will believe anything anyone tells him.'

'I was following the example of the justices in Norfolk who advised the general disuse of threshing machines as a friendly concession to public opinion.' She had picked the quotation from the newspaper for just such an occasion.

'Norfolk is not Wiltshire!'

'The Marquis of Bath ordered his farmers to destroy their machines,' she said defiantly.' At least I have not destroyed ours, only put it out of service for a while.'

Rupert could not articulate his anxiety over Harriet's taking a hand in such dangerous affairs. 'I should not have gone away and left you,' he muttered.

'You could not miss your brother's funeral, and you were forced to wait for Morna to arrive from the Continent.' Her voice took on a pleading note: 'Rupert, you have no idea of how severely the labourers have been hit by another cruel winter. You do not notice, when you go into Larkhill, the increase in the number of beggars. The Poor Rate brings their income to barely subsistence level, no more than that. You have protested against the meanness of the sums yourself. When I visit the cottagers on the estate, they may not be starving but they are near to it. Do not blame me for doing my duty.'

'Did you not read Lord Melbourne's proclamation?' he retorted angrily. 'He proposes a £500 reward for bringing rioters and incendiaries to justice, and advocates the enrolment of special constables and the formation of preventative vigilante groups. He specifically encourages magistrates to act energetically to quell the rioters.'

'And so they are. Mr West has sent I don't know how many poor creatures to await the Salisbury Assizes. But we have had no serious damage on our land and Lord Melbourne is in London not Larkhill. I did what I thought best at the time.' She sounded defiant.

'I hope you do not regret your impulsiveness, Harriet. I'm inclined to believe that a firm but fair hand is needed or the country will demand that the army be called out. The military deals in death, whereas Melbourne's measures keep it a civilian affair.'

'I did not act impulsively and I wasn't aware you had become a Whig supporter,' she said pettishly.

'If the dragoons are called out again there could be more bloodshed and Melbourne's proposals are the lesser of two evils.' He sounded annoyed.

'Whereas my solution has no evil in it at all,' she said standing up and flouncing out her skirt.

Rupert looked at his wife and decided to cut his losses. 'Very well. What's done is done. We cannot reverse it, for the moment.' He was not pleased but could not identify why he felt disappointed, apart from Harriet acting independently and going against his principle of not giving in to force. She had been pragmatic, as always, but a coolness rose between them.

Two days later on the eighth of December, Rupert opened his copy of *The Times* and read another circular from the Home Secretary regarding the labourers' demands.

'It is my Duty to recommend in the strongest Manner, that for the future all Justices of the Peace and other Magistrates, will oppose a firm Resistance to all Demands of the nature above described, more especially when accompanied by Violence and Menace; and that they will deem it their Duty to maintain and uphold the Rights of Property of every Description, against Violence and Aggression.'

He silently folded the paper at the relevant column, put it in front of his wife and left the room.

****

The children stood in the vestibule, dressed warmly in mittens and knitted berets. Miss Humble and Annie had been busy. Sophia and Rosa looked rather awkward in their new clothes.

'Now, Clement is to have the bill hook, and no one else is to touch it. Is that understood?' commanded Harriet looking from one child to another. 'This is the first time you have collected the Christmas branches on your own, without an adult to help you,' she continued sternly. 'You must obey Clement in all things. It is his land and he is responsible for you.' Harriet wondered if she were being unfair to put this burden on Clem but reflected that at his age some boys had already spent two years before the mast.

'Mr Browrigg says there are good holly berries in the plantation at Quennell House and great bunches of mistletoe on the apple trees in our orchard. Now get along with you. Both sledges are waiting for you in the stable yard with Martha and James.' Annie's older children were often playmates of the Darville children. 'You may take the dogs,' Harriet continued. 'No going off our own land, mind.' And with that she opened the great oak front door and ushered them into the blinding snow of the morning.

The yule log, destined to be burned over the twelve days of Christmas in the cavernous hearth of the Great Hall, was lying covered in tarpaulin behind the old brewery house, now the estate office for Mr Brownrigg and his son. The huge limb of ash had been a victim of the October gales and had been drying out in preparation for the holiday season. The children's role was to decorate it.

Harriet returned to her duties. She rang for Brownrigg and suggested they offer ditch-clearing or path mending to the unemployed. Again the estate would pay and it would perhaps stave off starvation as well as any temptation to do mischief. Brownrigg agreed and suggested she come to the office to study the maps of the estate. She was returning across the stable yard some hours later in pattens and a richly embroidered shawl when her daughter raced through the archway, rosy with exertion.

'Mama, Mama! We met some gypsies!' shrieked Lizzie, tearing off her beret and flinging her arms around her mother's waist in excitement.

'Where? Where did you meet these gypsies? You have been gone a long time. Did they speak to you?' Harriet felt momentarily anxious.

'They're from Wexford, near where Rosa and Sophia live.'

'How do you know?'

'Oh, we shouted across the stream,' said Lizzy airily. 'Martha and James were afraid, but we had the dogs so we knew we would be safe.'

'I have told you, never to talk to people we don't know, Lizzie.'

'Then how will I ever get to know them?'

Henry came puffing around the corner bumping the sledge over the cobbles, leaving a scatter of fir needles in his path.

'Henry, what's this I hear about gypsies?'

'They've camped on the other side of the stream, Mama, near Mr West's plantation.' Henry abandoned his laden sledge and shook his hands in his woollen gloves.

Harriet stepped to the archway quickly. She was relieved to see her two nieces trudging behind Clem who was dragging the other sledge laden with holly. Martha and James had gone home to their mother in the gatehouse. The dogs frisked around the straggling party.

'And we saw Mr West and he shouted at us,' cried Lizzie not in the least perturbed.

'Did he indeed?' Harriet's maternal hackles rose.

'He was shouting at the gypsies, Mama, not at us. He had two other men with him; I think they were the constables,' said Henry matter-of-factly. 'He told us to go home when he saw us watching.'

'Yes, well, it is of no matter.' She forced herself to smile. This tale would get about and was bound to be talked of at Bourne Park tomorrow. 'I hope you did not let the dogs trouble him.'

'It wasn't Peterkin and Lucky that caused the trouble. It was that great bull-mastiff of his that started a fight,' said Clem, coming through the archway and dropping the rope of his sledge with relief. 'He's an ugly customer, not trained all,' he added with knowledgeable concern. He had quite enjoyed the scrap between Mr West's brute and the Romany dogs, but the girls had been frightened and even the Darville dogs had stayed this side of the stream, barking bravely but safely. All the frenzied noise had spooked Mr West's skittish horse and inflamed the incident even further.

'Where did you find such splendid branches?' asked Harriet pushing this unpleasantness to the back of her mind until she had time to reflect on it. The boys unloaded the sledges and carried the greenery behind the old brew-house. Sophia and Rosa slipped away through the kitchen. Harriet called the stable boy to take the dogs away and feed them. Lizzie was hopping from one foot to another desperate to start decorating the yule log at once. Miss Humble appeared and hustled the children inside. Harriet turned to her nephew.

'Did you speak to the gypsies, Clement? I specifically told you not to go off our own land.'

'But we didn't, I promise you, Aunt. We stayed this side of the stream, I swear.' He thought Sophia had been most unladylike shouting across the little wooden bridge. 'Mr West was giving the gypsies the strongest dressing down for something. He'd brought Shaw and Hewitt with him, though they didn't join in. I thought he was going to have apoplexy. And then he told us to be off, which I thought was mighty unfair as we were on Darville land.'

'Never mind that now. You are back safe-'

'And I did not let Cousin Sophia use the bill hook,' said Clem handing it over with a flourish.

'How was Sophia?'

Schoolboy Clement would not split on anyone, let alone a girl. He gave an indifferent shrug.

Sophia's behaviour had been appalling. She had trailed behind, ignored James and Martha and threatened to run away. Only when they got to the stream had she shown any pleasure in the afternoon. Hearing the Irish voices she had run straight across the footbridge, the dogs following her.

Clem had attempted to drag her back struggling and kicking. There had been an intense stand-off between the dogs. Only Mr West's arrival on his huge Spanish stallion with his mastiff at his heels had finally sent Sophia and the Darville dogs back to the safety of the group.

'Thank you Clem. You have done a good day's work. Your uncle will be most pleased with your responsible attitude.'

'Think nothing of it, Aunt. I can manage the children,' he said loftily.

****

Finding the earl idly strumming the piano in the green drawing room, Harriet proposed an outing to their closest friends.

'We have a long-standing invitation to a Christmas party for the children, if you think it is right that Ladies Sophia and Rosa should go, and the Durringtons have their own grandchildren there, too. Please do not feel under any obligation to come with us, but there will be luncheon and company.'

In response to Harriet's hesitant suggestion he reassured her: 'Gerald would not have objected on grounds of mourning; I'm told he went hunting the day after the barmaid died. By all means, we will attend this party.'

He had no fear of exerting himself and the manor was beginning to pall; he needed a diversion. He saw it as an excuse to wear his dark blue coat and double-breasted waistcoat with the new pin-tucked shirt. 'But you will put me in mind of who exactly is going to attend, I beg you. I would like to know a little about your neighbours and I have the suspicion that sleepy Larkhill, underneath its gentility, is a hotbed of scandal.'

Harriet laughed. 'Larkhill has had its moments in the past, but not of late. We are all too middle-aged and respectable now to provide food for gossip.'

It was understood that the beautiful Mr Romero would be accompanying his employer. Harriet hoped Sir Charles would not be offended. Her suspicions were growing and this might be an occasion to examine them. Young though he was, Romero often spoke to the earl as an equal and was not backwards in putting himself forward. Perhaps this was the American way. She knew only that it annoyed Rupert.

Sebastian exclaimed aloud when the spectacular frontage of the tall, angular house first came into view beyond the circular drive. 'Why, it's in brick, not stone at all; just like the paintings of Hampton Court Palace. And take a look at that cupola and those oriel windows. How fine they are in the sun, like a regular kaleidoscope.' He was riding with the men. Such an outburst was greeted with silence, except by the earl who smiled at his friend's spontaneity.

Harriet, Miss Humble and the four children were wrapped up inside the barouche. Harriet felt she could not inflict Mrs O'Leary on her closest friends and was coming to think that the little girls disliked their nursemaid.

George and Lady Durrington greeted them in the entrance hall amid the usual shedding of wraps. Presently Sir Charles limped into view, leaning on a stick. 'Good, good, brought all the young shavers, have you? Miss Elizabeth, Henry.' Harriet's children politely made their obeisance. 'So these are Gerald's daughters, eh? Can't see the family likeness,' he said looking up at Rupert. 'I daresay they take after their mother.'

'I sincerely hope not,' murmured Ralph and then turned a bland face to his host.

But Sir Charles was still occupied with the children, the motive of his life after the navy. 'Miss Humble, take the children up to the long gallery; Clem, you know the way. Juliana's brood is there, causing mayhem as usual. Don't stand any nonsense from them or tell them they'll get hard tack for a week.'

'But-' Clem looked upset. He felt himself too old to make up one of the nursery party and had dressed in his best to appear in the Durrington's drawing room. Harriet touched his arm. 'Take them up and stay a little while. You can always come down to the company in an hour.'

'There's a long gallery?' interrupted Sebastian. 'You lucky fellow, Clem. What wouldn't I give to see that?'

Clem perked up and made to usher his new friend before him. 'I'll show you. We can play skittles if you wish.'

'Of course we have a long gallery,' replied Sir Charles. This is a seventeenth century house. Who are you young man?'

Hasty introductions were made and Lady Durrington led the adults upstairs into the warmth of the salon. Sun streamed through the great angular bay windows dimming the logs in the stone fireplace.

'Our daughter, Juliana, will be down directly,' said Lady Durrington to her visitors. 'She is a trifle indisposed this morning. But look who we have here to greet you,' said Lady Durrington drawing a plump bespectacled middle-aged lady towards her. The gauze peaked cap proclaimed her the widow.

'Mary! Mrs Wakefield. What a delight. Your mama kept this a great secret. It must be at least three years since your last visit. I was so sorry to hear of Mr Wakefield's untimely passing,' cried Harriet.

The two women embraced affectionately. 'Now dear Samuel has gone, I feel I can come home more often. I could not leave him in the latter years. And this time I have brought my youngest step-daughter, Charity, to visit her grandparents.'

She indicated a sprightly damsel of seventeen with an elaborate topknot, wearing an aggressively plunging gown with gigot sleeves.

Harriet held out her hand but Miss Wakefield was riveted by the appearance of Sebastian Romero. He tossed his floppy waves from his forehead like pony as he looked up to admire the coats of arms on the embossed ceiling.

'Is that the earl?' breathed Miss Wakefield, awestruck.

'His secretary,' replied Harriet in what she hoped were dampening tones.

'Gracious, no, Charity. The Earl of Morna is the gentleman talking to Grandmama. One can see the family likeness between him and Mr Darville, who I must say is looking very well, Harriet, despite his recent bereavement. You, my dear, never seem to grow any older.'

The two women moved away to a sofa to catch up on domestic news while Miss Wakefield trailed towards Sir Charles who was explaining the history of the house to the young American.

Clement appeared at the luncheon bell. Despite his misgivings he had enjoyed organising the children into team games but again he drew the line at eating in the nursery. Sophia had once more behaved badly, pushing the little ones aside in the races, cheating at snakes and ladders and refusing to share the hobby horse. Miss Humble and Georgiana had exerted their authority with the result that Sophia had sulked and refused to join in any more games.

'Ah, I am glad you have come down, Clem. We have laid a cover for you,' said Lady Durrington, following her guests into the dining room on the arm of the earl. Clem straightened his stock at the sight of Miss Wakefield and to his gratification was offered as her escort. Charity had hopes of Mr Romero but her myopic, stout step-mother was the chosen partner of this miracle of creation. For sentimental reasons Mary would much rather have been seated next to Young Clem.

Juliana had appeared in the course of the morning to give a fillip to the conversation and declared herself able to eat a morsel of the light luncheon put before them.

'Mr Darville, you are just the gentleman I must speak to. You must do something about those gypsies. They badly frightened poor Miss Williams and ruined her best pair of sewing shears. She was too scared to refuse them her custom and they charged her quite five shillings, you know. Such robbery! As if there weren't enough beggars in the town already and all now we have these labourers intent on insurrection. It cannot be borne! You must see them off at once.'

'I regret that I am neither a justice of the peace nor the squire', said Rupert. 'If you wish to avail yourself of the services of a magistrate I suggest you apply to your husband or to Horace West.'

'George refuses to do anything. He allowed them to come in the first place. But these criminals are on your land.'

'I think you are mistaken. I assure you that if gypsies were on my land then Brownrigg would have apprised me of it.'

'Perhaps not on your land precisely,' Juliana said dismissively. 'But on the other side of the stream which verges on the manor and Darville property.'

'Then they are on common land and no one may chase them off unless they have breached the law. I am confident that your husband knows all about them, as I do myself.'

George looked embarrassed; he had issued the travellers with a licence to cross the parish. He had not expected them to stay.

'But I am sure they have broken the law. They must have! Such rough men and impertinent women. The children are like the vermin they carry, begging in the street. None of us is safe from housebreakers. Mrs Talbot is convinced we shall be murdered in our beds. And when you consider the riots in Salisbury and Mr Shepherd's threshing-machine factory burnt down. Why, your own tenants were attacked and Harriet-'

'Hush, my dear,' said George. 'Do not agitate yourself so,' he said with meaning.

'I would not conflate Irish tinkers with agricultural labourers, Mrs Durrington. Both parties would give you short shrift if they discovered it.' Rupert returned to his plate.

'Harriet, make your husband mind me.' Juliana leaned across the table. 'Are you not afraid of an uprising, sir?' The lappets of her cap fell forward like curtains. 'Look what has occurred in France. Everyone knows our people are stirred up by French agents intent on spreading sedition amongst the poorer classes.'

'Their protest is economic, not political,' said Rupert shortly.

'That dreadful Mr Sharpe has been putting artful and treasonous ideas into people's minds. There are handbills everywhere, calling for revolution. I will never send my shoes to him again. You have been away for a month and do not know what Larkhill has come to!'

The earl broke in. 'There is no need for alarm, madam. I spent a few days in Paris on my journey to England. I can assure you the city was very quiet. The removal of one branch of the Bourbons for another cadet branch should not keep anyone awake at night. Everything has been most peaceful in Paris since last July.'

Rupert was about to draw attention to the secession of the Belgians from the Netherlands, when Harriet caught his eye and he accepted a veal cutlet instead.

'Talking of politics, Darville,' said Sir Charles. 'Not that I see the need for another election so soon. It was so careless of Winsmore to die like that, but tell us, have you decided to accept Lydiard's seat? We could do with a good man in parliament to protect our interests.'

As Rupert's interests were not quite the same at those of Sir Charles, he would have preferred not to discuss such matters in public. King George IV's death in June had led to a general election. The unfortunate Mr Winsmore had enjoyed the Larkhill seat for barely three months before being knocked down by a horse-bus while crossing Piccadilly. The seat had once again fallen vacant. Only Harriet knew that Rupert had rejected Lord Lydiard's offer. Rupert was aware of the nobleman's traditional views and felt he could not accept the nomination and then vote for Reform when once in the House. There was no doubt that Lydiard's candidate would win the seat; eight out of the fifteen electors for Larkhill borough were either the noble lord's tenants in the town or owed him substantial sums.

'The Whigs are bound to push a Reform Bill through in the next few years and then Larkhill will lose its seat entirely. We will be subsumed by the new Salisbury constituency,' said Rupert.

'All the more reason to fight it! Take the nomination and oppose all this franchise reform! '

'The mother country has many fine qualities but I'd rather live in an American democracy where every man who can read and write has a vote,' interposed Romero. 'Perhaps that's why your labourers are making trouble.' The table was momentarily silenced.

'Mr Romero, I applaud your patriotism but how can you support a nation that condones slavery? The poor negroes do not have their freedom, let alone a vote,' said Mary. Samuel Wakefield had turned her into a strong supporter of total emancipation.

'I know nothing about politics, ma'am, but the British have profited from slavery as much as the Americans. Where would your great cotton mills be without our southern plantations? My uncle is gentleman of Virginia.'

As Sir Charles had dabbled in the slave trade in his early years before his son had brought him to see the error of his ways, Romero's true but simplistic comment jarred on the company. Rupert looked about to speak but Morna jumped in before him.

'Forgive my friend, sir; the enthusiasm of youth and your remarkably fine claret have made him forget his company manners.'

Sebastian lowered his lashes in diffidence and turned to Sir Charles and Mary. 'I beg your pardon ma'am, sir, if I spoke out of turn.'

Clem felt embarrassed for Romero but admired his friend's *sang froid*.

Well, Darville. Will you take the nomination?' growled Sir Charles as though neither Romero nor the earl had spoken.

'I regret I am too busy with my next book and my duties in London. Recent events have put me badly behind my schedule,' said Rupert.

'The Board of Longitude has been dissolved. What can you be doing in London now?' asked his host.

Rupert looked embarrassed but the whole table was waiting for his reply. 'I have been asked to assist the Resident Committee for Scientific Advice for the Admiralty.'

'Ah, well! Congratulations, Darville; that's quite an honour. I would not distract you from vital work for the navy.'

'That means Mr West will have the seat,' said Lady Durrington in some dismay. 'He will become quite insufferable; though we may see a little less of him. Will you not save us, Mr Darville?'

Rupert shook his head. 'If ever there was a borough ripe for Reform then Larkhill is it.'

'I cannot bear Lord Lydiard's false teeth. He has the smile of a shark,' shuddered Juliana.

'Juliana!' scolded her mother.

'He's not half as obnoxious as Horace West,' said George. 'What can you make of a man who wears a magenta-stripped waistcoat?'

'The gentleman sounds most formidable. I am so looking forward to making his acquaintance,' murmured the earl to the table in general.

'Are you going to this, this conversazione, Darville?' asked Sir Charles. 'I would have thought you frowned on such chicanery. I cannot think why Maria has accepted the invitation.'

'I try to keep an open mind, sir. My wife insists we support Mrs West.'

Miss Wakefield, growing bored with the discussion and following the American's daring example, leaned across the table to the earl. 'My lord, how would you spend your Christmas in Italy?'

Mary Wakefield was mortified at her step-daughter's presumption. What were young people coming to?

The earl leaned back to allow the footman to remove his plate and answered affably. 'Not as pleasantly as here I'm sure, Miss Wakefield. Unlike in this country, in Italy the festivities end on Christmas Day and the children receive their presents on Epiphany, brought by a hag-like creature on a broomstick. Celebrations revolve around the church of course.'

'In Rome a gun is fired from Castel St. Angelo to proclaim the start of the Holy season,' said Sebastian in an effort to redeem himself. 'We were quite startled weren't we – my lord. Our friends had not warned us of this.'

The secretary's interruption made Sir Charles frown again.

'I could not wait for presents until the sixth of January,' said Clem. He had hopes of a new saddle for Minstrel Boy.

'I thought you considered yourself too old for presents,' said Rupert.

'Oh, yes, why, of course, I am,' Clem replied with a self-conscious glance at Miss Wakefield. 'I'm not a child any more but I know you would not give Lizzie and Harry presents, sir, without including me.'

'And now there will be Sophia and Rosa to consider,' added Harriet. 'I wish one could package good manners.'

'What would you wish for, Mr Romero?' asked Charity.

He gave a sideways look under his lashes at the earl. 'I can't say I know. I have everything I want - at the moment. Except maybe a carriage of my own. I had the smartest curricle in Boston, before I came to Europe.'

Everyone immediately began discussing the merits of the curricle over the latest style of phaeton and the performance of various carriage horses. The discussion naturally progressed to hunters and the Hinton Parva stud.

'You'll be at the hunt, won't you Darville?' asked George. 'Unless Hinton cancels it.'

'We all intend to be there. Why would Hinton cry off?'

'Didn't you hear? There was a riot at Pyt House Farm, not three miles from Hinton. About 400 labourers had armed themselves with the intention of destroying a factory and threshing machines. Hatchets, hammers, pick-axes; they were all fuelled with drink. Benett, the owner my lord,' said George in explanation. 'Benett read them the royal proclamation but it served no purpose. His barns were broken into and both his machines were destroyed before a troop of yeoman cavalry arrived. There was a pitched battle and one labourer was shot dead, several were wounded and twenty-five arrested. Melbourne has set up a Special Commission of Assize to try these cases. There are bound to be transportations.'

'I fail to see that as a reason for calling off the hunt. Why give in to threats of a mob which has been dispersed?' said Rupert.

Harriet toyed with her dessert and did not look at her husband. Her actions at Home Farm, although never mentioned, still hung between them like a cloud.

'Damned disgrace!' broke in Sir Charles. Half the blame lies with all these new beer houses. The labourers are permanently drunk since the new Act came in.' He held out his bumper for more claret.

Since October anyone could open a beer house on the payment of two guineas for a licence. Although intended to promote competition, in the present climate the gentry and the clergy feared that the peasantry would run amok or imbibe sedition with every tankard.

Sir Charles grunted: 'If I were still a magistrate I would not allow it.'

As this comment was a veiled criticism of his son's easy-going ways, the subject was hastily changed.

****'

Luncheon was followed by a tour of the house. Sir Charles felt he should educate the brash American, whom he grudgingly admitted had an eye for architecture but after half an hour he was forced to leave such duties to his wife and take to his bed to rest his ankle. Harriet chose to stay behind in the drawing room with Juliana and Mary. George and Rupert retired to the stables to view George's new hunter recently purchased from Will Hinton. To Rupert's surprise Young Clem chose to join the house tour.

'Who is that gorgeous boy?' asked Juliana resting on a sofa. 'Are the Romeros titled? And why is he American? What a peculiar way of speaking through his nose he has. Did you see his cravat? I would die for a gown made out of such watered silk, but it would be quite useless until next autumn.' She patted her abdomen.

'Mr Romero's father was an Italian musician. His mother was the daughter of a prosperous Bostonian sea captain,' replied Harriet, carefully avoiding Juliana's gaze by settling her pelerine about her shoulders.

'How romantic. Did they run away together?'

'And he is the earl's secretary?' asked Mary doubtfully. 'His features are certainly striking. The young man could model for a Botticelli angel. Perhaps he is artistic?'

'Oh,' said Juliana. 'A secretary? I understood him to be a friend of the earl.'

'Mr Romero is studying to become an architect, under the earl's patronage.'

'The young man is certainly very beautiful,' said Mary wistfully. 'Though I have always had a preference for blond gentlemen. Clem is so like his father.' She closed her eyes in sudden recollection.

'You'd be wiser to keep your eyes open, Mary. Miss Charity showed a distinct interest in Mr Romero at luncheon,' said Juliana with relish. 'If his parents eloped then you should keep your step-daughter close under your eye.'

'We have no idea whether Mr Romero's parents ran away together or not, Juliana. I'm sure they were married quite respectably.' Elopement was a tender subject for Harriet. 'Mary has no need to be concerned about Mr Romero's intentions towards Miss Wakefield.'

Thwarted of one piece of gossip Juliana eagerly found another. 'Do you think we'll see the black woman tomorrow?' she asked.

'I sincerely hope not,' replied Harriet frostily.

'Rupert has turned you into a prude, Harriet. You used not to be so straight-laced.'

Mary asked to be informed.

'Juliana has no doubt learned from her maid, who is cousin to the West's coachman, that Mr West has introduced his latest inamorata into Bourne Park. Though I cannot believe he has brought her under his roof; Euphemia would not countenance it,' explained Harriet.

'She may have had no choice. Dawkins says the negress is locked in the attics and that dreadful man has foisted her on the household as a maid. None of the other servants will speak to her. Mr West brought her from Jamaica; she is one of his slaves.'

'Not if she is residing in England surely?' said the knowledgeable Mrs Wakefield. Nearly sixty years before, *Sommersett's Case* held that slavery was unsupported in English law and no authority could be exercised on slaves entering English or Scottish soil.

'Poor girl,' said Harriet. 'How dreadful to be prey to Horace West and ostracised by her peers.'

'She may be a hussy,' protested Juliana, 'who inveigled her way into Mr West's bed and his pocket-book. Dawkins told my maid that his master is "moon-struck".'

'Juliana, this is not a suitable conversation for the drawing room, or for anywhere for that matter,' Mary rose, shook out her black silk and frowned at her sister. 'I think we should go up and supervise the children and I would dearly love to see Miss Humble again. Do not disturb yourself Juliana; rest here on the sofa. I will take Harriet up to the long gallery.'

Chapter 5   The Conversazione

The following afternoon, the coach from Andover trundled over the cobbles of the Three Crowns. Its squashed passengers levered themselves down into the yard; they included two young gentlemen who wove their way unsteadily into the inn.

''Tis a disgrace, such drunkenness,' mumbled a stout farmer's wife adjusting her bonnet. 'They should've been on the outside, swigging that bottle and causing' such a ruckus. No fit company for a respectable body. What the fat one said about his father was fair unchristian. They be friends of your'n?'

Bernard Butterworth knew Frank West by sight and Tom Talbot by reputation. 'No doubt the young gentlemen were a little overcome with Christmas spirit, ma'am,' said Bernard handing the woman her basket of cheeses. He was only glad they had not recognised him. He tipped his hat and turned to retrieve the well-wrapped parcel of books he had been sent to collect from the coach.

The two young men found themselves a corner by the fire and called for a jug of ale. After fifteen minutes loudly ridiculing their fellow passengers and customers, conversation lapsed; the hilarity of the coach journey punctured by the thought of another cold journey before they were home.

'I tell you, if it gets too sticky I'll high-tail it over to Cheney Court. You'll have me won't you, Tom?' Frank slopped a measure from a squat bottle into his tankard. 'I can just hear the old man now, nagging about my allowance. He has no idea what it costs a man of fashion to maintain his position in London.' Frank was stocky and plump like his father with a tiny triangle of beard and a smear of hair across his top lip. This effort at style was ruined by stained lapels and shabby cuffs.

'Better make this the last tipple,' said Tom, draining his tankard. 'Or you won't be able to stay in the saddle for more than a yard.'

'Just one more for the road.' Frank West called loudly for gin and water. 'It's easy for you; your old man sends a carriage to collect you. I'll have to rent a livery nag. Couldn't you take me home? I don't fancy the ride alone.'

'Courage man! You're not a farmer or a parson and you have your pistol. Bourne Park is five miles out of my way. Depend upon it, my father will expect me home before dark. I can't think where Fowler is.' He craned his neck towards the door in the hopes of seeing his father's coachman.

'I'm only here for my mother's sake,' said Frank gloomily staring at the bottom of his glass.

'Aren't we all?' replied Tom, getting to his feet and taking out his fob watch. Frank had reached the morose stage and was no longer fun. 'Don't brood too much, old fellow. The parents like to see us happy and carefree; it makes them think we've nothing to hide and they're more inclined to loosen the purse strings.'

'I'll never get another penny out of mine if he finds out I've raised money on my expectations.'

'I warned you that was a risky venture. No one likes to hear of someone else profiting from their death, least of all your own father.'

Frank knocked back the dregs of his glass and called for another. 'Then he should give me more now while he's above ground. I can't wait another ten years until he decides to snuff it!'

'Why should he? You've not exactly been the dutiful son, have you? They expected you at home three days ago.' Talbot was irritated.

'It's the hypocrisy I can't stand,' said Frank banging his glass on the wooden table. 'Prosing on at me about morals and behaviour when he's been acting the old goat for years.' He looked up at his friend. 'You know he brought a black woman home with him from his last trip, don't you?'

'Did he, by God?' said Tommy in admiration; he cherished this piece of gossip to relay to his family. 'That's more ammunition for you if your Pa cuts up rough over the debts. You'd be wise to make sure he doesn't get wind of your money-raising schemes,' he said picking up his portmanteau. He'd heard a wagonette rattle into the yard.

'To make things worse that brother-in-law of mine will be there, sermonising. He's a member of the Athenaeum.'

'What's wrong with that? It's a perfectly respectable club. My cousin's a member and he's a clergyman. You said Learoyd was an Archdeacon. Why should he get to hear about your affairs? You don't mix in the same circles do you?'

'I don't know,' said Frank in despair. 'But he always does – get to know about things, I mean. He spends more time in London than in Winchester; I'm always bumping in to him at Lazlo's.'

Talbot absorbed another choice morsel of information; Lazlo's was an exclusive gaming club which was hinted to cater for gentlemen of certain tastes. Perhaps there was a side to Frank he knew nothing of.

'I didn't think it was your kind of hell?'

'I just go there for the play. God knows why Learoyd frequents the place; he's as tight as a flea.' Warming to his theme, Frank continued: 'He's so earnest and short and he always reads me a lecture in that damned sanctimonious way of his.'

'I must go, old chap,' said Tom patting his friend on the shoulder. 'Fowler's here. I'll take you up as far as the livery stable if you come now.'

But Frank refused to stir from the fire.

'Then I'll wish you the compliments of the season, and if your Pa shows you the door you can always come to us. But after Christmas mind; we'll have a houseful before then, and I intend to keep my parents sweet by playing the prodigal.'

****

'How much longer will this go on?' hissed Juliana from behind her fan.

Harriet allowed herself a small shrug. 'Who knows? Lord Lydiard is already asleep.'

She returned her gaze to Mrs West, slumped in a chair, head on her chest, her wispy draperies adding to her ghost-like appearance. The lady still affected the high-waisted gowns and floating gauzes of her youth which gave the illusion of nightwear. The strings of her cap rose and fell rhythmically on her chest.

For the past fifteen minutes the company had been watching a dapper little man with bird-bright eyes and flowing moustaches make extravagant passes across Mrs West's face and form. His fingers skimmed her body, never quite touching, an intense look of concentration on his gnome-like face.

Someone coughed. There was a certain amount of restiveness among the spectators scattered thinly around the room. A low incessant hum came from the front row.

'Silence if you please,' said Dr Mazzotta with a pointed look at Letty Learoyd. 'I must 'ave complete quiet. The gravitational tides must be 'arnessed so that I can imbue the patient with the necessary magnetic force.' He returned to his arm waving and then took Mrs West's thumbs between his fingers. Mrs West trembled.

'You will observe, the magnetic force now passes from my body to that of Signora West,' the little man intoned. 'Complete balance and 'armony will soon be achieved.'

The earl, Rupert and Lord Lydiard had been coerced into sitting at the front of the audience. Rupert had mentally withdrawn to his own world. He sat with his arms stiffly folded across his chest, his eyes no more than slits. Lydiard was frankly snoring. The earl, however, maintained his polite interest in the pantomime before him and occasionally replied to Letty Learoyd's continuous whispered commentary.

Harriet looked about her. The drawing room was shuttered, illuminated by only a few candles and the firelight. In the gloom it was difficult to assess the attitude of the others; fascination, fear and boredom, she guessed. She could see Dr Makepeace and his young wife and dearly wanted to know what the physician was thinking.

Mrs West had been a patient of Dr Makepeace until Mr West had dismissed him with scathing comments regarding the doctor's failure to cure his wife and the exorbitance of his bills. Makepeace was well aware that he had been invited to be made to look incompetent. He had been persuaded to attend this "experiment" by his wife who wished her husband to be reinstated as the Wests' medical adviser and to further her own social ambitions. Makepeace could not resist the opportunity to expose the Italian "magnetiser" for the fraud that he was.

Sebastian and Archdeacon Learoyd stood next to each other at the back of the room, the slim athletic American a good head and shoulders taller than the fluffy-haired clergyman. The Durringtons and other guests were distributed on various sofas. A footman had provided a stool for Sir Charles Durrington's injured ankle. Mr West had placed his chair on the other side of Lord Lydiard and now did not know whether to wake his guest or not.

At last Mazzotta rose from his stool. 'The mesmeric link 'as been established. I will demonstrate this by inducing Signora West to follow me. You see she is calm, there is no crisis. The patient obeys my thoughts willingly.'

He then took five or six long strides between the chairs looking at the patient over his shoulder as he did so. After a brief hesitation Mrs West yielded to the influence and silently followed him. Lord Lydiard woke with a start as Mrs West's gauze shawl wafted against his face.

'Is she awake?' hissed Juliana.

Harriet did not know. Mrs West's eyes were open but unseeing. Everyone held their breath as Mazzotta led his patient back to her chair where she sank back into a state of insensibility.

'Ladies and gentlemen. I will now demonstrate the power of the 'ealing trance.'

From a small table at his side he took a hat pin. 'Signora?'

'Yes?' said the patient faintly, her head still on her chest.

'Tell to me what you feel,' and without hesitation he jabbed the hat pin into her arm. The audience jumped. Letty Learoyd let out a little scream and half rose. Mrs West gave no reaction.

'Do not disturb yourself, Madame. Your mother, she feel nothing. Her mind is in an altered state. The nerves are not receptive to any sensation. She feels only what I feel, thinks only my thoughts.' He returned to his patient. 'Ladies and Gentlemen, I will now show you 'ow the wonder of animal magnetism affects both the mental and physical properties of the body,' said the little Italian.

At a gesture from Mazzotta, two footmen placed a Chinese screen between himself and the patient. He slowly lifted his right arm above his head. Mrs West did the same. Each time the "magnetiser" moved a limb Mrs West, unbidden, mimicked him perfectly.

'She's like Georgiana's marionette,' giggled Juliana. 'How dreadful!'

After the experiments were repeated in other ways several spectators had to admit bafflement. Harriet wondered how any of this would help cure her friend's headaches and nervous complaints.

'I wouldn't like anyone to have such control over me,' whispered Juliana. 'Oh, dear. How much longer are we to sit here?'

On the mantelpiece an ornate bracket clock sweetly chimed three o'clock. The Italian made more intense passes over Mrs West's body whereupon her countenance and posture changed dramatically. Even in the dim light the lady took on a look of authority and firmness.

'Behold the transference of the vital fluid. The balance of the psyche and the physical is now completely established.' He leaned over his patient. "Ow do you feel, Signora? 'Ave you any pain, any disruption of the nerves?'

'I feel strong and well. I have no pain.'

'Will this animal magnetism mend my ankle?' chortled Sir Charles half aloud.

Mazzotta, sensing an opportunity said: 'Madame, will you please tell this gentleman what is wrong with him?'

Mrs West turned an astonishingly composed face towards her guest. 'I sense a weakness in all the bones. A regular iron tonic, and porter and an infusion of chalk should strengthen his constitution.'

Dr Makepeace snorted. As the proposed remedy was the accepted course of treatment, no one was very impressed. It was the lady's confidence that surprised her audience.

'Is there anyone else in the room who you are able to diagnose?' asked Mazzotta.

'My husband,' she said boldly. Mr West blustered some denial. It was acceptable that Euphemia make a fool of herself but he was not going to be the subject of this farce.

He had agreed to Mazzotta being invited only to keep the domestic peace after the debacle about Delilah. Lord Lydiard, now very much awake, clacked his teeth.

'My husband will die very soon-'

A gasp ran round the room. West leapt up. Dammit, he wished he'd never agreed to this public performance but he hoped to ingratiate himself with his neighbours by providing a learned entertainment, even if his wife were made to look ridiculous.

A few nervous titters rippled through the room until Mazzotta held up his hand for silence. 'It is perhaps wiser to end the demonstration 'ere, I believe.' He had seen his host's peremptory gesture of closure. He would win no clients this afternoon and may have lost this one.

'I do not wish to tire the patient further. 'Ave the goodness to retain your seats while I bring Signora West out of 'er trance.' He essayed a few passes across Mrs West's face, tapped her on her knee and bade her wake. Immediately her face fell into its usual fretful folds. She blinked, stared at her guests in embarrassment and sought for some control.

'Dear friends, how good of you to bear with Dr Mazzotta and myself for so long. Gracious, we have taken an age, but I hope some light has been shed on the wonders of animal magnetism for I swear I have never been in such good spirits until Dr Mazzotta came to us. Do forgive me, I am a trifle fatigued.'

This was a long speech for Mrs West. Letty went to her mother and helped her out of her chair. She invited the guests to partake of tea and sundries in the adjoining salon while she escorted her mother to her room. Mr West ordered the servants to douse the candles even though dusk was creeping in. After Euphemia's inexplicable revelation he would not encourage his neighbours to stay and wanted only to speak to Lord Lydiard alone. A footman moved the screen nearer the door.

Conversation over the tea cups was lively. A bowl of watery punch was also on offer among two plates of rout cakes and thin bread and butter. The ladies sat, the gentlemen clustered in knots of discussion.

'So poor West is destined for Davy Jones's locker eh?' said George with a grin. 'I'm not surprised, if he has to live on these rations.'

'We are all mortal, Mr Durrington. Mrs West did not predict exactly when she would lose her spouse or in what manner,' returned Makepeace, taking a bite out of a slice of tasteless pound cake and returning it to his plate.

Their host approached with his inevitable glass of sweet sherry in his hand.

'What d'you think of that, Makepeace? You heard my wife say she has never felt so well in her life. This Dr Mazzotta may not be one of your top-flight London doctors but a few sessions of animal magnetism have put an end to her megrims and pothers and the bills aren't as steep as yours, I can tell you.'

Makepeace put down his plate. 'I am gratified to hear of Mrs West's current good health. I assume you will not be needing my services when the influence of this "mesmerism" wears off?'

'Who's to say it will ever wear off,' blustered his host.

'Then I take it you are prepared to give this man shelter for the rest of your life, for however long that may be?' said Rupert.

Makepeace smothered a smile. West's face reddened. He would never have invited the Darvilles but for his wife, or Makepeace, for that matter, to be so impertinent under his own roof.

'You are of course familiar with the latest opinion in *The Lancet*?' challenged the doctor. 'The progress of quackery which prompts men to prefer the charlatan to the educated practitioner has long been criticised,' he half-quoted.

'Never heard of it,' interrupted their host. 'Ah, here comes another fool, short in inches and short on sense.'

Dr Learoyd was approaching and caught his father-in-law's words; with commendable self-command he ignored them. Sebastian followed looking mischievous.

'Now, now, father-in-law. Mrs West arranged this conversazione to discuss current matters of natural philosophy rationally and without rancour, like gentlemen.' He smiled placatingly at Makepeace.

'You've no call to poke your nose in! A clergyman is no cleverer than a physician, and not much more of a gentleman,' returned West.

Two angry spots of red appeared on Learoyd's cheeks. The men looked at their feet or their wine glasses. West knew he had gone too far but he was saved by an urgent summons from his butler. He turned on his heel and left the salon.

West's butler had managed to steer Frank straight upstairs to his own quarters but thought it best to forewarn his master of his heir's untimely arrival. After calling for some Madeira, Frank went to his mother's room to be bored by the account of her ailments and the wonder of Dr Mazzotta's treatment. His father entered and let lose a tirade of complaints and orders not to show himself to their guests. Euphemia collapsed into her usual nervous exhaustion and West left the airless room in a temper.

'I pray you will bear with my father-in-law, gentlemen. He is of a choleric disposition and has had many trials of late. He was undoubtedly shaken by his wife's unfortunate revelation,' said Dr Learoyd when West was safely out of the room.

'Which shows the danger of putting medical matters into the hands of non-practitioners,' Makepeace retorted coldly.

'Quite so,' replied Learoyd. 'As a man of the Church, I cannot approve of such tinkering with the unknown,' said the Archdeacon. He had been disgusted to find his mother-in-law in the thrall of this imposter. This was not the most unsettling discovery he had made that afternoon. 'God is the only power we should allow into our hearts and minds.' He stroked his pectoral cross piously.

'But you would not forbid the study of the human brain, surely? Imagine, if one could rid the world of disease without surgery or physic, by only manipulating the senses, think how many people we could save.' Like Rupert, Makepeace had seen the butchery of the battlefield.

'I am in the business of saving souls, Dr Makepeace. "Fear not them which kill the body, but are not able to kill the soul, but rather fear him which is able to destroy both soul and body in hell." Mathew ten, verse twenty-eight,' he said severely.

As this evoked no response, the Archdeacon rather floundered: 'I pray you will excuse me, gentlemen, Mr Romero wishes to see the chapel; the reredos has its own rustic charm.' He turned to Sebastian and indicated the open door. Sebastian smiled and followed with a jaunty step.

'West was damned rude but you will not think of taking this further, Makepeace?' said Rupert.

'No,' replied the doctor. 'He was lashing out in ignorance as that kind of man always does. Learoyd is forced to put up with it, but I am not. To that end, I think it better to remove temptation from our host's vicinity; I will take my leave of you.' He put down his glass and searched the room for his young wife.

'Don't go yet, Makepeace. Tell me, was our hostess in a state of complete catalepsy, do you think?' asked Rupert.

'How could one tell? In that poor light and with no opportunity to examine the lady I would not hazard a guess. She was almost comatose when we came into the room. Hypnotism works on any susceptible subject. There have been authenticated cures but no explanation as to why such methods work. Autosuggestion is not uncommon; the mind is a mysterious place.'

'What I do not understand is why anyone supposedly possessed of their senses ceases to be an accountable creature at the first opportunity,' said the earl, watching his secretary leave the salon. 'I fear that kind of influence.'

'What did you think of it all, Darville? You are the most learned one among us and have played with light and studied magnetism.' Sir Charles Durrington grimaced at his punch. 'Could it mend bones?'

'The Earth's magnetic field is not the quite the same thing, Sir Charles.' Rupert was his usual well-informed self. 'A French Royal Commission concluded the practise had no grounds in science as early as 1784; but even Laplace refused to dismiss the possibility of animal magnetism, on the basis that the nerves are the most sensitive instruments for the discovery of the "imperceptible agents of nature".' Laplace was an early hero of Rupert's and he would not denigrate the late-lamented polymath. The others, well used to his lectures, allowed him to talk on.

'Of course one cannot deny the cures but that does not prove that the body has a "vital fluid" controlled by internal magnetisation,' insisted Makepeace.

Rupert was about to concur when Lord Lydiard took him by the elbow and, with a toothy smile, steered him to a secluded corner near the lacquered screen. 'Tell me Darville, now this tomfoolery is over, can I persuade you to take the Larkhill nomination? I know you're not a high Tory and I'm not blind enough to think we can hold off Reform for ever. But if you take the seat for the next few years at least you can quash some of the more republican measures that Grey wants to bring in.'

'I hardly think broadening the franchise is a republican threat, my lord. The Prime Minister wants to avoid a revolution by giving the populace some say in how they are governed, which seems sensible to me. The Larkhill shopkeepers want reform and they'll be the voters of the future.'

'But for the present they'll elect who I tell them to! And I'd rather have you as my man than Horace West. Good God, what type of man allows such a lizard into his house to make a fool of his wife? You've better blood and are respected in the county and in London too. What you say will sway the House.' He bared his perfect set of dentures.

'But I will not be any man's mouthpiece my lord. I can only repeat that I am honoured by your confidence. However, I must continue to decline your flattering offer.'

Lydiard looked momentarily disgruntled and then shrugged. 'You're a fool then. I'm a man of influence and could have put you in the way of several advantageous schemes. You would have been privy to a deal of useful information.'

Lord Lydiard had made his money from the South Wales coalfields and the Kennet & Avon Canal on which his coal barges moved across the country. Nevertheless, for a forward-looking industrialist he had no truck with modern thinking in politics. He owned most of the land on which the town of Larkhill was built through his wife who had been a distant cousin of the late squire. He had settled on a vast estate in Somerset but held onto Larkhill for political reasons. As the town grew more prosperous he had been able to raise the rents of the properties and had increased his hold over his leaseholders by some judicial money-lending. It would be a foolish man who would cast his public vote against Lord Lydiard's candidate.

'Come, Darville, indulge me in this. I'll make it worth your while. We're distantly related through your wife and I cannot bring myself to dine with that blustering toady more than I have to.'

'I understand you have another member of the family who might be a more suitable candidate?'

Lord Lydiard looked wary. 'Mmm, I can say nothing as yet. I wanted to sound you out again and see if you were as stubborn as ever in your refusal.'

'I regret, my lord, I am.'

Lord Lydiard sucked his Waterloo teeth in disappointment. The two men moved away and Horace West emerged from behind the Chinese screen incandescent with rage. He wanted every man jack of them out of the house while he railed and swore and took himself off to Delilah. Instead he must continue with this humiliating party and had Frank to deal with at the end of it.

The men regrouped while Mazzotta ingratiated himself with the ladies.

'Do explain how you do such wonderful tricks,' begged Juliana from the sofa.

Mazzotta fluffed up his moustaches. 'No tricks, Signora, but a branch of 'Ippocrates' art which will sweep the world.' His bright eyes scanned them all, assessing each one's susceptibility. 'The founder of our science, Dr Anton Mesmer claimed there is a natural transfer of energy that occurs between all animate and inanimate objects; 'e called it "animal magnetism", which I 'ave been privileged to demonstrate to you this afternoon.'

'But you used no magnets, sir. I do not understand.'

'You are very observant, Signora Darville. Your 'usband is a famous man of science. 'E will explain to you the theory of fluid matter which occupies all of space and, because all bodies have pores, this fluid introduces itself into the body and flows in and out from other bodies – as if drawn by a magnet – which produces the phenomenon which we call "animal magnetism".' He beamed at the assembled women.

Harriet was used to long explanations from Rupert but thought she would not trouble him on this matter. Dr Learoyd and Sebastian reappeared and joined the women.

'The spirit of life is breathed in by the Creator; it is blasphemy to propose anything less,' said the Archdeacon.

'Ah, a priest would surely think so.' Mazzotta looked conciliatory. 'Monseigneur, the "fluid" we speak of consists of fire, air and spirit. Who is to say whether the spirit is divine or of nature? These are great questions for philosophers and theologians, not an 'umble *medico* like myself. To what extent the life of the mind is mechanical, and which spiritual matters are governed by natural law I leave to others cleverer than I.'

'But how can animal magnetism induce a state of mind which allows such experiments as you have shown us today?' Harriet persisted. Juliana rustled her fan impatiently.

'Madame is familiar with the properties of a fluid, no? Like all other fluids animal magnetism searches for equilibrium, therefore all bodies are drawn towards each other. *Naturelmente*, the stronger force will flow into the weaker.'

No one disputed that Euphemia West was the weaker vessel.

'Rather like electricity,' suggested Harriet, though she was not quite certain.

'Mama was not electrified,' protested Letty who now fluttered into the circle. 'She is sleeping quite peacefully with no recollection of the séance.'

'I did see her hands shake when you touched her, Signore,' said Lady Durrington, her sense of propriety a little disturbed.

'I beg, ladies, do not slander this treatment with the term "séance". You 'ave witnessed a scientific wonder which is dedicated only to 'ealing. Ask Signora West.'

'Whatever it is, it is a bizarre phenomenon,' said Mary. She was distracted by Charity who had slipped away to stand by the punch bowl in the hopes that Sebastian might offer to fill her glass. The young American was now deep in conversation with his patron. It was left to one of Lord Lydiard's tenants to offer Miss Wakefield a cup of the diluted elderberry wine.

Mazzotta moved on, satisfied he had intrigued the ladies of the district but wary of Harriet's blunt questions. The men, he knew, were harder nuts to crack.

In a little while the townspeople took their leave; it was never comfortable to mix with the carriage folk for long.

A few cryptic words and knowing looks were exchanged between Lord Lydiard and his leaseholders. Most of the electors were still uncertain where Lydiard's patronage would fall but none of them wanted to see Horace West as their representative in parliament.

'I see the secretary has come,' said Juliana when she and Harriet were alone. 'Dr Learoyd looked as though he had seen the Archangel when they were introduced. No man has a right to be as beautiful at that American boy.'

'I must go and rescue Letty. Rupert is certain to be expounding on some abstruse subject and she won't listen and he'll be cross,' said Harriet, unwilling to pursue the conversation.

Juliana looked around. 'How provoking, Mama and Papa are leaving and we have not yet seen the negress.'

'Don't be ridiculous, Juliana, even Mr West would not parade his paramour in the drawing room.'

'Do you know if Frank's coming home for the holidays? I wonder what he will think of it all.' The whole neighbourhood knew and tutted over the reprobate son.

'Letty said they expected him some days ago.'

'I wonder what horrors he would reveal if he were magnetised? No wonder Mrs West's nerves are always in shreds. I notice the Talbots are not here. Tommy is expected home today and Cheney Court is full of poor relations, so I hear.' Juliana picked up her shawl and her fan and pecked Harriet on the cheek goodbye.

Charity had at last lured Sebastian to the window. Topiary cones and low box hedges in intricate clipped patterns stood either side of the yellow sanded walks. The vista was lifeless and cold. A thin mist gathered over the river.

'Is there a body of water beyond that hedge, Miss Wakefield? It's growing so dark I can't quite make it out.' Sebastian craned his neck to peer out of the window, unconsciously moving closer to Charity. Her heart skipped a beat as a waft of mimosa filled her nostrils.

'I believe there's a river near here. I do not know what it is called. If it were summer how I'd love to take advantage of the water. Do you row, Mr Romero?'

'I do and sail too. My family has a place on the coast in Massachusetts; every summer we take a boat out off Cape Cod. I persuaded the earl to buy a yacht and we spent most of last August cruising the Bay of Naples.'

Charity sighed at the idyllic image. She was not pleased when the Archdeacon came up, almost trapping them against the glass. 'Do you like boats, Dr Learoyd?' asked Charity. 'Mr Romero sails a yacht.'

'I can manage oars as well as the next man but my preference is for hunting.'

Sebastian gave a dazzling smile. 'Why, isn't that just grand! I've been invited to a hunt on New Year's Day hereabouts. Some place called Hinton Parva. Are you going, Reverend?'

'Have you brought your horses with you?'

'Mrs Darville has lent me her mare during my stay. I love a good gallop after the fox.'

'Indeed. My father-in-law hunts so will be able to mount me.' He was surprised that Darville had not offered his guest the use of his second hunter.

'Then I guess I'll see you at the New Year, if not before. The reredos was quite beautiful.' This was said in such an arch manner that a slight tinge of pink came into the clergyman's cheeks. He gave Charity a quick look but she was distracted by a scuffle at the door.

Frank West strolled in and stared boldly at the company. His father stiffened. What other disaster could plague him this afternoon? All he wanted was to be out of it all and soothed and petted by a sympathetic woman, though that was another hopeless dream.

'I say, this is a fine welcome home,' said Frank clearly. 'My mother prostrate after some medical nonsense and all her neighbours gathered to gawp. My father too busy to send a carriage to collect me and no dinner waiting.' He looked disparagingly at the scanty table.

There was a great rustle of movement from the guests. Lydiard, who was committed to staying the night, stared at the young man with hostility.

'Francis has come down from London and has caught us unawares. You know what these young people are,' said West. For want of anything better to do and in a spirit of malice, Frank had sauntered downstairs expressly against his father's orders.

'The boy's drunk,' hissed someone.

'I wish I was,' said George and escorted his father and womenfolk to the door. Rupert, who had been immersed in a discussion on Lobachevsky's new mathematics with Hunniford's vicar was unaware of the undercurrents in the room. He did not notice Frank's arrival until Harriet whispered the information into his ear. Harriet caught Rupert by the arm and followed the others, murmuring their adieus to a bewildered Letty who was begging them all to stay. Morna made smooth farewells while Sebastian studied Frank with interest.

Within a few moments the salon was empty of guests.

The Wests, the Learoyds, Lord Lydiard and Mazzotta were left amid the debris of the tea cups.

****

That evening, Rupert and Morna settled over their port at the dinner table. Clem had been encouraged to join his aunt and Miss Humble in the green drawing room and Sebastian had been sent away to study catalogues and write letters.

Morna turned to his brother. 'What did you think of this afternoon's performance?'

'"Performance" is the right term. I'm inclined to agree with Makepeace: if the method works then use it, but there's still no evidence for this "universal fluid". We need a learned body to investigate all these claims; Brewster's trying to set one up to promote our patents and advance science generally in the national and international field. I would not go as far as Babbage in his recent *Reflections on the Decline of Science*-'

'My dear boy, pray do not to talk to me about natural philosophy; I am quite fatigued enough by the afternoon. All I know is that Mazzotta is no more Italian than I am,' interrupted Morna.

'No, indeed – from Hackney, I would guess.'

'The cakes were dry and the punch filthy.'

'Were they?' Food had never figured largely in Rupert's consciousness.

'I wonder what prompted Mrs West to foredoom her husband.'

Rupert thought for a moment. 'I have no idea. West is a hard-headed business man; this afternoon's little party was out of character. He's normally very dismissive of his wife, so Harriet tells me, but I think something, some crisis, must have forced him to pander to her ill-health. Or perhaps he was trying to make a good impression on the electors of Larkhill.'

'A noticeably unsuccessful attempt. What do you make of the son-in-law?'

'The Archdeacon?' Rupert did not make very much of anyone beyond his own family. 'I know nothing about the man apart from a civil nod in the street when he visits. As a senior member of the Anglican Church he is responsible for the welfare of his clergy in several Winchester parishes and takes charge of the maintenance of church buildings within the archdeaconry. Will that suffice?'

'Indeed it will,' said Morna thoughtfully and then shaking himself out of his petty mood said with his customary good humour: 'I am constantly surprised at how much you know about matters which do not concern you.'

'Know thy enemy,' said Rupert. 'Now, shall we join the ladies? I believe Clem intends to entertain us with his flute. Dunch, bring the port, would you?'

Chapter 6 Jacob causes trouble

Jem drove the gig into Larkhill with Jacob by his side. There had been no disturbances recorded for nearly two weeks, but Jem still carried the shotgun.

Rupert had sent his valet to the receiving office and Harriet had found herself short of several delicacies to satisfy the tastes of her visitors. Jacob was normally protective of his position as Mr Darville's personal servant, but he owed the Darvilles much and was glad of an opportunity to leave the bustle of the kitchen. He left Jem and the gig in the livery stable at the edge of the town and sauntered down the cobbled high street acknowledging the nods of various passers-by. He had finished his errands within the hour.

As he re-passed the grocer's shop he was arrested by the sight of a statuesque young woman looking worriedly at a piece of paper. She was a servant by her clothes; a grey merino dress, new boots and coarse cloak. Her bonnet was unadorned and from underneath peeped the frill of a mob cap. The face under it was the same colour as his own, a pale café au lait, but far prettier. He knew of her. The servants had heard the latest news from Bourne Park and although he tried to keep himself aloof from kitchen gossip, he knew that Horace West had installed a black girl as his mistress. He made to move on, but there was something about this girl's woeful stance that made him stop.

'May I be of service?'

The girl jumped, looked frightened and then paused at the sight of his face. 'Thankee, sir. I cannot read this lass word, sir. The ress I know but Cook will beat me if I doan't com back with everyting.'

Jacob gently took the paper and examined the cursive handwriting. He read slowly down the list, the girl nodding at each item. 'And finally, a pound of Málaga raisins.'

'Ah,' said the girl. 'The ress I remember, but there are so many loops in dat word-'

'Would you like me to come in with you, and speak to the shopkeeper?'

The girl hesitated. 'I doan't know. Massa said I was to speak to no one.'

'Who is your master?' he asked, not wanting to betray the fact that he knew her situation.

'Mista West of Bourne Park,' she muttered.

'I am Jacob Ombay, Mr Daville's man, of the Manor and Quennell House. There can be no objection to your speaking to me. And now you must tell me your name.'

'Delilah, Della for shortness.' She dropped a curtsey.

'Well, Miss Della, let us go into the shop and buy these raisins.'

Delilah looked even more nervous and fumbled in her reticule. She brought out a sovereign. 'Please, sir, could you help me wit' de money? Cook said I must bring back lotsa specie, coins.'

Jacob wondered why the purchases could not be added to the West's account. When they entered, Mr Bell and his comfortable wife greeted Jacob with smiles.

'Back again Mr Ombay? Did you forget something for Mrs Darville? How may we assist you?'

'You can rather help this young woman,' said Jacob, drawing a reluctant Delilah in front of him. 'She has a list of requirements for Mr West's cook and does not know the currency in England.'

'Mr West said he would no longer give us his custom,' said Mr Bell looking starchy. 'Not that we need it anyway.'

'It is an emergency, I think. I hope this young woman has not been sent on a fool's errand.'

Mrs Bell took pity on the forlorn girl. 'Well, his money's as good as anyone's and we don't want the maid blamed for her master's ill-manners.' It was plain she had not heard of Delilah's position at the Park.

Delilah gave Jacob a grateful look as he handed over the paper. Mr Bell licked his pencil and wrote the price by each item on the list, while his wife weighed and measured the dry goods. At the conclusion Mr Bell counted out and explained the change to Delilah. Jacob was an accepted figure in the town and the Darville family influential.

Their errands done, the two young people left the shop, Delilah thanking Jacob profusely but clearly wanting to hurry away.

'You must let me drive you back to Bourne Park. I have the gig,' said Jacob, hoping Jem would understand. 'It is not safe for a woman to be on the road alone. It is at least three miles and there'll be more snow before the day's end.' The road would take them quite out of his way but he did not want to say goodbye to this tall, flower-faced girl.

'No, no, 'tis no trouble at all to walk. I tank you sir, but I cannot be seen wid anyone.'

'I would leave you at the gates of the Park. Your cook must be impatient for her ingredients.'

They were walking towards the livery stable, Jacob carrying Delilah's basket, his own parcels under his arm. They were passing the archway of the Three Crowns when a figure on horseback clattered out into the street and nearly mowed them down.

'Out of my way there!' snapped the rider and then, looking down at his victims, drew on the reins so sharply that his mount reared and scrambled for a footing on the wet cobbles. 'Dammit, you'll have me unhorsed the pair of you!' shouted Horace West. 'What are you doing here, girl? And who is this?'

He steadied his mount with difficulty and levelled his riding crop at Jacob. Like many angry men he enjoyed mastering a big horse.

'I am Mr Darville's valet, sir,' said Jacob, expecting this would defuse the situation.

'Are you? Yes – well. It makes no odds; this girl should not be abroad.' West knew perfectly well who Jacob was but considered other people's servants beneath his notice.

'The young woman was sent into town on an errand for your cook, sir,' explained Jacob holding tight to Della's trembling arm.

'Silence! I was not speaking to you. Unhand my servant and take yourself off!' The mettlesome horse was becoming restive and a few heads were turned in their direction.

Jacob knew that whatever he said would make more trouble for the girl. He turned to the frightened creature beside him. 'Wait for me by the–'

The frayed leather keeper of West's riding crop flicked across Jacob's cheek with a resounding crack. The girl shrieked in alarm. Jacob faced his attacker with blazing eyes. He put his hand to his face and wiped away a few beads of blood. 'You should not have done that, sir.'

Horace West in truth had not meant to. He had wanted only to prod Jacob's shoulder with the crop to push him away from Delilah but Jacob's movement and the lunging horse had brought about this unlucky occurrence.

'Move away, move away!' blustered West as Jacob dropped the packages and took a step towards him. 'Your master shall hear of this insolence. I'll have you whipped out of town!'

'You will not sir. I am a free man and can speak to whom I please.' Jacob unconsciously tightened his grip on Delilah's arm. The girl started to sob and pull away.

West, shocked into outrage, raised his riding crop again. Jacob lunged at the stirrup of the restive horse and looked up into the turkey-cock face.

'You touch me with that thing again and I'll kill you,' he said with cold venom.

The onlookers gasped and drew together. Jem stepped out of the inn yard where he had been chatting to an ostler friend. He pulled Jacob by the shoulder. 'Come away, there, Mr Ombay, do. Leave the maid be. T'aint doing no good for her nor you.'

The brawny coachman looked up at Horace West. 'He don't mean nothing by it sir, you know what it is with these touchy foreigners.'

Jacob shook off the friendly hand and stepped back. Delilah had flattened herself against the inn wall, transfixed with terror.

'You heard that! You all heard him! I call you to witness,' cried West, encompassing the crowd with his crop. 'This devil threatens to murder me! I'm a justice of the peace. I'll have you up before the Assizes if you threaten me, you dog! Now get home to your master before I call for the constables.' He backed his horse away from the crowd and turned to the girl. 'Get up behind me.'

She clung to the wall of the Three Crowns staring at her employer in incomprehension.

'Have you lost your wits? Do as I say – here, get up behind me, now!' It was plain that the girl was too frightened to move.

'You there, you've got a lot to say for yourself; give the wench a hand,' he ordered Jem. The coachman coaxed the girl forward and lifted her up easily behind the substantial rump of Horace West.

'Cling on tight, maidy,' whispered Jem. 'I reckon he'll give you a rough ride home.'

Jacob stood smouldering with resentment in the crowd, dabbing his cheek with his handkerchief. There would be only a faint scar, unnoticeable among the three deep tribal incisions in his left cheek.

'And the basket,' demanded West impatiently. 'Give her the basket.' He was in charge now and wanted to show it. Reluctant hands retrieved the morning's purchases. As he watched the scramble on the wet cobbles, West said 'I won't leave my property unguarded for any nigger to act the thief. Is everything there? Have you found them all?'

'I reckon so, sir,' said Jem.

Jacob stuffed his handkerchief in his pocket and stepped forward, delving into the basket in his friend's hand.

'Wait! This, and this one and yes, this parcel belong to Mr Rupert Darville. I would not leave his property unguarded for any bully to act the thief.' This with a malevolent stare at West.

There was another intake of breath from the crowd. Someone thought they should fetch the constable but West lashed his horse into motion. He had made his point, he would not stay to bandy words with an uppity servant. Damn Rupert Darville and everything connected with him!

Delilah cried out in fear and dug her nails into the broadcloth of her master's greatcoat, the basket bumping perilously over her arm.

Jacob watched her go with anxious eyes.

****

The following day, Horace West entered his study, unsure what this call from the Honourable Rupert Darville portended. Rupert had never visited him alone before, no matter how hard Mr West had tried to ingratiate himself with the young aristocrat in the early days of Darville's marriage to Harriet. West wondered if Darville had changed his mind about refusing Lord Lydiard's nomination and had come to inform his rival. It was just the chivalrous gesture that the fool would indulge in. Or did he want to poach Mazzotta away from Bourne Park and take him to London for one of his fancy lectures? He'd be too late, West thought with satisfaction; he had packed the phoney Italian off the day after the conversazione despite Euphemia's pleadings. Nevertheless, this tall, dark, precise man always made him feel apprehensive. The possibility that Rupert had come to confront him over a servant never crossed his mind.

Greetings were exchanged, more on Horace West's side than Darville's. Rupert refused the offer of sherry.

'This is an unexpected pleasure, Darville. What can I do for you?'

'I'm here, Mr West, because I have heard a strange tale that there was some "altercation" between you and one of my servants in Larkhill High Street.' Rupert was not a man to dress up his thoughts in tact.

West shuffled some papers on his desk, caught by surprise. 'A minor incident I assure you. I have dismissed the matter from my mind. Think nothing of it.'

'But I must think of it. My valet has been brutally stuck in the face, for what reason he would not say. I cannot think that a gentleman would behave in this way, unless under the severest provocation. Do I dismiss my servant for gross misconduct? Because only that would warrant such an attack.'

Rupert's tone was perfectly reasonable if cold, which embarrassed West even more.

'No, no. Do not dismiss the fellow. Much was said in the heat of the moment. I can assure you, Darville; it was a storm in a tea cup. All best forgotten.' He took a gulp of sherry.

'My servant is scarred, sir. The town is alive with the incident. I give no credence to the wilder tales, of course, but as my valet will tell me nothing, I regret I am forced to come to you for an explanation.'

West felt himself backed into a corner. 'The man threatened me, sir,' he blustered. 'Me! A magistrate that could have him sent to the hulks. He almost brought my horse down.'

'My servant threatened you?' Rupert asked in disbelief.

'He said he would kill me! And I had to defend myself, as any man would, especially in times like these. I have received threatening letters from these insurgents calling themselves "Captain Swing".'

'I can assure you that none of my servants is involved with such disturbances. However, if you were threatened, Jacob must be arrested at once. Was this an unprovoked attack? Why did you not lay a charge against him? The constables would have taken him to the lock-up instantly on your word.'

West shifted in his chair again and cleared his throat. 'I'm not a vindictive man, Darville. And knowing the black was your servant I did not wish to inconvenience such a good neighbour. Gentlemen do not do such things.'

'But you see I am a vindictive man. And I am inconvenienced. And you are no gentleman.'

West's mouth fell open at the deliberateness of the tone.

Rupert continued: 'If you come within a mile of me and mine again I will take a horsewhip to you.' He rose. 'I will see myself out. Good day.'

'How dare you, sir! In my own house! Are you threatening me, sir? I've never heard the like! Like master, like man... When I'm Member of Parliament here-'

'And you're certain that day will come?' asked Rupert turning with his strong fingers on the door handle.

West paled as his intestines gave a stab of pain. It was all going wrong. He knew Lydiard could not be trusted. This damned opinionated pen-pusher may have turned down the seat but he could still wreck his chances of becoming a man of influence in the county. West tugged at the bell pull.

'Leave my house this instant, sir! Before my servants put you out.' His face was now purple with apoplectic rage.

'Nothing would give me greater pleasure.' Rupert walked out, his almond eyes narrowed, his nostrils flaring in disgust.

The butler wondered how many other people his employer would offend before the year was out.

****

Rupert knew exactly what had occurred from George Durrington. George had been standing in the coffee room doorway of the Three Crowns and had witnessed the whole episode.

'Nasty contretemps. I daresay West didn't mean to strike your man but half the town saw it. West behaved like a blustering fool as always and Jacob did not back down, more's the pity. I suspect because of the pretty wench involved. She's West's latest fancy, so Juliana tells me.'

'To the devil with West and his women.'

'He's got more to worry about than that. He'd just been into Salisbury to see his attorney and was cursing all lawyers. I'll wager he's cut Frank out of his will again. And he's seen off the "magnetiser"; no man likes to hear a prophecy of their own doom, especially from his wife.'

'And I fear the man is aware that Lydiard again offered me the Larkhill seat in preference to himself. Oh, don't look so hopeful; I turned it down,' he said to George's disappointment. 'But that added fuel to the fire of course. We have never got on.'

As Rupert could be as cold as Horace West was choleric, this was no news to his friend.

****

The following afternoon Dunch answered the jangle of the bell to admit Dr Learoyd.

'Good afternoon. I wish to have a private word with Mr Darville, if convenient.'

'Very good sir, if you care to step inside, I'll inform the master.' Taking the Archdeacon's card the butler disappeared, leaving the visitor stranded in the vestibule holding his hat. In the way of good servants, Dunch knew all about Rupert's quarrel with Horace West.

Hearing voices, Sebastian emerged from the Great Hall where he had been sketching the intricate carvings on the minstrels' gallery. He looked very dashing in shirt sleeves.

'Why Reverend, it's a pleasure to see you again. Come in and wait by the fire in here. What brings you to this lovely old manor?'

The Archdeacon became formal. 'A personal matter for Mr Darville's ears alone.'

'Then I wouldn't dream of intruding, sir,' said Sebastian with a small bow and made as if to leave.

'No, no, don't go, Mr Romero. I had hopes I might see you again. I so enjoyed our talk on church ornaments at the conversazione. I found it the only rational occurrence during the whole unfortunate afternoon.'

'Why, thank you, sir. It was a pleasure for me to talk with someone as conversant as yourself with all the architectural styles.'

'I regret my knowledge extends only to ecclesiastical buildings.'

'Fascinating edifices, sir. We have none such wondrous cathedrals in America and they are very different from the Romanesque churches in France and Italy. I so admire the gothic style; it's very romantic, don't you think?'

The man of the cloth paused and then attempted: 'Could I – perhaps,' he hesitated again. 'Would it interest you to be shown around Salisbury Cathedral? I flatter myself I know it almost as well as my own church, that is Winchester Cathedral, which I could also show you, if you have the time. He could hear footsteps and hurried on. 'The chantry displays the crocketed and finial ogee which marks it as being very early perpendicular. It is of modest interest.'

'Why surely,' Sebastian opened his hazel eyes wide. 'I'd be delighted to come with you. I would have to ask my patron if I may have leave but he is not like a regular employer and would encourage me to enlarge my experiences.' This was said with such a drawl that Learoyd was relieved when Dunch appeared on the threshold.

Within a moment Dr Learoyd was escorted to the library. Bernard gathered some papers and retreated to the school room. The Archdeacon took a seat and regretted his foolish impulse to come. Rupert, unsmiling as ever, looked at his visitor through gimlet eyes.

'How can I help you, Archdeacon?' Rupert knew instinctively what had prompted this call and felt contempt for the man.

Dr Learoyd spent the next ten minutes apologising for his father-in-law's temper. Nothing of which made any impression on Rupert. He listened in stony silence which unnerved his visitor even more. When the Archdeacon had used up all the excuses, he begged Mr Darville to exercise Christian forgiveness and not to break off all contact with Bourne Park because 'My mother-in-law is so very fond of Mrs Darville'. The precise speech faltered to a close.

Rupert said: 'What the ladies do is their affair. But Mr West and I have nothing to say to each other. I take it you are not acting as his messenger?'

The Archdeacon bridled. 'No, of course not. I am here in the spirit of Christian love and humility. Mr West has no idea I have come, but I promised myself that if I had a favourable welcome I would try to soften my father-in-law's heart in the matter.'

Rupert stood up. 'Even if Mr West did regret his intemperate behaviour, I do not regret mine. Good day, sir.'

He rang the bell for Dunch while Learoyd protested and hoped that his own presence and that of his wife was not to be shunned by the Darville family.

'I cannot prevent you from calling but would you risk your father-in-law's wrath if he came to hear of it?' asked Rupert bluntly. Learoyd swallowed. For once in his life, the Archdeacon felt himself in momentary sympathy with Horace West.

'I assure you that I am not my father-in-law's lackey! But I see I am wasting my time. Good day, sir.'

Just then, the butler appeared in the doorway. 'Ah, Dunch, Dr Learoyd is leaving,' Rupert said, not moving from his desk.

Chapter 7   Escape!

If Rupert had had a difficult afternoon, so had Harriet. The fishmonger delivered a cod instead of a carp and only one barrel of oysters instead of two and, although Dunch sent the wagoner packing with a sharp word, Harriet felt she should drive into Larkhill to insist on her correct Christmas order. At the same time she could enquire after their coal delivery which was already three days behindhand. It was at times like these that she wished for a housekeeper. Miss Humble was trying to keep order between Henry and Lizzie and Gerald's daughters and Harriet felt that the elderly governess needed more of her support.

After a cold drive and an unhelpful interview with the fishmonger she called in at the lodge to see Annie. Rupert insisted on keeping the gates to the manor closed in these troubled times. Annie's tardiness at the gate was explained by her anxiety over the baby; she thought little Paul had whooping cough. Harriet promised to send for Dr Makepeace and told the older children to come up to the house for various medicaments.

She was stripping her gloves off in the vestibule when Clem came rushing down the Grand Staircase like an avalanche.

'She's let Captain Blood go! She opened the cage and let him fly out of the window. Deliberately! Not an hour since.'

'Goodness, what do you mean?' Though in that instant Harriet knew exactly what had happened. Dunch stood woodenly by.

'Sophia has murdered Captain Blood! She opened the cage on purpose and pushed him out of the window just to spite me. She boasted of it! It's snowing again; he'll die of cold. He's a *tropical* bird. He's never been outside the house before. I must tell Uncle Rupert at once.'

'No, no,' said Harriet quickly. 'The parrot won't have flown far, he wouldn't have the strength. Get all the children to help you in a search party. And Jacob. Jacob's good with Captain Blood; the bird will go to him. You'll find the parrot somewhere in the grounds, I'm sure. Dunch, do what you can to assist Master Clement. Don't disturb your Uncle Rupert, though Mr Romero might offer to help you, if you can find him. He may have ridden into Larkhill, though I did not see him.'

Clem scampered back up the stairs.

'I will speak to Sophia. Send for Mrs O'Leary, Dunch.'

Fifteen minutes later, there was a knock on her bedroom door. Mrs O'Leary ushered in the drab figure of a mutinous Sophia.

Harriet looked at the child, from her lank hair to her resentful pale face, her bitten nails and stiff clothes. Harriet did not feel much charity in her heart.

'Leave us, Mrs O'Leary.'

'Oh, m'lady mam, you'll not be too hard on the sainted angel. A motherless child with only her ol' nurse to care for her. She meant no harm-'

'Thank you, Mrs O'Leary, you may go,' said Harriet from her dressing stool. Mrs O' Leary wobbled her way out of the room.

Sophia continued to stare at the carpet.

'Come here,' ordered Harriet. The girl shuffled forward.

Harriet sat with her hands in her lap and spoke with deliberation. 'Attend to me carefully. I know things are strange and new, and you miss your papa and your old life in Ireland. But there is nothing anyone can do to bring it back. You are old enough to understand that. We are your family now and you will conform to our rules while you are in this house. We have all been very indulgent towards you and I suspect you have tried Clem's patience in more ways than one since you have been with us. But to let his pet out to a certain death is cruel. He has had Captain Blood since he was five years old. Your Uncle Rupert brought it back for him from Brazil. I dread to think what he will say when he hears of this.'

For the first time a flicker of apprehension passed across Sophia's muddy features.

'What have you to say for yourself?' prompted Harriet.

'Nothin'. I didn't know the stupid bird was going to fly out the window.'

Harriet had been hoping for contrition and in the face of such stubbornness she hardened her heart.

'That is not what Clem tells me. Go to your room now while I think of a suitable punishment. You have seriously upset your cousin. I will have to decide whether you remain with us or not.'

'What about Rosa? If you send me away, can she come too?' There was a note of panic in the child's voice and Harriet had to steel herself not to weaken.

'All this will have to be discussed with your uncles. Go to your room and pray on your knees that the bird is found alive and unharmed.'

Young Clem marshalled his troops with a military precision that would have delighted his father. Sebastian had just returned and offered to search the priory ruins. Jacob searched the orchard. The children were ordered to scour the rose garden and the Yew Walk.

But the cold soon drove them indoors and Jacob had to return to the house to help his master dress for dinner. On Harriet's orders, he said nothing to Rupert about the hunt for the bird.

Despite the falling snow and the creeping twilight, Clem continued to tramp round the grounds for another hour until a flash of green plumage from the glasshouse in the kitchen garden gave him hope. The glass roof still held a residue of warmth from the brazier within and the parrot clung on more dead than alive. Gingerly, Clem held out a slice of dried apple in his frozen fingers and talking softly to the bird coaxed his pet onto his wrist. Very carefully he put Captain Blood in his coat and walked back to the house in triumph.

Harriet left the ecstatic children to fuss over the parrot's recovery and bade Clem hold his tongue. She would discuss the matter with his uncles when the time was right. Rosa was as relieved as anyone that the bird was found and begged that Sophia be let out of their bedroom. Harriet refused.

Clem was more concerned with his pet. 'I cannot leave the poor fellow tonight. I must keep him warm and fed. Could I have my dinner sent up to the nursery? Or perhaps I should keep the poor creature in my room tonight?' Now that Sophia was confined to the blue bedroom he had no quarrel with eating with the children.

'What are you going to do about Sophia?' he asked, following his aunt to the nursery door. 'She's a troublemaker. Harry and Lizzie don't like her.' This incident had destroyed any sense of chivalry he may have felt towards his distant cousin.

'That depends on your uncles but I think she and Rosa will have to go away to boarding school, then we may have harmony in the house again.'

'Good riddance,' he said in a rare show of vindictiveness.

****

The following morning, sitting up against the pillows, Harriet drank her chocolate slowly, her mind full of the problem of Sophia. Suddenly the nursery maid burst into the room. 'Oh, ma'am! I've just been to look and the young Irish ladies did not come for breakfast and are not in their bed!'

Harriet put down her cup. 'They are not with Miss Lizzie and Master Henry in the school room, I take it?'

'No, ma'am. Tilly came to lay the nursery fire and said the bed in the blue room was empty when she went to lay theirs at six o'clock.'

'Pass me my robe,' said Harriet sliding quickly out of bed and searching for her slippers. 'Perhaps they rose early and are playing somewhere, in the stables most probably.'

She went straight to the blue bedroom to find Mrs O'Leary beached like a whale on her truckle bed, grey faced and tearful. Her false curls lay on the dressing table like an enormous yellow caterpillar. The room reeked of whisky.

'What's the meaning of this? Where are the young ladies? They are in your charge! How dare you allow them to roam at this time of the morning? I particularly asked you to confine Lady Sophia to her bedroom.'

'Quiet as mice they must ha' been. I had no notion of them tippy-toeing about, the sweet tings. An' I'm sure they didn't want to disturb a poor body who slaves all day after them.' Mrs O'Leary wiped her eyes on the corner of her voluminous nightdress. 'Not to fret, ma'am. They'll be playing somewhere, that's what it is – in the gardens. They're so used to being will o' the wisp, little fairies that they are.'

Harriet picked up the whisky bottle. 'You are dismissed,' she said flatly. 'Gather your belongings and go.'

Mrs O'Leary let out a wail of protest. 'You wouldn't dismiss a body for takin' a drop o' the pure to keep out the bitter cold. I'm almost sleepin' on the floor on this truckle bed. The draft goes through my bones like a blade!'

Harriet hesitated. 'Wait, you had better see Mr Darville first and stay until we find the young ladies.'

She went to the closet. 'They have taken their outside things; at least they'll be warm. Where could they have gone?'

Mrs O'Leary struggled to her feet. 'Let me come with you ma'am, for the search. I've a thought where they might be. Carried off by the gypsies I'll be bound!'

'Nonsense!' said Harriet, knowing in some obscure way that it could be true. 'I must inform my husband at once.'

Rupert was dressing when she entered his room.

'My dear, what's amiss?' he said, taking one look at her anxious face. 'The children?'

'Sophia and Rosa have vanished. Mrs O'Leary was drunk. She thinks they have been taken by the gypsies.'

'That's hardly likely. We're long past the days of cradle-snatching. I locked up the house myself last night; no one could enter.' He continued to tie his cravat in a precise knot. Catching sight of his wife's face in the glass, he turned and took her hands in this.

'They have not been abducted, Harriet.' He said slowly. 'Put that fear out of your mind. They are playing somewhere in the house or grounds, or pestering Jem in the stables. Or they have gone down to Home Farm, as you yourself did as a girl.'

He turned back to the mirror. 'They are hiding to frighten us, after yesterday. They're a sorry pair and the sooner we send them away to school the better.'

'But we must find them first!'

The night before, Harriet had told the brothers of the incident with the parrot and tried to make light of it. Morna had laughed at her humorous account but Rupert had looked stern. As the distractions of the day faded, her anger had cooled and she hoped Rupert would give his nieces another chance. Rupert was unconvinced. Morna was sentimental but indifferent.

This morning Rupert thought his wife looked about sixteen with her hair in a long plait and without her matronly garb. He silently cursed this incident which stirred such ugly memories for her. Jacob helped him on with his black coat.

'Jacob, my compliments to the earl and ask him if he would meet me in the library as soon as possible on a matter of some urgency. Whether he likes it or not, the children are his nieces as much as ours and he should be informed at least.'

When they were alone, Harriet said: 'Then you do think they are with the gypsies? Their outdoor clothes have gone. What if they are walking on the road and are waylaid by ruffians?' She knew Rupert would not disturb his brother if he thought the children were playing in the attics or in the Yew Walk. 'The bed's been slept in so they must have crept out somehow at dawn, when the maids were up.'

'Field hands are not interested in children. Let us search the house and grounds before we move further afield. We need to question Clem and the children; they may be able to throw some light on the matter.' He tugged at the bell. 'There is no need to agitate yourself, we'll find them within the hour.'

When a maid appeared he sent for Dunch. Harriet went to the nursery. Her own children were wide-eyed with excitement.

'Have Sophia and Rosa been stolen by gypsies, Mama?' said Lizzie

'What nonsense have you heard? I'm sure Miss Humble does not fill your head with such foolish stories.'

'Certainly not, Mrs Darville; that dreadful Irish woman puts all sorts of unsavoury ideas into their minds.'

Captain Blood cackled ominously in his cage as though he knew something was afoot.

"Be quiet you horrid bird! This is all your fault.' Harriet threw a cloth over the cage and continued: 'Sophia and Rosa are merely playing somewhere or have wandered off and got lost. Nevertheless it is very cold outside and we don't want them to come to any harm, so Papa is organising a search.'

Harriet helped her daughter on with her apron and said casually: 'Have you any idea where they might be?'

'They've run away,' said Henry picking up his porridge spoon.

Harriet blinked. But of course they had. The unspoken threat of boarding school had probably driven them to flee. Harriet felt guilty, upset and anxious. She quickly tied the bow of Lizzie's apron behind her.

'Have you any idea where they may have gone?'

'Back home to Ireland,' said Henry with his father's cool logic. She could hear purposeful steps along the corridor, and doors being systematically opened and closed. The footmen and maids were searching.

'Would you like to help search the attics and go up on the leads?' As this was forbidden territory Lizzie was eager to start but Henry continued to eat his breakfast.

'It's not worth it, Mama; they're not in the house.'

'How can you be so certain?'

'They have either gone into Larkhill to catch the mail coach to Marlborough, but they would have to steal a lot of money for the fares. Or they have gone to the tinkers who said they would be leaving Larkhill today and going back to Wexford.'

'Clem said you had not spoken to the gypsies!'

'I didn't,' said Henry looking up from his bowl. 'I never went across the stream, but Sophia and Rosa did. They wouldn't come back when I shouted for them.' He looked at his sister who was twisting the corner of her apron awkwardly.

'Am I to understand that you've seen the gypsies since you collected the Christmas boughs?'

'Only once, Mama. The girls ran away to play and I thought I'd better follow them. Lizzie went and got them back.'

'I had to, Mama, they wouldn't do what Henry told them. We were there for hours shouting for them and I knew everyone would be cross and come looking for us so I went over the little bridge and dragged Rosa back.' This had taken considerable courage in the face of the Romany dogs.

'And Sophia?'

'She came after Rosa. She said we were not to tell and she was very cross.'

'I was very cross, too,' said Henry. 'They should mind what I say. I am the boy. I wanted to play in the barns at Home Farm.'

Harriet's mind raced. Would it be quicker to take a horse across the fields to get to the stream or should they go by the Amesbury road with the barouche?

She found her husband who was already on his way to the stables. She glimpsed a pistol at his waist and clutched at his coat. 'What's happening? Henry and Lizzie are convinced the girls are with the gypsies. They're leaving Larkhill today according to Henry and I cannot find Clem,' she said, her voice rising.

'Don't distress yourself Harriet. The girls are not in the house or grounds as far as I can deduce, so we will go to the gypsies. Clem is with Ralph. They will take the barouche in case of any - necessity. Jacob and I will go over the fields; it will be much faster.' He gave her a quick hug. 'Some villager is probably on their way to the manor now, with the girls, in the hopes of a fine reward. I'll warrant they have wandered into Larkhill to buy some Christmas trinket, nothing more.'

'Then I had better find some blankets for Morna to take.' Harriet hurried away to the lower regions.

'I will not come,' Harriet told her brother-in-law as she piled rugs into the carriage. 'It's me they're running away from after the scolding I gave Sophia.'

'It was my fault, Aunt Harriet. I told Sophia she was being sent away to boarding school.' Clem looked shamefaced.

'Nonsense, my dear. You must not blame yourself. Sophia's a difficult little baggage.' Harriet spoke distractedly. She was past caring as to how or when Clem had imparted this information.

'Morna, would you take Mrs O'Leary; the cold will sober her up and will be just punishment for her neglect. The girls might respond to a female face, however despised; she is familiar to them. Clem will show you the way. You will take care won't you?' she said, not knowing anything of Ralph's equestrian capabilities. Sebastian was already mounted, well muffled against the cold.

'Do not feel obliged to go after these silly children, Mr Romero,' she said.

'Yes, Sebastian, I have told you there is no need to disturb yourself. I have every faith in my brother to have rounded up the whole gang before we even get there,' said Ralph, swinging himself into the saddle. He did not ride much in the hills of Naples and hoped the horse was docile.

'Thank you, ma'am but I look forward to the jaunt and I've taken quite a shine to those two little ladies.'

Janet appeared from the kitchen with a hot brick wrapped in flannel and some gingerbread. 'And a bottle of small beer ma'am, in case the young ladies are thirsty.'

'Not for you, Mrs O'Leary,' said Harriet sternly, wondering if another whisky bottle was secreted under that wheezing parcel of shawls and jackets.

'No, no, m'lady mam. Not another drop shall pass my lips until the sainted angels are safe home again, so.' She crossed herself vigorously.

Clem was impatient to be off. The young men put their horses to a canter. Jem came behind them in the barouche, Rupert's rifle at his feet and Mrs O'Leary bouncing like a bundle behind him.

At the end of the drive they took the Larkhill road.

Their gallop along Larkhill High Street caused heads to turn and tongues to wag. Horace West, coming out of the Three Crowns coffee room, fulminated with rage at such cavalier behaviour from the Earl of Morna who's horse splashed mud over his best surcoat. After leaving the last cottages behind them the rescue party came out onto open scrubland bordering the Amesbury Road. Clem urged them on for another mile. At the signpost they paused to ease their panting horses and Clem indicated the left-hand fork.

'This is the old road that goes through Uncle Rupert's property and behind Bourne Park up to the Downs. It's not much more than a cart track now. This side of the stream is common land and that's where the gypsies will be, and Uncle Rupert, I hope.'

They reached the bend in the winding track and saw the wooden palings of the little bridge over the stream. Rupert was kicking over the ashes of a campfire nearby. Jacob scoured the brambles and trees. A litter of bones and dung showed where at least three caravans had camped. There were signs of a flurry of recent departure.

'Are we too late?' asked Morna, leaning down from his horse. Clement eased himself down to the frosty grass and joined Rupert. The dark water of the rivulet ran sluggishly beneath the old wooden bridge.

'Ah, they've gone, gone, spirited away by those evil tinkers. Sweet Mary, mother of Jasus, 'tis ashamed I am to call them my countrymen!' wailed Mrs O'Leary. The men ignored her.

'The ashes are still warm.' Rupert stared into the distance with narrowed eyes. 'I cannot think they would go by the old road; they know we can catch up with them too easily, and it's too exposed on the Downs. They must guess someone would be after them by now.'

'We did not pass them on the road unless we missed them at the fork,' said Morna looking around. 'Is there anywhere in the district they could lie low?'

'The other side of the stream is the manor demesne which gives rise to this small patch of common land. Over there is Quennell House land bordering on Horace West's park. He's a justice of the peace and is known in the county. They would not risk trespassing of any kind especially after he'd already warned them off.'

'Uncle Rupert! What about Deadman's Hollow? They could be hiding out of sight there.'

Rupert's face tightened. 'A foolish name that the young people have coined,' he said in response to Morna's look of enquiry. 'A man was shot by highwaymen there, many years ago. People avoid the place.'

'Then by jiminy let's try there,' said Sebastian to his unresponsive host. Clem leapt back into the saddle. The earl turned his horse's head to follow his friend.

Mrs O'Leary moaned as Jem pulled the barouche around and galloped the horses back along the old road. At the fork they retraced their steps along the Amesbury road towards Larkhill. Rupert directed them towards a distant stand of oak on the common. His face was very set. 'I can see no smoke from the hollow,' was all he said. He cantered off the road onto the high scrubland, Jem dragging the barouche and the protesting Mrs O'Leary after him.

At that moment a child on the watch rose up from the bracken and let out an ear-splitting yell. Rupert immediately spurred his horse forward and down the slope through the spinney with an expert hand. The others approached more slowly in an effort to stay in the saddle. Rupert brought his trembling horse to standstill in front of three Romany waggons. Several dogs barked viciously and were called off with difficulty. A gaggle of dirty children milled about the campsite.

A toothless crone with hoops in her ears came forward and cringed: 'Good day your worships. What would you be wanting with us this bitter cold morning?'

'I want two little girls of nine years of age, seen wandering in this vicinity not an hour since.'

'Give them up, ya dirty spalpeens!' shrieked Mrs O'Leary, brandishing her umbrella like a shillelagh.

'Be silent, Mrs O'Leary,' ordered Rupert.

The gypsy woman cringed. 'Ah, your worship, we've surely seen none like that, have we, Michael?'

A brute of a man with a broken nose and muscles like whipcord leant against one of the waggons, ostentatiously whittling something with an ugly-looking knife. He moved forward to stand behind the old woman.

Morna, Jacob and Clem brought their horses into line with Rupert's. Sebastian hung back with the barouche. Jem lifted the rifle onto his knee. Other figures were descending from the caravans; some women, a youth, two more men, all tense and wary. Jacob dismounted and stood by Rupert's stirrup.

'We'll be going on our way, sir. We don't want no trouble. We ain't seen no chavo but our own. Come away now, Ma,' said the man.

'Pity,' paused Rupert. 'There's a handsome reward for the two little girls.'

The earl shifted uneasily beside him. The crone's eyes glinted greedily. There was an angry mutter of Romany between mother and son and the woman turned back to Rupert. 'Nine years old sir? They'm big to be roamin'. But mebee I'd best ask the young'uns if they've seen anything of your young ladies. What did you say the reward might be, your honour?'

'Substantial,' said Rupert, taking a purse from his pocket and allowing it to chink in his palm. The gesture revealed the pistol at his belt. 'But if you say you have not seen them, then there is no help but to inform the justices that they are lost.' Rupert made to return the purse to his pocket.

'Now don't be so hasty your honour. 'Tis best to be certain. Let me ask if the little'uns have seen aught of your girls.' The woman scuttled away despite the man's muttered protests. The gypsy backed away but stood his ground when three other Romanies came to join him. One kicked his snarling dog into submission. The horses were restive.

'Can't we rush them?' hissed Clem.

'No. We don't know what waggon they're in, or if the girls are here at all,' said Rupert.

The old woman made a great show of going from cart to cart, talking to and scolding the ragamuffins. Rupert sat rigidly waiting. Mrs O'Leary, spoiling for a fight, waggled her umbrella and started to shriek abuse until Jem bade her hold her tongue. Eventually the crone pushed a sullen youth aside, tugged at the door of the last caravan and turned her toothless beam on Rupert.

'Lord be praised! They're found, your worship. The children saw them lost and cold on the road and 'ad never seen such pretty things afore. Out of kindness they thought to give 'em a wee drop of something and a morsel of bread before taking them back 'ome.'

'Bring them to me at once.' Rupert cut across her excuses with a voice of iron.

The wait seemed endless while the old woman once more pushed the glowering youth from the steps and clambered up into the caravan. There were some faint cries which again made Ralph shift in his saddle.

At last, with a great pantomime of concern, the old woman led Sophia and Rosa shakily down the wooden steps, blinking into the daylight.

'Let me have them, my little darlins',' shrieked Mrs O'Leary. 'If a hair of their heads have been harmed I'll skin ye alive, so I will!'

Clem gave a whoop of delight and Rupert leaned forward to grasp his reins. 'Hold still, boy.'

At the sight of the recue party the girls struggled to get away from their captors. Rosa was weeping, Sophia dazed and white faced. They were dressed in rags. The old woman kept a tight hold on Rosa who would not be separated from her sister. Her son took Sophia's flailing arm, the knife in his free hand. The four of them stopped a few feet from the riders. By now Mrs O'Leary was wailing enough to drown out the children. Sebastian leaned down and passed a hip flask across which miraculously reduced her to silent gulps.

'The reward, mister?' said the woman, holding up one clawed hand but determinedly gripping her prize with the other.

'Where are their clothes?' stormed Ralph. 'You'll be prosecuted for theft, if nothing worse.'

Rupert gritted his teeth. 'Put the children in the barouche and then you can have your reward.'

'What? An' see you ride off leavin' us with nothin'? I'd cut 'er throat first!' growled the man, putting the blade close to Sophia's writhing neck. She cried out pitifully.

'Then come here if you want your money.' Rupert threw the purse onto the grass in front of him.

The man gestured to the gypsy woman to take both children. Satisfied that the old woman now had fast hold of the two girls, the gypsy relinquished his grip. In that instant Rupert whipped his pistol from his belt and coshed the man on the side of his head as he rose from grasping at the purse, sending the gypsy and the knife spinning to the grass.

Everyone screamed. The dogs barked and charged the intruders. Morna had trouble controlling his horse but its thrashing hooves kept the curs at bay. The old woman dropped the girls' arms and fled to the nearest waggon. Jacob swept the children towards the barouche and, with Sebastian's help, threw them up beside Mrs O'Leary. Clem scrambled down from his horse to beat off the dogs with his crop and collect the purse. Rupert held his pistol over the groaning tinker.

'Count yourself lucky you've got no more than a sore head. I'll blow your brains out if you make a move. Call your dogs off! Jem, get the women out of here.'

****

'I beg your pardon if I have kept you waiting, gentlemen. The girls are settled now,' said Harriet taking her seat at the late luncheon table. She felt she could not eat a thing. 'Mrs O'Leary is standing guard like an avenging angel; I am quite *de trop*. I cannot bring myself to go to church today, though we should give thanks for the children's safe delivery.'

'You look somewhat fatigued yourself, my dear,' said Rupert, signalling for Dunch to pour the wine.

'Mere irritation of nerves, I assure you. The suspense of the morning and then the bustle of getting both children bathed. I've had those rags burnt and will have to go into Larkhill tomorrow to buy yet more clothes for them. I can ill spare the time and I do regret the boots.'

'Will you prosecute, Rupert?' asked the earl. 'You should at least inform a magistrate.'

Husband and wife exchanged glances. 'I think not. The tribe is probably long gone beyond the parish boundaries by now and think themselves well satisfied with the clothing.' Rupert dipped his spoon to his soup.

'But that's terrible,' burst in Sebastian. 'They would have abducted those little girls if you hadn't stopped them. At home we would have strung them up on the nearest tree! What if they try it again, in another parish?'

Harriet flinched and Rupert continued smoothly to the table at large: 'It wasn't abduction. The girls went voluntarily. I'll wager the gypsies didn't know what to do with them when they turned up at the stream this morning. Their first instinct was to decamp, and the second to sit tight in the hollow. There was certainly a dispute between the woman and her son as to whether to keep the girls or not. Nine year-olds are impossible to truly kidnap; they have a tongue in their heads. The clothes are what the gypsies were after; they'll fetch a good price. I imagine they've learnt their lesson.'

'Would you really have shot the fellow?' asked Morna.

'Of course. He was threatening Sophia with a knife.'

'I'm glad you did not give them any money,' continued Morna. 'It would only encourage such villainy. We know all about bandits and kidnapping in Italy, don't we, Sebastian?'

'Indeed, my lord; one must never give in to blackmail,' replied Romero dutifully.

'I was very tempted to pay them off but when I saw the knife I knew they had to be stopped. It does not do to yield to threats of violence.' He avoided looking at Harriet. 'Thanks to Young Clem's quick wits I saved myself some sovereigns.' Rupert smiled briefly at Clem.

'I am so glad I obeyed your command to hold back. I did not expect you to hit the gypsy on the head, sir.' Clement looked at his bookish uncle with new respect.

'Luckily neither did he.' Rupert saw his wife's drawn face at the end of the table and stopped.

'May I suggest we forget this whole business and turn our minds to pleasanter topics? There was a fascinating article in the *Quarterly Review* on the new Liverpool to Manchester steam railway. The success of the Rocket at the Rainhill Trials last year was mainly due to Stephenson's use of the multiple fire tube boiler in place of the single flue boiler previously used. The article claims that the locomotive can go faster than any racehorse...'

****

That night, in Harriet's room, Rupert came to bid his wife goodnight. Harriet dismissed her maid.

'Have you taken any valerian drops, my dear? You need a good night's rest.' He sat on the edge of the bed and took her hand. Her long dark plait lay across her bosom.

'No. I do not want to become like Mrs West. I will dream of course but that is to be expected.'

'Perhaps I should have taken you with me, to see it all and not be prey to imagination. You would have been more useful than Mrs O'Leary who never stopped shrieking the whole time.'

Harriet smiled. 'May we allow her to remain until after Christmas and see how the girls settle before making any decisions?'

'If you think it is best.'

She paused for a moment. 'Clement said you found the gypsies camped in a hollow on the common. Why does that make me uneasy?'

Rupert had never openly discussed his youthful duel and in this matter she had respected his reticence. He gave her a long look but her large brown eyes met his full of puzzlement.

'I knew the place as a boy,' he said slowly. 'Clem suggested we try there.' He could not bring himself to put a name to it. 'Your Uncle John once told me it was where highwaymen waited to ambush people, in the old days.'

As the implications filtered through her tired mind, she seemed about to speak, looked distraught and said: 'Forgive me. How stupid I am. I had forgotten. And I cannot even blame a sleeping draught.'

'Harriet, don't be unhappy. The girls are safe and what's past is past.' He circled her wrist between finger and thumb and shook it gently like a baby's rattle. 'To some extent I laid a ghost today.'

She turned from him with a troubled face. After a moment she looked back into his eyes and said: 'You mean you chose not to kill a man when you had the chance to do so?'

'Precisely.' He never had to explain anything to Harriet.

He leant forward and kissed her gently on the mouth. 'I'll come to you later,' he promised.

****

The adventure of the gypsies spread all over Larkhill within days. Now the rioting had faded away, people welcomed something new to talk about. No matter how the Darvilles tried to dismiss the affair it provided enough speculation to satisfy even the hungriest gossip. Rupert was the reluctant hero of the hour. Harriet kept the ladies Sophia and Rosa close to home. No one dared approach Rupert or the earl directly, but the American secretary and the Irish nursemaid proved wonderful sources of information.

Larkhill had no problem regarding the matter of the gypsies. Mr West would take the cat to the lot of them and revelled in the opportunity to condemn Darville for not reporting the matter to a local magistrate.

'The man's too soft,' he said to his son-in-law over port and cigars. Frank had taken himself off to the Three Crowns as soon as the covers were cleared. 'At every rate-payers' meeting he wants us to increase the Poor Rate for the labourers. What a bleeding-heart! Even a damned Whig like Melbourne expects us to use our powers to the maximum but then an arrogant pedant like Darville will think nothing of setting himself up against the Home Secretary.'

'I wouldn't call Mr Darville "soft". Mr Romero told me that Darville clubbed the gypsy to the ground.' His own interview with Rupert had shown him the man's mettle.

West gave the Archdeacon a speculative look. 'Been seeing much of that hermaphrodite, have you?'

Learoyd stiffened. 'A chance meeting in Larkhill High Street, that is all.' He pulled heavily on his cigar.

West tightened his lips. 'You are aware that we are no longer on speaking terms with that family or any of its – connections.'

'Your quarrel with Darville is no concern of mine, sir. I cannot conceive of any reason why Letty and I should not-'

'Why? *Why*? Because I say so! While you're under my roof you'll not hobnob with that stiff-backed star-gazer or anyone from the manor. You know his servant attacked me and that Darville threatened to horsewhip me?' West made a grab for the decanter. 'And don't think you can lickarse round the earl with your candles and your credo; people like that are dangerous and degenerate!' He drained his glass.

'Really, father-in-law, there is no need for such intemperate language. If it means so much to you then certainly Letty and I will cut the Darvilles, if we happen to meet them.'

West wiped his lips with his napkin. 'Do so, or you'll regret it. I can make life very difficult for you.'

George Durrington was begged not to issue any further licences to travellers and to ban all tinkers from camping on the common. Dead Man's Hollow enhanced its gruesome reputation. The Reverend Butterworth thundered from the pulpit on the need to update the ancient Vagrancy Acts and the Poor Law. This incident and the fear of further rioting put the townsfolk in a quake.

Sophia, too, had been badly frightened by the event. The squalor of the camp had not incommoded her and the girls were used to dogs roaming Castle Morna. When their clothes were exchanged for rags Sophia had felt far more comfortable although Rosa had fought valiantly to keep her new hat. But the arguments between the gypsies had thrown Sophia into a panic; perhaps they would not be taken home to Ireland at all, but sold or sent back to the manor. The heated altercations in a foreign tongue between the rough men and the old woman had alarmed her. She had understood enough to know that their fate was being decided.

They had been shut in the caravan at the sound of approaching horses and threatened with a beating if they made any noise. The gypsy's knife at her throat and Rupert's decisive action had stunned her. She had never experienced violence and had trembled like an aspen all the way home in the carriage.

The sight of Harriet's anxious face on their return had brought her no satisfaction; grown-ups were not supposed to be shaken out of their authority. Her aunt had uttered no word of censure while the girls were being bathed, inspected and bundled into bed but Miss Humble looked very stern.

'I like it here,' whispered Rosa tremulously. 'Don't let's run away again.' She turned on the pillow towards her sister, clutching a rag doll of Lizzie's. The blue bed curtains were tightly closed against Mrs O'Leary's snores.

'They'll hate us now and send us away to school for sure,' muttered Sophia. 'We must get home somehow.'

'Aunt Harriet was crying. If we're good perhaps they'll let us stay here. I want to play games at Christmas and have presents.'

Sophia, put an arm around her twin. 'Hush, now. We'll stay until after the holidays and ask if Uncle Ralph will take us to London with him. You like Mr Romero well enough don't you? I think he's lovely.'

'Yes,' sighed Rosa. 'I'd rather have him take care of us than O'Leary. He's so beautiful.' She started to cry softly.

'What's the matter?'

'I want my hat,' Rosa sobbed. The enormity of her loss had only just dawned on her. 'I knew we shouldn't have run away!'

Chapter 8   Sebastian

Rupert turned his face to the night sky. High above him between the drifting clouds he could just make out Orion's belt. He stooped to his telescope and adjusted the lens, searching for the bright stars. For an hour he made minute notes in his spidery scrawl, noting the position of the navigation stars and any miniscule changes from his previous observations. The constellations flickered above him and then intermittently faded behind a grey mist.

Eventually the cold drove Rupert down from the leads; his fingers were too numb to hold a pencil. He pocketed his notebook and blew out his lantern. As he wheeled his telescope into the hut on the flat roof of the manor he though he heard a sound below. He looked down over the guttering but could make out nothing in the fitful moonlight. Badgers or a fox scavenging for food, he thought and continued to pack his equipment away in the shelter. He momentarily warmed his fingers against the stones of a chimney stack then opened a trapdoor in the roof and descended into the attics, picking up the oil lamp, lit and waiting for him.

Passing along the back gallery Rupert saw a gleam of light under Young Clem's door. He raised his lamp high and approached the room. Giggles and scuffles and whispered exhortations came from the other side of the oak. Without hesitation Rupert turned the handle. Clem was at the window in his nightshirt, leaning out into the dark giving whispered instructions and hauling on a flailing arm.

'For goodness sake try and get a grip on the sill. Lord save us! It's my uncle,' choked Clem, losing his grip on the arm and turning to face a wrathful Rupert.

'What's the meaning of this? Come away from that window at once, Clement.'

A crash and a groan followed by muttered curses filtered up from the yard. Rupert stepped over to the casement and jerked it shut. He reflected for a moment, opened it again and looked down into the shadows. 'Mr Romero, if you are able to make your way to the kitchen door, I will unlock it.' He snapped the latch closed.

'Clement, what mischief is this? Get back into bed this instant. I am extremely displeased.' Rupert mastered his anger with difficulty. 'No, don't tell me; it's plain enough. I'll speak to you in the morning.'

'But sir! It wasn't my fault! Honestly! Yes, sir.' The boy hopped under the covers, too frightened to attempt any excuses.

'See me in the library after breakfast tomorrow. Meanwhile, you are not to stir from your bed again tonight.' Rupert blew out the candle and left the room. On the back stairs Rupert met Dunch in his nightcap and slippers wielding a poker and a very unsteady candle.

'I beg your pardon, sir but I thought I heard an intruder. I had forgotten you were at your astronomical observations on the roof tonight.'

'No matter, Dunch. You were quite right; Mr Romero has mistook the time and is at the back of the premises. You may leave the poker. I will let him in and lock up, but stay within call.'

'Very good, sir,' said Dunch with heroic constraint, desperate to know what the young American gentleman had been up to.

When Rupert unbolted the back kitchen door, the reek of cider fumes on Romero's breath explained all. The young man swayed in the moonlight and made a feeble attempt to brush the mud and lichen from his clothes. One sleeve of his expensive coat was badly torn.

'I'm so sorry, sir, to have disturbed anyone. I know you'll forgive me. I had no idea of the time. I got lost and we were having such capital fun.' He leaned heavily against the shallow stone trough in the kitchen, blinking owlishly.

'I see Hugget continues to poison the neighbourhood. You had better sit down before you fall down.'

Sebastian slumped into a wheelback chair before the banked embers of the kitchen fire. His hands were grazed but his face was as seductive as ever.

Feeling some explanation was called for, Sebastian began. 'Mr Frank West and Mr Talbot invited me for a hand of cards. I must have taken too much of what Mr West called "scrumpy". And then Mrs Darville's horse got lost. It wasn't my fault-"

'I do not wish to know the details of tonight's escapade but insist that while you are under my roof that you use the front door like a gentleman and do not sneak into the manor like a common house-breaker.'

'I didn't want to raise anyone, it was so late-' Romero put a finger in his cravat to loosen it.

'Precisely, and I insist that you leave my ward out of your calculations. How often have you gained entry through his window?'

'Never, sir, this is the first time, I swear.' His beguiling hazel eyes swam with honesty.

'And let it be the last. I will not have young Clement caught up in your follies.'

'You will not tell the earl, sir? Will you?' The beautiful face turned to Rupert with the innocence of a babe.

'I have no interest in what you tell your employer, but you will cease such activities while you are under this roof.' Rupert picked up the lamp and the whiff of whale oil made Romero gag. 'Meanwhile, I suggest you drink a quart of water before you find your bed and follow Gaston's advice to the letter.'

'Yes, sir, I beg your pardon. It won't happen again.' His head fell forward on his chest.

'Dunch! Come and give Mr Romero your arm. I'll hold the lamp.' Between them, they guided Romero stumbling up the back stairs to his room.

In the stables, Rupert found Juno trembling with cold. He gave her a vigorous rub down as a way of working off his own temper. With the help of the sleepy stable boy he settled Juno for the night, not for one moment believing that the mare did not know her way home. When Rupert at last returned to his own chamber he found Harriet waiting for him. She was in her dressing gown and night cap talking quietly to Jacob.

'There you are at last! I was about to send Jacob to find you. You must be chilled to the marrow. I've brought you some hot soup.' She leaned down to stir a bowl in the hearth.

Jacob tactfully retired. Rupert blew out the oil lamp and looked at his wife in the soft candle light.

'Did you wish to speak to me on anything particular, my dear, or is this your regular nightly scold?'

'Rupert, you make me sound like a shrew! I worry about you staying so long on the roof. I know your astronomical calculations are important but so is your health.' She sighed and gave up. 'But yes, I did want to ask if you had any objection to Mr Romero accompanying us to see the bishop tomorrow. Morna seems to expect it but Mrs Dalrymple can be outspoken in the extreme.'

'I doubt whether Mr Romero will be leaving his bed tomorrow.'

'Whatever do you mean?'

'I have just caught him attempting to climb in through Young Clem's window, drunk as a lord on Hugget's raw cider.' Rupert shrugged off his coat and slipped into his quilted robe.

Harriet looked horrified and then broke into laughter. 'At least it wasn't Young Clem. You know his father used to get up to just such tricks as that. He always said the quickest way out of the house was down the drainpipe and over the stable roof. Poor Mr Romero, was he very drunk?'

'I fear so. I hope so; it may teach him a lesson. English cider is not the same as that in America; it is far stronger over here, especially when fermented by our friend Hugget.'

'How do you come to know such odd facts? And how did Sebastian find his way to Mr Hugget's den of vice? I think no one should be riding the roads after dark.'

'George tells me that Romero is quite a favourite in the Three Crowns. Frank West or young Talbot took him along. They're an unsavoury pair.'

'I suppose all young men have to kick over the traces from time to time. He'll have a fearful head in the morning. I hope he pleads ill-health and cries off the invitation; that will solve my dilemma regarding the Dalrymples.'

'But what are we to do about Clem? I was too angry to speak to him tonight. How many times has he already helped the American in at his window? Romero swore it was the first, but can we believe him?'

'Clem is a trustworthy boy, ask him. Now Rupert, do not take on so. What was he to say if Mr Romero threw a handful of gravel at his window and begged to be let in, which I'll wager is exactly what happened. Clem would think it a great lark. What would you have him do?'

'Pretend to be asleep, or refuse to allow Romero access.'

'Don't be so mean-spirited! Young Clem is of an age to defy authority. Of course he was going to let his friend into the house.'

'And then what?' Rupert paused in the act of kicking off his shoes and gave his wife a challenging look.

'Nothing. Nothing at all. You worry too much. Mr Romero will be a chastened young man in the morning and I will invite Mary Wakefield and Miss Charity to tea in a day or two to distract everyone.' She stood up and kissed her husband's broad forehead. 'When you do speak to Clem on the matter, I would forbid him to allow *anyone* access through his window – if the occasion should arise again - but give him permission to ring for Dunch whose function it is to open doors in this house.'

Rupert laughed. 'How practical you are. But we cannot have Dunch being disturbed at all hours of the night and driven to give notice.'

'I will be very surprised if it happens again.' She smiled down at her husband.

'Won't you stay, my love?'

'No, not tonight. You need some rest and to drink your soup before it goes cold.'

****

As a conscientious landlord, Rupert regularly rode over to Quennell House to check on the empty property. This time he rode alone wishing to be solitary with his thoughts. He was not a man who often examined his feelings and certainly not in depth.

He needed to consider Morna and Romero. Rupert was used to men of that stamp and usually turned an indifferent shoulder. He may have avoided the phenomenon by being educated at home but he had seen passionate friendships at Cambridge and casual couplings aboard ship despite the threat of flogging or death. His three-year voyage on the *Neptune* had inured him to the instinctive revulsion he felt. Nevertheless he was uneasy about bringing such men under his roof and into proximity with his family. He was convinced that Harriet knew of their unnatural relationship but that she had chosen to say nothing as a dutiful wife. As an atheist, Rupert was not ruled by Christian tenets but convention tugged at his coat tails.

The risk that Young Clem, at his impressionable age, might develop an infatuation for the handsome American was worrying. He was already well on the way to hero-worship. Would Romero dare take advantage of it? Was the incident at the window really so innocent? Rupert's hands tightened on his reins causing Bounty to skitter. He calmed his horse and forced himself to think dispassionately.

He had never seen the American show any particular interest in Clem beyond boyish friendship. Instead, the young man had made himself a favourite with all the family except himself, casting his beauty like a beam of light around him. The little girls adored him. Even Miss Humble was captivated by his charm. Only this morning, Rupert had found her in the oak parlour sewing the rent in the superfine of Romero's coat. It was a relief to know that the young man was not always in the house, even if he was in bad company. Morna explained that, while Clem was in school, Romero had asked leave to ride around the neighbourhood sketching the picturesque sites and rural architecture.

'Are you not afraid for his safety?' asked Rupert with mixed motives, one day finding Ralph playing solitaire in the oak parlour.

'Sebastian is an excellent marksman; he tells me he can shoot a squirrel at twenty paces; whatever for I cannot imagine. How these Americans do amuse themselves. Be easy, everyone in Larkhill knows him now; he is such a popular boy. He makes friends with everyone; a result of his egalitarian upbringing, no doubt. It is just the same at Mimosa.'

Rupert kept his own counsel over the cider episode. Doubtless Romero had bribed the valet into silence, or Morna was being loyal to his secretary as nothing was said on the matter.

Such discretion could not be condemned but it irked Rupert. The boy loved to be loved, that was plain. Rupert's jaundiced eye could see that Romero was one of a string of companions that his brother would cultivate throughout his life; pretty and wanton in their search for adoration.

Rupert had been unsettled to find that he shared certain physical qualities with his brother. One evening, Morna had revealed himself to be an excellent pianist. Sitting beside Ralph on the piano stool Rupert had been disturbed to see their identical hands on the keyboard. But Rupert could not dislike his brother. Ralph's easy-going character, so different from own, was refreshing. Rupert was forced to concede that Morna had a claim to respect in his study of classical cameos although any intellectual rigour was missing. The earl was every inch the cultivated gentleman of means as so many of his London and foreign friends were. He knew if he questioned the sexual practices of some of his own colleagues he would be forced to some uncomfortable conclusions.

A partridge chittered across his path, brown, round and plump in the patches of snow. He resolved to invite Clem out shooting when he came home for Christmas. Rupert knew he would not make a very good fist of explaining his anxieties but at least he could discover Clem's feelings. If there was any problem, Harriet would have to deal with it.

In consequence, a few days later, Rupert and Clem walked up to the Downs after luncheon, their guns over their shoulders, Lucky and Peterkin at their heels, glad to be out in the fields. The sky was heavy, the scene empty of sheep, brought down to the winter folds in the lower, warmer pastures. More snow was imminent. They trudged on to Warren Hill in companionable silence until Rupert said: 'I'm glad to have your company; you seem always to be busy with Mr Romero these days. I'm surprised you didn't want to go to Bath with your uncle.'

As Rupert spent most of his time closeted with his papers, this was unfair. The earl, his secretary and the valet had taken the Darville's barouche to Bath early that morning, with the intention of staying overnight.

'Uncle Ralph did not ask me.'

'I expect they intend to buy presents for the children.'

Again Clem wondered if he were to be classed with the nursery party or be deprived of a gift after declaring himself to be an adult. He was secretly hurt at being excluded from the expedition.

'Let's see if we can get some rabbit,' said Rupert. 'I've quite missed not going to Winestead this year; Frodingham, Lord Halsham I mean, has some of the best coverts in Yorkshire. Your aunt will be short of Christmas fare unless we bag a few coneys for her. How's school?'

'Well enough,' shrugged Clem. 'My friend Carstairs and I are going to share a study next half.'

'Carstairs? Oh yes. His father is an ambassador, I believe. A dark boy, limps. Is he a particular friend of yours?'

'I should say so! We got up to some japes last term. Nothing terrible of course or the Head would have written home about it.' Clem looked anxiously at his uncle.

'Would you have liked company of your own age this holidays? The children spend all their time playing with Sophia and Rosa. Your aunt was concerned you might feel neglected.'

'Oh, no. With Uncle Ralph and Sebastian, I always have someone to talk to.'

'Yes, Mr Romero is very - outspoken.'

'Don't you like Americans?'

'I have not met many,' said Rupert. 'And no one of any sense can dislike a nationality *en masse*.'

'He is a capital sportsman and he knows such interesting things and has travelled all around the Mediterranean as well as America.'

Rupert shifted his gun on his shoulder. 'Clem, I must warn you: however fascinating the young man is, it may not be wise to become too intimate. Getting drunk with the dregs of the neighbourhood is not to be emulated. He is your uncle's employee as well as his protégé and Romero's first duty must be to the earl. Perhaps it would be as well to keep a little distance between you. He has his work to do and you will have a role to play here as squire which needs discretion. Mr Romero is a secretary who is passing through.'

'But he is my friend!'

'For a little while, perhaps.' Rupert paused in his stride and faced the boy. 'Romero is a good number of years your senior and much more experienced in the world than you.' As this was the attraction, Rupert felt he had not made the best of arguments.

'Jacob is nearly ten years older than me and he is your valet! You do not mind me being friends with a servant in his case.' Clem strode on in defiance.

Rupert had to concede to Clem's logic but quickly recovered. 'Jacob has been with this family since he was a boy. We know nothing of Mr Romero.'

'Uncle Ralph must know something about him and approve.'

'Nevertheless he may not be all that he seems.'

'What do you mean?' Clem's cornflower blue eyes widened recalling Sylvia's charming face. Rupert's courage gave out.

'He may be more than a friend to many men and never more than a friend to any woman,' said Rupert in exasperation. Such subjects embarrassed him and he was angry at himself for not being able to speak more plainly.

Clem said nothing, inwardly digesting his guardian's words, a slight crease between his brows.

Rupert gave up; he had no skill in the subtleties of relationships. He did not want to cause a breach with Young Clem and hoped that the pangs of adolescent adoration would soon pass, or transfer themselves to a suitable female. The Wakefields had come to tea but apart from a brief greeting he had not interrupted the visit.

They came to a chalk plateau above a coombe valley and waited by a clump of trees to take the lie of the land. Warren Hill was aptly named. The Trottman sons snared rabbits here regularly for the manor and the rabbits were out now feeding in the twilight.

'Hush, there they are. We must not scare them too soon. Pick your target and fire at my signal if you can and then we won't have to wait for them to return for a second shot.'

From a distance of a hundred yards, little brown bodies could be seen bobbing and nibbling at the cold grass. They were becoming more indistinct by the moment in the gathering gloom.

Clem prepared to load, gripping the rifle with his knees. He scrabbled in his cartridge pouch, bit the end off the cartridge, shook some primer into the pan and rammed the cartridge and ball into the muzzle with the ram rod.

Rupert watched him with satisfaction. 'Your father would have been proud of you, you know.'

Clem smiled awkwardly and shielded his face by raising the stock to his cheek.

Rupert broke the barrel of his new breech-loader and inserted a cartridge. They walked slowly closer to the feeding rabbits. Rupert raised the gun to his shoulder, counted softly to three and fired. The Downs echoed to the crack of gunfire.

Rupert shot his target cleanly through the head but Clem missed his aim and the rabbits fled underground.

'Oh, I can do nothing with this old Baker rifle,' said Clem, angrily. 'And it's too dark to see anything now.' He was not normally a bad loser but his guardian's veiled criticism had confused him.

The pointer remained quivering with excitement at Rupert's heels until he ordered: 'Fetch!' Lucky bounded away across the turf as he had trained her to do. In a moment she had dropped the warm body of the rabbit from her soft mouth and been rewarded by a treat from her master's game bag.

Clem looked disconsolate. 'I'm sorry Uncle Rupert. I know a good workman should not blame his tools but-'.

'You are a very good shot Clem. I've taught you well enough.' Rupert looked at the empty landscape. 'We'll have to wait for them to come out to feed again, but here, you may use my Pauly rifle for your next shot.'

Clem accepted the needle gun with reverence. Rupert gave him a quiet lesson on the percussion cap and showed him how to load it. By the time Young Clem had grasped the mechanics and the idiosyncrasies of this particular firearm, a few rabbits had dared to re-emerge to feed. The boy shot his coney. Rupert, feeling the chill of darkness, suggested they make their way home. He offered Clem a tot of rum from his flask, which the boy appreciated. 'This is to keep you warm until we reach home. Don't tell your aunt.'

Clem was in great spirits now he had bagged his game. He chattered happily about school and the impending pleasures of the Christmas holidays and New Year celebrations. 'Miss Wakefield says that to bring good luck to the house for the coming year the first person to enter after the clock has chimed midnight must be a dark-haired man carrying a piece of coal and bread and salt. I would love to do it but I am too fair.' He looked hopefully at his guardian.

'Lord Halsham told me of this northern tradition. We could ask your Uncle Morna to be the "first-foot", as they say.'

'But we are to spend New Year's Eve at the Hintons in preparation for the hunt.' Clem sounded excited at the prospect.

'Yes, of course. Your aunt arranges these things. There will be plenty of dark-haired gentlemen to choose from if Mrs Hinton wishes to adopt the custom.'

'I wish we were staying for the hunt ball.'

'Do you?'

'The Durringtons and Miss Wakefield will be there,' Clem said wistfully. Despite his vague hopes, Rupert was surprised to realise that Young Clem was already growing up.

Rupert was lost in thought when his ward said out of the blue: 'Sebastian is not like Mr Butterworth is he?'

'No. And I have every respect for Bernard.'

No more was said. Rupert did not know if Clem had understood the danger or whether the rum was talking but he felt he had done his duty and could do no more.

Chapter 9   Christmas at Larkhill Manor

On Christmas Eve Harriet studied herself in the glass. She wore a low-cut gown of dark green velvet edged with bugle beads. Around her neck lay the double strand of creamy pink pearls that Rupert had given her when Lizzie was born. She had ordered pearl buttons to be sewn on the wrists of her new gloves. She held out an arm to her young maid.

'Fasten my cuffs would you. Where is that button hook?' Tonight, she would wear a confection of ivy, artificial red flowers and Philippa's mother-of-pearl comb in her hair and hoped this would not be thought too frivolous for a family supposedly in grief.

Rupert knocked and entered. 'You look very festive tonight, my dear,' he said speaking to her reflection in the mirror. He wore the dark swallowtails and cream waistcoat that became every gentleman. The straps under his evening shoes tautened the trouser fabric and accentuated his long legs. Harriet still preferred the ruffle of his shirt front to the more fashionable flat pleats.

She smiled in welcome. 'Do not disturb us, pray. Jenny and I are at the most critical juncture. Another minute and I will be done.'

Rupert sat on the bed to watch his wife complete her toilette. 'I thought you might have worn the Darville emeralds tonight.' She was looking very beautiful in his eyes.

Harriet dismissed her maid. 'Don't be foolish, Rupert. How can I wear the emeralds while Gerald's daughters are here; they should have gone to their mama when she married your brother. And now I suppose Ralph will claim them when he marries. It would be the height of tactlessness for me to wear them in such company.'

Rupert abandoned the subject. He knew there were too many embarrassments associated with the family jewels for Harriet to wear them willingly.

'If you won't wear the emeralds perhaps you might care to wear this.' He drew a square leather box from his pocket and laid it in her palm. 'Happy anniversary my dear. I hope you like it. I saw it when I was up in Derbyshire with Froddy last. He says it's a good specimen and he is an expert on these matters.'

Lord Halsham had long succeeded to his father's titles but the Darvilles still referred to him as Viscount Frodingham between themselves. The eminent geologist was happy to advise his friend on a suitable present for the Nut Brown Maid.

'Dearest Rupert,' she said, knowing that whatever was in the box would interest him far more than it would her. 'Oh, how pretty,' she said taking the oval brooch out of its bed of white satin. 'What's it made of?' She examined the blue and whitish bands of mineral set in a chased gold rim.

'Blue John from the Derbyshire hills. It's fluorite.' He was about to embark on a geological explanation when she leaned forward and kissed him. 'Pin it on for me, won't you,' she said pointing to her plunging *décolletage*. 'And then we really must go down. I'm sure I heard the dinner bell.'

Dinner was light in expectation of the feasting of tomorrow. The carp was well cooked and the mutton unexceptional. Compliments on a side dish of fricassée of rabbit made Clem very proud. Everyone was in the best of humours.

'Did you have a successful visit in Bath?' Harriet asked her guests. They had returned with an interesting array of boxes which Gaston had whisked upstairs.

'Amazingly successful,' replied Morna. 'The Griffin Inn did us very well; it is so convenient for the Abbey. Sebastian was entranced by such perfection of architectural forms. I did enjoy the depiction of Jacob's ladder on the West Front; so amusing. We ran into an old acquaintance in the Pump Room; a gentleman we met in Rome last winter. He insisted on inviting us to a Handel concert in the Upper Rooms and promised us several introductions when we go to London.'

'I'm certain my cousins in Russell Square will welcome you most cordially,' said Harriet.

'Naturally, Harriet, and I am very much indebted to you, but it is particularly comfortable to have a connection of one's own, don't you agree?' It was obvious that the earl was pining for the sophisticated delights of the metropolis. 'I found Bath a shopper's paradise. For a provincial city, Bath can provide one with nearly everything that is most fashionable. We bought skates for Gerald's girls, but I hope I am not going to be asked to teach them. My days of athleticism are over; Sebastian will deputise for me.'

The young secretary nodded enthusiastically. 'The earl bought me some skates too, Mrs Darville.' He turned to Clem. 'I'll race you – if you can skate?'

Clem wondered if Uncle Ralph had bought him anything in Bath. 'I can skate but the river is not frozen; we have only the priory pond. We'd have to race round and round.'

'That's just dandy. I can beat you either way.' The sweetness of Romero's smile robbed the statement of any ill-feeling.

'Do be careful, Master Clement,' warned Miss Humble. 'The pond is very deep and perhaps not frozen to the same depth everywhere.'

Clem and Sebastian exchanged mischievous looks and then Clem looked down awkwardly at his plate.

'Will you join us, Rupert? You can advise us on the safety yourself,' suggested Harriet.

'No. I have far too much work to do. I do not recommend skating until we have had at least another day of solid freeze.'

Harriet smiled. 'Harry and Lizzie can skate; so, Mr Romero, you will have only Rosa and Sophia to teach, but I don't envy you that.'

'Lady Sophia seems mighty chastened by her adventure, ma'am. She won't go out of the house alone.'

'Good! I could not face them running away again. But does she confide in you, Mr Romero?'

'I can't say "confide", ma'am,' he tossed back his hair. 'You'll forgive me, but maybe because I'm not a member of the family, not a figure of authority, she talks to me quite naturally.'

'Then I hope she may trust you to teach her to skate. I will remain as a spectator on the bank, with you, Morna.'

'I look forward to it with pleasure,' said the earl. 'May I be impertinent and ask what is that pretty brooch you are wearing? I know something of cameos but that looks most unusual.'

'Rupert gave it to me this evening,' said Harriet proudly. 'Today is our ninth wedding anniversary.'

Morna and Romero said all that was suitable. Clem sat tongue-tied, not being aware of the occasion and, like most young people, entirely uninformed about his elders' past.

Rupert began: 'The purple-blue mineral veins of the Peak District were laid down in the late Carboniferous period. It is thought they were deposited by layers of crystals precipitating from hot fluids coating the walls of caves and other fractures in the limestone. No one quite knows why the colour emerges as it does; I suspect impurities. The mineral is semi-precious and of no real value.'

'Unlike emeralds, which would have gone so well with your gown tonight,' said Morna blandly.

'Oh, my lord, you must take them immediately,' broke in Harriet. 'They were merely put into my safekeeping by your mother and I never wear them.'

Endearing though it was, there were times when Rupert deplored his wife's generous impetuosity.

'Good Heavens, I do not mean to deprive you of them, Harriet. I think it most suitable for you to hold the jewels, and wear them, until I have need of them myself. Rupert, you should not boast of giving your wife ornaments of little value. She deserves better.'

'Blue John is a most rare and fascinating example of the chemical reaction of the strata of the Earth,' replied Rupert in surprise. 'If you were familiar with William Smith's *Geological Map of England and Wales* you would understand how massive forces under the Earth's surface have shaped the land we know and produced various gemstones.'

In her turn, Harriet's regretted being unable to always disguise her husband's lack of sensitivity. Happily, Dunch appeared as they were finishing their dessert. 'The quire has arrived already, madam,' he said, using the old term. 'The stable boy saw them coming up the drive. Everything is prepared.'

'Gracious, I was not expecting them for another half an hour. Thank you Dunch. We will be in the Great Hall directly. We will have our tea and coffee after they have gone. Miss Humble would you be so good as to fetch the children?' Harriet knew the servants would be clustering behind doors to listen to the Christmas music.

The Darvilles arranged themselves in the Great Hall. The Yule log was smoking fitfully and gave off little warmth. Nevertheless there was a reassuring glow around the edges and the candles and bodies in the hall would soon raise the temperature. After a few moments they heard a scuffle and a murmuring outside and then came the strains of *Good King Wenceslas* piercing the cold night air. St Saviour's choir consisted of several tenors, a few basses, a sprinkling of uncertain altos and Lydia Butterworth's sweet soprano. Before the advent of Mrs Butterworth's harmonium it had been accompanied by three violins, a recorder and a serpent. The musicians were out in force tonight.

When the last notes died away there was an imperious rap on the front door. Dunch opened it and a bitter draught swept in. The candles in the Great Hall guttered and righted themselves. A great clatter indicated a stacking of lanterns and wiping of boots in the vestibule. A short hiatus followed when the carollers spotted the mistletoe above their heads but, eventually, the singers divested themselves of their mufflers and proceeded into the Great Hall followed by the musicians carrying their instruments.

Henry stood next to Rupert in front of the huge hearth, consciously adopting his father's pose of hands behind his back. Young Clem stood behind the earl's chair. Sebastian had Rosa and Sophia at his knee. Lizzie stood with an arm about her mother's neck.

After a certain amount of shy greetings and shuffling for position, the choir sang *Remember Adam's Fall* and *Rejoice ye Tenants of the Earth*. Harriet called for a round song and, following Miss Butterworth's imperious finger, the Darville family joined in. Sophia and Rosa looked on in wonderment. After two more carols, the family applauded as Lydia Butterworth closed her music folder and turned to the spectators. She curtsied. Papa, she said, begged to be excused but he was saving himself for tomorrow.

At a sign from Harriet, Young Clem came forward and made a short awkward speech of thanks. He looked to his aunt who came to join him. 'And now you must all be thirsty after such splendid singing. Do help yourselves to the food, and take some home if you wish.'

There was a rush for the refectory table where plates of mince pies and meat pasties were piled high. Clem walked around with a jug of warm mead exchanging a friendly word with everyone.

'Are you going to any more houses tonight?' asked Harriet mingling with her guests.

'No, ma'am, you be the last; we always saves the best till last,' grinned Abel Trottman, munching a hot chicken pasty between empty gums.

'You know, of course, that Quennell House is still unoccupied?'

'Yes, ma'am. I told Miss Lydia that. We give it a miss this year that's why we're a bit before our usual time. And the short shrift we got at the Park put us ahead.'

'Were the Wests not very accommodating?' asked Harriet feeling guilty about prying but she was anxious for Euphemia and did not envy her neighbour's Christmas.

'We never saw the Wests, ma'am. A clergyman came to the door and gave us a shilling. We weren't invited in.'

'Mrs West has been ill, I believe, and probably did not wish to be disturbed.'

As this did not excuse the Archdeacon's parsimony she let the explanation lie. 'Now, Mr Trottman you must have another drink of something before you give us *Adeste Fidelis*.'

Mrs O'Leary was settled by the suit of armour, tankard in hand and talking nineteen to the dozen to anyone who would listen to her. The story of the gypsies became one of abduction and near murder and her own role exaggerated into a tale of either fighting frenzy or saintly fortitude. Meanwhile, her charges were left to themselves.

Sophia was fascinated by the serpent. Fiddles were commonplace in Ireland but the huge snake-like instrument was a novelty. With Romero's encouragement, she came forward and stroked the twisted leather tube.

Abel Trottman held it between his knees and allowed Sophia to approach the mouthpiece.'Now give 'un a good blow, Miss,' ordered the old man. Sophia blew. The girls went off into giggles at the crude notes resulting from Sophia's attempts.

Romero had coaxed the recorder out of reluctant hands and was playing a simple lively tune, drawing an admiring audience around him.

'Dear Sebastian looks positively Pan-like,' smiled the earl indulgently.

'Beware the cloven hoofs, my lord,' replied Harriet mockingly. 'What is he playing?'

'I believe it is called "The Old Colony Days". His choice is somewhat ironic but he would not be aware of the inconsistency.'

Clem raced off to find his flute. Elias Farley retrieved his violin and plucked out some melodic notes and the Darville children linked arms and swung each other around. Elias could see his daughter Violet from the kitchen peeking round the door behind the dais. He settled the violin under his chin and picked up his bow; he much preferred the old folk tunes.

'A dance! A dance!' called someone. Harriet smilingly gave her acquiescence and when the musicians had conferred and the recorder prised out of Sebastian's grip, Miss Lydia proposed "Sir Roger de Coverley". The servants hurried in to swell the numbers. Partners were seized, two lines formed in happy expectation. Harriet and Rupert, who had a surprising fondness for country dancing, led the set.

For the next half hour laughing couples advanced and retired, bowed, curtsied, corkscrewed, threaded-the-needle and got back again to their place. Abel Trottman clasped Mrs O'Leary by the waist and away they went down the middle, hands crossed and back again, red and perspiring, ending up in the wrong order amid good-natured laughter. Sebastian was captured by Harriet's maid and with a rueful glance at his patron allowed himself to be swept into the mêlée. The earl immediately bowed over Lydia Butterworth's hand and begged to be initiated into the mysteries of the dance. Clem was given a quick reminder of the figures by Violet, though Miss Humble had taught all the children to dance. Even Sophia and Rosa allowed themselves to be led and galloped and swung by many willing hands. Everyone enjoyed themselves until, panting for breath, Harriet and Rupert regained their place as top couple.

At last the carollers left with many a 'Merry Christmas' floating behind them. The children went to bed with token reluctance. Each one lit a candle from the Yule log and processed excitedly up the Grand Staircase under the watchful eye of Miss Humble and the watery gaze of Mrs O'Leary. The thought of presents the next day encouraged the children to seek their beds. Clem followed them, having had more mead than was wise.

'I will ask Cook to salvage as much as she can for the cottagers, though there's not much left,' said Harriet surveying the debris on the long refectory table. 'Morna, have you time for tea or coffee in the drawing room before I send for the chaise? You have at least three hours before Midnight Mass and it has stopped snowing.'

'I think we may risk a little delay. One of your tenants said the road is clear to Salisbury and the moon is bright. By all means–'

'Morna, will you favour me with a private word in the library,' interrupted Rupert. With an apologetic look to Harriet, Morna excused himself and followed his brother out of the hall.

'Now, Mr Romero,' said Harriet. 'What have you to tell me about Lady Sophia?'

In the library, Rupert lit another lamp with a taper from the fireplace. 'Have a seat,' he said, fishing in his waistcoat pocket for a small set of keys. He lifted a water-colour of Larkhill Manor from the wall to reveal what looked like any other wooden panel. Raising a candle, Rupert applied a key to a minute hole in the edge of the panel and the wood swung open.

'How ingenious,' murmured the earl. 'And what a pretty painting.'

'I keep it as a reminder.' Rupert did not explain further. 'This was Sir John's safe. It wouldn't keep out a mole.' Rupert put a hand inside the recess and took out three worn green leather boxes. He laid them on the desk in front of Morna.

'Here are the Darville emeralds. I would feel happier if you took them into your possession at once.'

Ralph looked surprised. 'My dear fellow; there's no need to take umbrage. I meant no offence by referring to them this evening. *I* have no wish for them. In fact it would suit me better if you kept them until I know what my plans are. I certainly have no wish to travel with a trunk full of gems.'

Nevertheless, Morna leaned over and opened the boxes. He raised his eyebrows. A tiara with five cabochon emeralds glistened at him. A diamond and emerald bracelet lay in a silver setting. A heavy corsage ornament with matching eardrops winked in the lamp light. After a moment he closed the boxes.

'Impressive.'

'There should have been a necklace but that was sold long ago by our grandfather to invest in the South Sea Company, Patrick says.'

'Surely these should be in the bank? Drummond's usually has the guarding of them, according to the lawyer in Wexford, especially if Harriet does not wear them.'

'They are paste, Morna,' said Rupert baldly. 'Our grandfather sold the originals in the hopes of clearing some of the debts on the estate. He couldn't of course; he was too fond of playing faro. Ask Patrick when you go to London, he knows all about it. If you had hopes of selling them, then I must disappoint you.'

Ralph looked stunned. 'Is that why Harriet won't wear them, because they are fake?'

'Good God, no. She saved them from being stolen once. It's just that she feels the stones rightly don't belong to her.'

'They don't belong to *any* of us now. I can't deny that this is a blow, Rupert. I had hopes of realising a substantial sum from them.' The earl looked shaken.

'I suppose that means you will definitely sell Castle Morna?'

'You must know that I could not keep the place going on my current income. And I have debts. The emeralds might have off-set the most pressing repairs but without them we can attempt nothing.' He squared his shoulders. 'Put them back in your safe, Rupert; we don't want the whole world to know they are glass. I must think about this.'

'I'm sorry that I can give you no better news.'

'Blame our grandfather if you must. And certainly blame our father for not telling us. But then none of us were beloved sons under his roof.' He rose heavily as Rupert returned the green cases to the wall. 'I shall go down on my knees tonight and pray with fervour that next year will see our fortunes repaired.'

'Or you must marry money.'

Ralph looked despairing. He shrugged hopelessly. 'As you did?'

'As I did.'

'But you love your wife. You know I cannot-'

'No, I suppose you must not,' Rupert agreed. 'Though such arrangements have been successful in the past.'

Morna shook his head. 'You don't know what you're asking.'

'No, I don't.'

'I should go. Your wife will have sent for the chaise and Sebastian will be waiting for me.'

'Yes, you should go,' said Rupert neutrally. He turned his back to re-hang the painting of the manor over the wooden panel. When he turned round again, his brother had gone.

****

Christmas Day dawned under a fleece of sparkling snow. A winter wonderland covered all of Larkhill. Morna declined to go to morning service with the family. At breakfast, Sebastian explained that the visit to Bath and the Salisbury Midnight Mass had exhausted the earl. He rather thought his employer was going down with a chill and felt he should remain at home with him. Rupert said he would accompany the family to St Saviour's.

Christmas Matins was joyful. Everyone bellowed the hymns and admired the green branches draping the pews and the rood screen. Even Sophia sat still and listened to the Reverend Butterworth's recitation of the nativity readings. This was the first time the runaways had been seen in public since their escapade but apart from a few jocular remarks from George Durrington about being "press-ganged", the girls were not troubled much. The rumour mongers were more interested in Rupert's dramatic rescue, but he was not a man to talk.

No one lingered in the churchyard after the service; everyone was anxious to be home for their dinner. On their return to the manor, the Darvilles found the earl recovered enough to join them. He was playing piquet with Sebastian in front of the drawing room fire, a cashmere shawl about his shoulders. 'We are all shriven of our sins and are free to sin some more. I would not miss an English Christmas dinner for the world,' he said.

Harriet produced oysters, a haunch of venison courtesy of the McAllister estate in Scotland, a crackling goose and the inevitable mutton, followed by a steaming Christmas pudding ablaze with brandy. The children were on their best behaviour dining with the grown-ups but they were anxious to have their promised presents. Out of consideration for the others, the gentlemen did not linger over their wine and soon joined the family in the green drawing room.

The next hour was full of tearing paper and unfolding of cloth and excited squeals from the children. The skates for Sophia and Rosa were an inspired gift. By the look on their faces, Harriet suspected these children had never received a worthwhile present before. Her own gift to each of them was a doll and though Rosa hugged hers with ferocity, Sophia merely thanked her aunt politely. Harriet knew she would have to get to know her niece a little better.

The unexpected success of the day was Rupert's gift of a thaumatrope for each child. The small spinning discs of card were a novelty giving the illusion of movement. Even Young Clem received one of a galloping horse.

'You may take it to school, Clem, and explain how it works. Mr Babbage said John Herschel introduced him to the "persistence of vision" principle; the brain is fooled into believing the objects are moving. An optical illusion, of course, to blend the two objects into one,' said Rupert, twirling the strings either side of the disc to produce a jumping man for Henry. The children were oblivious to the physics and clamoured to have their own magical moving discs.

Clement was overwhelmed by a new rifle from his uncle and aunt. He stroked the smooth wood of the stock and the intricate chasing engraved with his initials. He was even more thunderstruck by Morna's gift. The earl had volunteered to contribute to the much-wanted saddle even though Rupert explained the cost would be taken out of Clem's trust fund at his next birthday.

'But that won't be until the end of February and I may have taken my leave by then. Let me have the pleasure of being thanked,' Morna insisted. 'I like to see young people have what they want.'

'May we go ice skating, Mama, now Sophie and Rosa have their skates? And Clem can try out his new gun,' asked Lizzie.

'Clem is not going to shoot his gun over the pond,' snorted Henry.

'Or Mr Romero and I could go riding. I must try out my new saddle,' suggested Clem eagerly stroking the polished Spanish leather.

'Not today. It's growing too dark. We will play Blind Man's Buff instead. Let's push the furniture back to make more room. You must explain to Sophia and Rosa how we play it in this family.'

The children were off in a screaming whirl of blindfolds, chasing and kissing. Clem thought himself past all such childish games until he saw Sebastian don the blindfold. Even the earl joined in, growling like a bear. Morna stumbled about unable to catch the children who hid behind the furniture. Sebastian somehow got himself cornered by the piano and giggled when Morna approached with hands outstretched. The earl smiled. 'I know who this is! It's Mama!'

The children shrieked with laughter and denial.

'No, no. I believe it is Captain Blood with all his fine plumage,' he said, fingering Sebastian's wavy tresses.

Another wave of hysterics brought Rosa out from behind the piano stool. 'It's Mr Romero! It's Mr Romero!' she said, almost bursting with her own perspicacity.

The earl stroked Sebastian's face gently with his fingertips. 'I believe you're right,' he said pulling down his blindfold and smiling into his friend's eyes. 'How could I mistake him for anyone else?'

Sebastian for once, blushed.

'You must kiss him,' said Rosa.

The adults moved. 'No, Rosa. Only if Uncle Ralph had guessed correctly, but you told him.'

Rosa looked bewildered.

'*You* may kiss Mr Romero,' continued Harriet and then it will be your turn to be the blind man.'

They continued to play until everyone had taken a turn at being blindfolded, but the heart had gone out of the game. Clem pronounced it stupid and suggested a game of spillikins, which was eagerly adopted by the adults.

Eventually, the long case clock struck six. When the children had been sent off to nursery supper and bed, Clem took his new saddle out to the stables in the hopes of finding Jem, or at least the stable boy. He did not invite Sebastian to go with him.

'Well, Harriet, I cannot remember when I have enjoyed a Christmas more,' said the earl, sipping a glass of claret. 'Exhausting though I find the children to be. But I will desert you for an early night; I fear my cold is creeping on.'

'Oh dear, and the celebrations will not be over for days. We have our tenants due here tomorrow, after church. Clem is to hand out the Boxing Day vails. You need not appear, Morna. Then on Twelfth Night we all go out and bless the orchard and drink quantities of warm cider. The children love bobbing for apples. And the Hintons have invited us all to the Hall for New Year's Eve. The excuse is young Peter's birthday and Mrs Hinton wishes to compensate us for having to forgo the hunt ball. Do come with us; the invitation specifically included you and Mr Romero.'

'Are these the people who are more "my sort"?'

'Entirely so,' said Harriet. 'Mr Hinton is a great collector of *objets d'art* and has cabinets of treasures to delight you. They usually have charades or tableaux as entertainment.'

'How can I refuse such inducements? Sebastian, we must raid our trunks to see what exotic costumes we can devise.'

'Yes, my lord. You know how I adore dressing up.'

The earl sneezed.

Chapter 10   Boxing Day and beyond

The Great Hall was bustling with bodies. By now the Yule log was burning fiercely and looked to last the holidays. The refectory table had been moved to the dais where Brownrigg and his son stood guard over a pile of paper envelopes and assorted packages. Each was labelled and Brownrigg and his son compared labels with lists. There were the tenant farmers and their families, the manor servants, the tradesmen who had not already collected their Christmas boxes, all eager to come and all eager to be away to their families for the day. Harriet had warned her guests that dinner would be skimpy with only a skeleton staff at the manor.

Clem did very well. He formally shook hands with everyone whose name was called. Primed by Harriet he managed an appropriate word with each of them and solemnly handed over a suitable gift. In most instances it was money, in others, food, a shawl, baby clothes or a piece of cloth for a much-needed dress. Brownrigg and Harriet had been at work for weeks.

'How quaintly feudal,' said Sebastian to the earl. 'I guess this is *noblesse oblige* in action?' They were watching the scene from the privacy of the minstrels' gallery. The earl looked flamboyant in a gold brocade dressing robe, but his nose was distinctly raw.

'I would have to dispense such largesse in Ireland if I were to keep the castle. Could you bear it?'

'I could bear anything if I were with you, my lord.'

Morna was flattered and a little flustered. 'My dear boy, don't think you have to stay with me all day. Gaston will take care of me very well. I do not want to pass my cold onto you and intend to go back to bed this instant.'

'I guess I could go on my ride, even without the young squire,' said Romero throwing a casual glance over the balcony.

'Don't let your republican principles sour you, my boy; it quite brings a frown to your pretty face. Go and get some exercise and good air, but take my pistol; I do not trust these English peasants.'

When the Trottmans had received their "boxes" and a hearty handshake from Clem, Harriet called them aside and asked softly: 'I trust you have enough men guarding the stack yard? We want no more incendiary attacks. I hear there are gangs from other parishes on the move. You must be vigilant.'

'We've set extra posts round the clock, ma'am, but I don't expect no trouble; 'tis too cold for mischief and they'm that cause it will be wantin' to stay at home by the fire,' old Abel Trottman replied.

'Unless they want to start a big one,' said Michael belligerently.

'Very good. Mr Brownrigg will settle the bill for the extra watchers. Apply to him at the end of the quarter. By which time we should know whether this shocking unrest is finally over.'

'Thank'ee ma'am. There's little enough money about with the tithes and the rents to pay. Not that we'm complaining about the rent mind,' he said quickly touching his forehead. 'You be very good to us, like all the Larkhills, time outta mind.'

'Precisely. And I know you'll give your loyalty to Master Clem when he becomes squire.'

'Yes'm,' said the old man. 'Sir John would ha' been proud of him no matter where he comes from, an' that's a fact.' Abel Trottman was dragged away by his scolding daughter-in-law before anymore indiscretions could emerge.

Jem came forward all grins, James and Martha at his heels. 'Annie sends her respects, Mrs Darville,' he said turning to Harriet. 'She's at 'ome with baby Paul. He's doing nicely now thanks to your liniment but she thought it best not to bring 'im out in the cold so soon.'

'Quite right, Jem. Please tell her I'll be along tomorrow to see her. Do have some marchpane, James, Martha and take a piece for the baby.'

'Would 'e tell Mr Darville that the pond be safe for skating for the young'uns. I gave it a good bash with the iron pole, and it supported my weight even in hobnail boots. There'll be another hard freeze tonight so the ice should thicken up a treat.'

Meanwhile, in Bourne Park, a deadly fuse was lit.

****

Mrs West and the Learoyds gathered in the drawing room in response to Mr West's summons. The master of the house had not gone to Hunniford church with his family, complaining of stomach pains brought on by the previous day's rich Christmas food. But now he had sent word that he wanted to speak to them.

The Archdeacon took a chair by the fireside and played with his gold fob. He knew something was afoot; his father-in-law had been particularly belligerent since the conversazione. Doubtless he was about to threaten them with a change to his will. Euphemia seemed gently bewildered and murmured agreement to all of Letty's speculations. Frank appeared bleary eyed. He too had missed morning service because of his usual hang-over.

'What can it be about, I wonder? Papa is not truly ill is he? Is that why he missed church? Is his stomach', Letty blushed at the word, 'so very bad this morning? His digestion, I know, was never strong but Dr Makepeace will put it all to rights, now that horrid other doctor has gone. Mrs Makepeace assures me that her husband will attend you again, Mama, and if he comes to see you I see no reason why father should not consult him and as soon as the holidays are over you can order your cook to make slops and milk puddings, there's no need to continue with all the rich fare we have had, delicious though it was and much appreciated by the Archdeacon and myself I can assure you.'

The Archdeacon looked down at his immaculately pared nails and wondered when he could escape to Salisbury on diocesan duties for his bishop.

The door opened and in came the head of the household looking stern and carrying a leather portfolio.

'You are here, Papa. Are you feeling any better?' asked Letty.

West ignored his daughter. 'I will not keep you all long. I told Simpkins to put dinner back half an hour.'

Dr Learoyd chalked up another selfish act against his father-in-law. Frank was in no mood to eat.

West laid the portfolio on a marquetry table and looked round at their puzzled faces. 'I am leaving. I am taking passage to Kingston within the next three months. This house will be sold, as will the rest of the land. You, Euphemia, will be provided with a respectable lodging in Larkhill and a hundred pounds, unless Frank or your son-in-law offers you a home.'

Mrs West's weak eyes widened. 'Leaving, Horace?' Her hand went to her throat. 'Whatever can you mean?'

West looked exasperated. 'I cannot make things plainer. I will provide for you with what I can but I will live with you no longer.'

Letty gave a little shriek and clutched her mother's arm. A general babble of protest broke out.

West held up his hand. 'Frank and Letty will each receive a hundred pounds. Learoyd, if you chose to give your mother-in-law a roof then I will increase Letty's gift to two hundred pounds. All this is dependent on whether and how soon I can realise my assets.' He tapped the leather document wallet.

'Good God, Father, you must be mad! You cannot throw us to the wolves like this!' Frank had sobered up in an instant.

'My dear sir,' said the Archdeacon with concern. 'I fear your reasoning is affected. Pray let us call a physician at once.' He took a surreptitious glance at the sherry decanter.

'Nonsense! I am neither drunk nor incapable. I know perfectly well what I am about and have been planning this for some weeks. I have already asked Askew draw up the necessary papers.'

'I cannot survive on a hundred a year! My tailor's bill alone-' began Frank.

'Make no mistake. It is not one hundred a year but a single parting gift.'

'I'll starve!' said Frank, staring at his father in horror.

'Then try for a profession,' snapped West. 'I've been persuading you long enough. If there's sufficient money from the sale of the farms I will pay any premium required. I cannot afford to buy you a commission in the army and I don't think any regiment would have you, but business now, or the law, I could put you in the way of articles-'

'Oh, not a soldier, never a soldier,' protested Mrs West, clutching her son's arm. 'It would not suit Frank at all.'

Frank brushed off his mother's hand. 'I have no intention of going into the military or being some half-starved scrivener!'

The Archdeacon asked: 'Do you mean that Frank is not to inherit Bourne Park?'

'My God, am I'm being robbed of my birthright as well?' Frank cried in disbelief.

'Don't whine, Frank,' said his father with contempt. 'You've already received a considerable amount from the estate. I know all about the bills you've backed and the funds you've raised on the expectations of my death; I still have some useful contacts in the City.'

'Frank! How could you-?' Letty looked shocked.

Frank shrugged in embarrassment. 'A man must do something when he's kept on a pittance.'

'You deserve not a penny more of my money while I'm alive; you've almost bankrupted me as it is. You might consider yourself lucky to receive anything at all.'

Frank slumped back licking his lips in perplexity. He owed debts of honour all around Town as well as to bookmakers, let alone the money-lenders. 'But Pa! Bourne Park; this is my family home!'

'Balderdash, you come here only to bleed money out of me. The property is not entailed and it is mine to dispose of as I wish. If I make my way in Jamaica or the Americas I may leave something in my will to each of you, but do not depend upon it. And I intend to live a long time yet.'

'You are going to alter your will again?' asked the Archdeacon in some anxiety.

'I am going to tear it up completely! You can whistle for your wife's money. I cannot bequeath what I do not have, and make no mistake, I intend to sell up everything in England and be gone in March.'

'But the scandal!' wailed Letty. 'How will Mama live? What has she done that you are so cruel to her? What will people say? We will never be able to hold our heads up in the neighbourhood.'

'Then you'd better take your mother to Winchester to live with you.'

Learoyd roused himself. 'You cannot do this father-in-law. I will find a lawyer to prevent you. Askew will not let you do it, he is a sensible man. Frank will fight against this monstrous injustice, won't you Frank?' But Frank was distracted by the nightmare of disgrace, destitution and debtor's prison.

Letty started to sob. 'Oh don't leave us Papa! To go all that way and the climate so dreadful and all those wicked blackmen who would cut your throat! Who will take care of you? Mama, say something to prevent him!' But Mrs West stared uncomprehendingly at her husband.

'I won't stand for it!' shouted Frank. Fear made him ferocious. 'You disown me, do you? Damn your eyes! You'd leave me, your only son to starve? Well, I will leave you first! I know where I'm not wanted. I'll have a warmer welcome at the Talbots and I'll never set foot in this house again!'

Letty shrieked and half-rose to clutch at her brother but he slammed out of the room. Mrs West whimpered and fumbled among her draperies for a handkerchief. Dr Learoyd looked down at his highly polished shoes, his mind working furiously. Frank was such a child but his departure might work in Letty's favour.

'Let him go,' said West. His guts gave a cruel stab. 'He'll come back quick enough when he wants his share.'

'Father-in-law, sir,' said the emollient Archdeacon. 'If I or the rest of the family have upset you in any way, we beg your forgiveness. Pray do not do anything hasty. Sleep on the matter. I'm sure a few days of peace and calm will restore your equanimity.'

'Are you deaf as well as perverted?' snapped West. 'I have been planning this move for weeks and nothing will dissuade me from it. I will have no discussion on the matter. If you want to leave my house, like Frank, you may go as soon as you please.' He picked up his leather portfolio. 'I will take my dinner in my study. Euphemia, see to it.'

****

The priory pond lay to the south west of the manor. The long rectangular body of water was fed by a stream running down from the chalklands which eventually found its way into the Bourne.

Frost-covered ivy wreathed the remaining arches of the small priory church. Birds huddled amid the broken masonry fluffing their feathers against the cold. Grass scrunched underfoot as the Darvilles made their way from the house, wrapped in furs and laden with skates. The snow was deep and crunchy.

Sebastian guided Sophia and Rosa to a fallen block of masonry and began to buckle Rosa's skates onto her boots. Clem knelt down in the snow to do the same for Sophia. Henry and Lizzie were taking their first tentative steps hand in hand. Like most siblings, their body movements meshed; they moved as one and then crossing hands ventured further out onto the icy surface.

Sebastian was not as patient a teacher as was Clem; he was more concerned to display his own prowess. Rosa clung on for dear life or fell. Sophia seemed to have lost all her daring and did not take kindly to her cousin's instruction. Harriet stood on the bank in her sables and stamped her feet against the cold. Rupert appeared.

'Oh, you have decided to join us, my dear. Admit it; you could not bear to be left out,' teased Harriet.

'I had come to a natural break in my work and wished to have some fresh air. I thought I should ensure that the children were in no danger. Will you join me? I've brought your skates.'

'I think not. I'll stand here and watch you all for a little.'

Rupert produced his own skates and took to the ice with controlled and powerful strides. He soon relieved Clem of his hesitant partner and Sophia gained a little confidence under Rupert's strong hands.

Clem, left to himself, felt his jealousy rise at Romero's proficiency on skates. Sebastian pirouetted around in extravagant sweeping movements, coat tail flying like wings, his beautiful lips slightly open with pleasure. Rosa was now forlorn on the bank. Harriet walked around to the other side of the square pond to rescue the little girl and helped her to build a snowman. They had been enjoying the afternoon for not more than an hour when there was an interruption.

'Who's that?' said Henry, shading his eyes as a figure on horseback appeared on the old Priory Road below.

'Someone else wanting some fresh air, by the look of it. I believe he's coming to join us. Surely everyone knows this is private land,' frowned Clem.

The figure tied his horse to a thorn bush, climbed the stile and clumped up the slope of Priory field. The climb was steep and heavy through the snow, causing the small figure to take off his hat and wipe his brow. The winter sun illuminated the fuzz of pale hair like a halo around his head.

'Good Heavens, I do believe it's Dr Learoyd,' said Harriet. 'I daresay he wanted to get away from Bourne Park for a little.'

The Archdeacon came panting up the slope towards them, his top boots wet to the rims with mud and snow. He flourished his shovel hat in an elaborate bow. 'I trust I do not come inopportunely, Mrs Darville, Mr Darville? But I could not miss the opportunity of wishing you compliments of the season and hope that all will soon be well between our respective families.'

'How very kind of you, Dr Learoyd, to exert yourself in this way. I have no intention of deserting Euphemia, you may be sure, but are you wise to be riding alone? The clergy are very unpopular at this time, I'm grieved to say,' said Harriet holding out her hand in a friendly manner. 'I trust your mother-in-law is well, since Dr Mazotta's departure?'

'Let no one seek his own good but that of his neighbour, as First Corinthians puts it,' he returned piously. 'I have heard of no disturbance in the county for nearly a month now. I think we can thank God for a safe deliverance.'

Without a word, Rupert took Sophia by both hands and led her firmly back onto the ice. He felt that Harriet could be far too accommodating. Harriet made small talk. The Archdeacon answered absently, one eye on Sebastian's lithe figure.

'The earl is not with you?' asked Dr Learoyd politely.

'He has a chill; it would not be wise for him to stand about in this icy weather. I fear he may be confined to his room for some days.'

'Mama, may we go coasting tomorrow?' asked a breathless Lizzie, leaving her brother to make figures of eight on the ice.

'Coasting?' queried Harriet.

'Sledging, ma'am. We call it "coasting" at home.' Sebastian came across in a perfect glide and braked with one toe. 'Henry tells me there is a wonderful place called Lud's Hill with something called a long barrow, hereabouts.'

'Indeed there is but I would prefer the children not to stray from the grounds,' smiled Harriet. 'They could sledge down Folly Hill and, if Mr Darville will allow you the key, you may take shelter in Athena's Temple. Quennell House is still untenanted so you will disturb no one.'

'As you wish, ma'am. May we be permitted to take some refreshment with us?'

'Yes, why not make it a winter picnic? I will speak to Cook.'

Sebastian nodded politely to the Archdeacon, stooped to take Rosa's gloved hand and spun her up into the air. 'What balance that young man has,' said Harriet admiringly. 'Tell me Archdeacon, do you skate?'

'When younger ma'am, I have been known to attempt the ice. Your husband is a most powerful proponent of the art.' Rupert had left Sophia on the bank putting the finishing touches to the snowman. They watched the tall black figure powering his way up and down the frozen surface, with grim look of concentration on his face.

'What my husband lacks in style he makes up for in determination.'

'He is doubtless contemplating his next learned paper. But alas, I must desert this happy family scene,' said Learoyd with genuine regret. 'My horse will be suffering standing in this cold and I have had a most pleasant ride. If I have trespassed, do forgive me; I am not acquainted with all the byways around Larkhill.'

'You are welcome on any occasion, Dr Learoyd.'

'I trust that the New Year will bring more cordial relations between us all.' He tipped his hat and plunged down the snowy slope.

****

The earl recovered from his cold within a few days and was able to join the lumbering procession to Hinton Hall for the New Year celebrations. The journey was uneventful. Morna was enchanted with the house, once a Cistercian monastery, its pretty mistress and his host's fascinating treasures. While the children had their tea party in the nursery wing, Morna spent a contented hour wandering through the stately rooms in perfect amity with Will Hinton. Sebastian hovered at his patron's elbow. Catherine and Harriet followed the men at a discreet distance. Rupert and Young Clem had gone to inspect the stables in the company of Hinton's head groom.

'What a delightful selection of Cosway miniatures you have, Mr Hinton. I have a predilection for the delicate and intricate myself and I see these are exceptionally fine. You have an eye for the collectables of the future.' Morna peered over the glass cabinet in admiration. Rows of small paintings in square and round frames stared up from the velvet.

Hinton said modestly: 'They are extremely life-like and have just enough of the old-fashioned about them to make them quaint. I like to imagine our parents in wigs and frills carrying these pictures of their loved-ones. I confess I do not see the appeal of just some lover's eye.'

'The earl is a connoisseur of shell cameos. He has written a book about them,' said Romero with pride.

'Hush, my boy. Mr Hinton has a superb collection. One cannot compare such delicate pastels with the dull monochrome of a shell; he will mistake your enthusiasm for vulgar boasting.' But Morna's tone was pleased. He had not been feeling happy with his secretary of late.

Turning a corner of the corridor the earl was immediately struck by the mandarin's robe in a glass case. 'Good Lord, what magnificence is this? Chinese of course, and very old, if I'm not mistaken.'

'It is one of my favourite pieces. My husband bought it in '21,' explained Catherine, stepping forward. 'We were in London for the coronation of the late king. We had such an exciting time! Do you remember Harriet? All the trouble with the Velasquez and then the Devonshire's ball. But you fell downstairs, so perhaps there are not such happy memories for you.'

'How could I forget? Will you be in London for the next coronation, my lord?' she asked Morna in a bid to turn the conversation.

'I think I must, though I understand it is to be a far more modest affair than that of George IV.'

'Sir Charles Durrington thinks very highly of King William. They are both naval men.' There was a twinkle in her eye.

'And so wonderfully uxorious,' broke in Catherine. 'But not a legitimate heir to his name. Ten children by Mrs Jordan, all of them a FitzClarence, which is all very well but poor Queen Adelaide will not produce the next heir to the throne.'

'Who is the heir? I am sadly out of touch with the royal progeny, legitimate or otherwise,' asked the earl. 'I cannot go to London in ignorance.'

'The Princess Alexandrina Victoria. She is eleven and totally under the thumb of her mother the Duchess of Kent. The Duke died when the princess was a baby.' Catherine had not lost her fashionable connections in Town and always enjoyed the London Season. 'If you are to take a house there my lord, we would be delighted to see you in Park Street – and Mr Romero, of course,' she added smoothly.

Once Catherine had satisfied herself that her housekeeper had preparations in hand for the guests, she whisked Harriet away to her boudoir.

'Tell me, my dear, who is that pretty young man with the earl?'

Harriet was growing rather tired of the question. 'A perfectly charming young architect from Boston. He is certain to ask you all about your crenellations.'

'Goodness, I have not the slightest idea what you mean. He can ask away and I will refer him to my husband. There will be a dozen belles coming to the ball tomorrow who would have positively fought for his favours, but, alas, we have nothing but dowagers tonight. I wish you would stay, Harriet, for the ball; all your friends will be here. You need not dance and I will not be exerting myself. The earl doesn't seem to be a stickler for the proprieties.'

'He's not. But none of us has come prepared for a dance.'

'We can send over to Larkhill for anything you may need.'

But nothing Catherine could say would persuade Harriet to alter their plans. 'We will all enjoy the hunt and next week you may invite us to a private little soirée with all the artistic, intelligent people you know. That way we won't shock the county. I find that once the prejudices of society have been acknowledged one can do very much what one wants.'

'You are wicked Harriet. But talking of soirées, do tell me, what exactly occurred at the Wests' conversazione? Is it true that Mrs West predicted her husband would die? My sister tells me that "animal magnetism" is going to be the next craze in London. I want to hear everything that happened.'

Harriet gave a highly coloured account of the evening, making Catherine rock with laughter at her exaggerations. 'I'm surprised Mr West didn't charge us entry; it was such an extraordinary exhibition – more like a theatrical turn. And to cap it all Frank arrived, very drunk and then Mr West almost threw us all out! Poor Euphemia, she must have had a miserable Christmas.'

'And there was no sight of the black girl? No I suppose there wouldn't be. Did you know that Paton, Mrs West's own maid, is back in Hinton Parva, sobbing her heart out? West discharged Paton on the spot, you know, all because she was loyal to Mrs West; I have not heard the complete story. He really is a despicable man.'

Harriet told her about West's attack on Jacob and Rupert's hostile response.

Catherine was horrified. 'Will refuses to countenance Horace West. However, I fear he intends to hunt tomorrow on that vicious Andalusian stallion of his. This may be awkward for you all. I pray he does not bring Frank.'

'I pray he does not bring Dr Learoyd.'

'Whatever do you mean? The son-in-law, the short little clergyman? Has Rupert quarrelled with him too?'

'No, but his sanctimony offends Rupert,' said Harriet quickly. 'Mr Hinton should ask Mr West to bring back some artefacts from the West Indies for his collection and why will you not be exerting yourself tomorrow?' she continued.

Catherine coloured up a little and after some hesitation said: 'You were among the first to know about Peter so I may as well tell you, Harriet; we have happy expectations for the summer.'

Harriet caught her friend's hands between her own. 'My dear, I am so glad, and will pray that all goes well with you this time.' She herself yearned for more children; their absence was a source of unspoken sorrow to both her and Rupert.

Since Peter Hinton's birth nine years ago, Catherine had lost one darling daughter to scarlet fever and had suffered two miscarriages. 'So you see I will be sitting quiet as a mouse tomorrow night and would dearly love your company.'

'Gracious, there would be no room with all your admirers at your feet. And do not think about organising a special party for us. Hosting the hunt ball will exhaust you for a month and Mr Hinton should wrap you in furs until spring.'

Somewhere a distant bell rang. Catherine looked up, moist-eyed but smiling. 'Good heavens, we must dress for dinner. Let me take you to your room; we are all at sixes and sevens with so many people staying. But it is so nice to see you Harriet; you do me the world of good.'

The evening was one of jollity and laughter. Harriet wore her ruby pendant and glowed in burgundy silk. Cards, conversation and clever word games occupied almost twenty guests. An unexpected bonus of music was supplied by the Larkhill Manor party. The earl had a pleasant baritone voice and sang a lilting Italian ballad accompanied by Romero on the piano. Clem struggled through a flute sonata with Harriet's gentle guidance on the keyboard. After some persuasion Rupert left the whist table and was cajoled into sitting down at the piano with his brother to play a short duet. Even without practise both men managed to come up smiling in triumph at the end.

The only disappointment was the non-appearance of the tableaux. Catherine had exhausted herself in the hunt ball preparations and had not felt strong enough to organise costumes, sets and scenery. Harriet was relieved. The sight of the beautiful Sebastian draped in flowing silks and chiffon might be too unsettling for the rest of the guests; Larkhill was not Naples or Paris. Instead, the young American made himself the darling of the dowagers and was allowed to win more tricks at the card table than he deserved. He looked beautiful in a tight mulberry velvet coat with a set of diamond studs winking in his shirt front. Morna had been more than generous in his Christmas gift to his protégé.

Clem's artless referral to first-footing fell on unresponsive ears but he was allowed to stay up until midnight in compensation for not being able to dress up as a pirate.

A splendid dinner, copious alcohol and a late night did not trouble most of the gentlemen who were to hunt the following morning even though some of the ladies retired early. Will Hinton and his guests were able to raise their champagne glasses and welcome in 1831 in good heart and cheerful expectation that the worst of the agricultural unrest was over.

In Bourne Park, alone and morose in his study, Horace West had only forty-eight hours to live.

PART II: THE MURDER

Chapter 11   New Year 1831

A brilliant day of blue skies and light winds promised favourable for the hunt. The courtyard of Hinton Hall filled with horses, hounds, carriages, grooms, whips and servants offering up stirrup cups of port. A cacophony of noise and excitement rose above the mellow stone façade of the house. Steam and sweat wafted from the restless horses and riders.

Bounty trembled, ready for the off, ears flicking. Rupert looked well on his gleaming chestnut. Several men greeted him, others stopped to offer condolences.

'We don't see you out often, Darville. Brought that young ward of yours to be blooded at last?' A thin elderly man with snow-white hair and military bearing reined in his bay.

'I have, Colonel, and I have brought my brother to make everyone's acquaintance.' Rupert indicated the barouche filled with Harriet, four children and the earl. Sebastian rode at the side looking dazzling in russet and yellow nankeen even among the hunting pink.

'Who's the boy?'

'A friend of my brother.'

Colonel Talbot sniffed. 'He's got a very good leg for a boot but the rest of the rig out won't do; far too showy.'

'He's an American.'

'Ah, that accounts for it. I fought against 'em in the year '12. Damn fine riders, but a shambles in the line, a shambles. By the way, watch out for West. He almost brought me down last month, following so close behind when I took a fence. But then he's not likely to get near you is he, by what I hear?'

Rupert chose to ignore the enquiry. Clem looked intrigued; neither Jacob nor the family had spoken of the various quarrels with Horace West in his presence, but he had heard rumours, nonetheless.

'Is Frank West here?' asked Rupert.

'No, thank the Lord.' The colonel drew his snowy brows together. 'He and Tommy were out after some mischief last night. I left them stewing in their beds. I'll be glad when young West goes back to London. He's staying with us after some quarrel with his father.' He did not give Rupert time to respond.

'You met no trouble riding over, I trust? No disgruntled vagabonds? You heard that the Hinton Yeomanry shot one of the beggars? It's "justifiable homicide" of course. Things may have been quiet for a month but it's best to be prepared. I hope you have your pistols with you.'

Colonel Talbot touched his top hat and went in search of his wife who always followed sedately behind the hunt with her groom.

George Durrington coaxed his new hunter to Darville's side. 'Does the American know what he's doing? At least this filly will be familiar with the lie of the land around here; you can always trust Hinton to breed a good'un.' He patted his horse's neck. 'Now then Clem, stick close to your guardian, he knows what he's about. You might be given the brush if you do well today.'

Clem grinned. 'I'll do my best, sir but I have no hopes of being skilful enough to be awarded the fox's tail.'

West and his son-in-law sat on their mounts a little apart from the rest of the riders. The black stallion bucked and snorted. West was having his usual difficulty controlling the animal and the Archdeacon moved his grey a little to one side. Frank's absence heartened several timid horsemen; one erratic rider in the field was enough to cope with.

Hinton moved among his guests. The Master in his scarlet coat gave a signal, the huntsman blew his horn, whips were cracked and the pack was away to draw the first covert. A cavalcade of jingling riders followed behind the hounds. The carriages and the more sedate riders jostled for a place behind.

Jem did his best to follow the hounds in the barouche but after half an hour of waiting for the pack to cross their path the children grew fractious. Sophia said the hunts at Morna were far more exciting and her papa had allowed her and Rosa to follow on their ponies. She was obviously aggrieved and Harriet was about to suggest that they return to the Hall when in the distance they heard the pack give tongue. A few minutes later a stream of brown and white hounds cascaded over a low stone wall and raced across the road in front of them, tails wagging like catkins. The children screamed in delight, adding to the yelping of the pack.

They did not have long to wait before a parp, parp, parp of the horn heralded a thunder of hooves and the Master led his followers over the wall. A stream of scarlet and black riders burst out of the trees a few hundred yards away and cannonaded over the wall after the pack.

'Papa was not there, neither was Clem!' said Henry in alarm. He was standing on the box of the barouche and had a clear view.

'Don't worry. Papa is probably hanging back with Clem. Or they have taken a different route as this is Clem's first time out with the hounds.'

'I did not see Mr Romero, either,' said Morna anxiously. 'Perhaps he has had a fall and has gone back to the house.'

'Then that is what we shall do. Jem, take us back to Hinton Hall; the weather is far too cold to be outside any longer. We do not wish to see you relapse, my lord.'

****

Clem was a good horseman but this part of the county was not well known to him. Rupert stayed by his side, encouraged him over the fences and led him along safer paths, yet after an hour they were left behind with the slow-tops in the field. Clem felt embarrassed about spoiling his guardian's day.

'It is of no matter. I get no pleasure from killing a fox for sport, but my neighbours expect me – and you - to show our faces and Bounty likes a good gallop as well as your Minstrel Boy.'

'Then let's have a race to the top of that hill, where the copse is. There's no jumps.'

Rupert did not let the boy win; it was not in his nature to do so, but when they had caught their breath at the fringe of the trees, he complimented his ward's handling of the reins. They pushed through a track in the undergrowth to look down a steeply sloping field with a high hawthorn hedge at the bottom. A litter of stones covered the field beyond.

'By jingo, someone's come a cropper,' said Clem. 'He couldn't keep his seat across the hedge. He's been thrown right over by the look of it. Fancy letting go of the reins; how mutton-fisted!'

'It happens to us all, Clem, even the most experienced riders.'

'I think it's Mr West,' said his ward with glee.

Below them a crumpled form lay on the tussock grass, not moving. Some distance off, a big black stallion with rolling eyes twitched uneasily.

Dr Learoyd sat his horse and waited within a few yards of his father-in-law's body. Wearing a hunting topper made him appear taller.

'Why doesn't he get down and help?' asked Clem. 'I know we can't but what's the fellow waiting for? Mr West's hurt.' He looked to Rupert.

'Hush, give them a moment. We don't know what occurred. There, look, West is moving. He's not dead.' The fallen rider groaned and heaved himself up onto his forearms.

Still Learoyd sat his horse and waited.

'Yes but the Archdeacon isn't stirring a muscle to help him!'

'There may be no need. Come back a little. No rider likes to be seen having taken a toss.' Rupert took hold of Minstrel Boy's bridle and backed their horses further into the trees.

By now West had raised himself to his knees, at which the Archdeacon leisurely dismounted and went over to the winded man. West was rubbing the back of his head. Loud oaths drifted up the slope in the clear air. Learoyd gave his hand to his father-in-law and lifted him to his feet in one sure move.

Clem relaxed. 'He's up. It must have been a nasty fall. Shouldn't we at least help to fetch his horse, Uncle Rupert?'

'No. Dr Learoyd knows what he's about.'

The two men below exchanged a few words. At this point West staggered to the stirrup of Learoyd's grey and clung on while the clergyman walked down the field to the nervous stallion. It took him a while to coax the animal close enough for him to grab the reins but, once in his grasp, the horse soon recognised who was master. By the time Learoyd had walked the horse back up the field, Horace West was ready to get back in the saddle.

'The Archdeacon's very brave, especially for a litt – a clergyman,' said Clem. 'I've seen that brute kick out. He should have a green ribbon tied to his tail.'

West was still rubbing the back of his skull and refusing to put his topper on. Learoyd went to brush him down. Some sharp words were exchanged and then very slowly the clergyman helped his father-in-law to remount. At last the two men jogged across the stony field towards the gate and disappeared into a further clump of trees.

The sound of hooves in the undergrowth behind them made Rupert and Clem turn in the saddle.

'Where did you spring from? I thought you were with the rest of the field.' Clem greeted Sebastian with pleasure. The fresh air had brought colour to Romero's tanned cheeks. 'You've just missed Mr West falling off his horse.'

'I got lost,' said the American. 'By golly, the hedges are much higher here than in Fairfax county. I would not strain Mrs Daville's roan by jumping.' This with an ingratiating look at Rupert. 'I was misdirected by some jackanapes after I'd wandered down a cart track and through several gates. Are we far behind the others?'

At that moment, to their right came the strident blare of a hunting horn.

'They've found,' said Rupert. 'Over by Tidworth.' He had an unerring sense of direction. 'There's a short cut I know. You may be in at the kill yet, Clem.'

****

Two days later Dunch came into the library looking hesitant. 'I beg your pardon, sir, but a messenger has just arrived from Bourne Park. It seems they cannot find Mr West and wondered if we had had any sight of him.'

Rupert paused. 'Mr West is missing?'

Bernard's pen poised in mid-air; he thought it most unlikely that Horace West should visit this house.

'So the boy says, sir. According to him, the butler left Mr West in his study last night and the gentleman has not been seen since.'

'Surely his valet would have raised the alarm when Mr West did not come upstairs?'

Dunch could give no further explanation. 'The lad's still in the kitchen, sir.'

'Bernard, we will finish the letter to Faraday later. Send the boy to me, Dunch.'

After interrogating the lad, Rupert informed Harriet of the disappearance.

'Poor Mrs West. She must be in great distress. It would be just like the man to have gone into Larkhill and told no one.'

'I think not,' said Rupert. 'It appears West has not been seen since last night, and is nowhere on the premises. I questioned the boy myself. He says a search party is still scouring the Park.'

Harriet looked troubled. 'If that is the case then I must go over to Bourne Park directly. Either Mr West will have been found, with some perfectly good explanation, and he will not appreciate his wife rousing the neighbourhood, or, if he is still missing, his wife will be in great anxiety. In either case Euphemia needs a woman's presence. The house must seem empty enough as it is without her son or even that Italian man.'

'She has her daughter to support her.'

'Oh no. Have you forgotten? The Learoyds left yesterday.'

The previous evening, the family had been playing cards before the drawing-room fire. Rupert held no truck with the Lord's Day Observance movement and referred extensively to the Julian and Gregorian calendars in justification. No one argued. Dunch entered with a note. They had all been surprised when he approached Mr Romero and offered him the salver with an exaggerated bow.

Looking decidedly uncomfortable, Sebastian had read the note while play was suspended. He cleared his throat and looked around the table. 'I beg your pardon. It is from Mrs Learoyd. She assures me – and you my lord – a warm welcome in Winchester if ever I wish to continue my studies of ecclesiastical architecture.'

'How charming,' said the earl, 'but I regret we will be going up to London very shortly and may have to forgo such riveting pleasures.'

Romero stretched an arm behind him and dropped the note into the flames.

Harriet neatly laid a trump. 'I'm only surprised the Learoyds stayed as long as they did, Mr West is always so cutting to the Archdeacon, but I daresay his ecclesiastical duties for the bishop detained him.'

Rupert, frowning, went back to studying his hand and play continued. Romero seemed somewhat distracted and was the first to seek his bed.

This morning, the news of Mr West's absence put Rupert in a dilemma. He had sworn never to set foot in Bourne Park again but could not resist taking charge; however, he did not wish his wife to be inconvenienced. 'Do not trouble yourself, my dear. It is my duty to go.'

Rupert rode over to Bourne Park taking the boy back with him. Harriet knew better than to openly defy her husband and went to inform their guests of Mr West's unaccountable disappearance. She also sent an order to the stables. An hour later Harriet trotted the gig through the wrought iron gates of Bourne Park. She took Jem with her as groom.

Simpkins, the West's butler, informed her that Mr Darville was with one of the search parties but that Mrs West was closeted in her room, and that the housekeeper had not returned from her post-Christmas visit to her relations. He was a harassed man.

'Then I will go up to Mrs West at once,' said Harriet taking off her bonnet. 'There is no need to send for Mr Darville, but perhaps my groom could be of assistance?'

'Thank you ma'am, another pair of eyes would be welcome. The gamekeeper and his boy are searching the new plantation but they could do with some help.'

Harriet trod upstairs to Mrs West's bedroom and tapped gently on the door. Receiving no response she asked the housemaid. 'Is your mistress asleep? Has she taken a composer? Where is her maid?'

'Miss Paton left, madam, some days ago.'

'Ah yes, then you will have to do,' said Harriet recalling the domestic scandal but putting any enquiries to one side in the face of this emergency. She briskly turned the door handle. The curtains were closed and a strong smell of Kendal's Black Drops hung in the air.

'Mrs West? It's Harriet Darville. Come to see how you do. Euphemia?' she whispered into the darkness. She was inclined to let the poor woman sleep and station the housemaid in the room against her awakening.

'Harriet. I knew you'd come. Have they found him?' The voice from the bed was faint and resigned.

Harriet pulled one of the window curtains aside. 'I have only just arrived but I'm afraid there is no news. Oh, my dear, what a worry for you. But they will find him soon enough. Are you sure Mr West has not gone on a sudden visit connected with business, to Salisbury or even to London?'

Euphemia West pulled herself into a sitting position. She was fully dressed in an old fashioned round gown but she looked haggard and even paler than usual. A wisp of grey hair escaped from her cap. A soft shawl was draped over her stockinged feet. 'I have no idea where my husband is.'

'I did not mean to disturb you if you were sleeping,' began Harriet.

'I cannot sleep. Even my laudanum will not help. I knew someone would come. I'm glad it's you, Harriet.' Mrs West put her hand over Harriet's as she sat on the edge of the bed. The opiate had drugged her mind into lethargy. On the bedside table stood several sachets of Dover's Powder and an array of laxatives.

'Now, we mustn't be thinking the worst. Your husband will return as right as ninepence before dinner, you'll see and we will all look very foolish. Even my husband is out looking for him now.'

Mrs West gave her a long dazed look. 'Perhaps you're right. You are so very kind, considering the terrible quarrel-'

'Hush, hush, we will not talk of the gentlemen's foolishness. I am here to keep your spirits up.'

'Indeed; we do not know what has happened after all. But I fear the worst.' Mrs West looked blindly towards the white light streaming in at the window. 'If only he had not sent Dr Mazzotta away, and in such a manner too. I was ill for days afterwards and am still not myself. Now this quarrel with Frank -. The whole affair quite spoilt Christmas.'

'I'm sure he's sorry for it now. This will never do. Would you like some tea? I most certainly am in need of refreshment. And I'm sure your cook can find some of those delicious biscuits we had at your conversazione.'

Mrs West nodded absently and Harriet gave the necessary orders to the housemaid who promptly vanished.

Harriet's optimism was wearing a little thin by the time she heard the maid on the stairs. Privately, she thought that Horace West had most likely succumbed to apoplexy and lay dead among his flower beds. Mrs West listened politely to Harriet's platitudes, agreed occasionally and kept her own counsel. Her eyes again stared unseeing into nothingness, the pupils shrunken from the effect of the opium.

The bedroom door swung open to reveal a tall black girl struggling under the weight of a silver salver laden with a tea pot, hot water jug, a plate of muffins and a set of fine Worcester china.

'Here we are', said Harriet pulling up a small in-laid table to the side of the bed and nodding to the serving girl. She was surprised at what could only be the appearance of West's "piece of petticoat" but kept her countenance.

'Get Out!' screamed Mrs West, rearing forward. 'Get out of here, you harlot!'

'My dear Mrs West, calm yourself,' said Harriet sharply. But Mrs West was staring at the black girl as though she were a loathsome spider.

With shaking hands the girl set the tray on the table and backed away. 'Yes'm.'

'Get out! Get out of my house, you whore!' Mrs West's eyes were bulging, her face red, hands clenching. She snatched up a book from the bedside cabinet and made to throw it at the cowering servant.

Harriet leapt up. 'Euphemia! Control yourself!' The door slammed. 'The girl has gone. Whatever is the matter? There is no need for such an outburst.'

Mrs West subsided but continued to shoot venomous looks at the door. 'She is a fiend. She wormed her way into this house and behaves like a jezebel. It's all *her* fault!' Her hands shook.

'Then you may dismiss her,' said Harriet striving to keep calm.

'I will not have that slut anywhere near me. Keep her away,' said Mrs West viciously.

'Certainly, that is easily done. And your housekeeper may give the girl her notice when she returns.'

'I want her out of my house now!' said Mrs West, reviving.

Harriet thought Mr West would have something to say about that but answered: 'Of course. And so you shall. Mr Darville and I will take her away with us when we leave. You shall be troubled with her no longer. Now, here is your tea. Drink this and you will feel better.'

She was well aware of Mr West's reputation. He was the type of man who would tumble a housemaid whether under his own roof or another's. Harriet wished she had taken more notice of the black girl who was undoubtedly Jacob's Delilah. In the semi-darkened bedroom she had been more concerned to control Mrs West's hysteria.

In an effort to distract her friend, Harriet began to talk quietly about all the concerns of the neighbourhood and the New Year festivities at Hinton Hall. She could see that Mrs West was not paying attention, and her own ears were attuned to the comings and goings below, but after a while Euphemia's eyes began to close. Harriet carefully laid the shawl back over Mrs West, closed the curtain and tiptoed from the room.

She found her husband in the library staring out of the French windows. 'I didn't expect to see you here, Harriet,' he said with a slight frown. 'I told you not to come.'

'I couldn't leave Euphemia to the wrath of Mr West when he does appear. You gentlemen may be at odds but we ladies are far more loyal.'

Rupert picked up and set down the empty sherry decanter on the desk. 'This is a puzzling affair; we've had no luck as yet, which defies all reason. I can only think that he's lying somewhere in the undergrowth with a twisted ankle. West does not set man traps does he?'

'It would not surprise me in the least. Perhaps his bull-mastiff has carried him off. But, no; I must not be unkind. The poor man may have died of exposure overnight.'

'The dog is safely chained up. How's Mrs West taking the disappearance of her husband?'

'With too much laudanum, I would say. But you my dear, you must not catch a chill searching in the open air in this weather. That fire hasn't been laid long. I don't want you going down with one of your low fevers, especially after all the upsets we have had of late.'

'I have sent a message to George,' said Rupert, used to his wife's concern for his health. 'He will raise the Hue & Cry and get the constables to search the whole area. There is nothing more I can do here.'

'But we cannot abandon Mrs West. Her daughter should be with her and I have left her to sleep while I compose a letter to Letty. Mr West will not begrudge me some note paper and sealing wax, I'm sure.'

She moved around the heavy ebony desk and started to open the drawers. 'Euphemia gave me her daughter's address, but she said nothing about Frank. Do you think he should be informed, too?'

Rupert shrugged and picked up a leather portfolio from the desk. 'He can do nothing to help. I assume he is still with the Talbots or has gone back to London. I cannot believe he would be anything but pleased at his father's disappearance. We should wait until we have some definite news.' He idly let the portfolio fall open and glanced cursorily at the papers inside while Harriet chose a quill and examined its nib. A paper drifted to the floor.

'I won't be many minutes, Rupert, and then I can send one of the servants into Larkhill with this. It should go by the afternoon post. You, my dear, must go home to our guests.'

But Rupert was not listening. Harriet, quite used to this state of affairs, nibbled the end of her quill and set about composing her letter. Rupert picked up the document from the floor and read it with growing disquiet.

A frown appeared between his slanted eyes. He glanced quickly at his wife's bent head and slipped the paper into his inner coat pocket. Laying the leather portfolio back on the desk he said: 'I think I will stay here a little longer and wait for Durrington.'

'Very well. Oh, my dear, would you be so good as to allow Mrs West's black servant to come to us? She can ride with Jem in the gig; I think she's waiting in the hall now.'

'Whatever for? Doesn't Mrs West want her maid?'

'Not this one. I have reason to believe that Mr West was more set on keeping her.'

Rupert raised his eyebrows. 'And you would take her into our house?' His wife never ceased to amaze him.

'I would not have her thrown into the snow which is what Mrs West would wish to do.'

'Very well, do whatever you think best. But I would not want Horace West, whenever we find him, accusing us of poaching his servants. And what exactly am I to do with this girl?'

'Give her to Miss Humble. She can be the new nursery maid to help with Sophia and Rosa,' said Harriet briskly sanding her letter. 'Jacob will be pleased, and Mrs O'Leary may depart in a huff – one can but hope,' she added and then rang for a servant. 'There, that's my duty done,' she said as Rupert held the flame of a spill to a nub of sealing wax. Harriet watched the red wax splutter and drip onto the folded paper. Rupert impressed his signet ring into the soft surface. Harriet looked at him with satisfaction. 'What a useful man you are,' she said. 'I had better go up and see whether I can coax Euphemia to eat something.'

'Will you be home for dinner?'

'I think not. The housekeeper is visiting her family and there seems no one to take charge. The butler is new to his post, I understand. The men who have been out searching all day will need a hot meal. And what if Mr West were to be found, or to return with some perfectly reasonable explanation? I would not want poor Mrs West to face either of those possibilities alone. You might send someone over with my night things. I do not need my maid.'

'I will come and fetch you myself first thing in the morning,' Rupert said as his wife pecked him on the cheek.

'My goodness you need a shave.'

'Jacob has cut his hand. I had to valet myself this morning. Send for me at once if anything occurs.'

'Of course. Kiss the children for me and give the earl my deepest apologies. You gentlemen may indulge in a bachelor night without Miss Humble or I to spoil your fun.'

Rupert gave a wry smile and opened the door for her. He saw Harriet stop and speak to a tall quadroon girl in a rough cloak with a corded box, shrinking in the shadows, looking as if she were about to bolt. As Harriet disappeared up the stairs, he gave the girl a curt nod and retreated into the study. He was not yet ready to leave.

He returned to the French window to stare across the low white hedge and field beyond. Through the lacework of the trees his attention was caught by a glimpse of the whitened roof of the boat house, just jutting into view. When the butler appeared Rupert handed him Harriet's letter with an order to take it to Larkhill post office straight away. 'I assume someone has searched the boathouse?'

Horace West was no waterman but he kept an ancient rowboat for his bailiff to protect his riparian rights. The butler looked abashed and admitted that the boat house had not been thought of; Mr West had never been known to use it.

'We had better be certain,' said Rupert. 'I'll go myself. Has Mr Durrington arrived yet?'

On being informed that the magistrate had not yet appeared, Rupert sent for his coat and set out on his search. He took the circuitous path from the edge of the gardens down to the river, his footprints marking his route in the pristine snow. Silence crackled in the air. No one had come this way since dawn. The field beyond the ha-ha was empty, only the tufts of scratchy thistles and brown yarrow stalks stood up in the expanse of white. Soon the boathouse could be seen from a bend in the path. A former owner of Bourne Park had dug a small inlet in the river bank and thrown up an open-ended shelter to protect any pleasure boats. A short flight of slippery steps dropped down to the near end and the jetty within.

Rupert took care on the icy steps; he did not want to plunge into the water and end up a frozen corpse. Inside, the planks of the jetty lay under a thin covering of hoar frost. A rowing boat, covered in canvas, lay moored to the stanchions along the jetty. It was colder in here than outside. A thick layer of ice edged the water on the far wall of the boat house and trapped that side of the boat into immobility. In the middle of the stream, in front of the boat and alongside the jetty, the ice paled into a grey film. Below it the water looked black and still as marble.

Rupert immediately saw that the oars were in their rack. There was a layer of frost on the canvas. Rupert bent down and pulled it back; there was nothing untoward to be seen.

He rose from his haunches and scanned the walls. Something white on the slimy woodwork caught his eye. He reached up to finger the scar. A lead ball was embedded in the beam; the splinter was fresh.

After another careful scrutiny, Rupert made his way back to the house to find George Durrington waiting in the study.

'What's the damn fool done now?' said George, still wearing his cloak. He had been called away from a magistrates' emergency wages meeting. 'I got your message. That man causes a disturbance wherever he goes. That's the worst of these snappy fellows; they must be forever proving themselves or taking the slightest offence at nothing. Just like that business with Jacob.'

'That has all been settled. He will not touch one of my people again.'

Looking at Rupert's face, George could well believe it. 'He may not touch anybody again if we don't find him soon. He must be as frozen as a herring by now.' George rubbed his hands now released of their gauntlets. 'The butler says the grounds have been thoroughly searched. Is he to be trusted? He looks a poor specimen.'

'I ensured the search was systematic.'

'Then we may be certain West isn't lying in his own park. I roused the constables when I passed through Larkhill, but West isn't popular, you know. If he is in a ditch somewhere most people would be tempted to leave him there.'

Rupert shrugged.

'Have you questioned the servants?' continued George. 'I suppose I should.'

'The valet said West dismissed him at ten o'clock last night, saying he would see to himself. A not unusual occurrence his man claims, so he thought nothing of it. The butler swore he locked up everything but this study. There was no sign of a break-in. The butler was told to retire and left West drinking here at about ten-thirty; again, something which was not unusual. He did say he thought he heard the dog barking long after he went to bed; West had given orders that it should be let loose in the grounds. A housemaid found the decanter empty and the French windows open this morning.'

'You should have gone in for the law. Did you find any signs of disturbance?' George looked about the room.

'None. When West left, he left in good order. There was not a paper out of place when I arrived.'

'But where would he go at that time of night?'

'Somewhere close? All the outbuildings have been searched. Whatever took place, happened before the snow fell, so there's no helpful footprints, though there is one bald patch where West or an animal might have relieved itself, just outside the French window.' Rupert hesitated and then continued casually. 'You could widen the search along the river.'

'He wouldn't be going on a midnight stroll along the Bourne,' expostulated George.

'No, but he might not have gone willingly.'

'Pressed, you mean? But there would be signs of a struggle, surely?'

'Enticed more likely. I found something odd in the boat house and think you should come and give me your opinion.'

George was ready to follow, glad to have some clue to explain the disappearance. In the boat house, George reluctantly agreed that the water had been disturbed in the past twenty-four hours. The grey slush in front of the rowing boat meant that the ice had not had enough time to reform and solidify.

Rupert spoke. 'Perhaps someone took the boat out. It's difficult to tell. The oars are covered in frost as is the canvas, but that could have formed at any time. There's been some activity here within the last twenty-four hours. You must question West's bailiff. He may have taken the boat out for a legitimate reason.'

'No one goes fishing in December.'

'He may have been setting traps for eels or otters. It will do no harm to check.'

George said slowly. 'Do you think there has been foul play, Darville?'

'I cannot say, but what do you make of this?' Rupert pointed to the ball. 'The impact is of recent date; the splinter is new, though it will be impossible to pinpoint the day precisely.'

'Someone at the house must know,' said George looking worried. 'Someone must have heard a shot. Can you imagine any explanation for this ball being here?'

'No. Have you your knife?'

George produced a clasp knife from his pocket. 'I am never without it,' he said handing it to his friend.

Rupert carefully prised the ball out of the wood with his long, strong fingers. He rolled the ball in the palm of his hand. 'There's a faint line around the circumference. It's from a duelling pistol most like.'

'Who has a pair of those around here?'

'Any number of the gentry. Not a servant certainly. What servant has any kind of firearm? You could put some discreet enquiries in hand, George.'

'There may be a perfectly innocent explanation for this ball. Let's wait until West turns up shall we?'

Rupert did not press his case. A puzzling document lay within his coat pocket but he was not yet ready to reveal it. He, too, would wait until Horace West was found alive or dead.

Chapter 12   The late Mr Horace West

Harriet stayed the night at Bourne Park. George Durrington called off the search as the winter evening drew in and the temperature plummeted.

Rupert kept the discovery of the document to himself as he really did not know the implications of what he had found. On examination, the paper held a list of initials with what looked like sums of money next to them. There were various other notations which would take time to puzzle out. He felt he had done enough by giving George two clues to work on. The water in the boat house had been disturbed, but how and by what? What did the ball in the beam signify? And where was Horace West?

They found out the following day. The snow, which had frozen into crust during the night, had melted slightly in the weak morning sunshine. Clem took Minstrel Boy for a gallop around the lanes coming home via the old packhorse bridge. He was alone; Sebastian was snuffling with a chill, caught from his employer as was inevitable. This was Clem's last morning ride before returning to school.

It was Horace West's magenta-striped waistcoat that caught the boy's eye. At first he thought it was a bundle of clothes trapped against the stone piers of the bridge, prompting a wild idea that it might be his cousins' new garments abandoned by the gypsies. A second later he knew what he had seen. At nearly fifteen he was a confident boy and prided himself on his bravery, but he had to steel himself to dismount and investigate the corpse. The horse whinnied and stepped daintily backwards, sensing death. It was Horace West right enough, blue in the body from hours in the freezing water and scratched and bruised from his buffeting against the river banks.

Clem whipped his palomino into a lather to get back to the manor. He burst in on his guardian and George Durrington in the library discussing plans for the continuation of the search. Rupert took one look at his ward's dishevelled clothing and white face.

'Come in Clement. You have found Mr West, I see.' Rupert went towards the decanter of brandy.

'Yes, how did you know? Under the packhorse bridge, against one of the piers. It was horrible.' The boy shuddered. 'I would have missed him but for his waistcoat. I could not drag him out.'

'Drowned, I take it?' asked George. Clem nodded and sat down suddenly in a nearby chair.

'Here, get this down you,' Rupert thrust a brandy glass into the boy's hand. 'Did you see any obvious injuries on the body?'

George looked disapprovingly at his friend.

'There was a pretty severe gash at the back of his head,' said Clement. 'But I didn't look too closely.'

West's body had been a literal dead weight and after pulling the corpse to the side of the river, Clem had given up in horror and despair.

Rupert rang for Dunch and gave orders about a cart and who was to assist. 'This means you can call off the search, George. I suppose we must take the body back to Bourne Park?' He looked at Durrington for official confirmation.

'Of course. I'll fetch Makepeace; we should have a doctor examine the body before I inform the coroner. God knows what the fool was doing wandering down by the river in weather like this. You were right in your guesswork. I can only think he over-indulged in that sweet sherry of his then went for a midnight stroll to clear his head and fell in.'

Rupert had his hand on Clem's shoulder. 'Stay here and finish your brandy. Then find your Uncle Ralph if he has come downstairs. It might be polite to inform him of what's happening. This – mischance has made us very neglectful hosts. Not a word in the nursery, mind.'

'Is Aunt Harriet back?' Clem looked up hopefully.

'I was about to set out to fetch her when Lieutenant Durrington called. Mrs West will need her even more now that the worst has happened.' He squeezed his ward's shoulder sympathetically. He could not find words of comfort but hoped that Morna's smooth tongue and the guileless prattle of the children would mitigate the horror of Young Clem's find.

****

Three men stood around the corpse in one of the tumble-down sheds at the back of Bourne Park. The Trottman sons had brought the cart along the lonely lanes to the unused back gates of the park, Lud's Hill rising above them. The body had been laid on a hastily erected trestle amid a litter of old scythes and rusting rakes. Doctor Makepeace shooed out the ghoulish hangers on and held an oil lamp close to the corpse.

'He's got a nasty wound at the back of his skull,' stated the doctor, 'but no other injuries, apart from superficial lacerations from debris in the river.'

'No wounds from a firearm?' asked Rupert.

'None whatever,' returned Makepeace in surprise.

'Could he have got the head wound from colliding with the bridge?' asked Durrington.

Makepeace adopted an impersonal tone. 'It's possible. But he could also have been struck from behind with something heavy.' An uncomfortable silence hovered.

'The river is hardly fast-flowing in this weather; it's sluggish with ice. Would he have hit his head against the piers with such force?' Rupert sounded sceptical. He leaned down and fastidiously removed a tight bud of pussy willow from West's hair.

Makepeace shrugged. 'I cannot say, gentlemen. Medical dissection has not progressed sufficiently for me to make the distinction. You say your ward found West trapped under one of the arches, Mr Darville. Then a continuous buffeting against the stone may have caused such an injury. What I can tell you is that there was water in the lungs which indicates a drowning. He was alive when he went into the water.'

George visibly relaxed. 'And he wasn't attacked for his money,' he said looking at Horace West's pocket watch miraculously still threaded through his sodden waistcoat. 'So we can forget footpads or gypsies or even rioters. A simple accident you think, doctor?'

'But why did he disappear into the night without telling anyone?' interrupted Rupert.

'My dear man, you know as well as I do what a reputation West has – had. He may well have had an assignation with some female. In fact I'll lay my life that was why he was abroad after ten thirty. I've seen him myself, drinking in the Three Crowns until the small hours, and Frank is no better.'

"It is possible, but there was a domestic attraction under his own roof, I understand, and no one would go out in this weather without a greatcoat.' Rupert did not mention that Delilah was now at the manor.

'You mean the black girl? Then it was as I said when he first went missing: West had too much to drink, went outside to clear his head and fell in the river.'

Makepeace picked up his bag. 'I will leave you to your suppositions gentlemen. As a medical man I fear I can give you no further guidance on the matter and I have Mrs West to attend to. I take it the Italian person has gone?'

'Long ago,' said George with a chuckle. 'West told him to weigh anchor the day after the conversazione.'

Makepeace, looking smug, retrieved his hat and left the two men alone with the corpse.

George looked at his friend. 'Why not accept that this was an accidental death by drowning? No good can come of taking this matter any further. We have no proof of anything untoward. The melted ice in the boat house may mean nothing and there's no gunshot wound, you can see for yourself. Though it's deuced odd that his wife foretold his death.'

'It's a wonder how he escaped this long.' The paper from the document portfolio crackled ominously in Rupert's breast. 'Let's get back to the house,' he said. 'It's as cold as the tomb in here.'

****

Bourne Park was subdued but functioning thanks to Harriet's confident hand. The carpenter had been informed, the laying-out woman sent for. It needed only to contact Frank, and Harriet thought she could leave that duty to his sister. She believed there were titled relatives somewhere, though little had been heard of these since Rupert had settled in the neighbourhood. The Learoyds were expected within the hour. George said he would inform the coroner for form's sake; he would not encourage an inquest if only Darville would leave well alone.

George and Rupert were sitting in the study at Bourne Park, warming their hands on some mulled ale when the sound of a light carriage made them sit up.

'Let's hope that's the relatives,' said George. 'Juliana will let rip if I'm home late again today.'

A few moments later the butler announced that a Mr Askew had arrived. Rupert took the card from the silver tray.

'The gentleman says he has an appointment with Mr West, sir,' the butler explained apologetically. 'I didn't like to turn him away.'

'Very well, Simpkins, send him in.' Rupert handed the visiting card to Durrington. 'An attorney, from Salisbury.'

'Askew? Yes I've come across him in county matters. He's a pleasant enough cove.'

The two men sat back in anticipation as a stout man in his sixties clutching a heavy document case was shown in. His hair stuck out in pomaded whorls fringing his bald head. His spectacles steamed up in the warmth of the room.

'I beg your pardon, gentlemen.' He looked with some puzzlement from one to the other. 'I have an appointment with Mr West. He most particularly asked me to come today.'

'Brace yourself, Mr Askew,' said Rupert rising. 'I have the sad duty to inform you that your – client? – was found dead yesterday morning.'

'Good God!' said Mr Askew groping for a chair. 'Forgive me, gentlemen. This is so unexpected! If I had known. Today of all days!' He drew a large silk handkerchief from his pocket and mopped his perspiring pate, removed his spectacles and gave them a hard polish.

'Can you give me details, gentlemen? You are correct in your surmise, sir; Mr West is – was – my client. I regret I have not the honour of your acquaintance.'

Introductions were made. Mr Askew calmed a little on hearing that Durrington was a magistrate. 'Mr Durrington, yes, I thought we had met somewhere before. I take it you are overseeing Mr West's affairs, gentlemen?'

'Until the widow's family arrives. Tell me, Mr Askew,' said Rupert. 'What brings you to Bourne Park today?'

Mr Askew looked flustered. 'Really, sir. I must plead client confidentiality. I cannot divulge my client's affairs to just anyone. I, too, shall wait for the arrival of a gentleman of the family.'

'You may have to wait a while,' said George. 'They are not aware that Mr West is dead, only that he is missing.'

'Missing?' said Askew in confusion.

'And since found dead – drowned in the river Bourne,' explained Rupert. 'So you see your obligation to your client ended with his death. Mrs West or her family may not wish to retain you as their legal adviser and Lieutenant Durrington, as a local magistrate, has the authority to investigate this occurrence.'

George looked annoyed.

Mr Askew started to splutter with indignation but subsided with a shrewd look in his eye. 'Do you think there is something untoward, gentlemen, regarding my client's demise?'

'Let us say there are some loose ends to tie up before we can let the matter rest,' Rupert smiled.

George kept his thoughts to himself. 'Perhaps you could assist us, Mr Askew. Why did you come to Bourne Park today?'

Mr Askew took refuge in cleaning his spectacles again.

'Was it a matter of disposal of property or a will?' offered Rupert.

'How did you know? No one knew. I was sworn to secrecy, which was quite unnecessary in my profession. Did Mr West speak to you about this? I believed I was the only person in my client's confidence.'

'My dear Askew, why else would a lawyer attend on one of the most irascible men in the neighbourhood on one of the coldest days of the year unless the client demanded some urgent business of that lawyer? Buying or selling of stock, perhaps? Or since the family had been with Mr West for the so-called "season of good will", perhaps some change to his testamentary bequests?'

'Don't be such a cynic, Darville,' said George. He felt his friend was not showing sufficient gravitas in the circumstances.

'Mr West was a most litigious gentleman. I regret I am not at liberty to disclose details,' the lawyer replied primly.

'Mr Askew,' said George leaning forward. 'Your client has been found dead, with a nasty wound at the back of his skull. I would not advise you to obstruct an officer of the court in his duties.'

'No, no to be sure! But I cannot show you the draft documents; it goes against all professional ethics. My client's affairs are – were – private. The documents are worthless now and no good would come of my showing them to you.' He gripped his briefcase to his chest.

'I could insist that you hand over the papers,' said George in magisterial tones. He had no idea why Rupert was taking this line but he would support his friend and his own authority. Rupert remained impassive, an inscrutable look on his pale face.

'You may insist as much as you please, Mr Durrington, but until I have spoken with the family these papers remain in my possession.'

'The new arrangements,' interposed Rupert, 'were, shall we say, not quite what one would expect?'

'Indeed, sir, I do not consider them to be the actions of a gentleman,' spluttered Askew. 'But I know – knew - Mr West of old and can assure you that by Easter he would have reverted to a more sensible disposal of his property. Though I fear this time he may have meant it.'

Rupert put his fingers to his cheek. 'I take it the current settlements make a more generous provision for the family than the draft proposals?'

'I could not possibly comment,' said Askew and closed his lips.

Just then the sound of a carriage could be heard approaching. 'The Learoyds,' said Rupert, rising again. 'You may greet the bereaved family with a clear conscience, Mr Askew. Their fortunes are intact and you have let no skeletons out of the cupboard. And you have our word that we will say nothing of this – aberration of Mr West's.'

'I can assure you, sir, my conscience is always clear,' insisted the attorney.

'Ah, that we could all say the same,' said Rupert ruthlessly ushering him out. 'Would you be so kind as to wait in the dining room until called for? Lieutenant Durrington and I must break the sad news to the family.'

Harriet appeared at the foot of the stairs and took charge of Letty who demanded to be taken straight up to her mother. Dr Learoyd followed the gentlemen into the study. There followed a difficult half hour of explanations, suppositions, several glasses of brandy, and much effusive thanks from the son-in-law who looked very shaken at the end of it all. He did not ask to see the body.

Outside the bedroom door Harriet took both Mrs Learoyd's hands in hers, bid her hush and told her the sad facts. To her credit, Letty did not cry out but seemed unable to take in the tragic news.

'Dead? Papa cannot be dead! I saw him only on Sunday! I knew we shouldn't have left so precipitately!'

'Your mother is distraught. Let her sleep if you can. Once she knows that you and Dr Learoyd are here her mind will be considerably eased.'

Harriet led Letty into the darkened room and took a seat in the shadows.

'Mama! Mama! You poor darling! What are we to do? Dearest Papa, taken from us so cruelly and so soon I cannot believe it! But Mrs Darville assures me it is so, so it must be true. Drowned in the river! But I am here now and you can depend upon Martin to arrange everything that is necessary.'

'The Archdeacon is with you?' came Euphemia's faint voice. 'How forgiving.'

Her daughter dropped to her knees beside the bed. 'Of course Martin is here, Mama; he would not let me come alone, we had barely been home one night when Mrs Darville's letter arrived and you need not fear that Martin would allow a paltry quarrel to come between him and his Christian duty, even if Papa were only missing then. We came at once though dear Martin had an appointment to see my lord bishop and had so many other things to do, but no matter. We would have been here sooner but we were obliged to divert to Sallow's Cross again, the wretched coach spring broke once more, and imagine they gave us the same room as before, which is a blessing because I swear we lay on the same sheets as Sunday. They were damp of course the inn being so near the river, and I only pray no-one took the room the night between but I slept remarkably well for all that though poor Martin seems exhausted and then we were delayed for quite an hour in snowdrifts outside Andover, so full of people for market day. Why they hold it on a Wednesday I do not know but I daresay the farmers like it, though it does clog the roads...'

Harriet coughed to stem the flow of words. 'Perhaps we should allow your mother to rest? And I'm sure you'd like to take the opportunity to send a message to your brother.'

'Frank?' Letty sounded as though she had never heard of him. 'I do not know where he is. He could have gone back to London. He left Bourne Park early you know, in one of his pets, so he could be anywhere, staying at Cheney Court I have no doubt, with Tommy Talbot. They have been intimates since the university and I hold it is Tommy who leads them both into mischief, these young men-'

'Then perhaps you or your husband could write to both addresses in the hope that one letter will find him? Or we could send a message to Cheney Court in case your brother is still there.' She levered Letty to her feet.

'Oh, but I must say a few words in prayer to comfort my Mama,' said her daughter, attempting to sink to her knees again.

There was a moan from the bed.

'Perhaps your husband would be more suited to the task?' insisted Harriet propelling Letty to the door.

'Yes, of course, I'll ask him at once. But what was Papa doing by the river? He does not fish, he hates fish-' And the stream of verbiage continued down the stairs until they reached the salon where, to Harriet's surprise, Letty Learoyd burst into tears.

Eventually George and the Darvilles made their escape and said their goodbyes at the front of the house.

'A rum business,' said George from the saddle.

'It may be wiser to say nothing about the new will, if there was one, George,' warned Rupert as he patted the neck his friend's horse.

'Five years on the bench has taught me when to hold my tongue. What d'you make of it?'

A movement from the house behind them made them look up. Mr Askew was leaving.

'I trust your interview with the Learoyds went well?' asked Harriet.

'Yes, indeed Mrs Darville,' said the lawyer approaching the gig. 'I am retained to execute the will and to administer the late Mr West's estate.' He would say nothing of the scandalous draft documents in front of a lady. He ignored Rupert and looked up at George. 'I assume I will not be hearing from you, Mr Durrington?'

'Only if there is an inquest, and I'm not certain there are grounds for one. The son-in-law seems convinced that the death was an accident and there are no provable signs of foul play. I have no need to see your papers – yet. '

Rupert's hand tightened on the horse's bridle. George frowned and pulled his mount away. He was anxious to be gone. His magisterial authority displayed, he would not exert himself more than his duty demanded.

'Quite so. Better let sleeping dogs lie, I agree. Ah, here is my chaise. I'll bid you good day.' A modest town carriage appeared from the stables and Mr Askew made his way towards it.

'Shall we see you tomorrow, George?' asked Rupert, climbing into the gig beside his wife. Jem would ride Bounty back to the manor and doubtless relate everything to the servants.

'I imagine there'll be no wassail in your orchards tonight?'

'Good heavens, I'd quite forgotten it is Twelfth Night tonight. This ugly business had driven it right out of my head. I don't know if Harriet has arranged anything for the children but Clem may be glad of a diversion.'

'We'll think of something,' said Harriet, 'You and Juliana are always welcome, if she feels a need for some company.'

George touched his hat and declined but promised to ride over the following day to inform them of the coroner's decision regarding the inquest.

'Poor Mrs West,' said Harriet, whisking the pony into a trot. 'I'm not sure what comfort her daughter can give her. Letty never stopped talking; shock and her nerves, I suppose. She was complaining of the damp sheets at Sallow's Cross while her father lies dead in the barn. I'm glad to be out of the house, my head quite aches.'

'Once West's safely buried they'll find themselves vastly better off.'

'Once he's safely buried? You do think something's amiss, don't you?'

Her husband did not answer.

****

Harriet summoned Delilah to her room as soon as she had a free moment after her return to the manor.

'I see that you have heard the tragic news concerning your master.' Jem had been assiduous in telling the kitchen all he knew. The girl looked white-eyed with fear. 'There is no need to be alarmed. I have no intention of sending you back to Bourne Park, unless you are specifically asked for. And in this country you may choose your own employment. But strictly, the Wests did not hire you did they?'

Delilah blinked and shook her head but continued to twist her hands under her apron.

'I merely wish to ascertain if you will be a suitable nursery maid. How old are you?' Harriet eyed her up and down. Delilah was tall and willowy but looked to have a certain strength about her arms and hands. She was very pretty, Harriet had to acknowledge.

'Seventeen, ma'am, I tink.'

'What did you do before Mr West brought you to this country? Were you a house servant?'

'I was a dairy maid, ma'am an' I looked after de cattle on de plantation farm.'

'I see.' Harriet knew that one needed a certain amount of strength to milk beasts and churn butter. Whether the girl would be a good nursery maid was another matter.

Impulsively, because the topic was still uppermost in her mind, she asked 'Can you throw any light on how Mr West came to such an untimely end?'

'Ma'am?'

'Do you know why Mr West should fall in the river and drown?'

'Noa, ma'am, I know notting about it, notting at all.' The girl shook her head vehemently.

'Did Mr West visit you on the night he went missing? The night of the second of January?'

'I doan't know the dates of de calendar,' Delilah looked panic-stricken.

'I refer to last Sunday. The day after Mr West returned from hunting. The day the family went to church.'

The girl nodded as if grasping at some straw.

'Did Mr West visit you that night?' Harriet repeated. She had no hesitation in asking such an indelicate question of a servant.

'No, no, ma'am. I never saw him a bit. I never saw him, no way at all dat night. I was locked in de attic.' Delilah's face shut down.

Harriet sighed. 'Very well. We will say no more about the matter until the inquest is over. When a jury will decide on the cause of Mr West's death,' she explained to Delilah's blank face. 'After that we may have to reconsider your position here. No one will lock you in at the manor. If you wish to leave us you may, but I don't advise it.' She thought that Delilah would be inclined to stay while Jacob was there to protect her.

'No, ma'am, no, ma'am. I gonna stay as long as I can.'

'Good. The world is harsh and cold and you would bring yourself under suspicion if you ran away. Do you understand?'

'Yes, ma'am. I been branded once for tryin' to escape. I woan't never do it again.'

Harriet was appalled. 'No one will brand you in England. You are a free woman.'

She dismissed Delilah with instructions to obey Miss Humble in all matters and sat staring into her bedroom fire. If the inquest jury concluded accidental drowning then Delilah, if suitable to the duties, could remain as nursery maid, but if there was a hint of illegality concerning the death then Harriet had no scruples about dismissing Delilah instantly. No one could risk having a possible murderess in charge of their children.

On the other hand, Delilah's fall from virtue did not disturb Harriet a jot. The girl was a obviously a victim of West's unbridled philandering; there seemed nothing of the coquette about her.

Which is more than could be said of Mr Romero. Harriet had long made her mind up about her two guests but she had no inclination to demand that Rupert turn them from the house. Her Bible told her that such a sin was an "abomination" but Leviticus also said that eating shell-fish was an abomination and she had no intention of denying Rupert his oysters any more than she had of depriving him of his brother. She wondered how Ralph reconciled his conscience with the demands of his religion and came to the conclusion that confession was a very convenient ritual. As her two visitors made no great demands on the household, nor made a spectacle of themselves, she was content to follow her husband's lead and turn a blind eye. There were far too many other problems to manage.

****

Harriet abandoned her plans for the wassail that night. The discovery of their neighbour's body was too horrific to allow a tipsy celebration to bless the orchards. Young Clem was still shaken by his find although he made a valiant effort to conceal it. He made no request to attend the funeral; it was nerve-racking enough to be called to give evidence if there were to be an inquest.

But the evening was not a gloomy affair after all. A tacit agreement not to discuss the grisly discovery and some entertaining tales from the earl occupied the dinner table. The dessert was followed by the appearance of the Twelfth Night cake. A waft of brandy and spices came from the huge plum cake lightly iced and decorated with sugared almonds. The children were summoned to the dining room and Lizzie, as the youngest, was helped to cut the first slice.

'Whoever finds the bean will be king or queen of the feast,' explained Lizzie. 'Have you the paper crown, Mama?' Her own piece had been mined thoroughly without finding the prize.

To everyone's satisfaction Sophia found the bean. She looked around helplessly at the smiling gathering. 'Do I have to eat it?'

'No, no, stupid,' teased Clem. 'But I'll eat your slice of cake if you don't want it.' Harriet was pleased to see his spirits improved.

Lizzie snatched up the paper crown and inexpertly sat it on Sophia's drab hair. 'Now, you must come and sit at the head of the table. Papa, would you please move. And, Sophie, you can make us do whatever you like for the rest of the party.'

Sophia sat, looking rather lost at the head of the table, staring round at them all.

'What do you wish, oh majesty?' curtsied Lizzie, entering into the spirit of the occasion with gusto. Sophia looked nervous until Sebastian gave her a warm smile of encouragement.

'I want Rosa and me to stay here and not be sent away to school.' Sophia looked at Harriet with apprehension.

'That's just dandy,' whispered the young American.

A silence fell. All eyes turned to Harriet. She looked at her husband who frowned. Morna shrugged. Clem looked tense.

'Now is not the time to discuss this but we will postpone the boarding school plans until after Easter. Your uncles and I will talk about it again in the light of your behaviour. But meanwhile you are not to concern yourself, both you and Rosa may stay here with us.'

Rupert may not have been pleased but Sophia beamed with relief. It was the first time Harriet had seen the child smile. Lizzie clapped her hands.

Sebastian leaned over to straighten the crown 'There, Miss Sophia, your majesty, I should say. You will be able to put a shine on your skating and go coasting again if we have more snow.'

'Will the priest come too?' asked Rosa. 'I don't like him.'

'What priest?' asked Harriet.

Sebastian was about to reply when Henry interposed. 'She means Dr Learoyd, Mama. She thinks he's a priest not an archdeacon, the silly.'

Sebastian tried again. 'Dr Learoyd joined us when we were sledging down Folly Hill. It was a chance encounter, Mrs Darville. He was most interested in the Temple of Athena, particularly when I told him we had visited the original in Athens, my lord.' He smiled winsomely at the earl.

'My grandfather's folly is modelled on the Temple of Athena Pronaia at Delphi. It is not like you to be so mistaken, Sebastian; I daresay your mind was on other things,' said the earl.

'You spent forever in there with the Archbacon,' said Lizzie who had resented being abandoned at Dr Learoyd's appearance.

'Archdeacon,' corrected her bother.

'You said nothing about this, Clem,' queried Rupert.

The Archdeacon's sudden arrival at the folly had annoyed Clem. He had taken refuge in piling Sophia and Rosa in front of him on the sledge and whirling down the hill as fast as the snow would take them. He would have mentioned the intrusion in the normal course of events but he felt uncomfortable about the situation. Although he did not quite know the significance of his guardian's warning, he knew that Rupert did not approve of the young American. The talk on Warren Hill tied his tongue; he did not want to get his friend into more bad odour. Since then there had been the discovery of Mr West's body to occupy all his thoughts.

The boy shrugged. 'I didn't think it was important,' he muttered. 'May I have another slice of cake, please?'

'You must ask Sophia,' said his aunt, her thoughts elsewhere.

'How pleasing that the good doctor has such an interest in architecture,' said the earl. 'What a lot you two must have in common.'

Romero squirmed under this blatant sarcasm. 'The Archdeacon promised to give me a tour of Salisbury cathedral. I suppose that will be impossible now Mr West is dead.'

This unlucky remark led to the breakup of the party.

Chapter 13   The Inquest

George Durrington was in a bad mood. 'That damned officious parish constable has gone and informed the coroner about the death, just get his fee I'll be bound. As if there isn't enough charge on the parish already, what with the Poor Rate being demanded by every working man in the parish. There's no need to have an inquest, I'm convinced, and I would have had a quiet word with Sir Archibald if Shaw hadn't overstepped the mark. West was three sheets to the wind, fell into his own river and drowned and that's the end of the matter.'

Rupert looked closely at his friend and offered him the cigar box. 'I may not entirely agree with you but that's not all that's ruffled your feathers, is it?'

'I think I prefer you when you have your nose in a book; you are not wont to be so sharp.' George took a spill from Rupert's hand and made a business of lighting it from the fire. He needed a moment to decide how much to tell his friend. He took a long draw on his thin cigar, studied the glowing tip and said at last: 'If you must know, there's nasty rumours going around the town, concerning your Jacob. I heard some ugly things hinted at in the Three Crowns as I came through.'

'The fact that Jacob threatened to kill West? Do you think there will be any repercussions?' It had been Harriet who had been worried about wagging tongues if the death looked suspicious. Rupert's logical brain had at first dismissed the possibility but now he was resigned to it.

'Yes, but I was there, I saw the whole thing. It was pure bravado on Jacob's part, we all know that. Still, I wouldn't want the lad to be charged with anything. Where was he on Sunday night?'

'I do not spy on my servants.'

George looked thoughtful. He did not care to say that suspicion had brushed against Rupert; his quarrel with West was another rumour relished by the scandal-mongers.

'Perhaps an inquest would be the best thing – to exonerate everyone. Not that I can prevent the damn thing now that Walcot has been informed of it officially. More bother and expense and I shall have to spend an hour tramping the river bank with him. What a way to end Christmas!'

'I've kept Clem home from school until this business is over. I assume you will have to subpoena him? He found the body.'

'I brought the subpoena with me. I don't feel easy about calling a youngster but he isn't under suspicion in any way.'

'There are others who might be. Surely you are curious about the contents of the draft documents Askew holds? If West had been planning to change his will or sell his holdings to the detriment of the family then any of them would have a motive for murder.'

'I know that! I could see what you were getting at when you were questioning the lawyer,' said George unhappy to have his vague unease spoken aloud. 'But as they must have known that he always saw sense after a few weeks, there was no point in bumping the old boy off. We have nothing to raise our suspicions apart from a cracked skull.'

'And the pistol ball in the boat house?'

'Could have got have there any time. And your theory of the ice being disturbed is hardly proof. I've seen ice in the Baffin Straights do funny things; you cannot rely on it.'

'You can rely on the natural laws of physics, but as you say, everything is circumstantial.' Even West's piece of paper, now locked away in Rupert's desk, would prove nothing. 'Tell me, if the verdict is murder, would you investigate?'

'To what end? I can issue an arrest warrant only after the culprit has been found. We don't want another murderous attack in the neighbourhood just to catch the criminal in the act. I discharged the special constables at the end of December so have only Hewitt and Shaw to call on and they are barely paid to keep the peace let alone search out criminals. And it's not my duty to junket around the county poking into people's private affairs. If West was killed it was by one of the "Bread or Blood" mob and I could be next on their list. I don't propose to stir up a hornet's nest without some hard facts.'

'Even if a magistrate has been murdered? The Lord Lieutenant will be expecting somebody to take the blame.'

'It would be like looking for a needle in a haystack. Most of the ringleaders are already being tried; I would have to question all the farmworkers and their families in the county. You're asking the impossible.' George did not like to think about it.

'Then we shall have to see what verdict arises from the inquest. For your sake I hope it is "misadventure".'

'I'll ask Makepeace to give evidence that West drowned, which he did. I hope he doesn't expect to be paid, though I'd tip him out of my own pocket if necessary.' George drew heavily on his cigar. 'Here,' he said drawing a red-sealed, important looking paper from his breast pocket. 'Clem's subpoena. I'll leave it to your judgement as to whether you show it to him or not.'

Rupert laid it aside. 'Are you sure you won't stay to dinner? You could explain the procedure to Clem yourself.'

'You can do that just as well. I must be on my way. Juliana sends her regrets but it is too cold to venture out and my mother has something planned tonight before Mary and Miss Charlotte leave us. My compliments to Harriet and the earl and tell Young Clem that Sir Archibald will call him to give evidence first, so it will soon be over.'

He stood and threw his cigar butt into the flames. 'I do not want to be at odds with you over this, Darville but, whatever the outcome, my hands are tied unless someone furnishes me with proof.'

****

Fifteen good men and true were sworn in and seated in wooden pews in Larkhill's Moot Hall. The benches were packed with townsfolk, squashing together for warmth in the wood-panelled court room. Dr Learoyd and Frank West appeared wearing black arm bands. They both looked drawn. Chairs were found for the bereaved brothers-in-law. Nods were exchanged with the Darvilles and George Durrington but the men made no move to speak to each other.

'A large turn out,' commented Rupert, under his breath.

'They can't believe West is dead and want to be certain,' replied George. 'He rubbed a lot of people up the wrong way. Look, that lawyer fellow from Salisbury is here.'

Mr Askew had found himself a corner nook at the back of the room and was absently polishing his spectacles.

The medieval Moot Hall had been the old manorial court which now served as the town council meeting room. The Royal Coat of Arms positioned above the dais provided the only spot of colour in the weak sunlight. The long table had been dismantled and the space filled with benches for the onlookers. Those who could not push their way up the wooden staircase remained under the pillars below and demanded a running commentary from their luckier fellows in the court room. At last the constable slammed the door against the intrusive crowd. A sprinkling of the gentry occupied the front benches, the Earl of Morna among them. Romero had been granted permission to stay at home and nurse his cold.

'All rise,' ordered the clerk. A cloud of dust and body odour rose with the spectators.

Sir Archibald Walcot, justice of the peace and coroner for the county, took his seat on the dais, adjusted his wig over his cadaverous skull and glowered at the court. After a dry and brisk introduction he asked for the first witness.

Clem felt a mixture of importance and fear when he was called, but the faces around him were familiar and he told what little he knew with no hesitation. Sir Archibald dismissed him kindly.

Dr Makepeace took the stand next and explained that he had been summoned by the other district magistrate, Mr Durrington, who was in some quandary as to whether the death had been the result of a "Visitation from God", misadventure or foul play. When he had instructed the men to lift the body from the river, a quantity of water had gushed from the deceased's mouth. This indicated that the deceased had inhaled a substantial amount of water, which meant Mr West was alive and breathing when he went into the river. He would not be drawn on the head wound.

Frank West looked agitated and was calmed only by the Archdeacon's whispers.

The valet and the housemaid repeated their stories which enlightened no one. Rupert noted that neither mentioned hearing a gunshot. The butler took the stand and told his tale.

'You said there was no evidence of intruders but that you heard the dog bark? What time would this be?' questioned Sir Archibald.

'I cannot say, sir, perhaps a few hours after I retired,' replied the butler.

'And you did not get up to investigate?' asked the coroner in surprise.

'No, sir. Mr West did not appreciate being disturbed in the middle of the night.'

There was a snigger from the lower orders.

'Then it seems hardly worthwhile letting the dog loose! Did Mr West have any enemies in the district?'

George stared straight ahead. Mr Askew looked blandly unconcerned. No one spoke, though several instinctively glanced at Rupert. The Earl of Morna picked an invisible speck of fluff from his lapel.

'Is any member of the West family present who can give evidence on this point?' insisted the coroner.

Dr Learoyd stood up, the motes of dust dancing about his hair in the sunlight. 'The Venerable Martin Learoyd, sir, Archdeacon of Winchester. I am, was, son-in-law to the deceased. My late father-in-law, though a perfectly just man, had had occasion to sentence several of the agricultural rioters to transportation or long terms of imprisonment.'

Sir Archibald nodded sympathetically. 'Well deserved I'm sure. A difficult time for us all, sir.'

'I know my father-in-law had received a threatening letter from some miscreant signing himself Captain Swing. I saw the letter myself. He was extremely troubled by it.'

'With every good reason in this time of anarchy.' The coroner looked towards the parish constable. 'Have we any indication as to whether any attempt was made on Mr West's life? Had there been any altercation with a specific individual?'

The spectators shuffled their feet. Constable Hewitt looked at the floor.

'Constable, can you throw any light on this?' insisted the coroner. Learoyd resumed his seat next to Frank who was suddenly looking alert.

'No complaint wus laid, sir, from Mr West, except 'gainst the gypsies that is. But they'm long gone.'

The account of the argument with the gypsies was gone into. Rupert's granite face persuaded Hewitt not to mention the presence of the Darville children as spectators. Clem looked very nervous.

'So, this gang of Romanies as well as various radicalised peasants had reason to resent Mr West? Is there anyone else we should consider, Constable? Though goodness knows that is sufficient.'

Frank West pulled himself from the Archdeacon's restraining hand and stood up rather shakily. 'My father was threatened by Mr Darville's black servant, in front of the whole town. He said he would murder him!' he said looking accusingly at Rupert. Clem looked frightened and the Archdeacon angry.

Immediately, George got to his feet. 'I beg your pardon, Sir Archibald, but I was a witness to the unfortunate event and can explain the matter.' The court all turned to look at the magistrate.

'Ah, Mr Durrington.' The coroner relaxed at the sight of a known figure of authority. 'Do enlighten us, if you please. Be so good as to take the stand.'

'Do you want your father exposed as philandering bully?' hissed the Archdeacon to his brother-in-law. 'Keep quiet and let us brush through the business as best we can.'

Duly sworn in, George said: 'Mr Horace West was coming out of the inn yard at the Three Crowns when, I believe, his horse slipped on the wet cobbles, inadvertently knocking Mr Darville's manservant to the ground. I understand the servant's cheek was grazed, with the result that harsh words were exchanged, purely in the heat of the moment, I assure you. The incident was a momentary accident; I witnessed it all from the coffee room door.'

Several people glanced again at Rupert. His knuckles whitened as he gripped his arms. Not even the rats squeaked. Frank was about to protest when his brother-in-law held him down, whispering fiercely. 'You cannot contradict a magistrate; and you were not there! And at least the family's name had not been besmirched.'

'I see,' said the coroner. 'I assume that there is no indication that this servant took any further action against Mr West?'

No one spoke. In the face of this mute response the coroner concluded: 'So, apart from these general threats, Mr West was well thought of in the neighbourhood, I take it?'

No one demurred.

'Mr Francis West, are you in a position to comment on your father's state of mind?'

Frank stood up slowly. 'He was not suicidal, sir, if that's what you're thinking. He had his whole future mapped out ahead of him.'

Mr Askew was all at once captivated by the wooden bosses on the ceiling. Rupert looked up sharply to see the Archdeacon half rising again. 'My father-in-law was a very Christian man; self-destruction would be abhorrent to his beliefs. The family was all together for the Christmas holidays, nothing could have been more conducive to our mutual happiness.' Learoyd broke off as if in distress. George, who had resumed his seat on the benches, nudged Rupert in disgust.

'Have you *any* idea how your father-in-law may have fallen into the river?' asked Walcot.

'Upon my honour I could not say. My wife and I had already left Bourne Park that morning; I wanted to be back in Winchester to minister to my own flock.' He hesitated, looked a little embarrassed. 'Far be it from me to speak ill of the dead, let alone a respected member of my own family, but Mr West did like to indulge in several glasses of sherry in the evening. I know myself that he had a strenuous outing with the hunt the previous day, on the Saturday that is. My father-in-law went to bed early when we returned from Hinton Parva. He complained of a headache after a serious fall. My wife and I left the following morning. We were not in residence when the tragic event took place.'

Learoyd sat down neatly, his hand clutching his pectoral cross.

'How convenient,' thought Rupert with faint unease. Yet death could have been the result of concussion after the fall. In his travels he had known men succumb to brain injuries days after the blow or accident. But that did not explain why the back of West's skull was staved in or the leadball in the boathouse wall.

'I see. You are implying that Mr West, perhaps to alleviate this headache, may have taken a little too much fortified wine, gone into the garden for a breath of fresh air and accidentally fallen into the river?'

'I fear that this may be so,' said Learoyd sorrowfully.

'But what about the dog?' cried Frank, leaping to his feet.

'The dog? What about the dog?' The coroner sounded testy. 'Please take the stand, Mr West, if you have anything relevant to tell us. I will not have these constant interruptions.'

Dr Learoyd made way for his brother-in-law but did not look pleased.

'My father's mastiff has a great cut on its muzzle,' Frank began. 'The groom tells me he first saw it on the Monday morning my father was discovered to be missing. Of course he could not say how the animal came by it but there must have been an intruder on the Sunday night.'

The groom was called and confirmed what Mr Frank had said. No, sir, he did not see how the wound could have arisen naturally but of course could not swear to anything. The cut, he thought, had been inflicted by a knife or some such implement. The groom resumed his seat feeling uncomfortable under the stares of his betters.

Frank was on his feet again. 'I contend someone broke into the Park or else why would the dog bark loud enough to wake the butler? The murderer obviously struck the dog when it attacked him!'

'Control yourself, sir. This court is here to determine in the first instance whether any crime has been committed. I will not allow wild assumptions to colour the outcome of this hearing.' The coroner eyed Frank with dislike. 'Where were you, Mr West, on the night of January the second?'

'I was staying with my friends the Talbots at Cheney Court, some miles away.'

Rupert looked around for the colonel but could see neither the white headed gentlemen nor his son in the court room.

The coroner was unimpressed. 'Thank you Mr West, you may be seated. You have sought to muddy the waters mightily even if you know nothing about the matter. However, we are not here to point the finger of accusation but merely to determine cause of death.'

He shuffled his papers impatiently and looked at the jurymen. 'If no one else has anything to say I will proceed to my summing up. I have no intention of staying in this ice-house any longer than is necessary. I am not at all sure this case should have been brought at all.

We have no evidence of Mr West's state of physical health. Dr Makepeace says he was never called upon to attend the gentleman. His valet has told us that the deceased suffered from severe indigestion and frequent stomach pains. Mr Francis West assures us that his father had everything to live for, so I think we can rule out death from the crime of suicide. We have heard from a member of his own family that Mr West was in the habit of drinking substantial quantities of liquor late at night.

After a particularly exhausting previous day in the field, resulting in a fall, he may have over indulged, sought to clear his head with a walk in the garden and, in his stupor, mistaken his way or his footing and slipped into the river. If you believe that this is what is likely to have occurred you must bring in a verdict of misadventure.

However, if you think the dog barking – and it could have been at a fox or a badger – and the cut on the dog's muzzle, which could arise from anything, indicate that there may have been an intruder, then you must consider foul play, though the connection is slender in the extreme. Furthermore, if you think the wound on the back of Mr West's skull was not caused by contact with the stone piers of the bridge but by human agency, then you must bring in a verdict of death by person or persons unknown.'

There was a great shuffling of bodies in the pews as the fifteen men of property turned around to consult with their neighbours. Rupert looked speculatively at the brothers-in-law. They were not speaking to each other. Mr Askew deliberately avoided Rupert's eye. The jury asked leave to go off and consult in a corner. Sir Archibald Walcot ostentatiously took out his watch and put it on the table in front of him.

The jury, after much heated whispering and counting of hands, returned to their places. The foreman stood up clutching his hat and coughed.

'What is your verdict?' asked the clerk.

'Murder by person or persons unknown, yur honour, sir.'

An audible gasp ran through the room. Someone groaned. The Earl of Morna looked intrigued.

'Damnation,' muttered George between his teeth. 'Walcot won't like that.'

Sir Archibald Walcot snapped his hunter shut. 'And so it shall be recorded, though I must add a rider to the effect that it goes against my better judgement.' He surveyed the stunned faces in the court room. 'In the light of this – extraordinary -- verdict it is my duty to ensure that every effort is made to apprehend the criminal in question, when he is discovered. Court dismissed.'

And with this peremptory pronouncement he pocketed his watch and stiffly rose from the bench.

'All rise!' called the clerk caught off guard.

'What possessed them to bring in a verdict like that? We're in for stormy weather now!' hissed George. 'I'd better go and have a word with Sir Archibald. He's certain to want to explode at someone.' He disappeared towards the back of the hall.

'What will happen now, Uncle Rupert?' Clem asked in alarm. 'And what was all that about Jacob? I don't understand.' Rupert took the boy's arm to steer him through the crowd pushing down the stairs. The earl led the way, his elegance and rank clearing their path.

'Nothing will happen, I suspect. Unless a murderer confesses or is caught committing a similar deed, the constables have no authority to search out offenders. All we'll have is uninformed speculation for a few months; there's no hope of a rational examination of the events.'

At the foot of the wooden staircase Frank was expostulating with the Archdeacon. 'I told you! Someone broke into the Park and killed him. Why does no one listen to me? Whoever attacked the dog attacked my father. Even those hay-seeds could see it was no accident.'

Dr Learoyd looked anxiously up the High Street in the hopes of seeing their carriage. He would not argue in public; Frank really was making an unseemly spectacle of himself. George reappeared and pushed his way through to the brothers-in-law.

'I have just spoken to Sir Archibald. He instructs me to give you my co-operation as a local magistrate,' said George woodenly. 'Though how we are to search beyond the parish I do not know. The gypsies were long gone and any common labourer would be mad to try to attack your father in his own house with the servants within call.'

Frank's red-rimmed eyes glinted with malice. 'Someone could have lured him into the garden and hit him with a rock and then tossed him in the river! I'll bring a private agent from London; he'll find out the truth.'

Dr Learoyd looked startled. 'My dear Frank, think of the talk, the newspapers! Our aim must be to live down this dreadful verdict, not noise it abroad. Surely that is more than enough for your mother and sister to cope with?'

Frank would not be placated and then suddenly burst into tears. He groped for his whisky flask. The Darvilles looked on in embarrassment.

'At least wait until after the funeral before you make any decisions,' Learoyd continued whispering. 'You are in no fit state to know your own mind and this is neither the time not the place to discuss such matters. I apologise, gentlemen. My brother-in-law is severely shaken; I must get him home immediately.' And with a splayed hand on his brother-in-law's back, Dr Learoyd steered Frank towards the carriage, like a busy tug boat nudging a bedraggled schooner into port.

'When he's sobered up and counted the money he won't be so keen to set hares running,' said George as the West's carriage bowled away from the staring crowd. 'Let's hope Learoyd can talk sense into him. Will I see you both at the funeral?'

'Certainly,' said the earl promptly. Larkhill was proving most entertaining.

Rupert shrugged. 'I suppose I must attend though it goes against the grain; everyone knows West and I had quarrelled. Harriet will want to stay with Mrs West and Letty for the interment. But I must thank you, George, for your most timely intervention. You may have saved Jacob from being taken up for murder.'

'Nonsense! I wasn't going to have that drunken buffoon slander your name in public.'

The crowd thinned; there was no need to stay longer now the Wests had departed. The warm taverns and a chance to discuss the tremendous news over a steaming mug of porter were far more tempting. George made his goodbyes and headed for the Three Crowns where his horse was stabled.

Mr Askew edged alongside the Darvilles as they made their way up the High Street. 'May I accompany you, sir, my lord? My chaise is lodged in the livery stable.'

'Of course, so is ours. What do you make of it all, Askew?' asked Rupert.

Morna and Clem fell behind discussing the proceedings, the earl intent on easing Clem's troubled mind about Jacob and the quarrel with Horace West.

Mr Askew panted in an effort to match Rupert's stride. 'An unfortunate verdict, Mr Darville, you will agree. It leaves a nasty taste. Sir Archibald will be displeased, though he is duty-bound to support the verdict. Larkhill will feel quite terrorised with a murderer in its midst. I trust Mr Durrington will do all he can to lay fears to rest. I am on my way to advise the family. Such a shock! Such an unfortunate stain on the name.'

'Did anyone know of West's intended plans with regard to his property or bequests?' asked Rupert quickly.

'I sincerely hope not; unless my late client informed the family of his intentions himself. They have said nothing to me to indicate that they were aware of Mr West's schemes. Not a word has passed my lips either before or after this tragedy, as I trust none will pass yours sir, nor Mr Durrington's. I do not know how much you have guessed but the unsigned documents became worthless the moment Mr West died.'

'Have you destroyed them?'

'I have filed them away safely in my place of business.'

'I trust you have a good lock on your office door, Mr Askew,' said Rupert dryly. He wondered why the lawyer had kept them at all. He needed to get home and study that scribbled list again.

Chapter 14   The Funeral

A lone funeral bell tolled over the frozen fields. The service was held in St Mary's, Hunniford where a trickle of the county came out of duty. Lord Lydiard did not brave the snowdrifts to come up from Taunton. After the obsequies, the ladies retired to the house; only the gentlemen followed the coffin to the graveyard. The ground was so hard that the sexton and his boy had been forced to pour boiling water on the earth before they could dig a spade in. No one lingered over the interment apart from Frank who sobbed noisily and resorted to a hip flask when he thought no one was looking. Dr Learoyd behaved with dignity although he felt too distraught to give the eulogy.

In Bourne Park, Harriet worried that Rupert would catch a chill and hoped the icy wind would not reawaken the earl's cough. Mr Romero was still absent, confined to the manor by his cold. Mrs West had retired to her room in the care of the reinstated Paton and the ladies clustered around Letty like fussing crows. Harriet found herself cornered by Mrs Talbot, an intense woman with an air of delicious doom about her. The surprising verdict was discussed *sotto voce*.

'Well, Mrs Darville, what do you think of this tragic affair? We have never had a murderer in the neighbourhood before, at least not for twenty years and I do not count highway robbers or a dead Frenchman.'

Harriet was uncertain whether this was meant to be an advantage or not. 'The verdict may not be a true one. Lieutenant Durrington tells me that no real evidence was brought for ill-intent,' she replied looking towards the magistrate.

George had escorted his step-mother to the funeral. Sir Charles had refused to come; he had never liked Horace West and would not stand long upon his ankle. Juliana's delicate condition gave her the perfect excuse for not attending.

'George Durrington is as soft as butter for all his naval ways.' The colonel's lady allowed a shade of contempt for the senior service to colour her tone. 'During the riots he did nothing but post bills all over the parish offering a reward for information. Our parson was most rudely attacked and had mud thrown at his carriage, yet no one came forward,' she said in disgust. 'Thank God for the yeomanry.'

Harriet asked: 'Will your parson reduce his tithes? The farmers would be in a better position to pay their workers an increase if some compromise could be reached.'

'I hear you came to some such compromise, yourself.' sniffed Mrs Talbot.

'I have no influence over our Rector's income. The living is in the gift of my husband,' replied Harriet neutrally.

'I would like to know what your husband has to say about these uprisings and the murder of Mr West. George Durrington will certainly not bestir himself to find the killer amongst us; he much prefers an easy life.'

'My husband has not said much at all.' Rupert had been more uncommunicative than usual.

'Mr Darville never does say much of interest to a lady but he thinks a great deal.' Mrs Talbot leaned a little closer and put a lace-mittened hand to her cheek. 'I do not hold Frank West in very great esteem; he leads my son into all sorts of scrapes.' Tommy Talbot was standing next to his father, looking sober and uncomfortable. He and Frank West had hardly exchanged a word.

'Frank stayed with us for a few days after Christmas, after another disagreement with his father, and was wickedly drunk most of the time. In the end, the Colonel had to ask him to leave. But I would not wish this calamity on my worst enemy. Euphemia will never recover. Murder; what a disgrace! And young Clement found the body, I hear? He must have had such a shock, poor boy. My husband's subalterns often fainted clean away when they saw their first corpse. I trust the boy will suffer no unpleasant repercussions.'

'I believe Clem looks forward to returning to school to tell all his friends.'

'Young men are so insensitive about these matters. Although I am forced to admit that Frank seems properly chastened by his father's murder. I am only thankful that he is intent on bringing the malefactors to justice before we are all done to death.' She looked around nervously as though the culprit were hiding behind the chintz curtains.

In an attempt to lighten the mood Harriet said: 'It is my belief that the jury *wished* Mr West had been murdered. He was very much disliked and his unfortunate drowning gave them the perfect excuse to have their revenge at second-hand and puff their own importance.'

Mrs Talbot disapproved of Harriet's levity. 'Oh, you are a mind reader are you Mrs Darville? I heard that Euphemia was subject to a mesmerist before this tragic event and predicted her husband's death; it sounded most improper.' She looked scandalised. 'Frank claimed that the man had disreputable motives. The Colonel would not attend such a sacrilegious display even though we were invited; I hold it does no good to meddle with the occult.'

She looked over at the cluster of women by the fire. 'Euphemia will go to live with her daughter. She'll regret it; Letty will talk her to death. And we will have Frank but a few miles away.' She did not sound pleased.

'Surely Frank will spend most of his time in London, if he's as wicked as you say.' But Harriet's irony missed its mark.

'And bring further disgrace on the family no doubt. Bourne Park has never been lucky in its occupants. You are too young to remember the Blunsdons; they were dreadful people who absconded with thousands of pounds.' She looked around the tall spacious salon. 'Such a cold house and the enfilade of rooms so old fashioned. I would not care to live here myself; there is an air of melancholy about the place.'

Harriet attempted to move away but Mrs Talbot detained her. 'We have not had the pleasure of seeing you at Cheney Court for far too long. All is well at the manor I trust? You have not been able to find tenants for Quennell House, I hear. The children are in good health? And how are those two Irish nieces of yours? Have they settled in or -?' She left the sentence hanging in the hope of some complaint from Harriet who perversely felt a wave of protection for Gerald's daughters.

'The ladies Sophia and Rosa have settled in wonderfully well,' replied Harriet calmly.

'No winter chills like the one that carried off dear Betsy? Gracious, how long ago was that now? My condolences on the loss of your brother-in-law but I have often thought how unhealthy the bogs of Wexford are. Was it the typhoid fever?'

'The late earl died in a hunting accident.'

Mrs Talbot immediately shook her grey corkscrew ringlets. 'I knew it! Reckless riding; the bane of the hunting field; I see it myself far too often. I saw Mr West fall you know. He was riding as if the devil were after him; the foolish man. There was no need for such showing off. I believe he was trying to catch up with the Archdeacon and another gentleman. But then he could never control that great brute of a stallion. I was too far away on the road to be of assistance and then a few moments later I saw your husband and Clement appear at the top of a little rise so I knew they would attend to the matter. I sent my groom to enquire, for one cannot be too careful about such accidents. Even Mr Darville, so proficient, so controlled, can give the Colonel a nervous moment or two.'

'How often has my husband said the same of you, Mrs Talbot,' Harriet smiled sweetly.

'We have not yet had the pleasure of being introduced to the new Earl of Morna. He will not be staying with you for much longer, I imagine? Some visitors sadly outstay their welcome after a few weeks, but one has one's duty to the more unfortunate members of the family.'

'Morna is going to London soon to bespeak a house for the Season.'

Mrs Talbot looked solemn. 'The lure of London always beckons; it is the downfall of so many decent men. It is not wise for a gentleman of his years and build to be "racketing around" as Tommy would say. My brother was much the same and had apoplexy within a twelve-month of moving to London. And where is the young American secretary we have heard so much about?'

'Indisposed. Do excuse me Mrs Talbot, I must have a word with Lady Durrington.'

The gentlemen began to appear in the salon in ones and twos. They rubbed their hands against the cold and accepted hot toddies from the footmen.

The ladies made room for the Archdeacon on the sofa. Being a small man they tended to fuss over him as if he were a boy which he liked. He distracted all attention from his wife who subsided into unusual silence. Frank made straight for the well-stocked cabinet. He looked pale and more hung-over than usual.

In the corner, under a dark portrait of a Flemish matron, Will Hinton was saying that he had no idea that Horace West had suffered a fall. Only when he had enquired as to West's non-appearance at the hunt ball had he been informed of the accident and Mr West's decision to go straight home. In an obscure way Hinton felt some measure of responsibility for the unfortunate death. However little he had been acquainted with the deceased he felt it was only good manners to attend the funeral. His pleasant square face looked troubled.

George spoke up: 'Don't concern yourself; if it is murder then you cannot be blamed. You didn't bash him on the head. Not that I give a fig for the verdict. I still say it was the fall and the drink that killed him.' This ambiguous response did not make Hinton feel any better. George tried to repair his blunder: 'Or at least it led the man to go a-wandering. Askew's here to read the will, look; the roly-poly man talking to Darville. Let's hope the inheritance will settle Frank's nerves and there'll be no more nonsense about sending to London for one of these new-fangled Peelers.'

But Frank was determined. After bracing himself with a warm whisky and water he came over to solemnly thank Durrington for his efforts in finding his father.

'It was Darville who organised most of the search and Mrs Darville was a great support to your mother, I understand.'

Frank did not want to hear this. He believed Darville had cut him at the conversazione and he was well aware of Rupert's dispute with his father. His own encounters with the Darvilles over the years had been cool at best and embarrassing at worst.

'I intend to discover who did this terrible deed,' he said, the little wisp of beard on his chin trembling.

'My dear fellow, it will be very difficult,' said George kindly. 'Where would you start?' George had hoped that Learoyd had talked some sense into his brother-in-law by now.

'A Bow Street Officer or one of the new Peelers would know where to start well enough. Learoyd may want none of it and think only of his career and his blasted bishop but it is my father who has been murdered, not his.'

'And how does your mother take to your idea?'

'My mother is in no fit condition to know what she thinks. I am head of the family now.' The effect was spoiled by a distinct swaying on Frank's part.

'Like father, like son?' asked Hinton watching Frank weave his way back to the bottle-stacked side-board.

'Horace was a sherry man. Frank will drink anything.'

Rupert came over, his thin face taut with cold. St Mary's church had raised unsettling memories for him. 'We should be leaving. Askew is anxious to have his legal business done with the family. Where is Harriet?'

'With Morna, doing the pretty with the neighbours. And I must weigh anchor too; my mother-in-law is looking quite fagged. Did you speak to Tommy Talbot? The Colonel kept him pretty well tied to the mast, I thought. I can't see him and Frank getting up to any more hijinks. Let's hope this business will sober them both.'

****

The Darvilles had barely been home an hour when a note was brought from Bourne Park. Rupert read the letter in silence, chewing his lip. 'Forgive me. I have to return to Bourne Park at once. It seems that Jacob has been caught trespassing.'

'Jacob?' cried Harriet in disbelief. She was cosily installed in the drawing room with a cup of hot chocolate discussing their neighbours with the earl.

'So Learoyd informs me. I am summoned to take charge of my property.'

'Allow me to come with you, Rupert,' said Morna. 'The whole family fascinates me.'

'There is no need; I'm quite capable of settling my affairs alone.' Irritation made Rupert brusque. He suspected his brother of being lightly inquisitive.

'No one doubts that, my dear,' said Harriet. 'But if Ralph can bring any influence to bear – and don't try to persuade me that Dr Learoyd or Frank would not be influenced by the presence of an earl - then it is better to have your brother there as a witness.'

'Very well. Meet me in the vestibule in a quarter of an hour, if you will, Morna. Be so good as to ring for the chaise, would you, Harriet.'

The earl was reluctant to depart without some talk. 'What do you think this all means?' he asked when Rupert had left the room.

'I could not say. The only source of attraction in Bourne Park is now living under this very roof. Why Jacob, of all people, should be found in the grounds is beyond my comprehension.' She tugged the bell pull.

'Source of attraction?'

'Oh, Delilah, my new nursery maid. I took her in when Euphemia grew hysterical and wished to be rid of her; another of my impulsive gestures, Rupert would call it. I have been told that Jacob has an interest with her.'

'You allow followers?'

'It would be ludicrous to try to prevent it. They are both under my eye. I have no idea how far the courtship has gone but unless it impinges on their duties then I see no cause for alarm.'

'Then I had better find Gaston and get ready. We cannot have your husband charging over to Bourne Park with a horse whip in his hand.'

'I am obliged to you, Morna. You are just the person to pour oil on troubled waters.'

When the earl had departed Harriet ordered the chaise and then went in search of Miss Humble.

Harriet found her old governess in the school room preparing lessons for Sophia and Rosa. A warm fire gave a glow to the room. 'Ah, Miss Humble. I beg your pardon for disturbing you.' She picked up a dog-eared alphabet primer from the desk.

'My goodness I remember this. You taught all of us and Young Clem and the children from it.'

'I find the children like the pictures. Though I had a little difficulty with Jacob at first; he was so much older and had little knowledge of English ways.'

'Was it you who so neatly bandaged his hand recently?'

Miss Humble became occupied with her pencil. 'He did not want to disturb you when you have been so busy.'

'Of course. How came he to be injured?'

Miss Humble looked more uncomfortable. 'He said he'd cut his hand on one of Mr Darville's razors.'

'So I heard. But you didn't believe him, did you?'

The governess hesitated. 'I must confess the wound recalled your own unfortunate encounter with Beauty, the original Beauty that is, when you were a girl. But when I referred to the incident, Mr Ombay insisted that I make nothing of his "accident".'

'Are you saying that he was bitten by a dog?'

'I believe so, though Mr Ombay denies it. He most particularly asked me to be discreet. I hope I did nothing wrong.'

'Gracious, no. Men are foolishly sensitive about these matters. I do hope it wasn't Lucky or Peterkin who attacked him. I didn't think Jacob had much to do with the dogs. He's not a young man to torment anything.'

'Mr Ombay did not give me his confidence. He mentioned only cutting his hand on Mr Darville's razor.'

'Well, it is a trivial matter; we'll say no more about it. Now tell me, how is Delilah taking to her duties?'

Miss Humble agreed that if one could overlook the girl's unfortunate past then she was a good and willing worker. She thought the other servants were coming to accept her as certainly the ladies Sophia and Rosa were. This unsettled Harriet. She did not know what to do about her suspicions and resolved to have another talk with her new maid. Mrs O'Leary, on the other hand was still proving troublesome, mainly because she had nothing to do and spent most of her time in the kitchen annoying the maids. Harriet added this to her list of preoccupations.

****

The butler's pantry in Bourne Park was stiff with silence. Jacob sat on a hard chair, his face grey, with a wodge of bloody rags around his left leg. The bandage on his hand was torn and filthy.

Dr Learoyd stood next to Frank who was seated at the butler's desk. Mr Askew had taken a chair by the small fire and looked as though he would rather be elsewhere.

'Your man was caught trespassing sir! While I was at my own father's funeral,' shouted Frank looking remarkably similar to his late parent in his fury. 'He will give no credible explanation of his presence on my land and I have no option but to bring charges against him. I strongly suspect he is my father's murderer! I don't care what Durrington says, the whole town heard his threats!'

'Hush, Frank, there is no need to be so intemperate,' advised the Archdeacon.

Rupert looked at Frank coldly. 'You may sue for trespass if you wish; it is a civil not a criminal offence. I will pay the fine. But I will counter-sue for the illegal use of man-traps.'

Lawyer Askew had sudden recourse to polishing his spectacles. He had had a most uncomfortable day.

Dr Learoyd looked nervous. 'I can assure you we do not want to prosecute-'

'Yes I do!' avowed Frank. 'The nigger swore to kill my father not more than a fortnight ago, in front of witnesses. The Darvilles made my father's life a misery and turned him against me.'

In reality, the news of his father's diminished fortune had turned Frank against the world. He was determined to take his rage out on someone.

'Control yourself, Frank. This will do none of us any credit,' the Archdeacon snapped.

'Should we not hear Jacob's explanation of why he was in your grounds?' suggested Morna, taking the other armchair unbidden.

Rupert turned around and looked at his servant. 'What have you to say for yourself?'

Jacob winced slightly. 'Please, sir, I meant no harm. I thought I would walk over to the Park to collect some of Delilah's belongings. She could not carry them all when she came to us.'

As Rupert recalled a substantial box, he believed Jacob no more that the rest of them did. 'There, he has a perfectly reasonable explanation.'

'It's a lie! None of the servants were expecting him and the black bitch certainly never left anything behind when you shamelessly abducted her. I wouldn't be surprised if she took some of my mother's jewellery with her. There are several pieces missing.'

When questioned, Mrs West had been irritatingly vague on the subject of her jewels and Askew suspected his late client of selling off some of his wife's gems for ready cash.

Again Dr Learoyd clapped his hand on Frank's shoulder. 'This is getting us nowhere. I advise some moderation especially in a house of mourning. Though I feel we are entitled to some explanation.' He eyed the earl, wondering exactly why he had accompanied his brother.

Frank smouldered. 'Why did he not come to the front door?'

Jacob said quickly: 'I am a servant. I use the back door, and walking across the fields and along the old cart track is the quickest way into Bourne Park from the manor. I did not want to walk up the drive; it is another half mile out of my way, and I did not want to be seen on a day like today – out of respect.'

'You came over the wall like a thief!' pronounced Frank.

Jacob remained stubbornly silent.

'Did my servant have anything of yours in his possession when you found him?' asked Rupert.

'Nothing of mine, but this must be yours!' Frank scrabbled among the litter of account books on the butler's desk and threw a bill hook down in front of Rupert.

'I regret I have no familiarity with agricultural implements.'

'See! There are the letters L.M. branded into the shaft. It is the property of Larkhill Manor; you cannot deny it.'

'Then I will thank you to return it to me,' said Rupert calmly taking it up.

'Give it back, sir, it's evidence. Askew, I call you to witness–'

'And where exactly did you find this implement?' asked the earl.

'Within a hand's reach of the nigger. He used it to cut my dog on the night my father was murdered. Look at his hand. The mastiff gave as good as he got.'

'I would warn you against slander, sir. You can prove none of your wild accusations.' Rupert's tone was sharp. 'My valet had an accident with my razor.'

'My dear Mr West, because a bill hook was found near Jacob today it does not follow that he was anywhere near Bourne Park on the night your father died. No lawyer would give credence to your accusation; you would be laughed out of court.' The earl was at his most urbane.

'My lord is quite correct in his surmise,' said Askew at last, seeing which way the matter would end. 'While Mr Darville's servant was undoubtedly trespassing today, that is: undertaking unjustifiable interference with the land whether harm was done or no – there are no legal grounds for any other accusation. And the man-traps are undoubtedly illegal, Mr West, even in your current state of anxiety. I did advise you of the law before this interview. Even your father did not stoop to laying them, despite the threats to his life.'

'Do not tell me what I cannot do and what I have not got! Or I'll find someone sharper to look after my interests.' Frank sounded vicious.

'As you wish, Mr West. You are at liberty to instruct whom you wish to handle your legal affairs.' Askew made to rise.

Dr Learoyd said quickly. 'My dear sir, please remain. The family cannot do without your invaluable assistance, especially at this tragic time. My brother-in-law meant nothing by his remarks.'

Askew reluctantly sat down again.

'And now I will take my servant home,' said Rupert. 'He needs medical attention, which should have already been sent for in all humanity,' he added acidly. 'I see no point in prolonging this distasteful scene.'

Learoyd looked embarrassed but made no objection. He had dreaded this meeting. Frank's wild accusations of murder and Askew's threat of withdrawal worried him. Thankfully the fight had gone out of Frank in the face of Rupert's resolve and the earl's bland reasoning.

The Archdeacon opened the pantry door and beckoned to the butler as Rupert and Morna hoisted Jacob from the chair. 'I bitterly regret this distressing scene, my lord. I seem to be forever apologising for this family's extreme behaviour,' said Learoyd following the Darvilles down the narrow passage to the back kitchen door. 'Grief has quite deranged Mr West. He must blame someone for his father's death.'

'Then I suggest he look closer to home,' replied the earl. Morna meant only that Frank's own disgraceful behaviour had probably been a factor in his father's drinking, but the Archdeacon looked taken aback.

The Darvilles left the house and eased Jacob into the chaise. They drove straight to Dr Makepeace.

By the time Learoyd returned to the house, Frank had broached a bottle of whisky in the butler's pantry. Simpkins was too scared to object; it was his master's malt after all. Resentment now took over from aggression which spilled out at the sight of the Archdeacon. 'This blatant trespassing has convinced me something untoward is going on! You cannot fob me off with talk of my mother and Letty. I will write for a private investigator from London. He should be here within three days, and then we'll see.'

'My dear Frank, we talked of this before. You will cause us all only more distress,' said the Archdeacon, failing to prize the bottle out of his brother-in-law's grasp.

'I mean what I say, Martin. I won't have these people make a fool of me any longer!'

****

Doctor Makepeace was at home and shook his head at the sight of Jacob's mangled leg. 'A man-trap? I thought those filthy things had been banned.'

'It did not happen on my land,' said Rupert shortly.

Makepeace knew it was useless to expect any further explanation and continued: 'The boy's lost a lot of blood. I'll reset the bone and sew up the wound. If it happened only a few hours ago he should not succumb to gangrene. Thank God the weather is cold; I can pack the wound with ice while I work. You may collect Jacob in a day or two; there's no point in waiting about here.'

'I'll stay until after you have performed the surgery,' said Rupert.

'Morna, would you take the chaise back to Larkhill? Harriet will want to know what has happened. Jem can return with my horse. If you are asked, it would be best if we say that Jacob fell on the ice and broke his leg. And Makepeace, I trust you to put about the same story.'

'If you wish it, Mr Darville.' The doctor did not sound happy. 'Do you intend to prosecute whoever is responsible?'

'No.'

'It will take several weeks before Jacob can put any weight on that leg but I know he'll be well tended at the manor. I will say nothing, if you so wish. If you must wait, then let me take you up to the parlour; my wife will be more than happy to entertain you.'

Mrs Makepeace was rather flustered to find Rupert Darville in her best parlour. She was the daughter of a comfortable glove-maker and had been educated to be a lady. As a doctor's wife she had hopes of being accepted among the provincial gentry. However, being less than a year married she was still technically a bride and after one round of calls had not had many opportunities to mix with the cream of the county, as she liked to describe them in her weekly letters to her parents in Nottingham.

The sombre figure of Rupert Darville and his monosyllabic responses did not put her at her ease. A servant's accident provided no very exciting speculation. On the other hand Jacob Ombay was a figure now notorious in Larkhill for his attack on Mr West; this unnerved the doctor's wife even further. Conversation was stilted, refreshments were refused, until in an excess of nerves Mrs Makepeace came out with: 'Of course I blame that dreadful Mazzotta person for all the disasters that have befallen the unhappy Wests.'

'Indeed? In what way? Has the man returned to Bourne Park?'

'Thank the Lord, no. But you saw how he ordered Mrs West about and manipulated her very movements. Goodness knows what influence he brought to bear while he was with them and what harm may have resulted to the family. The whole afternoon was to be deplored on moral if not medical grounds.'

Rupert looked uncomprehending. Mrs Makepeace, out of loyalty to her husband, continued: 'Such charlatans cannot know what they are dealing with when it comes to matters of the mind. I dread to contemplate what thoughts passed from him to the lady. It seemed most improper; our vicar was of the same opinion.'

'I beg your pardon? Do I understand that you believe Mazzotta implanted some undesirable suggestions in Mrs West's mind?'

'It could be entirely possible,' averred Mrs Makepeace, gamely sticking to her guns. 'I know very little of such matters of course and far be it for me to discuss my husband's patients, former patients, but Mrs West, everyone agrees, is a lady of no very firm character and Dr Mazzotta – if he really was a doctor – comes from a very volatile and revolutionary race. Your brother the earl was telling me all about the banditti in Italy and what a scourge they are.'

A sharp cry was heard from the doctor's room below. Mrs Makepeace ignored it and offered her guest a plate of macaroons.

'No, thank you,' said Rupert. 'May I ask whether your interesting opinion is held by many people of your acquaintance?'

'Certainly,' she said with a touch of defiance. The Larkhill ladies had had much to discuss during the previous week.

Rupert's eyebrows shot up.

'Oh, I would not say it is a decided opinion, merely a possibility,' said Mrs Makepeace hastily back-tracking. 'I would not dream of suggesting that Mrs West was involved in any way in her husband's unfortunate death; the poor lady is prostrate with grief, I hear. But it is only human nature to speculate on the outcome of such an unwholesome spectacle, especially as the lady herself foretold her husband's passing.'

Garbled details of the West's conversazione had swept through the town like the wind. The parish sewing circle was horrified at the thought of a foreigner making a slave of Euphemia West. In the tap rooms and coffee parlours, hands were rubbed over her prediction of her husband's demise. There was still a healthy regard for the myths and fairies of the district; the general feeling being that it was best not to flirt with the supernatural. The local clergymen, of whatever denomination, did not approve of such goings-on and even West's own son-in-law had condemned the exhibition. Larkhill was divided between those who considered themselves enlightened intellectuals and those who saw the somewhat extreme wrath of a Christian god manifest in West's corpse.

'I fail to see what motivation Mazzotta would have for bringing ill to the household,' said Rupert.

'But Mr West dismissed him the day after the conversazione!'

'Quite so,' said Rupert with impeccable logic. 'Until then he had every reason to be in charity with the Wests. I would imagine that Mr West forbade his wife an interview of any sort with the doctor after the conversazione.'

Mrs Makepeace looked deflated. To the relief of them both the door opened to admit her husband. He had stripped himself of his bloodied apron and washed before joining his wife in the parlour.

'There it is done,' said Makepeace, tightening his cravat. 'A neat job if I say so myself. I would not move the young man just now. My assistant has made a bed up for him in my surgery. I've given your man a composer. He has a strong constitution and is a brave young fellow.'

'Indeed he is,' said Rupert standing to shake hands. 'I cannot thank you enough, Makepeace. I would deem it a favour if as little were said about this incident as possible.'

'Of course. I have a shrewd idea who is to blame but there are enough appalling rumours about the Wests without adding this calamity to the list.'

His young wife went a little pink.

Chapter 15   Rupert in confusion

The inquest verdict had put Rupert in a quandary. He had already spent several hours studying the half-sheet of foolscap which had fallen from Horace West's portfolio. He now felt he could identify the stocks, shares, property holdings and various sums which he assumed were to be distributed to members of the West family. But the scribbled notes were not clear or comprehensive and several things puzzled him. He had no way of knowing if the sums were more or less favourable than the bequests in West's current will and therefore he had no evidence for suspecting foul play. He did not even know if Horace West had truly intended to act upon his jottings or had merely forgotten to destroy a scrap of paper drawn up on a whim; the man could have been idly calculating his assets. Nevertheless his instinct told him that Horace West had been murdered, and most likely by a disgruntled relative.

Yet the only member of the family in residence on the night of the second of January had been his wife. However unbiased he tried to be, Rupert could not visualise Euphemia West braining her husband and throwing him into the Bourne. He envied George's ability to throw off his responsibility while he himself was being drawn further into the mystery by Jacob's incomprehensible behaviour.

He immersed himself in his work to avoid any discussion of his valet's activities, or the inevitable re-hashing of the inquest. Harriet was forced to rely on the earl's account of the interview with Frank West and the Archdeacon.

A few days later, Jacob was conveyed home, weak, pale and in pain. Harriet persuaded Rupert to curb his impatience and allow his valet to recover his strength before questioning him.

'So that he may get his story straight?'

'So that he may answer you like a sensible man. I assure you Jacob is innocent of any wrongdoing, and you know it. You may speak to him tomorrow. Are you not going to Salisbury this morning for a landowners meeting with the protesters?'

'Yes, I am to collect Butterworth and, for your sake, Harriet, I will try to persuade him to reduce the percentage of his tithes, which should help your tenants. But I suppose the increase in his stipend in lieu will eventually come from my pocket.'

'Oh, thank you, thank you! I'm convinced it is the wisest course. Mrs Butterworth says she sells the surplus peas and beans from the farms so she is certain to feel the loss of that income. By-the-by, Miss Humble begs some lemons for Mr Romero and Cook tells me there's not one to be had in Larkhill since Christmas. I wish we had not shut down your hot houses. Could you bring back a dozen from Salisbury if you have the time?'

'I object to being an errand boy for that whippersnapper!'

'He is our guest, my dear, and this cold of his is bound to spread through the house, so we must be prepared in case any of the children succumb.'

Rupert spent the journey to Salisbury convincing Butterworth that a reduction in tithes was an inevitability. By the time the chaise had decanted them at the Assembly Rooms the Rector was almost persuaded; it was a brave man who would cross Rupert Darville or dispute his logic. When he saw the hostile crowds gathering in protest he finally succumbed and agreed to reduce his tithes at the next audit.

In the Assembly Rooms the meeting was rowdy. The Rector stuck close to his patron. The property owners jibbed at an increase in the Poor Rate. The farmers grumbled at the increase in the minimum wages proposed by the magistrates. Everyone demanded a reduction in the tithes paid to the clergy. Two hours of wrangling over the difference to be paid to single or married men, winter or summer rates and a thousand local anomalies resulted in stalemate. It was not until Rupert stood up and revealed that Larkhill's parson had agreed to give up five per cent of his tithes that others followed and eventually a compromise was reached. The Rector was rewarded by appearing to be an enlightened and liberal Christian and later by receiving an assurance from his patron that he would be compensated financially.

After the meeting, Rupert and George dined together at The Haunch of Venison. The Rector took himself off to colleagues in cathedral close.

'Let's hope we've seen the last of the riots,' said George tucking into his steak and oyster pie. 'We've done enough to satisfy everyone today, surely? We've sent too many of our people to the Assizes already; nearly three hundred by the last count. I can only hope that Melbourne's Special Commission will deal with them fairly. Do you want to go along to the court house and see what's happening?'

'No.' Rupert toyed with a leg of chicken.

'At least the wages meeting was some sort of distraction from Horace West.'

'West would have hanged them all. Thank God magistrates can't judge capital crimes.'

'I heard Frank has brought in a Bow Street Runner – a regular thief taker.'

'Nothing was stolen,' said Rupert instantly.

'No, and he won't find anyone who committed violence either. Frank's a fool.'

Rupert forgot the lemons.

The following day, Rupert ordered Bounty to be saddled and took off across the snowy Downs towards Tidworth. Lizzie had sneezed and looked limp; Harriet was worried. He offered to look for lemons. Some hours later, errand satisfactorily completed and tired from the ride, he reached Lud's long barrow. Rupert paused to survey his property in the valley below. Athena's Temple stood out on Folly Hill. It was time he made another visit to Quennell House. On the way down the coombe he would stop at the temple.

Rupert tied Bounty to a laurel bush and walked up the steps of the folly. Even from here he could see that the door was ajar. The lock had been damaged; someone had been careless or in a hurry. He pushed the door inwards. The circular room was furnished with an old Empire sofa, a paint-stained wooden table and chairs, and a cold, ash-filled brazier. A wing chair lay on its side amid a heap of sacking. Crumbs of bread and an empty wine bottle littered the table, perhaps the remnants of the children's feast when they had been up here sledging; perhaps not. Someone had thrown an old horse blanket over the mildewed sofa adding to the tawdriness of the place. A rare ray of winter sun filtered through the transom windows circling the walls, bringing out a faint hint of tobacco smoke. Rupert turned his head quickly and swore he smelt mimosa. A glint of diamond amid the dust caught his eye. He bent to retrieve a shirt stud.

A blinding thought struck him into immobility. There might be one other suspect, motivated by something other than money, which would hideously complicate matters. If it were true, the Darville family would be smeared, his brother ruined, his own reputation put in jeopardy by gossiping tongues. His fist closed over the stud. He could not bring himself to believe it. To pursue that avenue would be madness. He dare do nothing for fear of what he might uncover. He could do nothing; he would do nothing.

Rupert rode down to the house, taking the Hobsons unawares, but there was nothing amiss. He left his butler a trifle confused. No, he had seen nothing of Mr Romero or the Archdeacon. Were either of the gentlemen or the earl perhaps thinking of renting Quennell House? The American gentleman had been very complimentary about the Turkish salon when he and Master Clem had ridden over for a game of billiards.

At Rupert's terse denial Hobson wondered what had prompted his master to ask the question. He watched Rupert turn his horse in the direction of the manor. The winter and this terrible murder was taking its toll, he thought; the sooner Quennell House was tenanted again the better.

****

Harriet gave out that Jacob's broken leg was the result of jumping from the chaise onto treacherous ice. She kept her thoughts to herself as to the real reason he had been trespassing but a quiet interview with a distraught Delilah enlightened her wonderfully. Her only difficulty was knowing how much to tell Rupert; he seemed more unapproachable than ever. Clem had to be dissuaded from tiring his friend and it was to the patient's relief when the earl again took Young Clem back to school on Sunday and remained in Salisbury to attend evening mass.

When Makepeace had pronounced the patient to be mending satisfactorily, Rupert went to his valet's room.

'How do you feel today? Any stronger?' Rupert looked at the tented bedclothes and the array of comforts on the rattan bedside table. 'Do you have everything you need?' The room struck him as chilly.

'Yes, sir. My leg hurts but I have all my senses.' Jacob did not take his eyes off his master.

'Then,' said Rupert lifting the chair up to the bedside. 'You can tell me exactly what you were doing in Bourne Park last Monday, if not on the night of January the second.'

Jacob swallowed. 'How do you know about that?'

'I can reason as well as Frank West.'

Jacob looked at his master's face. He knew he would have to confess everything as Mrs Darville had advised. 'I met Delilah, Mrs West's maid, by accident in the town before Christmas.'

'Yes, we know all about that.' Harriet had explained the romance to her incredulous husband. 'I assume there were other meetings?'

Jacob nodded reluctantly. 'She's a good girl, sir. I won't have anyone thinking she—'

'Good God, her morals are no concern of mine, though I feel sympathy for any woman in West's employ. Did she reciprocate your sentiments? I suppose she must if she agreed to meet you again.'

'Yes, sir. We want to be married.'

Rupert flexed his shoulders. 'You will have to consult Mrs Darville on that matter. What I must know is what drove you to break into Bourne Park on the night Horace West died.'

Jacob looked terrified. His slight accent thickened. 'I did nothing wrong! You cannot think it was me, sir! I never laid eyes on the gentleman at all.'

'Convince me that it wasn't you.'

Jacob swallowed again and shifted awkwardly under the bedclothes. He knew his master's demand for precision; plain facts would serve him best. 'Della and I had planned her escape that night. I was going to hide her in the Athena's Temple until we could get away from here. Did you know that he told her she was still a slave, even in England? She thought she was his property for life. We were going to run away together.'

Rupert was surprised, not at Horace West's deception of the girl, but at Jacob's intended desertion. 'Forget Horace West. Tell me exactly what happened.'

'I took the field paths to the old Downs road until I reached the back of Bourne Park. I cleared the bushes with the bill hook and got over the wall. I expected Della to be waiting for me but there was no light in the house; that devil had locked her in her room in the attic.'

Rupert waited impassively until the young man had collected himself.

'Then I heard the church clock chime the three-quarters in the distance. I'd been waiting almost an hour and was frozen. In desperation I sprinted across the yard to a corner of the stables to get closer to the house. But there was no sign of her. All of a sudden I heard this scuffle from the side of the house. I jerked back into the doorway of the stable. One of the horses let out a nicker. The snuffling swelled into a growl and, before I could escape, a huge bull-mastiff burst round the corner, its mouth open, snorting and slavering.' Jacob shuddered at the recollection.

'I ran. It was the wrong thing to do, but I remember what it's like to be hunted.' He paused for a moment, his childhood terror rearing up into his eyes. 'I knew better than to climb a tree and be trapped, so I ran for my life.'

He stopped again and Rupert silently poured him a glass of water. Jacob took it gratefully and gathered his composure. 'The dog came after me, yelping and barking. I knew I must get back over the wall but I got caught in the brambles and stumbled. I found myself with my back to the wall.' The scene replayed itself vividly before his eyes.

'The dog stopped, snarledled and leapt. I lashed out with the bill hook across the dog's face. I aimed for the eye but the brute twisted his head at the last second. He snapped his jaws over my hand forcing me to drop the bill hook. But the blade had done its work and, when I kicked the dog between the legs, the animal let go and backed off.'

There was a silence and he handed the glass back to Rupert saying shakily: 'That gave me enough time to get over the wall. I knew I should go back for the bill hook but my hand was bleeding badly and I thought no one would ever search that part of the grounds.'

'And what else?' asked Rupert replacing the glass on the table.

Jacob looked puzzled. 'There was nothing else, master, except it started to snow.' The tramp home had been long and cold.

'You heard no noise, no gunshot perhaps?'

Jacob thought. 'The woodland is full of noises at night and maybe the branches were cracking in the frost, but I heard no gunshot. I had no time to think of anything but the dog. Although there was a moment when it was distracted by something, the church clock at midnight I think, and turned its head.'

'Very well. You got yourself back to the manor and made up the story of cutting your palm with my razor.'

'Yes, sir. It was the first excuse I could think of.'

'And you returned to Bourne Park on the afternoon of the funeral in the hopes of retrieving the bill hook?'

'Yes, sir. As soon as I heard the verdict of the inquest, I knew they would be looking for someone to blame. The Park would be searched for a sign of intruders; I had no notion there would be man-traps. I hoped the snow had covered the bill hook but it was melting now. I knew it could be identified as belonging to the manor.'

Rupert looked severe. 'It never occurred to you to come to me with all this?'

'No, sir.' Jacob looked uncomfortable.

'I'm disappointed in you Jacob, for trying to deceive us in this way. You've had a lucky escape in more ways than one. I will inform the earl and Mrs Darville of the truth of the matter, though I have every expectation that my wife knows already.'

'I'm sorry, massa,' Jacob lapsed into his old ways in his misery.

Rupert rose. 'We'll say no more about it, but I shall not forget. I shall tell Dunch to send someone to mend your fire.' With his hand on the latch, looking at the tired young face against the white pillows, he said: 'Master Clem will be home again soon; he is most anxious to see you improve. Let's not disappoint him.'

Larkhill Manor felt very subdued after the drama of the inquest and the solemnity of the funeral. Jacob's broken leg was not spoken of outside the household. Some of the servants were suspicious of the accident but, this time, Dunch did not encourage speculation. Delilah and Miss Humble attended the patient and did not deviate from Harriet's story.

Rupert complained of being without a valet and of the clumsiness of Edward the footman, Jacob's temporary replacement. When he was not being irritable he became silent and shut himself away more than ever.

The manor returned to its daily routine. The January cold turned to fog shrouding the house in morning mists. It lingered in the valleys and veiled the watery sun. The earl took his secretary and his valet to London to see his brokers and to secure a house and staff for the London Season.

'I am almost loathe to leave you, Harriet, for fear something even more exciting will happen while I'm away,' said Morna, dressed in his great travelling cloak. 'London cannot offer such thrilling diversions as Larkhill, I am sure.'

'All this unpleasantness will have blown over by the time you return. At least I hope it will; I have no great reliance on Rupert's ability not to take it upon himself to find the murderer,' she half joked.

'He is too lost in his books and star calculations, my dear. Do not worry.'

The children hopped about on the low slab threshold. Harriet was envious when she saw Sophia and Rosa bestow a goodbye kiss on Mr Romero. Rupert, as usual, ignored the young American. The earl had already distributed his parting pennies to all the children.

'Do give my dearest love to Sir Hamish and Lady McAllister and any of my cousins you may meet in Town. We so look forward to seeing them all in the spring,' said Harriet.

'Is it ever spring in this country?' Morna peered through the chill morning mist.

'We shall be all jonquil and crocus for your return,' promised Harriet.

Rupert shook hands with his brother and slammed the door of the chaise behind him. 'Jem is well armed, but I hope you have your pistols about you. One cannot depend on these stagecoach guards, though you should be safe on the turnpike roads.'

****

Harriet and Rupert were alone in the drawing room with the heavy green brocade curtains closed against the winter night. Beauty lay sprawled in front of the fire in blissful warmth. Rupert opened his *Monthly Notices of the Royal Astronomical Society* and smiled at his wife sitting comfortably at the other side of the fireplace. He stretched out his long legs and took a sip of Madeira.

'I'm glad we're on our own again. Visitors are all very well but one does have to make conversation.'

'You never address a word directly to Mr Romero. Don't you like him?'

Rupert hesitated. 'I have an aversion to that type of man.'

She knew her husband's reasons exactly. 'He's still only a boy at heart. The children adore him.'

'Even Clem?'

'Oh, the hero worship is fading I think. He was much smitten by Charlotte Wakefield; did you not notice? She and Mary are to visit Durrington Hall again at Easter.'

'Surely Miss Wakefield is too old for Clem? He is still a schoolboy.'

'At this point of course, though three years is not so much of an age gap later on in life. Have no fear, Clem will fall in love half a dozen times before he is twenty. He is quite safe from Mr Romero's allure, I assure you.' She suspected Sebastian may have directed his charms elsewhere.

Rupert felt a tightness lift from his chest. Since his finding in the folly, he had been doubly anxious about Romero's influence on his ward and was glad to see him gone from the manor.

'And what should we do about Jacob?' Rupert depended on Harriet to keep his household running smoothly. Emotional disturbances were beyond his competence.

'Jacob? His leg is healing beautifully according to Dr Makepeace. He managed a few steps across his room today, so Miss Humble tells me.'

'I was not referring to his injury.' He narrowed his eyes at his wife. 'You've known all along about Jacob breaking into Bourne Park on the night West died, haven't you?'

Harriet admitted she had learnt the whole story from a weeping Delilah when Jacob's bandaged body had been brought home from Dr Makepeace.

Rupert was confused and indignant. 'Why did you say nothing about this to me?'

'Delilah told me in confidence; she was in desperate fear of being accused of murder. You do not usually concern yourself with domestic matters and I thought it best Jacob should tell you himself – man to man, when he was ready.'

'But what am I to make of his deception? To consider leaving us on a whim! I would never have thought Jacob capable of disloyalty after all these years in my service.' The scientific journal slipped through his fingers to the floor.

'My dear, Jacob is a no longer an untutored boy of fourteen. He is a young man, deeply in love. He would find it shaming to come to you with this affair of the heart and expect you to make things right for him. He was forced to choose between this house and Delilah. In his place what would you have done? You are not the most sensitive of men, my love.'

'Then why did he not confide in you?'

'He might have but as you brought Delilah to the manor the following day, there was no need.' She held up her little silk hand-screen against the flames. 'Do you think we have heard the last of the murder now that Jacob has confessed to a love frolic? No one would dispute his story if he were forced to tell it. And no one would dare contradict the unimpeachable character you would give him in any court of law.'

'Unfortunately we are not done with it yet. Frank West has hired a Bow Street officer to nose around. The fellow has already made himself known to George who kindly informed me of it. I thought better of Learoyd and hoped he would dissuade Frank. What induced that blockhead to take such a course I cannot imagine; he will gain nothing by it.'

'Except an easing of his conscience. As an undutiful son, I daresay Frank wished his father dead a hundred times this past year and now he is horrified that his wish has come true.'

'If he ever sobers up he won't be so keen to have anyone prying into the family's affairs too closely. Learoyd has returned to Winchester, I understand.'

'Meanwhile this dreadful crime, if there was a crime, hangs over the neighbourhood. I am not as foolish as Mrs Talbot but it is uncomfortable, all the same, to think there may be a murderer in the vicinity.'

Rupert's conscience pricked him. He considered revealing all his suspicions to his wife and at once dismissed the idea. He did not want to admit that the manor could be sheltering a killer.

Harriet looked across at her husband. 'At the start of it all, you yourself thought there may be some suspicious circumstances surrounding Mr West's death. But now you know Jacob is innocent do you intend to forget about the whole terrible episode or do you intend to investigate it?' She sounded very matter-of-fact.

'I never for one moment doubted Jacob's innocence.'

'In your heart, no, but your head was not happy until you had discovered the truth of his actions. Is that not so?'

She knew him too well. Rupert's enquiring brain was tempted to solve the mystery on an academic level but he did not dare probe any further. Romero's escapades out of the house could not be accounted for; there was no knowing his movements on the night of the murder.

If Horace West had threatened to expose Learoyd's infatuation then the secretary might have taken a hand in West's destruction and the Darvilles would be brought down in the scandal. He could not let that happen.

Rupert looked at his wife's intelligent inquisitive face, half shadowed from the flames. He would not embroil her in this; the lead ball in the boathouse wall indicated possible violence. West's cracked skull confirmed the danger. He instinctively threw a protective wall around his family and could not afford to become involved.

His own interests and commitments warranted his attention to the exclusion of solving the mystery of Horace West's death. He had missed the first appearance of the bright comet in the January skies because of these domestic distractions. There was a book to complete and scientific papers to write. The demands of his new post meant that he would be in London more frequently. Discretion dictated that he take the matter no further. Yet unfinished business tormented him.

He picked up his journal but found he could not settle to it. He gave up and moved to the piano to lose himself in a Bach fugue. Harriet stared into the fire with her own thoughts while her husband attempted to soothe his troubled mind.

PART III: RESOLUTION

Chapter 16   Rumours

'I beg your pardon, madam, but Mrs O'Leary is desirous of having a word with you. Master Clement is with her.' Disapproval dripped from Dunch's tongue.

'Very well,' said Harriet, wondering what new domestic disaster this heralded. 'I will see her in the oak parlour.' She continued on her way, a bowl of snowdrops between her hands.

When she turned around Clem stood before her, smeared with mud, with a handkerchief to his bloodied nose and a rapidly closing eye.

'Good Heavens! Whatever has happened to you? Dunch, ask Miss Humble to come here directly. We must attend to Master Clem. Are you very much hurt?' She took hold of his shoulder in an attempt to make him look at her and saw him wince away.

'Dere's no need to fret yourself, m'lady mam; sure an t'was nottin' but a bit of a barney with the village lads. Master Clem fought something ferocious so he did and could have flattened them all if he hadn't been outnumbered.'

'What were you fighting about?' Harriet asked in amazement. Young Clem usually got on well with the town children.

''Bout Peterkin,' snuffled Clem quickly. 'Dick Ponting called her a useless hearth rug and said she was no good for catching anything! His mangy-looking cur can catch nothing but fleas-'

'Never mind about the dogs. You have quite ruined your jacket. As long as you're not badly hurt?'

'Dere's no harm done ma'am; I saw the dirty ruffians off before they could murther him.' Mrs O'Leary brandished her umbrella in demonstration.

Clement shot her a malevolent look. It was Jem who had set about the older boys with his whip and pulled a still-fighting Clem from beneath the pile of arms and legs.

'Brave as a Turk he was, m'lady ma'am, a pleasure to watch. I ha'nt seen a mill like that since Paddy O'Laughlin laid out Bruiser Kelly in five.'

'I suppose you will want another day off school?' said Harriet ignoring this pugilistic reference and turning to her nephew. 'You don't deserve it for fighting like a common navvy. What your uncle will say I dread to think!'

Rupert was putting up in Bath overnight to give his astronomical lecture.

'Please don't tell him, Aunt,' pleaded Clem in alarm.

'He will have to know. What excuse could you give for your bruises?'

'I'll say I took a toss. A rabbit hole or something,' he mumbled.

'You'll say nothing of the kind! I will have no falsehoods in this house.' She was more surprised by Clem's willingness to lie about his horsemanship than by his fighting.

Miss Humble appeared in the doorway, took in the situation at a glance and carried her favourite off to have his wounds bathed. 'Dear me, two invalids in the house now; whatever next?'

'Thank you, Mrs O'Leary, that will be all.' Harriet wished to send for Jem and hear his version of events. She was not satisfied that she had heard the truth.

'Oh, m'lady mam. If I could just have a word, in private like.' The nursemaid looked meaningfully at Dunch. Harriet realising something else was afoot, dismissed him, much to his annoyance.

'Now Mrs O'Leary, sit down. What do you have to tell me? What was the fight really about? Master Clem has a sweet nature as a rule. Something serious must have driven him to such behaviour. How come you were a witness to it all?'

'To be sure there never was such an angel of a boy.' Mrs O'Leary settled herself down for a good gossip. 'Well, m'lady mam, Cook had a list as long as your arm this morning so out o' the kindness of my heart I said I would keep Jem company goin' into Larkhill. I was passing the Drover's Arms, just passing you understand, when I heard this turrble commotion, barking and shoutin', enough to scare the daylights out of a body. It was a dog fight sure enough and with half the town looking on and laying bets. Imagine my surprise when I saw Master Clem shouting for his dog to slaughter the other!'

'You cannot mean that Clement agreed to this dog fight?' Harriet sounded appalled.

'I could not say, ma'am, but that Peterkin is turrble fierce in his barking and drove Dick Ponting's dog right up the High Street with his tail between his legs,' she said smugly.

'And that's when the fight between the children started?'

'Children – huh! Ponting is more than a child, the great hulkin' brute. He didn't like to be shown up to his friends and started insulting Master Clem's dog. He said he was no ratter and was all bark and no bite and a lot more besides; it was enough to try the patience of a saint. And then Master Clem hit him a smacker in the face.'

'With no more provocation? What exactly did this boy say that upset Master Clem so much?'

'He only accused Mr Darville of being the murderer, so he did!' Her eyes grew round with gleeful horror.

'Dear God!' Harriet paled.

'I blame that trouble-maker da of his, Joe Ponting, who's got nottin' better to do than slander good people to wheedle a free mug o' porter. His son takes after him. He's a great bully just like his father but Master Clem defended your husband's honour something fierce he did. He's a boy to be proud of.'

Seeing Harriet's stricken face Mrs O'Leary grew concerned. 'Now don't you go takin' on so, Mrs Darville. Young Clem doesn't know I heard what that eedjit said. Shall I send for your maid, ma'am, you're looking as white as milk.'

'No, no I am perfectly well, thank you. You did right to inform me of what is being said about my husband.' She looked directly at the nursemaid. 'How widespread is this preposterous rumour?'

'I couldn't say ma'am, never getting beyond the manor gates from one day's end to the next, and not a word of gossip would I allow to pass me ears,' she said plaintively. 'But the whole town knows of the argument with Mr West over Mr Ombay, and if the servant didn't do it, then the master could have done it, Mr Darville being known as a violent man.'

'Violent!'

'The gypsies, ma'am. I told them 'till I was blue in the face what a hero Mr Darville was, rescuing our two sainted angels, but some people like to think the worst, may they be forgiven.' She crossed herself.

Mrs O'Leary's account had entertained the tap room of the Drover's Arms many a night and been embellished with each telling.

'Yes, thank you, Mrs O'Leary,' said Harriet faintly. 'I can quite see how the incident with the gypsies could have been blown out of all proportion.'

''Tis all moonshine o'course; I tell 'em so. Mr Darville is a quiet, book-reading gentleman, I tell them, who wouldn't hurt a fly. To my mind such wicked tales are as unchristian as saying poor widow West did her husband in under the devil's orders.'

Harriet gathered her wits. 'You must mention the fight to no one, no one do you understand? Any unfounded rumours will soon be dispersed by the Bow Street officer's investigations. We must leave him to find the culprit. There is no need for you to defend the family, or be involved in any way.'

'Oh, right you are, m'lady ma'am,' said Mrs O'Leary somewhat taken aback by Harriet's tone. She did not want to be deprived of her audience in the kitchen. 'Sure an' I'll not breathe a word to a soul. I'll be as silent as the grave.'

If only Harriet could believe her. Harriet's strained smile faded as the oak door closed behind the rotund Irish woman. She pulled the bell cord.

'Dunch, bring me a glass of Madeira, would you. And send a message to the stables to ask Jem to come here at once. Then I must go up and speak to Master Clem.'

Half an hour's quiet reflection and a word with Jem eased her mind a little. Jem assured her the fight had been nothing but a boyish scrap. The dogs had taken a dislike to each other; the boys had defended their pets. Having lost the dog fight, the bigger, slower boy had hurled any insult he could think of in his opponent's direction. Jem explained that there had been few onlookers apart from himself and Mrs O'Leary who had run into the side alley of the Drover's Arms in time to hear the insults. They saw Clement throw the first punch.

'And while I don't doubt Master Clem could have bested Dick Ponting by hisself; I don't 'old with four settin' onto one.'

'And the accusation against Mr Darville? Have you heard this before?'

Jem looked embarrassed. 'Folk dursn't say anything to me ma'am; I'd take my whip to them if they did.'

'But this is not the only time you've heard something of the sort, have you? Come Jem, you have been with us for twenty years or more, you must not keep such things to yourself.'

'I did hear something at the Sallow's Inn,' he admitted reluctantly. 'I was fetching a basket of eels for Cook. Not being local they don't know Mr Darville like we do, nor what truly happened 'bout Mr Ombay. Of course it don't help to have this Bow Street Runner nosing about asking questions. It stirs people up is what I say.'

'Thank you, Jem. I would be obliged if none of this reached Mr Darville's ears and if you could do what you can to quash this nonsensical rumour.'

'As you wish, ma'am.'

Rupert returned from Bath the following day. The jaunt away from the manor had done him good. His lecture had gone well and he had put another notice in the *Bath Chronical* advertising Quennell House to let. Unfortunately, the newspaper was full of wild speculation about Horace West's murder; the Swing rioters being implicated with a suitable amount of horror. The illogicality of it irritated him again.

The reason for Clem's bruises and extra day at home was passed off as a fight over the dogs and nothing more. The younger children treated their cousin like a wounded hero and Clem was as happy as a grig to have another day off school.

****

The tap room of the Drover's Arms was crowded. It was market day and the place was littered with straw and reeked of manure from the stockmen and small farmers who congregated to slake their thirst. Thick veils of smoke hung in the air from the cheap tobacco pipes favoured by the customers. Joe Ponting muttered into his tankard of ale, hoping there would be another drop at the bottom. Like many casual labourers he had lost his winter income to the greater efficiency of the threshing machine and what work his wife could find barely fed his growing family. The Trottmans had refused to re-hire him because of his drinking. He had just come from a humiliating meeting with the Parish Assistance Board where he had been sent away with only a few shillings. Most of this had been spent in the Drover's Arms.

A stranger sat in a dark corner of the inglenook. He was a middle-aged, thick-set man with a confident bearing. He removed his tall hat to reveal grey and grizzled hair. He sipped his cider with unconcern and made idle jottings in what could be mistaken for an order book. No one took much notice of him after a first glance; there were always strangers passing through Larkhill on market day. They were too busy discussing Horace West's murder. Those who had not been into the town since New Year were agog at the news and the locals paraded their superior knowledge.

'Well 'tis all black magic, I say. 'Tis his wife what killed him under a spell from that they "magnetiser" man, so my Daisy says an' she should know being 'ousemaid at the Park.'

'You'm talking a loada fustian, Elias Farley. The magician were long gone, afore Christmas Day. Mr West were bashed on the 'ead. I heard crowner say so. No woman coulda done that.'

'You ain't seen my Susan when she's in a bait.'

When the laughter had died down someone said: 'Then I'll lay odds 'twas gypsies. Hewitt reckoned West took a whip to 'em when he found them camped on his land – only it wasn't his land. They come back for revenge.' The speaker stabbed the air with the stem of his clay pipe for emphasis.

Various heads nodded. It was convenient for everyone to blame the gypsies. They were all anxious to deflect suspicion from themselves; too many had been part of roaming mobs that winter. No one mentioned friends and relatives now languishing in Salisbury jail destined for transportation.

'What about the black woman?' asked someone. 'What your Daisy 'ave to say about *'er*?'

Elias shrugged. 'Daisy's a respectable girl and keeps herself to herself. She says Mr West kept the black woman out of sight, locked in an attic. The wench is livin' at the manor now; the Darvilles have took 'er in.'

There were various sorrowful murmurs and head shakings at this news.

'And did you hear about Mr Ombay?' asked Dr Makepeace's assistant. All eyes turned to the respectable young man in expectation. He held out his empty glass knowing someone would refill it. In response he continued: 'He got caught a week after the murder, trespassing in Bourne Park, on the very day of the funeral. He broke his leg in a man-trap; serve him right, I say.'

'Them things is illegal,' snorted Elias who was known for his very deep pockets and cleverness with wire.

'Going back to visit the scene of the crime, I expect.' Nathaniel Haycock nodded knowingly. 'He did threaten to murder Mr West, not long afore Christmas. Half the town 'eard 'im, an' that's the gospel truth.' Haycock was an occasional shepherd when he was sober enough to do the work. He was a Darville tenant who took labouring work where he could.

A silence fell. Jacob was not one of their own but they were reluctant to point a definite finger at someone connected with the manor.

'Why not one of the gentry?' said Joe Ponting in the hopes of prolonging the discussion to scrounge another drink. 'West and his son 'ated each other, we all know that. The young'un could 'ave brained the old 'un outa spite.'

'Nah, our Daisy said Mr Frank skipped the coop long afore his dad got done in. Look to your own son, Joe Ponting. Just 'cos a boy's running wild don't mean he's a murderer. Though, I agree with 'ee, it looks bad for young Frank coming into the property like that.'

'What about parson?' asked someone else.

'Who? Miss Letty's 'usband? Daisy said they'd gone 'ome too.' Elias let out a guffaw. 'He'd be too short to hit West on the noddle.'

''Twas a deed done in temper and if it weren't one of the family we all know who half killed an Irish tinker and threatened Mr West with a gun. He's a crack shot is Darville for all his 'igh and mighty ways.' Ponting was not prepared to be contradicted.

The drinkers stirred uneasily. They knew Darville as a precise and detached landlord. His intellectual pursuits baffled them but as long as Mrs Darville and Mr Brownrigg were there to listen, they knew they would get fair dealings. But Ponting was right; Rupert Darville was known to be a superb marksman.

'Have a care, Joe; Mr Darville is mighty thick with Magistrate Durrington. He had no call to kill Mr West - that we know of. Horace West had quarrelled with 'alf the county; it could 'ave been anyone.'

'And I thought you said this Horace West was bashed on the head and drowned,' said some out-of-town small-holder. 'Who got shot, then?'

'No one! Sup yer ale.'

The stranger underlined something in his notebook, and resolved to make further enquiries.

And so the stories went round and grew until they eventually reached the ears of the Reverend Butterworth who felt his patron should be made aware of this slander. Meeting Dr Learoyd in the Salisbury cathedral close one day – the Archdeacon bemoaned his continuing business for the Bishop of Winchester - the two clerical gentlemen commiserated on the wickedness of idle tongues. However, the Archdeacon thought it best to leave well alone and excused himself to go in to his meeting in the chapter house.

The Rector understood the Archdeacon's reluctance to discuss the ramifications of his father-in-law's death, but he could not rid himself of the notion that Mr Darville would know how to put a stop to idle talk. To his disappointment, Bernard agreed with the Venerable Archdeacon. The secretary felt his employer was too immersed in his studies to be aware of vindictive speculation and that the rumours would soon die away.

' "He who conceals hatred has lying lips",' quoted the Rector. 'I would feel easier in my mind if Mr Darville knew.'

'"And he who spreads slander is a fool",' said Bernard, continuing Proverbs ten, verse eighteen. 'I do not wish to contradict you, father, but you can do no good by interfering and Mr Darville has an uncertain temper these days; he will not thank you for the information.'

'Really, my boy? He has always been courtesy itself to me and your mother. He could not have been more generous regarding the tithes. But no doubt you and the Archdeacon know best. As long as the Darvilles are not upset in any way.'

However, when Harriet next drove into Larkhill she was conscious of the odd looks, the dropped conversation in the shops and the whispers beneath the bonnets when she changed her library books in Mr Jackson's book shop. Other people went out of their way to accost her in an over-hearty manner, intent on showing their support. She hoped she was imagining things until a sharp-looking stranger followed her with his eyes as she drove the gig past the Three Crowns. It could only be the Bow Street officer from London. Harriet came home feeling a little nauseous.

****

The man told the hired chaise to wait and said a few words to someone inside the vehicle who pulled his head back sharply to avoid being seen. When Dunch answered the imperious bell pull, the visitor, in an assertive tone, asked to speak to the master of the house on business. Dunch looked the man up and down in his most frosty manner. 'Your card, sir?'

'I don't carry such things; there don't seem to be much call for them in Whitechapel. You just cut along now and tell Mr Darville that Inspector Cuttle of the Bow Street police court is here and would have a few words with him.' Cuttle's voice was full of the strangled vowels of the metropolis.

Dunch stalked off to the library, wondering what the world was coming to and whether he could eavesdrop.

'What is it, Dunch?' asked Rupert breaking off from his dictation to Bernard. 'I'm very busy.'

'A person, sir, from Bow Street, wishes to have a word with you, sir.'

'The devil he does! What manner of man is he? I really do not wish to be disturbed.'

'Respectably dressed, sir, but no gentleman.' Dunch thought that the Runner should have presented himself at the back door.

'I could say the same of many of my acquaintance,' Rupert said, taking off his spectacles. 'Very well, you may send him in. Bernard, stay where you are. You can make yourself useful by taking notes.'

Mr Cuttle came into the room and bowed. 'Mr Darville? The name is Inspector Cuttle. I daresay your butler explained that I'm attached to the Bow Street police court in London and I'm down here at the request of Mr Francis West.' He sounded brisk.

Rupert rose from his desk but did not offer Cuttle a seat. 'How may I help you, Inspector?'

The inspector was rather taken aback by Rupert's slanted eyes and high cheekbones. He looked at Bernard in enquiry and back to Rupert. 'I was hoping to have a word in private with you, sir, if you've no objection.'

'This is my secretary, Mr Butterworth. You may say what you will in front of him.'

'Very well, sir; a relative of the good Rector, no doubt?'

Bernard did not reply but found a clean sheet of paper. His father had not appreciated the inspector's inquisition regarding his flock's nefarious tendencies. The Rector might condemn some of his weaker congregation himself but would tolerate no word of reproach from an outsider.

'How can I help you, Cuttle?' A shade of impatience coloured Rupert's tone. 'I am somewhat occupied this morning.'

'I'm here to arrest Mr Jacob Ombay for the late Mr West's murder.'

Bernard's steel nib spluttered on the paper. Rupert's face froze.

Inspector Cuttle had had a profitable time in the Drover's Arms. Plied with the local cider, the regular customers were happy to regale him with their views that the murder was the devil's work or Delilah's. From the black maid to the black valet was a short step.

Everyone had heard a garbled version of Jacob's threats and trespassing, which caused much speculation. And weren't he and the wench both now living under the same roof at the manor? If this was not enough, Rupert's own aloofness had exacerbated the talk. No one would dare to accuse Mr Darville outright but after several tankards, Mrs O'Leary's tales were resurrected and those who had experienced Rupert's indifference took their petty revenge by implicating his valet, if not himself.

Cuttle needed a culprit fast before Frank West grew tired of paying him by the day. You could never trust the gentry; his client did not appreciate the amount of time spent in the various ale houses of Larkhill. Frank's offer of fifty guineas reward had made Cuttle settle on the valet as the most vulnerable "collar" on his list of suspects.

'Let me see the warrant,' ordered Rupert. He could not believe that George had signed it. 'Ah, so you went to Sir Archibald Walcot.' He handed the paper back to the inspector; he saw Frank West's hand in this.

'Yussir, it's all legal, so if you would have the goodness to send for Mr Ombay-'

'You cannot arrest a man on rumour. What facts have you discovered?'

'I was told that Mr Ombay was roamin' in Bourne Park on the night of the murder, and went back again some days later to retrieve a weapon he'd dropped. That's enough for the magistrate and for me to make an arrest, sir. I'll leave the rest up to the lawyers.'

'I would think again, Mr Cuttle. You have nothing but hearsay. There also seems some doubt as to whether the death was murder or an accident. And if it was murder, while I don't deny that my servant was in the vicinity a week later, there is no proof that he had any encounter with Mr West on the night of his death.'

'The inquest said murder and my client does not believe Mr Ombay's denial regarding the second of January. Sir Archibald was satisfied. Now if you would send for Mr Ombay we could get the matter over with without any unpleasantness.'

'I'm afraid I cannot help you.'

'I have to insist, sir.' Cuttle was uneasy in this man's presence; he was more at home in the flash houses of Covent Garden. The gentry were tricky coves and stuck together.

West had promised to pay him something on account if a culprit was charged even before the case came to court. Frank West was just the kind of weakling to change his mind and Cuttle wanted to claim his reward for the arrest before this could happen. The inspector wondered whether to call the reluctant Hewitt from the chaise in support.

Rupert pulled himself up to his full, dark height. 'Confound your impertinence! To come here demanding to arrest a gentleman's servant on nothing but other people's lies!'

The fifty guineas chinked in Cuttle's ears. 'I am an officer of the law and I am hired by Mr West to find his father's murderer,' he said doggedly.

'Well, you can look elsewhere; it is not my valet!'

Bernard coughed. 'He has a warrant, sir. Sir Archibald is an influential gentleman.'

'Hold your tongue, Bernard!'

The young secretary flushed. But his intervention was sufficient for Rupert to calm himself. He leant his hands on the desk, his fingers splayed, his thumbs bloodless with pressure. After a few moments he said: 'Very well, I will send for Ombay. Perhaps he can convince you that he has nothing to do with the murder.' Rupert pulled the bell rope sharply.

''T'aint up to me, sir; that's for the court to decide.'

The ensuing scene was unpleasant. Jacob was in pain, protesting and terrified. Rupert, pale with anger, assured him they would procure his release as soon as possible. Harriet arrived and, once over her indignation, became her usual practical self, finding food for Jacob to take with him.

'Where will you put him, Inspector?' she recognised Cuttle as the man who had watched her drive down the High Street. 'Surely there's no need for those handcuffs? He cannot walk without his crutch.'

Cuttle, having won his prisoner, thought it best to be gracious. 'Very good, ma'am. I've a chaise outside and we'll put him in Larkhill lock-up tonight.' The lock-up was a tiny stone cell on the edge of town near the pack horse bridge.

'He'll freeze to death! Can't you see he's injured? How long do you intend to keep him there?'

The Inspector shrugged and escorted his prisoner across the vestibule. 'According to the magistrate, I'm to take him to Salisbury jail tomorrow morning; they're expecting him.'

Rupert and Harriet could only comfort a trembling Jacob. Delilah appeared, sobbing and distracted, to be held back by Dunch and Bernard. Miss Humble thankfully kept all the children in the nursery though the servants gravitated to the vestibule in response to the commotion.

'Ah, Mr Hewitt,' said Harriet, catching sight of the shame-faced constable. 'You can help us, I'm certain. There has been a silly misunderstanding with the result that Mr Ombay is to go to the lock-up. Now I'm sure you, as one of the parish constables, could find him a secure bed for the night? In your own cottage perhaps? We would of course pay for Mr Ombay's lodging.'

Hewitt knew what was required. He liked the Darville family and would be in Larkhill long after Cuttle had disappeared back to Bow Street. 'Certainly ma'am. I've a stout lock on all my doors and Mr Ombay can't get far with that leg of his. The missus and I'll take him in.' He was glad to ease his conscience; he had not wanted to come on this embarrassing arrest in the first place.

Cuttle did not look happy but could find no reason to object, especially when Hewitt belatedly invoked his parochial authority. He was more concerned with claiming his reward and getting back to the smoke. The whole affair had proved an unsatisfactory business with a drunk and unstable client, little chance of anyone who was abroad that night peaching on his fellows; there were too many locals in jail already, some of them thanks to the deceased himself. He could not touch the gentry and having met the daunting Mr Darville, he would not dare to try again. He retrieved his tall hat from Dunch, nodded to the Darvilles and slammed the carriage door behind him.

Rupert stood with his arm around his wife's shoulders watching the hired chaise trundle down the drive. 'Don't fret, my dear, we'll have Jacob back at the manor by the end of the week. I'll ride into Salisbury directly and see Walcot.'

'And if we can't get Jacob back, what are we to tell Clem?'

Chapter 17   Good Deeds

Sir Archibald Walcot was adamant. Word had come down from the Lord Lieutenant of Wiltshire; a magistrate had been murdered, a sacrificial lamb must be found and slaughtered. Nothing Rupert could say would persuade the lawyer to rescind the warrant. The coroner wondered if this solemn and somehow unworldly man had heard the whispers against himself; they were foolish, of course, but corrosive.

Walcot sat behind his desk, a fur cape about his shoulders. A fire roared in the grate but the book room in the tall, thin house in Salisbury still felt chilly. The room smelt of stale snuff and musty volumes. In the street below, the drainage channels gurgled and overflowed with icy rain. Rupert shivered.

'If I release your servant, then we would have to charge another miscreant and I understand there are not many to choose from.' He gave his visitor a significant look which Rupert deflected. 'Due process has begun and must be continued, for justice's sake.'

'Sir Archibald, do you realise the boy might perish in Salisbury jail? He could be there for months. With an open leg wound he won't stand a chance of surviving a week, let alone against the cold and the typhus. Ombay will die before you get him to court.'

The Special Commission Assizes might be over but the jail was full to bursting with prisoners serving their terms or awaiting transportation. The overcrowding and squalor were intolerable. Ordure, lice, rats and starvation were the norm.

'I'm sure your wife will supply him with the necessary comforts.' Nevertheless, Walcot felt uneasy; Darville had a point and he did not want to lose his prisoner. He ran a bony hand over his bald skull. He knew he was on thin ice with the charge but he was not a man to offend the Great Ones. Even the High Sheriff of Wiltshire had shown an interest in the case.

'The Home Secretary won't appreciate being robbed of a scapegoat if Jacob dies before you can hang him,' pursued Rupert.

'Now look here, Darville. What do you expect me to do? Your man was found in Bourne Park with a weapon. He had threatened to murder West – several people heard him; we have witnesses. I cannot release him; Melbourne expects us to come down hard on these criminals.'

'My valet has nothing to do with the Swing rioters and you know it! The Special Commission has moved on to Dorchester along with the disturbances.' The stupidity of the premise amazed Rupert.

Walcot shifted uncomfortably. 'That's debateable. West received a Captain Swing letter and was dead within weeks. We must be seen to be active. The Government fears sedition, with good cause.' He rustled among his papers. 'Have you seen this handbill?' Walcot thrust a torn and muddy poster towards Rupert. 'These were plastered all around the town.'

Rupert read. *"Englishmen! Is it to be wondered that the productive poor are found starving in the highways, hanging and drowning themselves to get rid of a wretched existence while non-productive gentlemen take so much from their hard earnings? Remember what the French and the Belgians have done! One hour of true liberty is worth Ages of slavery! Consider, is it not more praiseworthy to meet an honourable death in defending your rights, than quietly die of starvation. Starvation stares while your oppressors are rolling in luxury and wealth."*

Rupert handed the poster back. 'I repeat, you know that Ombay is not involved and that handbill is at least two month's old.'

Walcot shook his head and replaced the muddy paper among a sheaf of documents. 'I would assist you if I could, Darville, but there's nothing I can do.'

'What you can do is allow Ombay to stay in the custody of our parish constable until his trial. Hewitt is a good man, very firm about his duties. Jacob cannot run off with his leg wound still healing. And there would be no danger of your prisoner dying before the Easter Assizes.'

Walcot gave him a considered look; as a lawyer he appreciated the compromise. 'It might be done.' He pulled his fur cape further round his hunched shoulders. Frank West had annoyed him with his ridiculous demands for justice; Walcot knew malicious revenge when he heard it. West's insane accusations against Darville had been ungentlemanly and the involvement of a Bow Street officer had added insult to the irritation. As the lesser of two evils, Walcot had preferred to move against a black servant instead of the brother of an earl.

After a moment he said. 'If I agreed to your suggestion, would you stand a recognizance for your servant?'

'Most willingly. Any amount.'

'And I would have your word that you would produce, what's his name – Ombay - for trial when the case is called?'

'Of course. I will be instructing lawyers on his behalf.'

'I am not happy about this, Darville, but between ourselves, it might be the wisest course. West was insistent on the arrest and I am being pressurised from Whitehall to set an example. However, I'll make it as easy for your man as I'm able, until the court decides.'

'Thank you, Sir Archibald. I will wait while you write the necessary cancellation to the superintendent of the jail. I will ride over with it directly and we can keep Ombay under lock and key in Larkhill until you send for him.'

Walcot knew he was being stampeded and considered being obstructive, but after one look at Rupert's granite expression, he picked up his quill and began to write. He was not a man to procrastinate once his mind was made up.

****

It was George Durrington who thought it best to tell Rupert of the unsavoury rumours touching the Darville family. George's knew his duty to his friends even if it did not extend to actively hunting for a killer. He was rather shocked to see how worn Rupert had become.

'You do not surprise me, George. I had half picked up on some facetious remarks when I was in Bath and certainly rumours have reached Salisbury.' The irony of the situation struck Rupert as ludicrous. He dare not follow his suspicions for fear of exposing his family and as a result his servant was charged and he himself was under a cloud.

'I must say, hearing such nonsense launched me into action but I may have done your cause more harm than good,' said George with regret. 'As soon as that Bow Street Runner arrived I wrote to the magistrates in the next district and I set a man to trace the route of the gypsies to the coast. As far as anyone can tell, they made a steady progress north to Bristol and took ship to Wexford within three days of leaving Larkhill. It's impossible to say whether or not one of the men doubled-back to take his revenge on West two weeks later, but I think it unlikely. West only gave them a tongue-lashing after all. You were more likely to be their target after your encounter with them.'

'I agree,' said Rupert. 'Gypsy families tend to stay together and any stranger in the vicinity would have been spotted. You've done well George. No magistrate could have taken a more thorough line.'

'But that doesn't help you. As to any rioter being the murderer, you may take your pick of hundreds. Though I thought we'd rounded them up by the time Horace West disappeared. Larkhill was relatively peaceful compared with other parts of the county.'

'An unemployed labourer isn't going to tell a magistrate or a Runner anything, particularly in the light of that Captain Swing letter. As no one has yet come forward in response to the reward offered by Frank West then I believe no one will.'

'And what if wasn't a murder, but an accident all along as I've always said? You'll never prove your innocence then.'

'I won't have to. No one has a shred of evidence against me, except that West and I had quarrelled and that argument applies to many people. The rumours will die away eventually. I have a thick skin. However, I don't want Harriet or the children to be upset in any way. Perhaps it is best to say no more about it. Thank you, George, for apprising me of my unpopularity in the district; I will not let it bother me.'

This was not true. Rupert was exasperated by the stupidity of his neighbours. He threw himself into his work once more and avoided going into Larkhill. The family would have to ride out the storm. What he would say to Morna on his return, he had no idea.

The murder of a magistrate had made the London papers and, with no explanation to hand, the crime was the common talk of the day. The earl and his secretary found themselves in great demand in the fashionable salons because of their Darville connection. While Morna knew how to be discreet in public he saw his young friend courted on all sides for what he could tell, especially when Jacob's arrest was the subject of an adverse editorial comment in *The Times*.

The McAllisters were staunch defenders of the Darvilles and being Tories naturally blamed the Swing rioters for the killing. The family had been sympathetic to the Duke of Wellington's desire to repress all civil disturbances by force. London was in fear of the agricultural uprising spreading to the urban poor and doubted if the new Home Secretary's handling of the situation would avert class insurrection. But Sir Hamish contended that, with the Horse Guards within call, there was no need for alarm and Elspeth thanked her Maker for not being born a country cousin.

****

On a rare dry, bright afternoon, Harriet decided to take parcels to those tenants who were in most need. Rupert thought Brownrigg should attend to the matter but Harriet said she wanted to "blow the winter cobwebs away" in the fresh air, and assured him she would be well protected by Jem and the shotgun. The county had suffered no disturbance for a month and Rupert reluctantly allowed her to go on condition that she used the chaise and was back before sunset.

'Nathaniel Haycock, today, Jem. He did not come on Boxing Day; I can only hope he stayed home to care for his wife.' Harriet settled herself in the chaise and examined her list. 'Young Mrs Trottman told me that Dorcas was very poorly again.'

Jem cracked his whip and the chaise bowled down the drive over the remnants of snow. James opened the manor gates and waved to his father and Mrs Darville as they passed.

The Haycocks rented a small cottage at Sheep's End, tucked in the shoulder of the Downs near the manor's sheep pastures. The country track was heavy going but Harriet enjoyed the patched whiteness of the fields and the hoar frost glistening on the hedges. Everything seemed clean and pure. She drank in the silence and the peace of having no one demanding her attention. The slushing of the wheels and the rhythmic clop of hooves would have soothed her anxieties over Jacob and the murder but for the jolting of the carriage through the neglected pot holes.

When they came to the isolated cottage, Harriet was alarmed to see no wisp of smoke from the chimney. The cottage consisted of two up, two down and a sty for either a pig or goats. Being Darville property she knew Brownrigg would see that it was in reasonable condition but there was an air of dereliction about the Haycock's home. Frozen cabbage stalks poked up through the snow in the front garden. The shadow of the Downs kept the cottage in a pocket of cold.

She climbed down with her basket of provisions. Jem rapped on the wooden door with his whip. A baby's wail came from within. 'This is a desolate place in winter, Jem. We must not be late home.'

A mite of about five years of age dragged the door open and a tremulous voice croaked 'Who is it?'

'It's Mrs Darville, Dorcas. I see you are not at all well.' A figure wrapped in blankets lay on a straw mattress in front of a dying fire trying to stifle a hacking cough. A baby whimpered at the breast. Two more children huddled on the hearth. A girl of about nine hovered protectively over her mother. They were all slovenly and in rags.

'Goodness, how long have you been like this?' Harriet put her hand to the woman's forehead. 'You're burning with fever! Jem, fetch some kindling; we mustn't let the fire go out.'

The room was bare; everything had been sold months before; rugs, furniture, candlesticks, superfluous crockery, clothes, even the cradle had been pawned. Only the unused crook stood in the corner. What had once been a serviceable cottage for a farm labourer's family was now as empty as a broken eggshell.

For the next hour Harriet worked with what she had and made others do the same. One of the children was set to scouring the porridge pot, encrusted with burnt oats from Nathaniel Haycock's efforts at cooking. Kitty was sent to milk the goat. She spooned the cook's broth into Dorcas's mouth, fed the children on bread and bacon and promised to send a message to Mrs Haycock's sister.

'Can she read?' asked Harriet.

'No, mum, but she'll come if I ask. She ain't got no situation at the moment; there's no work about.'

Just when she was satisfied she could do no more, Harriet heard men's voices and heavy footsteps approaching the cottage. The door opened and Nathaniel Haycock pushed into the darkening room, closely followed by Jem.

'What you be doin' 'ere, missus?' growled the shepherd.

'Looking after your wife, as you should be.' A nauseous sweet smell reached Harriet's nostrils.

The man's voice was thick, slurred and indignant. 'I been spreading manure over at Figheldean, for Farmer Shrewton and then I been beggin' at the Assistance Board in Larkhill.'

The younger children gathered round their father, tugging at his thin hessian coat. In better times he had brought them sticks of barley-sugar from Larkhill. Haycock tried to beat them away saying petulantly. 'I ain't got nothin' for ye, get away now.'

Harriet picked up her empty basket. 'I know times are difficult but if you stayed sober you would have a chance of more lucrative employment,' she said. Shrewton was known to be a tight-fisted master. It was obvious that Haycock had taken a drink on his way home.

'If you gentry paid us a living wage and the Assistance Board weren't so 'ard then we wouldn't 'ave to drink!'

At that moment one of the children gave a final tug at his father's pocket. The thin weave shredded in the child's hand and a glittering sovereign fell to the earth floor.

'Ah,' said Harriet. 'I see you are not so destitute after all. I suggest you re-stock your larder and buy some medicine from the apothecary; I recommend Balsam of Violets and goose grease. The sooner your wife is on her feet again the better.'

'I tole you, I been working and then to the Parish Vestry,' said Haycock, quickly stooping to retrieve his booty. The movement made him stagger and he leaned against the wall, gasping.

Harriet knew the Larkhill Assistance Board did not meet on this day of the week, nor did it give out money to someone who was not working within the parish. Figheldean was three miles from Larkhill's borders. Neither did any Board give out so much money; a shilling a child was the most that local parishes would offer. He had stolen the sovereign from somewhere; from Farmer Shrewton, perhaps, or some lonely traveller.

Harriet said nothing, twenty shillings would keep the family in food for a few weeks.

Dorcas started to cough in fear. Harriet immediately bent down to her and said softly. 'Now, now Mrs Haycock, do not become alarmed. Your husband has got good wages it seems and will soon be his own self after young Kitty has made him a pot of tea. I have left a twist of Assam and some sugar in the cupboard. Do not fret yourself.'

Haycock slid down the wall in exhaustion, leaving smears of manure on the whitewashed wall. He really had been working in the fields all day and had walked to Larkhill and back. Harriet's conscience smote her.

'I will send for your sister as soon as I can,' she said to Dorcas.

'We doan't want no extra mouth to feed!' snarled Haycock looking up.

'Keep a civil tongue in your 'ead,' said Jem cowing the man into submission with a look.

'Your sister-in-law will take the younger children and Kitty can remain to care for your wife while you work. Apply to Mr Brownrigg, there may be drainage work for you to do, or timber felling.'

'Time be getting on Mrs Darville. The master'll be expecting us 'ome.' Jem was insistent.

'Kitty, boil the water for tea. I'm sure you're all parched. I have left some candle ends on the dresser, so you need not be in the dark. Send for me if your mother does not improve.'

And with that, Jem ushered his mistress firmly from the cottage.

****

Lady Durrington came to call, braving the weather, the gossip and the roads. 'I think we are quite done with all that horrid business of rick burning. George says the rioting has moved into Dorset and Somerset. I do hope Lord Lydiard's property is well guarded.'

Juliana was left at home with the children. Harriet rang for tea to be laid in the oak parlour. Over the mixing of the leaves and bringing the kettle to the boil, the two women spoke of the children, Juliana's interesting condition and how Jacob was faring in captivity. When they were settled with their cups and Janet had left the room, Harriet leaned forward. 'I am pleased to have this opportunity of speaking to you alone, ma'am. I need your advice on a matter of some delicacy.'

Lady Durrington immediately put down her cup. Had Harriet discovered the nature of relationship between the earl and his friend? She felt for Harriet in this predicament. 'My dear, if I can be of service in any way. But it is your husband who should advise you in all matters.'

'It is my husband who troubles me.' Harriet sounded serious. 'He is his own worst enemy in this situation.'

Lady Durrington had a sudden thought of the temptress Delilah but immediately dismissed the idea of marital infidelity and waited to be informed.

Harriet related Young Clem's fight in defence of his guardian. 'I tried to keep the talk from Rupert but somehow he knows that he is regarded as one of the suspects, as much as Jacob or Delilah or anyone in the vicinity. I am sure Frank West has helped to spread this slander as an act of spite.'

Knowing the young man, Lady Durrington could only agree. The shrewd suspicion that her son-in-law had been the bearer of the bad tidings to the Darvilles had prompted her visit.

Harriet, for once indulging in a rant, continued. 'I believe Rupert is more angry than hurt by the vile rumours that are attaching themselves to him. He cannot understand it; such suspicions have no basis in truth. He shuts himself away in the library with Bernard or spends hours on the roof with his telescope and refuses to talk about the murder. He'll catch pneumonia if he continues like this. Worst of all, he will not talk to me about how he feels.'

'Rupert has never been in the habit of confiding in anyone,' said Lady Durrington with regret.

'There are times when he is not the most – comfortable of men. He is deeply anxious about Jacob and now these ridiculous rumours only irritate him more. You must have heard the talk yourself. The newspaper accounts are despicable, full of innuendo. Our London friends have been very kind but every letter of good-will exacerbates the sore.'

'George did express some concern at first at various whispers he had heard; he thought they would soon fade away. I had no idea matters were so openly spoken of. It is to Young Clem's honour that he defended Mr Darville but I can see how that would cause tongues to wag.'

Harried sighed. 'Clem is back at school now but I know he is still being teased. He looks troubled every time he comes home and covers up by getting into mischief. The very idea of Rupert being in any way concerned in Mr West's death is preposterous. Yet he has no verifiable alibi and, according to the town, is a man steeped in violence who had a grudge against Mr West; Rupert's argument with him is common knowledge.'

'The fact that Lord Lydiard had dropped Mr West as a parliamentary candidate in favour of Rupert would have added to the antagonism between the gentlemen, of course. They are saying that Lord Lydiard has now dropped Rupert.'

'Stuff and nonsense! Rupert refused Lord Lydiard's offer. You know that.'

'And I tell them so, but alas, I do not frequent public houses where these slanders begin. I suppose the episode with the gypsies does not look well in a certain light,' Lady Durrington added pensively.

'A month ago my husband was the hero of the neighbourhood. Now the very same action has rendered him capable of murder! It is a terrible thing.'

'My dear Harriet, do not distress yourself. This will all blow over and be forgotten, or the real murderer will be found. We all know that Jacob did not do it and certainly neither did your husband.'

'But what if there is no murderer? Horace West could have died accidentally. If we cannot prove it or find the real villain, Rupert or anyone may always be subject to this wicked calumny.'

Lady Durrington took another sip of her tea. 'If someone came to you with the self-same problem, my dear, what would you advise them to do?'

'I would tell them to search out the murderer themselves,' Harriet replied instantly.

'I had a feeling you would say that,' said Lady Durrington.

'But I'm not so foolish as to think I can do this alone. I cannot question everyone in the neighbourhood in the hope that they may know something of use. But I have to do what I can to help Rupert.' She looked desperately at her friend. 'I am so afraid that all this dreadful talk will lower his spirits and cause another attack of the malaria; his weak heart cannot stand any more fevers.'

Over the years, Harriet's impetuosity had been tempered by concern for her husband's health. Maria Durrington found this praiseworthy but she did not like to see her friend at such a loss. She was disturbed to find the practical, prosaic Harriet so harassed and perplexed.

'People will confide in you, Harriet; you are well thought of in the neighbourhood. The scandal surely has not attached itself to you?'

'No, no. I think they pity me for harbouring a household of assassins.' A glimmer of humour softened her face. 'I am only thankful that Morna and Mr Romero are in London to be spared any other gossip,' she said unguardedly.

'I always thought Euphemia had the desire to kill her husband,' said Lady Durrington absently. 'You could begin by questioning her. You are friends, are you not?'

'I cannot visit Euphemia while someone, anyone, from the manor is accused of murdering her husband!'

'I agree that such an intrusion may be considered by some to show a sad want of sensibility but I would have thought that was the perfect reason for clearing the air.'

Harriet looked thoughtful and Lady Durrington pursued her advantage. 'Sir Charles has always admired your boldness, Harriet. Did you not face down an angry mob? A visit to a neighbour is nothing in comparison. It can do no harm, and may bring some good.'

'Do not ask me how I know, but I am reasonably convinced of Delilah's innocence.'

Lady Durrington looked sceptical but said nothing.

Harriet continued. 'Rupert would not question Euphemia or Letty, but there's no reason why I shouldn't probe a little more.'

A spark came into her dark brown eyes. 'I could call unannounced and hope Mrs West does not refuse to see me. Perhaps I can gain a clearer idea of what really went on in Bourne Park that night. Of course Frank could show me the door; he and Rupert are now implacable enemies.'

'Frank West has gone to London. Now he's done his mischief he is off to spend his father's money.'

****

Harriet's visit to Mrs West was difficult. Euphemia's pupils were nothing but pinpricks in her weak blue eyes. Today, words tumbled out like grain from a sack; it was as though her husband's death had released all the pent-up speech she had suppressed during her married life. Harriet could see from whom Letty had inherited her loquacious tendencies. Euphemia talked of abandonment, destitution, Frank going for a soldier, all the while threading a frill of torn lace between her hands. Among the stream of half-sentences and unfinished thoughts Harriet could discover only that there had been a series of arguments among the family during the holidays. Mazzotta had been expelled, Frank had stormed out and the Learoyds had left prematurely.

'What was all the quarrelling about?' asked Harriet innocently.

'Shh, I'm not supposed to say. But I got rid of her didn't I? She killed him you know, not me, but Martin says we are not to speak of it and we are all rich again and I am to go and live with Letty. Frank doesn't want me here,' her eyes filled with easy tears. 'It makes no odds; I hate the place, he can keep it. His father hated the place too and was always intoxicated, the amount of sherry he consumed was disgusting but it finished him in the end didn't it? I saw to that.'

After another half an hour's incoherent rambling and confusing pronouns, Harriet took her leave. Daisy, one of the housemaids slightly known to Harriet, hovered in the entrance hall. The butler did not reprimand her for being above stairs.

'Why Daisy, what are you doing here?' asked Harriet, retrieving her driving cloak from Simpkins.

'Please, mum, I've come to aks about my sister Violet.' Daisy's eldest sister Violet worked in the kitchen at Larkhill.

'Her burn is healing nicely. You may tell your mother that Violet is on light duties until she can remove the bandage.'

Daisy bobbed and then said in a rush. 'Can I come and visit 'er, mum? We don't 'ave the same afternoon off.'

Harriet smiled. 'I see no harm in it. Why not come now and I'll give Violet leave to spend an hour with you.' Harriet believed in striking while the iron was hot.

The butler frowned but was distracted by the arrival of Jem with the gig. Simpkins had a lot of respect for Mrs Darville who had taken over during the housekeeper's absence but he felt she was being a little high-handed.

'I will explain to the housekeeper – Mrs Fletcher – is it? You fetch your bonnet and shawl. Go along with you now.'

Daisy, overwhelmed by the sudden whims of the gentry, bobbed several more grateful curtsies and vanished to the back stairs.

Once arrived at the manor, Harriet ushered the girl into the oak parlour.

'Come in Daisy. There's no need to be afraid; you've done nothing wrong. You may even be able to help me. Sit down.'

The maid was still in her frieze cloak and best bonnet. She looked a little bewildered at not being sent to the back door, but Harriet was generally well-liked in the neighbourhood and Daisy was eager to please. She had hopes that Mrs Darville would offer her a position; she would give anything to be out of that damp, unlucky house by the river and longed for the next Mop fair.

'Now, Daisy, my husband and I are trying to discover if there is any little thing that might help Mr Ombay. You must be aware that he has been unjustly accused of Mr West's murder.'

'Yes, mum.' Daisy had admired the handsome young valet from afar and had been shocked by his arrest.

'I am not asking you to be disloyal to your master in any way; he would want to see the right person brought to justice as much as we do. And I'm sure Mrs West would be only too happy to help us if she were in better health.'

Daisy hated Frank West, having suffered from his drunken advances more than once, and felt sorry for her poor, distracted mistress.

'Tell me, Daisy, do you remember the night that Mr West went missing? Good. Was there anything particular about that night that you can recall?'

'Mum?'

'Any noises, any unusual movement in the house?' Harriet tried not to lace her fingers in anxiety.

'I'm in the attics, mum, I don't hear much after I go off, I'm that tired.'

'Of course. But did you hear the dog bark? Mr Darville tells me it was mentioned at the inquest by your butler.'

If Mr Simpkins had admitted hearing the mastiff then there was no harm in speaking out, thought Daisy. 'Oh I 'eard the dog bark something fierce, but a bit far away like, on the other side of the house. It woke me up. And then the clock struck but I couldn't rightly count all the chimes because of 'er banging on 'er door fit to wake the dead.'

'Her? And who would that be?' Harriet probed gently.

Daisy looked awkward. She didn't want to mention the black girl even if the Darvilles were giving the slut shelter.

'Do you mean Delilah?'

'Yes, mum. He'd locked her in.'

'Mr West, I take it. Did you let her out?'

'No, mum!' Daisy said in horror. "T'aint my place to do that.'

Harriet felt a wave of relief sweep over her. She sat back. 'I see. Did you hear anything else? Was anyone creeping about?"

'No, mum. I 'eard nothing 'cept 'er shouting.'

'What was she shouting?'

Daisy looked contemptuous. 'Let me out, it's midnight, I've gotta go, he's waitin' – fit to wake the dead it was.'

'And nothing else?'

'Well, there was shoutin' after dinner,' said Daisy, willing to please.

'From Delilah?'

'No, I don't think so. I 'eard the Reverend's voice and the master 'aving 'igh words in the study.'

'Did you hear what they were saying?'

'No, mum. I was carrying the tea tray to the drawing room, an' it's mortal 'eavy, I dursn't stop.'

'What time was this?'

Daisy thought. "Bout five o'clock, mum. Mr West 'ad 'is dinner on a tray in 'is study, like 'e 'ad all week.'

Harriet smiled. 'Thank you Daisy. You have been most helpful.' She stood up and tugged at the bell. 'Janet will take you down to the kitchen and give you your dinner. Violet is waiting for you.' Harriet went to a small bureau and took out a purse. She pressed a half-sovereign into the girl's hand.

'Thank you, mum.' Daisy bobbed and followed Janet to the nether regions.

Chapter 18   Another attack

'My God! Askew's been shot!' Rupert shook out the *Salisbury Journal* and settled his spectacles firmly on his nose. He felt as though the very pistol had been fired behind his ear.

Harriet paused, a piece of bread roll in her hand. 'Shot? By whom? Was he attacked on the road? Are the labourers rioting again? Is he badly hurt?'

With a crease between his brows Rupert read out: *"'Fifty Pounds Reward. Murderous Outrage and Arson Attack. On Saturday the twenty-ninth of January at about nine o'clock in the evening a shot was fired through the window of the premises belonging to Mr John Askew, attorney-at-law of Castle Street, Salisbury. Mr Askew had descended from his private quarters to investigate a suspicious noise and smell of smoke. While endeavouring to save his property from the flames, supposed to have been wilfully occasioned as a means of decoy, he was barbarously wounded by a pistol ball and left for dead. The building and its contents were destroyed. Whoever will give such information as may lead to the detection of the perpetrator or perpetrators, shall on conviction, receive the above reward.'"*

'Wounded? Then he must be in the care of relatives and friends. I wonder if the Wests know of this?'

'I'm almost certain they do,' said Rupert. The list of figures locked in his desk leapt into focus.

'This must exonerate Euphemia and Delilah,' said Harriet. 'And I cannot for one moment see Letty wielding a gun or setting a fire.'

'What are you saying?' Rupert looked at his wife in astonishment.

'Exactly what you have been wondering for weeks: Who killed Horace West?' She put down her roll. 'You believe this shooting to be connected to Horace West's death, I presume? You cannot cozen me my dear, you have been worrying at this murder like a puzzle in a newspaper. Gentleman that you are, you could not bring yourself to accuse the ladies, though suspicion surrounded them all. Now, Mr Askew's shooting means you can put them aside and concentrate on tracing the culprit – who is more likely to be a man.'

Rupert stared at his wife; he felt out-manoeuvred and rather alarmed. 'Why are you so certain of the women's innocence?'

'I paid a call on Mrs West recently and made some discreet enquiries of my own.'

'I forbid you to go to Bourne Park!' Rupert was shaken by the implied criticism of his own inaction.

'I beg your pardon? You and Frank may have quarrelled but Euphemia is still my friend.'

'A man was brutally done to death and an innocent one is accused. How could you cross that cursed threshold?' Fear that Harriet might put them all in danger made him speak more sharply than he intended.

Harriet knew how to placate him. 'I will not go again. Neither of the two gentlemen were there and Euphemia is removing to Winchester soon. I discovered nothing of note - or nothing that would interest you.'

'What did you discover?' His almond eyes were piqued with curiosity.

She smiled winningly. 'Only that I'm certain Maria Durrington was right; Euphemia always wanted to kill her husband. Happily, she managed only to intoxify him – is there such a word? Anyhow, I am convinced that she drugged his sherry with laudanum in the hopes he would never wake up.'

Rupert blinked for a moment. 'Then she crept downstairs in the morning and emptied the dregs of the sherry decanter onto the snow,' he continued slowly.

'Yes, of course! You found the melted patch by the French windows, didn't you? How clever of you, Rupert.'

'You must leave this matter to me, Harriet. There could be danger. I can say no more; there have been too many vicious rumours, I will not add to them.'

'My dear, I am not a court of law, I am your wife. Did no one ever tell you it is vulgar to be mysterious?' she teased.

Rupert remained serious. 'Very well. As you have involved yourself so much, perhaps it is better to forewarn you. I have circumstantial evidence that suggests Horace West may have been killed before he could disinherit his family.' His suspicions of Romero could not be voiced.

'Are you certain it is one of the family, not a labourer or passing vagrant? And why would Mr Askew be attacked?'

'Because he drew up the necessary documents to disinherit them. George has made enquiries and we believe we can eliminate the gypsies, but I cannot say the same of the world in general. I believe the family had most to gain by West's death, although I can prove nothing.'

Harriet was not concerned with the world in general. 'If the ladies of the family are exonerated then it must be either Frank or the Archdeacon if it is a matter of inheritance.' She had a disconcerting way of getting to the root of the matter with no fuss.

'And you must stay away from both of them.'

'Frank is in London and I assume the Archdeacon is in Winchester when he isn't haunting Salisbury cathedral or Bourne Park.'

But the thought of one of them being a killer made her pause for a moment. She could not credit it and for the first time felt afraid.

'However did you discover all this?' asked her husband.

'I might ask you the same,' she said.

Harriet gave Rupert a brief account of her interview with Mrs West. 'Poor woman, she was almost incomprehensible but she said enough to show me how her mind was working. I knew she could not have dragged her husband to the river but she undoubtedly tried to kill him. So would I if he had forced his mistress onto me as a personal maid.'

'What?'

'You know what I mean, Rupert. It was the last straw that broke the camel's back; the unassailable motive. Mr West ordered Paton, Euphemia's own maid, from the house and tried to put Delilah in her place. I saw the result myself.' Harriet calmly reached for the marmalade. 'No wonder Euphemia wanted to get rid of the girl. She was quite violent and hysterical when Delilah came into her bedroom.'

'Are you sure of this?'

'Yes,' said Harriet simply. 'And I confirmed it with Delilah.'

'What about Delilah, herself? She is tall and strong enough to have cracked West's skull, and by what Jacob told me, she had a motive to kill him. He was taking her back to slavery in the West Indies.'

'Delilah swore West had locked her in her room all night. I believe her to be a truthful young woman and I have the satisfaction of knowing that one of West's housemaids corroborates her story.'

'You have been busy! I take it you dismiss Mrs Learoyd because she was not on the premises? Then you must dismiss the Archdeacon too, leaving only Frank, also nowhere near Bourne Park.'

Harriet's spoon hovered over the marmalade pot. 'It may be nothing, but Letty said something odd, when they returned to Bourne Park. Do you remember me complaining of her incessant chatter when I took her up to see her mother, the day they returned to Larkhill?'

Rupert did not; his mind had been occupied by the interview with Askew and his own discoveries.

Harriet continued hesitantly: 'Letty complained about the damp sheets at Sallow's Cross Inn and said they had been given the same room as they had on the previous Sunday night. To my understanding that means they did not get home to Winchester on Sunday evening but stayed at the inn instead. Which is no surprise as they did not leave the Park until after dinner, according the the maid Daisy. It was dark and the roads are treacherous. Though why they went to Sallow's Cross, I have no idea.'

Rupert sat up in his chair. 'Then Learoyd lied at the inquest! He said they'd left in the morning and made no mention of any detour to Sallow's Cross. Harriet you are a wonderful woman!' If Learoyd had no alibi for the night of the second of January, then he had opportunity and there was a chance that Romero had nothing to do with the killing. Unless they had done the deed together. Rupert threw down the newspaper in frustration.

Harriet was still talking. 'But Sallow's Cross is more than twelve miles from Bourne Park and it's a terrible road. At night it would have taken at least two hours to ride back. I have puzzled at it myself and have come to the conclusion that Dr Learoyd could not have arrived back at Bourne Park until the small hours. And you said you had found no footprints of any kind in the snow. The whole thing is a mystery.'

Rupert was standing now. 'No matter. I must inform George of this. If we can place either Frank or the Archdeacon in Salisbury last Saturday night when Askew was attacked, then Jacob has a chance of being freed.' He did not think Romero would have travelled all the way from London in order to shoot the lawyer. Yet he could not be sure of anything.

Rupert turned back from the door. 'I had persuaded myself that no good would come of my making enquiries, that my investigations might stir up more trouble; it seems my anxieties were justified. You must not meddle, Harriet.'

'I have finished my meddling, I promise,' she said tranquilly and bit into her roll. She was happy to see the old spirit of action in her husband rather than his brooding bad temper.

****

Rupert rode over to Durrington Hall. He could wait no longer in the hope of some easy resolution. Harriet's headstrong dabbling had at least cleared some of the way.

George was in the stables waiting for a groom to saddle his horse. 'Good day, Darville. I was just about to ride out. But I'm glad you're here. You've heard the news about Askew, I suppose? I was the one who rescued him. I want to see how the poor fellow does this morning. Do you intend to come?'

He did not seem too concerned and had trusted to the newspaper to inform his friend of the attack. While the groom rubbed down and watered Rupert's horse, George had plenty to tell concerning the arson. He had been in Salisbury for a meeting of the justices which had ended in a good dinner at the Bugle coaching inn. Riding home, on the outskirts of Salisbury, he had seen the glimmer of flames.

'It was a pretty bad business. I think they fired his house because it was easy to do so, being on the edge of the town and a little isolated. I sent a lad for the fire engine but by the time it arrived most of the ground floor had burnt to ashes; the rest of the place collapsed. Only the chimneystack remains. That's the trouble with these old timber houses, they look picturesque but go up like tinder. I've seen ships do the same.'

'Do you think it was an incendiary? A rioter? Or perhaps an unhappy client?'

'I didn't see anyone, the fog was thick and they'd long gone before I got there. Askew did have a stock of hay and oats; I heard he did a little arable dealing on the side. That went up first and must have caught the house. He's been involved in the trials at the Assizes, so it could have been someone set on revenge. Someone told me Askew was a member of the select vestry for his parish, which also wouldn't have made him very popular in the town; it's a bit of a sinecure.'

'Keeping the Poor Rate at starvation level wouldn't make him popular with the rural labourers, either.' The closed committees of self-appointed worthies who administered the Poor Law were another institution ripe for reform.

'But why shoot the man? He is a harmless enough fellow. I think some fool got carried away or was drunk,' said George.

'I'll ask again: how many field workers do you know who have access to a pistol?'

'Well, none. But the firearm could have been stolen.'

'Did you make enquiries at Bourne Park about the lead ball in the boat house?'

'You think this attack is connected to the West affair?' George looked uncomfortable. 'It slipped my mind, I admit. I was busy with the body and the inquest and rate-payers' meetings and then tracing the gypsies. I thought we'd agreed that anyone could have fired the shot at any time from any gun; I cannot go around asking all my neighbours to let me inspect their firearms.'

'Are you proposing to do anything about this?' Rupert sounded exasperated.

'Look here, I dragged Askew from his front garden, got him to a surgeon and delivered him safely to his sister's house. What more can I do?'

'I want to examine the ball taken out of his arm.'

'Ah, you mean to compare it with the other ball, I take it?'

'Just so; if Askew has kept it. Besides, I want to ask him some questions and he may be more inclined to reveal what he knows with a magistrate who is also his rescuer at the end of the bed.'

'You're a hard devil! If your horse is rested, we can go together and find out what the lawyer remembers. You don't seriously think this attack has anything to do with Horace West do you?'

'Yes, and I'll explain why after I've spoken to Askew.'

Durrington refused to be kept in the dark, so to placate him Rupert revealed what Harriet had said about the Learoyds and the implications of their putting up at Sallow's Cross on the night of West's death.

George pulled a face. 'That's easily verified of course. But your wife is right; that inn is nearly twelve miles by road to Larkhill. I would not fancy a ride on that road in the dark, whether I had pistols or not.'

****

Askew was lying propped up in an old fashioned four poster bed. His left arm was supported by a sling and many frilled pillows. The singed hair had been cut away and his round face plastered in grease against the burns. The tapestried counterpane was scattered with papers. The room was gloomy and smelled of coal tar. Miss Askew, acting the nursemaid, displayed her brother like a new-born baby.

'I cannot say how much we are indebted to you, Mr Durrington for rescuing my brother. And now you favour us with a call. Have you come to tell us that you've arrested the murderous scoundrel responsible for such wickedness?'

'Now, Martha, hush. Mr Durrington has done more than his duty in that respect. We do not know who the perpetrators are and may never know.' Askew removed his spectacles with one hand and made a clumsy attempt to polish them on the corner of the sheet.

'I regret, Miss Askew, that the culprit or culprits have not yet been identified but Mr Darville and I are here for that very reason, to ascertain if Mr Askew can help us with our enquiries.'

She had only the vaguest notion of who Mr Darville was but as a friend of her brother's saviour he would always be welcome, despite those odd cat's eyes. He looked like another lawyer.

Miss Askew leaned down to straighten the sling around her brother's arm and shoulder. 'Thank you, Mr Durrington. We are all at the mercy of these terrible vagabonds; they should be put in the stocks! Now you must not tire yourself, John. You know what the doctor said. Allow me to send up some claret for you gentlemen. John, you are to have no more than one glass or I will not be responsible for the result.'

When the door closed behind Miss Askew, George encouraged the solicitor to retell his tale. It was no more than what the *Salisbury Journal* had reported. From time to time Mr Askew put his hand up to his raw, burnt face and grimaced as he spoke. The claret arrived and Askew made a grab for his glass.

'Did you see anyone, or hear anything unusual?' asked Rupert.

'Really Mr Darville, I have made it quite clear that all I saw, or rather smelt, was the smoke coming up through my floorboards. I rushed downstairs to find one wall of my office ablaze. I started to remove some of my papers by throwing them out of the window into the garden. I left the document boxes until last in the hope that they were fire-proof and that I would be able to extinguish the flames. If I had not been attacked in such a cowardly manner I would have saved everything.'

'Did the box containing the Wests' files survive?'

He hesitated. 'The West estate? Alas, no. In the total conflagration which followed, very few boxes were salvaged with the papers intact. The intense heat melted the cheaper tin, I fear. My business is ruined.' His bloodshot eyes filled with tears.

'You were lucky to escape with your life,' returned George heartily. 'Surely a smart man of business like yourself will have insurance? You'll be back at your law books in no time.'

'All thanks to you, Mr Durrington.'

Askew turned to Rupert. 'The impact of the missile threw me to the floor. I was momentarily stunned. When I came to, the whole room was an inferno. I managed to crawl to the front door and drag myself into the garden where, by God's providence, Mr Durrington found me and pulled me to safety.'

'And you have no idea who could have done this thing?'

'None whatsoever,' he said putting his hand up to his blistered face.

'Mr Askew, did the surgeon by any chance give you the ball as a souvenir?'

'Indeed he did. It is on the wash stand in a little glass dish. Some may think it ghoulish but my sister wishes to net a small pouch for it so that I may hang it on my watch chain.'

Rupert got up and retrieved the ball. From the pocket of his waistcoat he took a piece of cloth and unwrapped it to reveal the pistol ball taken out of the woodwork in West's boathouse. Both missiles had the identical faint scratch on the surface. Rupert held them out to Durrington who nodded his head in agreement.

If Romero had been in London, then he could not have fired this second ball. But he may still have been involved in West's killing. Each revelation was inconclusive.

'Do not lose it, Askew,' he said returning the ball. 'This may be valuable evidence.'

The lawyer looked surprised. 'What can you mean? A pistol ball is a pistol ball; hundreds are sold every day.'

'Would you care to enlighten us now as to the contents of those papers of Mr West which were so sadly destroyed?' Rupert said casually.

'Certainly not. No power on Earth would induce me to discuss the family's affairs – of any kind.' He would not be badgered in this way.

'Askew, someone has just shot at you and ensured the destruction of the only written evidence that may provide a motive for a murder. Would you put the ethics of your profession above your own life? The perpetrator may try again.'

'Darville! What are you implying?'

'You said you were not a fool, George; you know perfectly well what I am saying. I am suggesting that one of the family may have murdered Horace West to prevent him changing his will and that whoever it was then attempted to kill Askew who had proof of the new arrangements. You thought so, yourself.' Rupert turned back to the figure cowering on the pillows. 'Why did you keep the documents? You must have known there was a risk.'

Askew swallowed. He was exhausted, in pain and frightened at the thought that his attacker may return. George's magisterial authority and Rupert's succinct deduction punctured his bravado. It would be a relief to unburden himself of this nagging anxiety.

'I do not deny that a similar thought had crossed my mind, Mr Darville, ridiculous though it sounds,' mumbled Askew as if ashamed. He plucked at the sheet with nervous fingers. 'If the coroner's verdict had been misadventure, then I would have said nothing - the circumstances are so contradictory,' he protested helplessly. 'But murder! I felt that I should retain the documents which Mr West intended to sign, as evidence, if any arrests were ever made. I have long had the habit of keeping every scrap of paper pertinent to a client's estate.'

'No wonder the place went up like a haystack,' said George. 'Then you, too, think someone in the family murdered West?'

'No, no indeed, how could I? It is absurd! Only Mrs West was in residence at the time. You are surely not suggesting that the lady cracked her husband's skull and pushed him in the river? It is not possible.'

He looked appalled. 'And, at the time, there were - other suspects with credible motives.' He avoided Rupert's penetrating gaze. 'I was merely being prudent with regard to the documents.'

'And now they are gone,' said George.

'Not entirely,' said Rupert, reaching into his coat for his pocket-book. To Askew's amazement he unfolded a piece of paper covered in jottings and lists of figures. He handed it to Askew. 'What do you make of this? It is in your late client's handwriting is it not?'

'Yes,' he breathed in alarm. 'Where did you get it?' He looked up anxiously at the two men.

'Study it. Am I correct in thinking that the column of initials refers to members of the West family, followed by sums of money? And the abbreviations underneath relate to stocks and shares and various property holdings of Mr Horace West?'

Askew nodded carefully. Rupert extracted the document from the lawyer's clutch and gave it to George. 'I found this in West's study the morning he went missing, or rather on the floor where it had fallen out of a portfolio. It struck me as rather curious.'

'You should have shown me this before, Darville,' protested George. 'E.W. one hundred pounds; F.W. one hundred pounds; L.L one hundred pounds.' George read out the figures. 'I take it this is an allowance per quarter or per year, or are they paltry one-off bequests?' He squinted at the paper again. 'B.P. must be Bourne Park, ten thousand pounds – was West intending to sell the place?'

Askew looked miserable. 'I might as well tell you as you know so much. Mr West was intent on realising all his assets in England and returning to Jamaica. The current will was to be destroyed. There was no new will because he said he did not know what his future income would be. That list you have in your hand refers to the lump sums he would give to his dependents before he left the country. I took no pleasure in drawing up the relevant documents, I assure you. But then I expected him to change his mind within the month.'

He took another mouthful of claret. 'Mrs West was to have the use of a small cottage he owned in Larkhill if she did not choose to live with her daughter. The amounts designated were single gifts to be taken from the sale of his stocks and shares. He was a warm man when it was all counted up, though not as wealthy as his son had hoped.'

'God rot the man! He was going to run out on them and leave them in penury. No wonder someone killed him.'

'But who?' asked Rupert, pleased that George had openly accepted what had been obvious to him for weeks. George was reluctant to say more. Much as he wanted Jacob to escape the charge, it was another thing entirely to accuse one of their own class.

Rupert thought for a moment. He looked at the trembling lawyer. 'You said no one in the family knew of the impending changes?'

'Not from me. Mr West may have informed them of his intentions during the holidays. And I, naturally, said nothing to that officer from Bow Street.' He shuddered at the recollection of the interview with such a sharp, common fellow.

'Nevertheless, someone guessed why you were at Bourne Park before you were sent for. The murderer knew or guessed you were the one man who knew about the documents that would rob them of everything. I think we should pursue this matter, Askew, for your own safety.'

'But West would have changed his mind! He always does, did. There was no need to murder him.' Askew gave a cry of anguish.

'Perhaps not, but they've nearly murdered you. We must put a stop to this.'

'And who knows if Darville or I are safe, or anyone who suspected what was in the wind. The killer may strike again. We should all be on the alert.'

'Quite so, Mr Durrington.' Askew was sweating freely now. 'If you will forgive me I am a little tired. This horror has been preying on my mind for many days. I will sleep with my own gun under my bolster tonight.' He swallowed the last drop of his claret and put the glass on his nightstand. He picked up a little bell and rang it furiously. 'My sister will show you out.' he said, sliding beneath the covers.

****

Darville and Durrington rode back to Durrington Hall. Once out of the blustery wind and settled with a warm negus in front of a good fire they fell to discussing Askew's revelations.

'Surely you cannot think it was one of the ladies? They have not the strength or the spirit to club a man over the head.'

'Don't be so hasty George. If we're to find the real killer, and clear Jacob of the charge, let alone me of suspicion, we must rid our minds of all preconceived ideas. As Butterworth would say "Examine all things and hold fast to that which is good". Do not expect me to provide the reference.'

George raised his eyebrows at Rupert quoting scripture. 'I refuse to believe Euphemia West killed her husband, even under the influence of that Mazzotta person.'

'That is mumbo-jumbo, I agree. But I believe she doctored her husband's sherry with laudanum, with the intention of killing him.'

'Good Lord! What makes you say that?'

'Harriet, mainly. On the Monday morning that West disappeared, I found the sherry decanter empty but unwashed. There was a stain on the snow just outside the French doors. There could be several explanations but Harriet believes that Mrs West doped the decanter with laudanum, and I agree with her. When her husband's body was not found slumped over the desk in the morning, terrified at what she had done, Mrs West slipped downstairs into the library and emptied the dregs of the mixture onto the grass.'

'So West, drugged to the gills, fell into the river, drowned and bashed his head on the bridge piers. I said so all along. That's not premeditated murder and you can prove nothing against Mrs West,' said George with relief.

'Someone wanted him to die.'

'A lot of people, I agree, but whatever did his wife want to kill him for? The man was a scoundrel but she'd put up with him for years. Of course, she might have known about the Jamaica plan and preferred being a rich widow.' He was reluctant to believe it.

'Harriet told me that West had tried to force the black girl onto Euphemia as her personal maid. No woman could tolerate that, she says.'

'You will not take this accusation any further surely?' George was worried now.

'No. I think Mrs West's part ended with the sherry decanter, and you're right, I can prove nothing.'

They discussed Euphemia's culpability for a few moments, George shaking his head and longing to get upstairs and tell Juliana. He leaned forward in his chair.

'And what about the black wench. Did she kill him?' He rather hoped she had.

'Delilah is tall enough and strong enough, I grant you but, according to her, West had locked her in her room. I think he'd got wind of something.'

'What do you mean? Do you believe her?'

'Harriet does. One of the housemaids heard Delilah banging to be let out at around midnight. Jacob was hoping to elope with Delilah that night but she never appeared. He has admitted his presence in the Park. But such a disclosure would hang him, George. We must say nothing about it.'

George sat back to digest this news. 'If the girl was thwarted in her effort to escape, might she have killed West? She had a strong enough motive.'

'I agree. West told her she was still a slave even in England and he'd be taking her back to Kingston with him. That might have been enough to make her kill him if she had the opportunity but she was locked in her room all night and, as in the case of Mrs West, none of this explains the fresh pistol ball in the boat house, the broken ice or who shot Askew.'

George looked puzzled. 'And we agree the same person must be concerned in both affairs?'

'Certainly the same gun was involved.' The sickening thought that two people may be implicated caused Rupert's heart to shudder in his ribs. He was playing a dangerous game.

'That leaves only the Learoyds who had gone back to Winchester by then, or were stranded in Sallow's Cross, and your same objections apply.' George's relief was palpable. 'Frank was with the Talbots so it cannot be him. After all, he paid for the Bow Street Runner to snoop around and put up a reward for information. We will have to put the death down to misadventure. I wonder if we can appeal the inquest.'

'And the attack on Askew?'

'It will be deuced difficult to prove whether Frank or the Archdeacon were in Salisbury on the night of the twenty-ninth of January.'

'That won't help Jacob. We must bestir ourselves; there's not much time until the Easter Assizes.'

'But you've got your lawyers onto it haven't you?'

'Harriet's cousin William McAllister is to take the case; he's a K.C. now.'

'There, Jacob is bound to get off! I'm sorry I can help you no further, Darville, but this has been a most enlightening exercise. The Salisbury constables will have to chase up Askew's attacker. At least Jacob cannot be blamed for that.' He slapped his hands on his thighs with finality. 'I'm glad the Wests are cleared of any suspicion. I knew I was right all along.'

Rupert rose and punctiliously took his leave. He realised that George would not help him implicate his neighbours but Rupert had too much to lose to let the matter rest. He had either to exonerate the American secretary completely or, if he were guilty, cover up the deed somehow. Either way he had to discover the truth. And he knew he had to catch whoever was starting to panic; a panicked man was a dangerous man. He could not risk taking the easy option of inaction any longer. George's withdrawal left Rupert solitary in his search for the killer and he knew he had delayed too long.

Chapter 19 Alibis

February was no kinder than January; the days were full of drenching rain and sharp winds. Rupert rode Bounty hard over the Downs until they were both in a sweat. The exertion helped to lift his mood and clear his mind, though the perspiration dried clammily on his skin.

As yet he was uncertain of his approach to the Archdeacon and did not want to undertake the journey to Winchester without some positive proof of Learoyd's involvement. Instead, he was in a hurry to get to Cheney Court to resolve at least one part of the puzzle. He could not escape the hope that the murderer could be Frank. He believed that bringing in the Bow Street officer had been a bluff, with disastrous results for the Darvilles. Rupert was as prejudiced as the next man and wanted to see Frank West in the dock.

Colonel Talbot, delighted but surprised at his visitor's appearance, ushered him into the morning room talking of shoots and gundogs. When he realised the purpose of Rupert's visit he immediately became serious. In some embarrassment he admitted that Frank had been absent from Cheney Court on the night of his father's death.

'I had no idea the fellow claimed he was still staying with us! We did not go to the inquest. I wanted to cut all ties with the family by then. My wife insisted we go to the funeral as a mark of respect. Frank turned up here on Boxing Day – most inconvenient; we still had a house full of people. He'd had some dust-up with his father but wouldn't say about what. Money, I expect. It's always money with these young men.'

'And when did he leave?'

'The day after the hunt, it must have been. My wife and I returned from morning service to find the place in an uproar. There was some trouble with a housemaid.' The colonel harrumphed. A scene of hysterical weeping and drunken denials had made Colonel Talbot order Frank West's immediate departure. 'I don't allow that sort of behaviour under my roof; it upsets the servants. One must keep discipline in the ranks.'

Rupert felt a surge of satisfaction. 'Where did Frank go after he left you?'

'I have no idea; we never saw him again until his father's funeral.'

'Do you know whether he had a pistol with him?'

'He most certainly did. The villain took a pot-shot at the weather vane, so my steward tells me. He missed, I'm happy to say.'

'Do you happen to know what kind of pistol it was? A duelling pistol perhaps?'

'I have not the faintest idea. He kept it well out of sight when my wife and I were around. You're not suggesting that Horace West was shot are you? I thought he drowned in the Bourne.'

Rupert persevered. 'Did you miss a pistol by any chance, at about that time?'

'Certainly not. Why do you ask? I am the only one with keys to the gun cupboard and all my firearms were there yesterday. I'd just bagged six brace of pheasant. You shoot with Halsham, don't you, in Holderness?'

'Not this year, Colonel. Would your son know where Frank went after he left Cheney Court?'

'Tommy? He may. I have sent him to my brother's in Bute; he can do no mischief there. Is this important, Darville?' Tommy had protested against his friend's expulsion but had eventually come to heel. Mr West's death and Frank's erratic behaviour had cowed him into obedience.

'What has prompted you to act now, Darville? The man has been in his grave for more than a month. You cannot pay any attention to the gossip-mongers, surely?'

'I cannot say more at the moment. There have been too many unsubstantiated rumours of late, but I think the killer has made another attack.'

'Good God!'

'If I can identify the perpetrator it will exonerate my valet.'

'Ah, yes, your servant. In the lock-up I hear. Bad business. Upset the troops has it?'

'My wife is as cheerful as ever and I am confident we can put up a good case.' They were now walking back across the flagged entrance hall.

'You're not a military man, Darville are you? Nevertheless attack is the best form of defence, mark my words.' The colonel walked Rupert to the door.

'I see myself as more of a sapper,' said Rupert with a wintry smile.

'Ah, undermine the foundations and finish with a big bang, eh?'

'Something of the sort.'

Rupert rode home cogitating. If he could discover where Frank had been on the night of the murder and place him in Salisbury on the night Askew was shot then he would be some way to proving him the killer. He would have to ride to London and confront him. Perhaps, away from Bourne Park, he would be able to get the truth out of the young libertine.

****

Harriet would not hear of Rupert riding to London. The strain on his constitution would be too severe, she protested, and the earl and his entourage were expected to return to Larkhill the following day.

'It would be the height of ill-manners to pass them on the road,' she cajoled her husband. 'If you must go to London, then take the coach, like any other civilised man, but wait until your brother has returned.'

She hoped Morna's return would provide Rupert with a sympathetic male ear. She knew that Rupert was hiding something and George Durrington was conspicuous by his absence. If her husband refused to unburden himself to her then she had hopes of his brother.

The earl returned very pleased with himself. A desirable lodging had been fixed upon in Pall Mall; Morna was to take up the lease at Easter. Kind messages from the McAllisters and the Beaumonts cheered Harriet considerably. Morna had enjoyed himself in the sophisticated metropolis, returning with novelties for the children and gifts for all.

'I warned Harriet that I should not go away. Arson and attempted murder in Salisbury! The London papers were full of it, especially after the West affair. Larkhill is quite notorious. And Jacob arrested! How do you go on without a valet? I'm sure I could not appear in public without Gaston's ministrations. The sooner Sebastian and I are safely back amid the *ton* the better.' Morna stroked the cat on his knee, which purred in bliss. 'But forgive me, I can see that it is no subject for levity.' He was not an insensitive man and he was alarmed by his brother's haggard looks.

There was indeed a tension in the house. Harriet and Sophia had arrived at an uneasy truce; Jacob was feeling confined in Hewitt's cottage and more frightened as spring moved on. Delilah was crushed with fear and her misery conveyed itself to the other servants. Harriet guessed that Young Clem was still being ragged at school and her own children were being unnaturally well-behaved. There would be eruptions soon. It was a relief to have the genial earl back on the premises even if Rupert cut Mr Romero to his face.

The following afternoon, Morna confronted Rupert alone in the library.

'Forgive me, but I feel I have to mention – and I may be quite at fault here - but I have the distinct impression that you do not care for my secretary.'

Rupert, his mind forever turning on a wheel of hideous possibilities, was startled into the truth. 'I find him a manipulative young puppy.'

'I am distressed that you should think so. I find his confidence charming. So different from the servility one comes across in one's inferiors in this country or on the Continent.'

'No man is inherently superior to any other, Morna. I disapprove of his manners and his behaviour, that is all.'

'I am well aware of Sebastian's night-time excursions, if that is what you mean, and have taken him to task on the matter, but he is barely out of adolescence and although he does duty as my secretary, he is a free spirit. I cannot continually keep him shackled to my side.'

'Then you know when he went out of this house?'

Morna looked puzzled. 'He rides out frequently during the day. I do not keep a diary of my secretary's movements.'

'But at night?' Rupert asked urgently.

'I have no idea, nor have I any idea why you should wish to know.'

'I'm trying to catch a murderer before he can strike again.'

Morna leaned back in amazement. 'And you think Sebastian is the culprit?' He gave a snort of laughter. 'I cannot think what motive you can ascribe to an innocent young man who has no connections with the West family at all. You may dislike Romero but it is ridiculous to suspect him of murder, based only on the indiscretions of youth.'

His tone changed in the face of Rupert's stony expression. 'Good God, Harriet was right. You are on some kind of witch hunt. You cannot seriously mean to accuse Sebastian? How exactly do you think my secretary is involved?' He masked his own discomfort with indignation.

'I accuse nobody, but Learoyd was besotted and Romero did nothing to discourage him, providing a ripe situation for blackmail. We've had it from his own lips that blackmail is not to be tolerated.' Rupert said harshly. He was embarrassed at being forced to speak openly of such matters.

It was now Morna's turn to bite his lip. He considered a blustering denial and then looked at his brother's face. He shrugged. 'I regret you have a point. I know there was an attraction there but, believe me, I curbed it when I could. You must be mad to think that Sebastian had anything to do with West's murder.' .

'Where was your secretary on the night of January the second? A note was sent from Bourne Park, saying what exactly? To beware danger? That they were discovered? That Horace West was about to expose them to the world? It was no woman's handwriting. Romero burnt the letter before our eyes. Did he sneak out that night and confront Horace West?' Rupert's pent-up anger came out like a fusillade.

'I will vouch for Sebastian,' said Ralph hoarsely. 'He never left my side all night.'

'If you tell me so, then I must take your word.' Rupert's face was a mask.

He turned away but curbed his bitter reaction. With an effort he regained his usual analytical tone. 'My reason for considering your secretary is that I suspect Horace West knew and disapproved of the liaison. We cannot know what threats he held over Learoyd, and thereby your secretary. Fear of exposure would provide either man with a motive for murder. We'll ascertain the whole truth if we confront them face to face. I only hope to God that I am wrong.'

'Do you expect Sebastian to tell me where he was when Horace West was killed?' asked Morna, aghast.

Rupert noticed his brother's back-tracking. 'Only you have the right to ask.'

****

In a burst of anxiety, Harriet confessed her fears for Rupert's health to Morna. She hoped the earl would persuade her husband to confide in him directly and ease his mind. But while Rupert suspected Romero, he would say nothing more until Morna had revealed something of the American's movements.

After two days, Rupert would wait no longer. He wrote a note to Bourne Park requesting an interview with Frank West. Harriet knew that Frank had been seen in Larkhill and was relieved that Rupert would not have to suffer the journey to London, but she was nevertheless apprehensive about the outcome.

"What if Frank becomes violent?' she said to Morna. 'He is such a hothead.'

'Rupert will freeze him to the floor with one of his stares.'

However, Morna dutifully offered to accompany his brother to Bourne Park but was cooly rebuffed. The earl was relieved; since their interview he preferred to leave his brother to his own devices. Morna gave his secretary leave to visit the abbey at Amesbury, advising him not to be away too long as heavy rain was forecast.

'Are you riding in my direction, sir?" Romero asked Rupert as they were saddling up in the yard.

'No.'

Rupert swung himself up onto Bounty's back. He left Romero to ingratiate himself with the stable boy and galloped out under the arch. He cantered along the Amesbury Road, eager to escape Romero and to have the distasteful interview over with.

To his chagrin, Rupert was denied entry to Bourne Park. Simpkins, looking embarrassed, explained that Mr West was indisposed and was at home to no one that day.

"Your master has engaged to see me. Take my card up to him.'

'He won't see you, sir.' Simpkins knew this for a fact. He had left his master up and about but a wreck after an excess of brandy and another dose of mercury. 'He's very poorly today, sir.'

Rupert looked astonished at such a response from a servant. 'Do what I ask,' he ordered and scribbled something on the back of his card.

Simpkins ushered Rupert into the hall and disappeared. He returned a few moments later. 'I'm sorry, sir, but Mr West regrets he is unable to keep your appointment today; ill-health confines him to his room. He requests that you have the kindness to call on him again next week.' The butler had had time to think and he did not want to antagonise the Darvilles.

'Is Mrs West at home?'

'Mrs West is in Winchester, sir, with her daughter.'

Rupert gave up and, tight-lipped, called for his horse. Suppressing his anger, he cantered back along the Amesbury road towards Larkhill. Thankfully there was no sign of Romero. On impulse, to work off his frustration, at the fork in the road he turned onto the old cart track, put his horse to a hedge and galloped across the common land towards the manor. The sky was heavy with grey cloud. A faint drizzle pitted the air. He wanted to get home before the storm broke.

Suddenly, a shot rang out, echoing from between the boles of the trees behind him. Rupert felt as though someone had punched him on the shoulder. The impact twisted him in the saddle. Bounty reared in panic but Rupert did not let go of the reins. The stinging pain in his shoulder was made worse by the need to keep the horse in check.

'Calm down, whoa there. Damn fool,' was his first thought. 'Who's shooting rooks in West's plantation?' He looked down at his shoulder but saw no dark stain, only a few pitted scorch marks on the surface of the cloth. "Missed, by God', he muttered aloud and looked about him quickly. Bounty, sensing his master's slackened grip, bolted for home.

All would have been well if Bounty had kept to the field paths but, arriving at the wooden bridge over the rivulet, she veered across taking the shortest route back to the manor. As Rupert vainly tried to pull his horse back, an ominous crack of wood threw up splintering planks and horse and rider toppled sideways into the stream.

Rupert crashed to the water. He hit his head a stunning blow on a jutting stone. He did not know for how long he lost consciousness; all was blackness until he thought he heard footsteps running towards him across the grass. With an effort he opened his eyes, saw nothing but a dark blur of a figure silhouetted against the grey sky, and groaned.

After a moment the icy stream revived him and he was able to drag himself to his knees. He thought he heard footsteps receding; he was hallucinating. He shook his head and wished he had not.

He groped his way to the bank and was dismayed to find that Bounty had continued his mad flight to the stables. Still half dazed, he slumped down onto the muddy grass trying to focus his eyes on the distant trees. He was not sure if he could see a movement there, a figure behind the broken wall. It was impossible to tell and his head ached with the effort.

In the end he gave up, aware of the chill seeping through his bones. He emptied the water out of his boots and removed his heavy greatcoat. He examined the shoulder. The singe would develop into a hole but he was lucky the pellets had not struck flesh. He ripped the hole into a larger tear and looked about him. The figure in West's plantation, if there had ever been one, had gone.

He thought for a while. He could differentiate between a pistol shot and a fowling-piece. No one knew he was coming this way. It would be best to say nothing of the event. It could all be construed as an accident, but he would send Brownrigg to examine the bridge. Meanwhile, a brisk walk home would warm him through; they would be worried at the house if Bounty arrived riderless.

By the time he had trudged over the fields and up the slope to the manor, the rain had saturated him. Jem had organised a search party. Harriet was white faced in the stable yard when Rupert appeared, sodden and abstracted. His only response to all the enquiries was that a supporting timber must have cracked in the recent frosts and it was foolish of him to have attempted to ride over the wooden bridge in the first place.

'Ask Brownrigg to see to it this afternoon, would you, Jem," he said. 'The children must not stray down there.'

Jem, touched his cap. He was not about to argue but had severe reservations about the whole episode.

"I'll send for a hot rum and butter," fussed Harriet, drawing her husband towards the house. "You must take those wet things off at once."

"My dear, there is no need. My greatcoat had a slight wetting but I am dry enough underneath. I fear I may have ripped the shoulder on a rock in the stream. I trust Jem gave Bounty a good rub down?'

"Of course. But you have a nasty bruise on your head. You must rest and get warm at once. I will not send for Dr Makepeace until I have to."

Rupert meekly allowed himself to be led away. He would not burden Harriet with the truth and needed a quiet hour or two to plan his next move. His head ached abominably.

****

Morna appeared in Rupert's room a few hours later, followed by Dunch bearing warm punch and saffron cakes.

"That's a nasty lump," Morna said when the butler had departed. "Harriet told me you'd taken a toss and had a drenching. I thought you were a *non-pareil* when it came to horses. I fear you are losing your famous control.' He had not forgiven his brother for his accusations.

'Someone took a pot-shot at me.'

Morna almost choked on his saffron cake. 'A shot! Then things have become truly serious. First the lawyer and now you! My God, what are you going to do?'

'I most particularly do not want it known. We must keep this between ourselves. Bounty bolted at the noise and I was distracted enough to let him attempt the bridge. I don't think whoever it was meant to kill me, only to wound me enough to incapacitate me and put me off my enquiries.' He had a sudden recollection of the footfall on the grass and wondered if he were being too sanguine. 'The ducking in the stream was an unexpected bonus, I suspect.'

'Could it have been Frank?'

'Possibly. He refused to see me, which was very convenient. But how he knew I would return home by the old cart track, I have no idea. I didn't know myself. That's why I think no serious harm was intended. If it was him, and who else could it have been on West's land, then it was a spur of the moment idiocy."

'Are you suggesting that he shot at you for the fun of it?'

'To scare me. On the other hand I may have scared him. I wrote on my card that I had been to see Colonel Talbot. Frank West does not like me and he is also an habitual fighting drunk.'

'Indeed he is.'

'Nevertheless, this "accident" convinces me that I have no more time to waste. I must confront my suspects, all my suspects.' Rupert looked meaningfully at his brother. 'Whoever is responsible is getting rattled and I have no intention of being the next fatality.'

Morna eventually took his leave with an air of hesitancy about him.

****

Rupert's rest was disturbed by an urgent request from Mr Brownrigg. All matters to do with the farms were usually referred to Harriet and he wondered what was afoot. He came down to the study to find his land agent and a labourer in a smock whom he vaguely recognised standing on the carpet looking agitated.

The land agent spoke up. 'Pardon me for disturbing you, sir, but this isn't truly estate business and I don't wish to trouble Mrs Darville as it rightly concerns yourself.'

'Very well, Brownrigg. And who is this?'

'Nathaniel Haycock, sir, up at Sheep's End,' replied the labourer. The man looked more than usually shabby and wrung his cap between his hands in anxiety. A faint whiff of beer came from his open mouth.

'Ah, yes. What is this about Brownrigg?'

'Go on, Nat. Tell Mr Darville what you saw. You won't get into trouble and might do yourself some good,' added the agent significantly.

'I saw 'im shoot you sir!'

'Him? Whom do you mean by "him"?' Rupert was very calm, but his mind worked furiously.

'Why, Mr Frank, sir, young Mr West. He was behind the wall in the plantation and he saw you ride by.'

'I can assure you I have not been shot at.' Rupert allowed a faint disbelief to colour his voice.

'But the 'orse bolted sir, and you fell in the stream!'

'I admit that my horse was frightened by a gunshot this morning. I daresay Mr West was shooting pigeons. It pains me to admit that the horse slipped on the bridge and brought us both down. I can promise you nothing untoward occurred. I have no idea where you have got this absurd idea. What were you doing in the vicinity? Not trespassing I hope?'

Haycock looked bewildered. 'I saw 'im, sir. He raised 'is gun and aimed at you as you rode past!'

'I do not for one moment believe it; I would not wonder if the rain confused you,' said Rupert. 'You are mistaken, but I thank you for your concern. I would be even more grateful if you did not mention this incident to anyone. A man does not like to own up to such a foolish tumble.' He gave one of his rare smiles. 'How come you were such a timely witness?'

'What were you doing there?' translated Brownrigg. Rupert's denial did not ring true but Haycock could have been drunk, a frequent state of affairs these days.

'I'd gone over to Netheravon to see the childer. I come 'ome over the Downs. I told the missus and she sent me straight to Mr Brownrigg. After what your lady done for the wife, an' for not tellin' on us like about the thrasher, Dorcas said we 'ad a duty to come and tell you. Though I don't 'old with getting involved with the gentry,' he said sullenly. He was annoyed that his story had been dismissed and that he'd had a cold, tiring and unprofitable day, lengthened by this fruitless walk to the manor.

'Thank your wife, but I think you may be in the right, Haycock; it's best not to jump to conclusions. Mr West would not like to hear of you spreading such tales.'

'No, no, sir. I won't say nothin', sir.' The man suddenly felt alarmed and sought to justify himself. 'I did run over and see if you was still livin', but when I saw you was, I thought I'd best be on my way. 'Twas only Dorcas what made me come.'

By now Rupert had shaken a few coins from a leather pouch in his desk and pressed them into Haycock's calloused hand.

'Then we'll keep this between ourselves. Thank you Brownrigg. That will be all.'

****

The earl was in his shirt-sleeves, nervously fingering the watch chain in his satin waistcoat. Sebastian lay on the chaise longue at the foot of the earl's tester bed. He was in his stocking feet, blowing smoke rings to the ornate ceiling, knowing full well that no one would chide the earl for the scent of tobacco smoke in his bedroom. The smoke drifted up to the heavy yellow silk hangings.

'I wish you wouldn't do that, Sebastian,' said the earl testily. He picked up and put down a heavy cologne bottle.

'Why not?'

'Our hostess does not approve.'

Sebastian smiled lazily and took another puff. 'Mrs Darville would forgive me anything, I'm sure. And you won't tell.'

After a few moments of hesitation, the earl plucked up courage. 'I hope you are not still indulging in your nocturnal activities. Apart from being foolish and ungentlemanly, you must realise that you put yourself in jeopardy.'

'Of what and from whom?' replied Sebastian languidly blowing another smoke ring.

'Of becoming the victim of scandalous rumour and from the roaming mobs, especially at night. Darville also thinks West's murderer is still at large and may strike again.'

'Did the professor split on me? What a bad sport he is. Is he afraid I'll seduce his precious ward?'

'No, he did not "split" on you as you put it, and I will not have you speak in that way about members of my family. Remember your position!'

Sebastian's smiled faded but he continued to smoke.

Ralph did not look at Sebastian directly but rearranged the silver-backed combs and brushes on the dressing table. After a moment he continued.

'My brother says that while we were in Town he heard unsavoury talk about your friendship with Dr Learoyd,' he prevaricated. 'I warned you against becoming too involved with the man. Country people are not sophisticated or tolerant, but neither are they blind nor stupid.'

'Mrs Darville and her friends don't seem to mind, even if Mr Darville disapproves. You once told me that sodomy was known as the "English vice". Why should the yokels concern themselves with my affairs?' said Sebastian with a slight laugh, allowing ash to fall on the Aubusson carpet.

'Dear boy, you know how much I dislike such coarse remarks. I assure you the rustics will roger anything, even sheep, as long as it's an English sheep. But you are an American, a foreigner and the English hate foreigners on principle. Twenty years ago you would have been shot as the enemy. They will blame you for everything: starvation wages, bad harvests, dead cattle, even West's murder.'

'I thought I was supposedly in danger of being the next victim. Now suddenly I am the killer? This is all crazy!'

'My brother fears your indiscretions have brought you under suspicion as having a strong motive to silence Horace West and, as none of the family were anywhere near Bourne Park that night, the gossips are short of someone to blame.'

Sebastian swung his legs to the floor and threw away his cigarette. 'But Darville's valet is charged. How can I be implicated?' He sounded put out.

'I can and will swear to you being in London on the evening of the twenty-ninth of January, the night West's lawyer was shot. Goodness knows there are enough witnesses to confirm that you were flirting with that fat fop Stephen Everard at Lazlo's. But people here are asking where you were on the night West was killed.' He did not clarify that only Rupert had voiced his suspicions. 'Things could turn nasty for you if Jacob is proved innocent.'

Sebastian's beautiful mouth opened. He went up behind Ralph and put his hands on the earl's shoulders.

'You know I was with you on the night Horace West died,' he said softly into Morna's ear.

Ralph turned to face his lover. 'Even if I were clear in my mind about dates, it is a fact I would not confirm publicly,' he replied levelly.

Sebastian took a step backwards, scanning the earl's face. It was as implacable as his brother's. With a shock, Sebastian realised that Ralph would abandon him to save his own reputation. For once his confident, selfish heart misgave him.

He swallowed and said: 'You may not choose to believe me, my lord, but I have witnesses who can prove I was under this roof at midnight on the second of January.'

'My boy! That's wonderful! Not for one instant did I think you were involved in this ghastly business. I knew Rupert was fussing over nothing.' Morna held out his arms.

But Sebastian was shrugging on his coat and searching for his shoes. 'You will excuse me my lord, but I must speak to Mrs Darville at once.'

****

'My dear, I have just heard!' Harriet flew into her husband's bedroom like a whirlwind. 'Mr Romero has come to me in great distress at the idea of being implicated in Horace West's murder. Though I, for one, have heard of no such rumours. I admit that the thought had crossed my mind, I dismissed it at once, naturally. Did you think -? But you said nothing!'

'Dear heart, calm yourself,' said Rupert, taking her by the waist.

Harriet put her hands to her husband's lapels and looked up at him. 'He said you suspected him of being the murderer. Why did you not tell me? We should have no secrets from each other; look what misunderstandings it brings. I had no notion that the poor boy was part of your investigations or I would have spoken immediately. I know exactly where Mr Romero was on the night of Mr West's death.'

Rupert felt momentarily light-headed with relief but only took his wife's hands in his and kissed them.

It appeared that on the Sunday night that Horace West went missing, Sophia and Rosa had made another bid for freedom. When the long-case clock struck midnight, the girls had left an intoxicated Mrs O'Leary on her truckle bed and had crept from the blue bedroom clutching bundles of clothes and their small hoard of money.

To their mixed fear and relief they had seen Mr Romero wandering the corridor in his Japanese silk kimono. He had halted with his hand on the earl's door when he saw the children. Whispered words had been exchanged between the wanderers before the young man had escorted the girls back to the blue room. Rosa had been a reluctant adventurer from the start and only Sophia needed persuasion to abandon her plans. Romero extracted promises of good behaviour and made many of his own in return. He had mentioned the incident to Harriet in circumspect terms and she had not wished to antagonise her husband with another account of a domestic rebellion.

'I have spoken to Sophia and Rosa myself, alone, without Mr Romero or your brother being present. Sophia admitted they tried to run away again, definitely on the night that Mr West died. They said that they had met Mr Romero in the corridor at around midnight. I suspect the Rector's sermon that morning had been too much for them and they were more than homesick after the New Year hunt.'

'Do you believe their story?' Rupert was still holding her hands.

'Of course, the girls would have no reason to lie and Mr Romero spoke to me about it in the most guarded terms not long afterwards. He begged only that I would not betray his confidence to the children. But of course he gave permission for me to do so after Morna had informed him of your suspicions. He bitterly regrets his evenings at the Three Crowns and Hugget's and realises now how his actions have brought him into disrepute. The silly boy, he is too embarrassed to face you and he begs to have his dinner in his room tonight.'

Rupert saw that Romero had charmed his wife into forgiveness but he felt no remorse for his distrust of the young American. He blamed the youth for his irresponsible behaviour and the unhappiness it had brought. But they were not out of the woods yet.

'I was very discreet with the children,' continued Harriet, 'and said only that their escapade had come to my notice. I would not have them dislike Mr Romero for doing his duty.'

'But by Twelfth Night Sophia was begging to stay with us. I do not understand.'

'Bribery. Mr Romero promised that we would buy them each a pony and take them to London for a visit.' She smiled up at him. 'That's not so very much, surely, for domestic harmony? You know you were going to teach Henry to ride properly this summer.'

'Damned impertinence!' But Rupert was too relieved to take serious offence at his wife's explanation. He let the welcome news filter through his tired brain. 'That means,' he said, 'if Morna can also vouch for Romero being in London on the night Askew was shot then I am free to pursue the real murderer.'

Harriet groaned inwardly.

****

The following morning, in a rare attempt at mending fences, Rupert took Morna into his confidence and gave an exhaustive account of his deductions and conclusions. 'I have been working to find the real killer. But I have proof of nothing as yet, or certainly not enough on which to issue a warrant.' He would not mention Romero again.

The earl looked somewhat stunned and stroked the tabby on his knee thoughtfully. 'What suspects do you have left, now you have exonerated dear Sebastian?' Morna may be his usual affable self but he was masking a serious quarrel with his secretary.

'The West family. I believe they all stood to lose a great deal if Horace West continued to live. He was about to desert them and return to Jamaica after selling up.'

'You had better be sure of your facts, Rupert. This could blow up into another nasty scandal. I regret to have to tell you, in some quarters *your* name was linked to the murder. The idea is ridiculous of course, and only just this side of slander. For a scholar you have a fearsome reputation.'

Rupert grimaced. 'I read the newspapers; they can produce nothing but speculation. I have no taste for the bones of the business but Jacob is unjustly accused and the Darville name has been besmirched. I have to bring the felon to book.'

'How chivalrous; you sound quite medieval,' said the earl faintly, his mind working. 'I suppose I should help you all I can. Do you think either Frank himself or the Archdeacon is the killer?'

'You are as direct as Harriet. I have no idea where Frank was when his father was killed nor on the night that Askew was shot. I would ask him to his face but I have no faith in his answers, and he refuses to see me. I only know that the Talbots had shown Frank the door on the Sunday afternoon of the night West died and that Frank was not in Bourne Park last Saturday when Askew was attacked.'

'No, he was not!' said the earl unceremoniously pushing the cat from his knee. 'Frank was in Town. Sebastian and I saw him at Lazlo's dipping fairly deep, I must say. He was working his way through his father's fortune with abandon. I didn't think he was such a flat.'

'He was lucky to have anything to gamble with. But are you sure? On Saturday the twenty-ninth?'

'Undoubtedly. At about ten o'clock. He cut us both most publicly,' Morna said in amusement.

Another load fell from Rupert's shoulders. His brother had just provided Romero with an unimpeachable alibi for the attack on the lawyer. He now mentally dismissed the American.

'Then Frank could not have shot at Askew. But that does not exonerate him of his father's murder. We have no knowledge of his whereabouts on the night of the second of January.'

Just then Bernard came quietly into the room. 'I beg your pardon, sir, for disturbing you. My lord. I need the big atlas for the children's lesson.' He approached the bookcase. 'We are studying the Thirty Years War with special reference to the Peace of Westphalia.'

'How erudite and respectable your children will be,' murmured Morna. 'Unlike that reprobate who now looks to be our number one suspect, if he cannot prove where he was on the night his father died.'

Rupert frowned at his brother's casual and audible indiscretion.

Bernard hesitated with his hand to the shelf and then slowly turned to face the two men. 'I beg your pardon, if you are referring to Frank West, my lord, he was with me.'

'With *you*!' Both men stared at the secretary.

'Yes, if you are alluding to the night of his father's demise.'

'Why have you said nothing of this before?' said Rupert.

'I was not asked,' replied the secretary stiffly. Rupert's reprimand in front of Inspector Cuttle still rankled. 'I thought the incident of no moment and it is not my place to spread tittle-tattle.'

'Explain yourself, Bernard,' ordered Rupert.

The young man calmly placed the atlas on the desk in front of him. 'With pleasure; there is no mystery attached to the matter. My father had been called out to attend Mr Sillitoe. The old gentleman wasn't expected to last the night. Indeed, he died of dropsy in the early hours. I would not allow my father to drive about the country unattended after dark, times being so very uncertain, so I offered to drive the dog cart.'

'But how come Frank West was with you?'

Bernard would not be hurried. 'On our return we came across Mr West on the edge of town, standing by his horse; he seemed somewhat - er - the worse for drink. Because he was so vehemently opposed to returning to Bourne Park or Cheney Court I suggested taking him back to the Three Crowns. I had the impression that Colonel Talbot had asked him to leave. My father insisted that, as a Good Samaritan, and in order to remove Mr West from further alcoholic temptation, we provide him with a bed at the rectory.' He looked between the two men. 'Which we did and he was sick as a dog all night.'

Morna and Rupert looked amazed. 'You have just given Frank West a cast-iron alibi for the murder of his father.' said the earl.

'I am truly sorry, my lord.'

'Thank you, Bernard. Your account has eliminated at least one problem,' said Rupert.

'I am glad to have been of service, sir. As I said, I had no idea Mr Frank West's whereabouts were pertinent to his father's death or I would have spoken earlier. I did not want to add further disgrace to an already unhappy event. Will that be all, sir? The children are waiting and the young ladies grow a trifle restless if I am away from the schoolroom for long.'

'Yes, of course. Wait! What time would you say you met West on the road?'

Bernard thought. 'We left the Sillitoe's house at midnight. I heard the church clock chime. The old gentleman had slipped into insensibility by then and there was no point in keeping my father from his bed. I would say that we came upon Frank when the clock chimed the quarter. He was really in no fit state to do anything, sir.'

'And when did Frank leave the rectory?'

'About nine o'clock on Monday morning. I put him on the coach to Andover myself. He intended to return to London.' Breakfast at the rectory had been most embarrassing.

Rupert dismissed him. Bernard picked up the big atlas, bowed and left.

'What an invaluable young man. He may not be in the first mode of fashion but he is indispensable nonetheless,' said the earl lightly. 'Would that I could depend on my own secretary-' He broke off.

'This means we can cross Frank West off the list of suspects,' said Rupert his face tightening. He did not like the way his investigations were leading him. Only the Archdeacon remained and the Learoyds should have been miles away snug at home in Winchester. Even if Harriet was correct, and they had stayed overnight at Sallow's Cross, neither of the Learoyds could have returned to Bourne Park in time to murder Horace West.

'You do not sound happy, Rupert. Could young West have killed his father and then drowned his guilt in the bar of the Three Crowns before your secretary found him?' asked the earl in a tone of mild enquiry.

'I doubt it. Whatever happened to Horace West happened around midnight. Jacob heard the clocks chime and his encounter with the dog would probably mask the noise of any other disturbance. Particularly as the Wests' servants seem adept at turning a deaf ear.'

Rupert cogitated for a moment. 'If Frank was carousing or drowning his sorrows in the Three Crowns beforehand, then someone will have seen him. I'll have a word with Drinkwater, the landlord, before we go any further.'

Drinkwater confirmed Frank's presence in the Three Crowns until around midnight on the night of the murder. The young man's alibis were water-tight. But Rupert still delayed visiting the Archdeacon.

He wanted some kind of evidence before he confronted the venerable clergyman; he realised he was still on uncertain ground and could not quite believe where his investigations were leading.

The next day, Rupert rode over to Sallow's Cross and ascertained that the Learoyds had stayed at the inn on the night Horace West died. Harriet had been correct in her assumption. Their carriage had broken a main spring and the Learoyds had been forced to walk the vehicle to the nearest blacksmith's in a small village two miles north off the main Andover Road. Unfortunately, at that hour the forge was closed. The landlord said they had arrived at his door at about nine o'clock in the evening. His wife had found them a bit of supper and they had retired after ten, the lady in an exhausted state.

Despite its name, Sallow's Cross Inn was little more than a tavern. Its popularity depended on the clutch of rowing boats used by courting couples in the summer and the eel traps in the winter. It did not boast extensive stables nor more than three bedrooms. There was no possibility that anyone had taken a horse out that night; the one stable boy slept in the hay loft of the barn where the Learoyd's horses had been sheltered.

On a good day, with a halt at the toll gate, the canter from Bourne Park took Rupert, an expert horseman on a thoroughbred mount, at least two hours. He did not see how a rider could do it in the dark in less than three, and besides, the toll gate keeper had made no record of a lone horseman passing the gate late that night.

A half-sovereign changed hands; Rupert inspected the keeper's tally book. Nothing had been registered after a farm cart passed through at five o'clock in the evening. But the keeper may have been bribed to silence, or just pocketed the fourpence and not entered the horseman in the book.

Rupert still had nothing definite to go on regarding Archdeacon Learoyd.

Chapter 20 Explanations

Clem's fifteenth birthday at the end of February was a subdued affair. His friend Carstairs came for Sunday but Clem invited no one else, despite his erstwhile popularity. Harriet felt helpless to protect her nephew at this vulnerable, awkward stage of his life. However, the younger children took great delight in Mr Romero's company; the young man wisely did not stray far from the manor and spent much of his time in the nursery teaching the girls rudimentary Italian. Rupert continued to lose weight; his cheek bones stood out under the hollows of his eyes.

April would bring the Easter sittings of the Assizes to Salisbury. Someone from the manor went to visit Jacob every day; even the children were taken in Delilah's care. Apart from anxiety, Jacob did not suffer greatly and his leg was healing well, if a little crookedly. Nevertheless, the spring days were moving faster and Rupert was no nearer finding evidence to implicate Archdeacon Learoyd. Harriet, now fully reconciled with Rupert after the interview with Sophia and Rosa, was, as always, stoutly optimistic.

A short visit from William McAllister K.C., brought everyone hope. His sharp, intelligent face below thinning sandy hair gave him the air of a fox. He had that indefinable London polish. He and Morna had hit it off instantly in London, recognising in each other a certain indolence and love of the dramatic at a distance. Romero sulked a little at not being the centre of the earl's attention and resumed his solo rides on Harriet's horse. Whenever he came home from school, Clem now only had time for Jacob. The date of the Assize court sittings drew closer.

'What do you think of Romero, eh?' said William, ever alert for a juicy titbit of scandal.

'He's nothing but a pretty face,' said Rupert. Wild horses would not make him say more.

'Yes, but what a face! He caused quite a stir at Lazlo's, I heard. And Morna made himself very agreeable everywhere. You've gained some notoriety yourself if Grubb street is to be believed.'

He and Rupert were sipping brandy and soda in the library at the manor, supposedly discussing the probable outcome of Jacob's case. Rupert brought the conversation back to the known facts, or lack of them.

'My dear man,' said William, after hearing the account of Jacob's forays into Bourne Park. 'The prosecution do not have a leg to stand on! It is all supposition on their part.

We will deny that your man was anywhere near Bourne Park when West disappeared; they can prove nothing to the contrary. It's all circumstantial evidence. In my opinion, someone was too hasty to point the finger. With my unassailable defence and you as a character witness the case against your man will fall. I have no doubts on the matter.'

'And who will the newspapers blame after that, I wonder?'

William steepled his fingers on his waistcoat in a gesture reminiscent of his father. 'Put that right out of your mind. This nonsense will all blow over by the summer. The new Attorney General will look a fool if he pursues this. Would you like me to have a word in high places? If I can't get the charge withdrawn, to save the government humiliation, I can at least discover who will be the circuit judge.'

'Have as many words as you like as long as Jacob gets off. I have my hands full trying to find the real killer.'

'More deeds of derring-do?' asked William from under arched eyebrows. 'I thought you would be too old and respectable for any more heroics. You don't exactly look in the pink, now.' He was not a physically adventurous man despite his love of sensation and he thought Rupert looked as taut as a bow-string. 'We want no repeat of that dreadful business with Harriet. You and Andrew rowed to some godforsaken place-'

Rupert sat bolt upright. 'Wait! God Almighty! What a fool I am! You're right, I must be in my dotage. I think you may have hit upon it, William.' He leapt out of his chair and went to Sir John's old desk. After a rummage around he tossed out two or three scrolls of parchment. 'I was too concerned with trying to exonerate certain people.' He turned to the shelves behind him and, running his fingers along various spines, hooked out the County Atlas of Hampshire.

'I must have been blind not to see it! I should have concentrated on the geography before the human element. Hard facts will never let one down. Come over here and tell me if you think this is possible.'

William obliged. Rupert unrolled the hand-drawn maps of the local area and then found a particular page in the atlas.

'Here, this is the town of Larkhill. This is the manor, here is Quennell House and down here by the river is Bourne Park.' He then turned the atlas towards William. 'Here is Winchester,' he said pointing further south on the page. If I marry these two maps together, one sees the complete topography, even though they are of different counties. They're not to the same scale but they're good enough to give credence to my idea.'

'Which is?' asked William, already guessing the gist of the answer.

'Learoyd has always said that he and his wife left Bourne Park on Sunday morning, whereas Harriet has discovered-'

'Harriet? Surely you have not involved her in all this?'

'I have never been able to keep Harriet out of anything. She has discovered,' Rupert continued, 'that on Sunday the second of January the Learoyds did not set out until after dinner; sometime after five o'clock in fact, and were forced to make a diversion along this minor road and break their journey at Sallow's Cross, here.' Rupert indicated a hamlet two miles north off the main Andover road on a straggling off-shoot of the Bourne.

'According to the landlord, there was some trouble with their coach and it was too dark to continue to Winchester. The blacksmith's forge at Sallow's Cross was shut so the Learoyds were forced to put up at the inn, twelve miles away by road from Bourne Park.'

'Are you suggesting that Learoyd rode twelve miles back to the Park, gained admittance to the house without being seen, struck his father-in-law over the head and threw his body in the river?' William enjoyed playing devil's advocate.

'He didn't ride, he would have been spotted at the turnpike, and he wasn't. It's impossible to ride cross-country in the dark and would take twice as long. I don't think he reached the house at all.'

'Explain yourself, sir!' said William, grinning.

'Learoyd *rowed* back to Bourne Park. Look here, by river the journey is barely two miles. A determined man could cover the distance in an hour.'

'And there you have it, m'lud. Opportunity and with money as the motive, I submit that the Archdeacon is guilty and should be hanged by the neck until dead!' He slapped Rupert on the back. 'Well done, dear fellow. If you can collect corroborating evidence at this, this Sallow's Inn? What an unusual name.'

'It's old English for "willow"' said Rupert, only now remembering the early bud he had idly taken from West's hair.

'And if you can place the Archdeacon in Salisbury when your lawyer friend was shot then we've got him!'

'It's him, of course it's him; there is no one left who it could be. Proof of opportunity for his father-in-law's murder may be enough to confound him. I knew something had gone on in the boat house but I couldn't understand why West's boat had been taken out that night. It hadn't, of course; another craft had been pulled into the boathouse; the ice had been disturbed and had not had time to refreeze.'

'Don't go all scientific, old fellow; it's wasted on me. I think we should go through the whole sequence again to see if this clergyman's river journey really was possible. Does he row?'

'I have no idea. But it's not that difficult for a desperate man. Learoyd may be short in the leg but he has powerful arms. I've seen him master a panicked horse. He must have been mad but God knows he had more than one motive for murder.'

'I thought being cut off from a tidy sum would be enough. You said his wife stood to inherit several thousand as long as her father didn't abandon the family. I've known people kill for far less. But how can you accuse the man without evidence? Your ice has melted.'

'I'm not sure,' said Rupert, following his own train of thought. At last everything seemed to slot into place. The mists cleared from his brain. 'He either enticed West out into the garden, or he found his father-in-law wandering by the boat house. There must have been a quarrel and Learoyd hit West on the back of the head. I suspect he may have tried to shoot him first and then, missing his aim, he used an oar to crack West's skull like an egg.'

William looked sombre. 'A shooting? And nobody heard? I find that hard to believe. Must you complicate matters?'

'I like to be thorough. I can only imagine that the sound of the dog barking when it attacked Jacob and the chime of the church clock masked the sound of the shot in the boat house. Durrington and I found a fresh pistol ball in the woodwork. I'll lay odds Learoyd possesses a gun which fires a scratched ball.'

'Well, I'm sure you have reasons for all your assumptions, which I pray you will spare me, but what about the incendiarist attack on the lawyer? Considering the crime attracts the death penalty, I can't see a clergyman risking it. Learoyd could have been respectably asleep in Winchester.'

'He could, but he had every opportunity to be in Salisbury. Butterworth, our local rector, told me he'd seen him several times in the cathedral close on his way to meetings. Learoyd had been attached to the Salisbury diocese for the past three months. We can always confirm the dates.' Rupert recalled the Rector's protestations of obligation among the stumbling hints of scandal.

'And if everything fits, what do you intend to do about it?'

'When I have worked out the timings as accurately as possible I will confront Learoyd and hope to God he confesses.'

'A rather risky proposition, I would have thought. But go to it, my dear man. Ride over to Winchester or wherever he preaches, challenge the reverend gentleman and see what comes of it. You need not fear benefit of clergy these days.'

Rupert gave a slight smile. 'I prefer to tackle him on my own ground.'

****

William returned to London promising to do what he could to have Jacob's arrest warrant withdrawn. He would not stay for the denouement claiming that, as a respected King's Counsel involved in the case, he had to remain in the background. Rupert's hopes were not high. Frustratingly, the Reverend Butterworth had not been in Salisbury on the day of the attack on lawyer Askew and could give his patron no pertinent information about Dr Learoyd's movements.

The morning after McAllister's departure, Rupert asked his brother for help. 'I do not wish Harriet to know of this, but I intend to confront Dr Learoyd with my conclusions.'

'Are you not being rather foolhardy? You cannot know how he will react. Or Harriet, for that matter.'

'There is no help for it. I will be safe on my own property and Durrington and you will be there as witnesses.'

'We will?' responded Morna in alarm.

'Yes, and Romero too.'

'Sebastian! Why Sebastian?'

'That young man is one of the underlying causes of all this misery.' Romero may be innocent of murder but Rupert wanted to make the youth pay for all his deceit. Goodness knows where he was at this very moment.

'Will you invite Learoyd here?'

'I have no intention of bringing the man here. Not to the manor, nor to Quennell House; I want no taint of this near my family. Romero shall invite him to an assignation in Athena's Temple.'

'You cannot mean - he'll never do it.' To his credit Morna did not completely condemn the idea.

'He has in the past, I'll swear to that. He should count himself lucky the trap is not being set for him. Romero will cooperate if you ask him and – show him the error of his ways.'

Morna looked very uneasy. 'Who's to say if Learoyd will come? He will be committed to his duties in Winchester, surely?'

'Harriet tells me he has been seen in Larkhill again. I assume he is here on estate business for Mrs West.'

'That does not mean he will have a secret meeting with my secretary. I do not know if they are still in communication. I cannot face another painful interview - such unjust accusations-'

'Come, Ralph, you know he and Learoyd met in the temple when the children were there and I have reason to believe that that was not the only occasion.' The diamond shirt stud lay in his waistcoat pocket. He would produce it only if necessary. 'You cannot be wilfully blind.'

Morna was silent. His own suspicions were justified. Certain unaccountable absences could now be explained. He felt his heart shrivel. 'If I do what you ask, I may lose someone I hold very dear,' he said quietly. 'Sebastian will leave me as soon as we get to London.'

'Learoyd killed his father-in-law, he will let Jacob hang and he tried to kill Askew who knew too much. Learoyd might also assume that Durrington and I know what the lawyer knew. I told you, I do not intend to be the next corpse – at whoever's hand.'

There was a moment's pause while Morna stared into the coals. 'Very well, but you must let me handle Sebastian in my own way. I shall insist that he break things off with Learoyd at one last meeting, if he hasn't done so already.'

'As you wish. Though the knowledge that he's been dallying with a killer might bring him to his senses.'

'You cannot ask Sebastian to be present; it would be too cruel.'

'On the contrary, I am only astonished at my own forbearance.'

And then seeing his brother's distraught expression, Rupert shrugged, sick and tired of the whole affair and willing for once to compromise if he achieved what he wanted. He had not expected Ralph to be so shaken.

'It may not be strictly necessary for Romero to be present but I wish to see the letter before it is sent.'

'That is understood. What will you do if Learoyd denies his guilt?' The earl privately had no doubt that the Archdeacon would come when summoned.

'I think we have enough to draw up an arrest warrant. I am to see George Durrington this afternoon. Whatever Learoyd says, he will have to languish some time in Salisbury jail before being tried for his life; I'm not sure which experience is the worst.'

'The whole business is a catastrophe, Rupert; I have no wish to be part of it.' The earl's easy-going nature shrank from such a sordid matter.

'No more do I. But you are my brother. Would you oblige me in this? My family has been troubled and I cannot allow that to go unpunished.'

The two men looked at each other.

'Very well, I will do what you ask.'

Rupert did not enquire what inducements Morna used to get Sebastian to write the invitation to Dr Learoyd who was again staying at Bourne Park. It was a simple note, innocuous at first glance, as between two gentlemen with architectural interests. Rupert was shown no reply but Morna assured him that the Archdeacon would come. Sebastian did not appear at dinner that night and the following day Morna sent his secretary back to London on some trivial excuse.

'Can we trust him not to forewarn Learoyd?' asked Rupert.

'I think so. He says he cares little for the man and he knows he would have nothing to gain by siding with a murderer. I have promised him a curricle of his own when we are in Town.'

George Durrington was more difficult to persuade. Every instinct revolted against charging a senior member of the clergy with a capital offence. He could not refute Rupert's reasoning but said: 'I cannot legally draw up an arrest warrant for West's murder when Jacob is already charged with the same crime!'

'Then draw up a warrant for arson and Askew's attempted murder.' Rupert was losing patience.

'But you've got not a shred of evidence on that score!'

'He's not to know that. There is still the possibility that someone will place him in Salisbury on the day Askew was shot. I need to call his bluff. I need to threaten him with the law, present what we do know against him and hope we scare him into a full confession.'

'And if you do? Have you considered what the outcome will be? Larkhill will be in turmoil again and none of your neighbours will thank you for bringing one of their own to book. The Church will be against you. God knows what the bishop will say! You will be ostracised. The Wests will have to emigrate.' George looked seriously disturbed.

'I know; somewhat ironic, I feel,' said Rupert with regret. 'Listen, George, I'm well aware of all the damage this may cause. Things may not be as bad as you fear. I have an alternative plan. My primary aim is to have Jacob released and hint at a miscarriage of justice. You mentioned yourself that we might appeal the inquest. If that means the Archdeacon will escape legal punishment then I'm willing to accept that. But I would need your support.'

It was George's turn to start pacing. 'I've sworn on oath to uphold the law; I don't take these things lightly, Darville. I did what I could for you at the inquest but you cannot embroil me further.'

'If we can end this business with the minimum of fuss then the better it is for us all. I am not asking you to break the law, just draw up an arrest warrant. You may safely leave the rest to me.'

'I don't know what scheme you've got in your head but I don't want my jurisdiction to be talked about either in the coffee houses or in Parliament. If this got out we're all finished and we will most likely end in the brig ourselves.'

'I promise that what I have in mind will be known only by you and me, Morna and Bernard Butterworth.'

'Butterworth? Your secretary?'

'Yes, but I am assured he is not a bit like Mr Romero,' said Rupert with a rare glint of humour.

'But what if Learoyd doesn't confess? If he is innocent he will sue us all for slander. We would be ruined in the county, and your reputation in London would be finished. The Anglican Church has a way of taking care of its own.'

'I am well aware of that. If you really feel you cannot lend yourself to this entrapment then I understand and we'll say no more about it.'

'But you would go ahead without me?' George stopped pacing.

'Without a doubt.'

'Phoney warrant and all?'

'Possibly.'

George squared his shoulders. 'I can't have you putting yourself in breach of the law, Darville. I think it best you tell me exactly what you intend to do.'

It took a full hour before Rupert, detailing his plan and all the possible ramifications, was able to persuade George to draw up an arrest warrant and agree to accompany him and Morna to the assignation in Athena's Temple.

Chapter 21   Denouement

'Quiet, I heard the sound of a horse. Take your places.' Rupert laid his pistol carefully on the wooden table within reach of his hand. Durrington went to stand behind the half-open door of the temple. The earl took the wing chair, just out of sight. Bernard sat quietly at the end of the table, pen, ink and paper before him. The sound of footsteps on the grass made them all stiffen. The warped door scraped open over the flags and the short figure of the Archdeacon stood silhouetted in the doorway.

'Gracious, Mr Darville! I had not expected – forgive me – you must wonder why I am here.'

'Not at all. Won't you come in?' said Rupert smooth as a cat.

Learoyd edged round the door and stopped. The Earl of Morna rose with all his elegant style. 'Good afternoon, Dr Learoyd. No, do not go. I regret my secretary is unable to keep his appointment with you. Urgent business of mine calls him to London.'

Durrington slammed the door behind the Archdeacon and leaned his shoulders against it.

'Gentlemen, what does this mean?' Learoyd looked around in innocent bewilderment. 'I come here in good faith to discuss the temples of Apollo with an architect friend, to find I am made captive by my neighbours.' he gave a nervous laugh.

'Won't you take a seat?' Rupert indicated the low sofa. The Archdeacon sat awkwardly, one hand straying to the cross on his breast, the other clutching his shovel hat.

'I have important business with the bishop in Salisbury. I am visiting my brother-in-law in Bourne Park; he will be anxious if I do not return in an hour.'

'Our talk will not take so long. Provided you supply us with a truthful account of your actions on the night Horace West was killed and when lawyer Askew was shot.'

Learoyd visibly blenched. 'Really! I must protest! This is absurd. I know nothing of either matter. How dare you trample on my most sacred sorrows-'

'There is no point, Archdeacon. We know of your father-in-law's intentions to sell up and quit the country, leaving the family destitute. Askew managed to salvage the relevant papers, despite your efforts to burn his house down. We have all the proof we need.'

George did not move a muscle at the lie. He was under orders and knew how to obey them.

'And on this flimsy pretext you judge me a murderer? Forgive me, gentlemen, but I have no intention of lending myself to this cruel farce.' Learoyd rose and made for the door.

'Sit down,' Rupert said sharply. 'We know how you carried out the murder. You took a boat from the Sallow's Cross Inn and rowed back along the river to Bourne Park. You killed West, put his body in the boat, rowed as far as you could downstream to Larkhill and dumped his body in the water by the packhorse bridge. Then you rowed back to the inn. Do you deny it?'

'Of course I deny it! I know nothing of what you mean. It is outrageous that I, a man of the cloth, should suffer such an insult at the hands of those I thought my friends.' Learoyd was throaty with indignation. 'You shall hear from my lawyers, sir.'

A flicker of unease crossed the earl's face but Rupert was unmoved.

'Do you admit that Horace West died at your hands?'

'I admit no such thing,' said Learoyd baring his teeth. 'I insist you let me go at once!'

Rupert gave the nod to George. 'I have an arrest warrant with your name on,' said Durrington brusquely, coming forward and unfolding the paper.

'What foolery is this? Let me see the charge; it is nothing but a malicious hoax.' Learoyd moved his hand from his pectoral cross and slid it inside his coat. 'My spectacles.' He took them out and put the wire loops over his ears with a shaking hand. "Forasmuch as-". He read his own name and the words, "attempted murder", "arson", and saw the heavy red seal beneath. The rest of the copper-plate script was a blur. He handed the paper back to George, removed his spectacles and slowly inserted them into his inside pocket.

The next moment there was a pistol in his hand. He fired at Morna. The earl slammed back into the wing chair which fell backwards onto the slabs. George leapt for Learoyd's gun and wrenched it out of his grasp, pushing the smaller man to the floor. The noise of the report boomed around the stone room making Bernard jump. Rupert snatched up his own pistol and aimed it steadily at the Archdeacon.

'Make another move and I'll put a ball through you. And I don't miss my aim. I'm considered to be a violent man. Are you hurt, Ralph?' he asked urgently, never taking his eyes off the clergyman.

'No, no,' came the winded reply. 'He missed. The ball hit the chair. My apologies to your wife; you will not inherit the title today.'

The earl staggered to his feet and righted the wing chair. The back rim was shredded. The ball had reduced the frame to a few splinters and had embedded itself in the wall of the folly.

'Show me the ball,' ordered Rupert. His gaze never wavered from the Archdeacon who had started to shake uncontrollably. 'Secure him, George.' Rupert took a coil of thin rope from his pocket.

George produced his knife, sliced a piece and tied the clergyman's hands in front of him. 'You'll not get out of that in a hurry,' he said, tightening a handcuff knot with professional pride and some enjoyment.

'Forgive me! I'm sorry. This is insane. There is no need - I didn't mean to – it was an accident. I don't know what came over me. You cannot arrest me. My calling, my lord bishop-'

George hauled Learoyd back onto the sofa and looked at him with contempt. He took his penknife to the wall.

A little colour came back into Rupert's cheeks. 'Do you always carry a primed pistol about with you? You did when you rowed back to Bourne Park to kill your father-in-law.'

'No, no! It is West's pistol. His initials are carved on the handle. He shot at me. I was forced to defend myself. You must believe what I'm saying. I didn't go there to kill him, but to plead with him.'

'About your wife's inheritance?'

'Yes.' Learoyd cast a swift look at the earl who was brushing dust from his coat.

George retrieved the pistol and the ball. 'There's H.W. carved on the handle, right enough. And the ball has the same hairline scratch as the others.' He laid the pistol and spent ball on the table in front of Rupert.

'You'd better tell us your side of the story, Learoyd. George, wipe his face. Morna, are you sure you're uninjured?'

'Perfectly. I am just a little shaken but my trousers are quite ruined.' The earl sat down gingerly in the remains of the wing chair. 'Do carry on.' He fortified himself from his hip flask.

Learoyd remained silent, his mouth working, his eye's still darting about for a means of escape.

'Look at me. If you tell us the truth, and we believe you, there may be a way of settling this matter with the minimum of unpleasantness. But first we need your full and signed confession.' Rupert spoke deliberately.

Learoyd turned his gaze back to Rupert. 'How can you guarantee-?'

'I can guarantee that if you don't tell us everything you will hang for attempting to shoot an Irish peer in the presence of a magistrate and two other witnesses.'

Learoyd looked between the four men and the unwavering gun. 'Put that thing down for pity's sake; I can do nothing now. It's too late. I have nothing to lose but my life.'

Reluctantly, Rupert put his pistol on the table but kept his finger on the trigger. He nodded to Bernard who started to write in an unsteady hand. 'Tell us what happened.'

'Why should I tell you anything?'

'Because there may be a way of getting you out of this predicament.'

Learoyd hesitated until Rupert said: 'Tell us or tell the circuit judge at the Assizes. The choice is yours.'

'Very well. I see I must take my chance with you. But I have done nothing wrong.'

It took some moments for Learoyd to gather his thoughts. 'I hated Horace West. He delighted in humiliating me in public, you saw for yourself. He harangued me in the vilest terms in private; a man can tolerate only so much.' He swallowed. 'Christmas was hellish. I escaped to Salisbury as often as I could. We were not a happy family. Then, after we returned from church on St Stephen's Day, my father-in-law informed us in the harshest manner that he was selling up everything, giving his family a pittance and leaving for the West Indies with his black woman as soon as possible.'

Put so plainly it seemed brutal to the listeners even though they already knew the facts.

'Frank stormed out and went to the Talbots. I knew West was prone to these spiteful alterations to his will and then regretted them, so I played the dutiful son-in-law for a week until the day of the hunt. It did me no good; West taunted me unmercifully. I wish he'd broken his neck on that damned vicious horse of his; it would have released us all. My wife and I were due to leave Bourne Park on the Monday and West had not modified his plans or attitude in the interim. The fall at Hinton had made him talk even more wildly and my wife and Mrs West were seriously disturbed by his behaviour. After dinner I went to the study to reason with him. It was impossible. There was a terrible argument, with the result that my wife and I left, immediately.'

'We know all this. Forgive me, but the money was not the only reason for the argument, was it? You sent a warning note regarding your father-in-law's intentions to Mr Romero before you left.'

Learoyd flushed. 'Do I have to confess my sin in public?' he asked bitterly.

'We are all aware of your inclinations and I presume so was Horace West. There is no need to record any of this, Bernard.'

In gratitude Learoyd continued, in an odd way relieved to get his justification out into the open. 'He guessed. He sneered and was offensive at every opportunity. He was as vulgar and ignorant as a savage. He said if I tried to prevent him from fulfilling his plans, he would inform my bishop. He had no proof of course but the merest whiff of such scandal could not be ignored. I would be finished in the Church and in England.'

There was a silence. Morna straightened his cravat and crossed his legs somewhat self-consciously.

'What made you go back to Bourne Park that night?' asked Rupert with genuine curiosity.

'Does it matter?' said Learoyd in despair. 'I wanted to beg for his silence. I had left in denial and righteous anger. Like a fool I thought if gave up any claim to Letty's money he might be satisfied and not tell my lord bishop of his suspicions. I did not know if it was merely a malicious threat or whether he was serious in his intentions to expose me. I could not live with such a sword of Damocles hanging over my head.'

He buried his face in his hands and groaned. The men shifted their positions; they were unsure whether to believe him.

Rupert continued with his examination, giving Bernard a nod to continue writing. 'You left Bourne Park at about five-thirty on the Sunday evening and then what happened?'

'There was trouble with the carriage spring. Nothing would induce me to turn back to Bourne Park or Larkhill. Our coachman said there was a blacksmith's at Sallow's Cross, so we walked the carriage and horses to the village but the smithy was shut and it was too dark to continue. We managed to get a room at Sallow's Cross Inn. I gave Letty a sleeping draught; not that she needed it. She was already in nervous hysterics when we left her father's house and was exhausted after walking the last mile or two to Sallow's Cross.

I could not sleep. I was frantic to get back and confront West about his intentions. I saw some rowing boats drawn up on the bank for the winter, under the willows. It was easy enough to slip out into the garden, slide a boat into the stream and row the two miles back to Bourne Park.'

'Damned cold though,' said George having experience of being on the water in freezing temperatures.

'Rowing kept my blood circulating. The moon came out at one point.' Desperation had kept him going against the current. The shrouded moon had danced like a temptress on the water in front of him.

'I rowed the boat right into the boat house.'

'Breaking the ice,' interposed Rupert. George raised a rueful eyebrow in acknowledgement.

'Yes, of course. I was about to go up to the house. West often stayed up late in his study; I prayed this was one of those nights. Perhaps I hadn't thought my plans through but I was a man driven by demons. I heard a scuffle on the path. It was West, reeling and weaving and waving his pistol, swearing damnation to all rioters and anyone who had ever crossed him. He was in no fit state to be reasoned with. I don't know if he was drunk-'.

'Drugged,' said Rupert, pedantically. 'And probably suffering from concussion.'

'Yes, I hoped it was so. I cannot be blamed-' He looked up, searching for sympathy.

'I leave that to your conscience. We are here only to uncover the facts.'

Learoyd gave a hollow moan and wiped his nose on his sleeve. 'West refused to return to the house and forced me back into the boat, trying to get me off his property, he said. He followed me, threatened me with his pistol. When he fired I swung out wildly with my oar. I was trying to keep him at a distance. The report of the pistol made him stagger. Either that or he was startled by the dog barking and some clock chiming. He seemed to slip and flailed round with his back to me. The oar caught him on the back of the head, and he fell.'

There was a silence. 'May I have something to drink? Water would do.' He was a beaten man.

Morna came forward and put his hip flask in the Archdeacon's hands. Learoyd raised it to his cracked lips. Their eyes met with wordless understanding. Learoyd choked a little.

'What did you do then?' Rupert was remorseless.

'I lost my head. I should have left him there, but he would have frozen to death, I knew. I dragged him into the boat and hauled for my life out into the river Bourne. I rowed in the direction of Larkhill. I wanted the body as far away from the Park and Sallow's Cross as possible.'

'Did you not think to check if he were still alive?' asked Durrington.

'No. I was only thankful that the brute was no more. I rowed until I could see the packhorse bridge round the bend and tipped the body in the water. I thought he would float much further downstream.'

He had rowed three miles back to the inn and slept like the dead.

Rupert looked slowly around at the others who nodded in acceptance. Learoyd had given them enough that they could believe.

'What will you do with me now? I have told you all I know. I struck West in self-defence; I did not mean to kill him.'

'Was it you, guessing that Askew knew about the draft documents, who set the fire and shot at him through the window?'

Rupert had the incriminating pistol ball but needed to hear a confession from Learoyd's own lips. Bernard's steel nib scratched on.

'I am heartily ashamed of it. But Frank had brought in that damned Runner. I didn't know he was going to blame your servant, Darville. I thought he would discover things none of us could afford to have revealed. Cuttle interviewed Askew and I had no idea what had been let slip about my father-in-law's plans. My life has been a nightmare for months.' He twisted his roped hands together in torment.

'Not entirely, surely?' said the earl

'Every moment was torture, I assure you,' he said meeting Morna's eyes.

'Ah, the cruelty of youth,' sighed the earl with bitter satisfaction.

'Loosen his hands, George.' Rupert's shoulders relaxed. 'Bernard, have you finished? Then give Dr Learoyd your seat so that he may confirm what you have written.'

Learoyd read and signed every page of his confession without demur.

When he had finished, Rupert stacked up the sheets and asked idly. 'Bye-the-bye, did you make any attempt on *my* life?'

'Good God, no! Whatever makes you think that?'

'Nothing of any moment.'

Learoyd looked confused and asked anxiously 'What will happen now?'

'If you return to Bourne Park and persuade your brother-in-law that the information he laid against Ombay was incorrect and that he should accept unreservedly my servant's story of nothing more than trespass on the day of West's funeral, then we may come to some mutually satisfactory agreement.'

'That's impossible! Have some pity!' A wild look returned to Learoyd's eyes. 'I cannot tell Frank it was me who killed his father!'

'I have not the slightest interest in what means you use, but Frank West must withdraw the charge against my servant. You might find him more understanding than you think. I believe he himself is in danger of being charged with attempted murder. You may wish to impress upon him that I have an unimpeachable eye-witness. However, you may tell him I will not be pressing charges if he cooperates. '

'I have no idea what you are talking about,' said a bewildered Learoyd. Neither did George or Bernard.

'Ask your brother to explain, preferably without a shotgun in his hand.'

Morna repressed a grimace and Rupert continued. 'I'll give you four days until I approach Sir Archibald Walcot with your confession.' He paused to allow the ultimatum to sink in.

'Even if the charges against my valet are dropped you may wish to consider a change of career. I hear the Anglican Church is in need of missionaries in Tasmania.'

'You may as well transport me now,' Learoyd moaned.

'It's either that or hang.'

'And if by some miracle I can get Frank to do what you ask, what happens to my confession?'

Rupert paused. 'I keep it as insurance. The day you embark for Port Arthur, someone will put it into your hands.'

****

Harriet guessed something momentous had happened. That night, Rupert and his brother kept up an innocuous flow of conversation over dinner and it was impossible to raise such matters in front of the servants. She would have to speak to Rupert alone. Ralph retired early; the delayed shock of the attack rocked him where he stood. Gaston sent for a brandy and put his shaking master to bed like an infant.

Harriet went to Rupert's room and demanded to be informed of the day's events and the true reason for Romero's dismissal. 'We promised we would have no more secrets from each other and here is Morna practically fainting on the stairs and you wound like a spring.'

'I promised nothing, if you recall. Do not concern yourself, Harriet. This business about West is nearly over. Jacob will be home with us very soon.'

'And then will you rest?' She put her arms around him. 'You look ill, my dear. What exactly have you and Ralph been up to? It's something to do with the Archdeacon isn't it? It's no use trying to protect me, Rupert. If I know what happened I can be prepared for what may come. We should share our troubles as well as our joys.'

Rupert kissed her forehead and put her gently away from him. 'You were correct in your supposition; once you had cleared the women that left only Frank and the Archdeacon as suspects in the family.'

'And foolish Mr Romero.'

'I fear Morna will never forgive me for denigrating his friend.'

'There will be many other "friends". Why did you send this one away? The children are very upset.'

'I, for once, am not responsible for causing dissention in the household. Morna packed Romero off to London to be out of harm's way. Thanks to the incomparable Bernard, Frank West has an alibi, which meant that today Ralph, George and I confronted Learoyd.

We wrung a signed confession out of him. He admitted the killing to prevent West absconding with the family fortune.'

Rupert would not discuss any other motive openly. 'Learoyd has four days to make Frank West withdraw the charge against Jacob.'

Harriet sat down heavily on the bed. 'Did he admit to the murder and the attack on Mr Askew?' Her brown eyes grew large in wonder.

'Manslaughter is all he will answer to as far as Horace West is concerned, though he confessed to the attack on Askew and the firing of his barn. We should be satisfied with that. Incendiarism is a capital offence. It seems we have enough to allow Walcot to release Jacob.'

'And the poor man has to tell Frank? Rupert, you do not think you may have driven him too far?' asked Harriet in alarm. 'What if the Archdeacon does something foolish to escape the shame?'

This had not crossed Rupert's mind. He considered for a moment. 'Then suicide would confirm his guilt and we still have the confession.'

Harriet despaired of her husband's attitude but reminded herself she should be used to his impersonal logic after nine years of marriage. 'Let us hope he also regards self-destruction as sin,' she sighed. 'Very well, so we must wait for four days and see what happens? What torture. I'm only pleased that George Durrington was there to lend some respectability to your efforts. But why did you involve Ralph?'

'We could not have achieved anything without him. Though I suspect he felt sorry for Learoyd.'

'After all that flirting by Sebastian? Your brother must be a saint.'

'No, just a fellow sinner.'

****

Harriet would always say that the next four days were some of the longest in her life. Rupert became monosyllabic and retreated to the roof despite the rain and the cloud cover. Harriet wormed the whole story out of Ralph and was suitably impressed by his account of the dramatic confrontation in the folly. The thought that Rupert's ultimatum may not be met, worried her. They had Learoyd's signed confession secreted behind the wood panel in the library which would absolve Jacob of all charges, though it would open a Pandora's box of trouble if it had to be used. As she tried to occupy herself with her daily round of tasks and the fractious children, only Ralph brought her any comfort but she knew he wished to be away from the manor and the nerve-racking situation.

Whatever Learoyd said to his brother-in-law at last resulted in a terse letter from Sir Archibald Walcot to Rupert Darville. Rupert ripped open the seal. Frank West had withdrawn all charges but political expediency demanded a prisoner in the dock.

The Crown intended to continue the prosecution because Ombay's presumed presence on the murder scene was considered sufficient grounds for the indictment. Walcot regretted this and thought the Lord Lieutenant was making an ass of himself but his hands were tied; he was sure Darville would understand. Consequently, Jacob was to be conveyed to Salisbury jail as soon as possible in preparation for the Quarterly Assizes.

Rupert crumpled the letter in rage. 'Damn all politicians, I'd like to pitch them all to purgatory!'

He rode into Larkhill to forewarn Jacob and Constable Hewitt; his mouth in a tight line. Harriet cried out in dismay, and then pulled herself together. She had to comfort Delilah and Clem when he came home. The children sensed the anxiety in the house and went quiet. They missed Sebastian as did the earl.

Morna was indignant. 'You mean we went through all that unpleasantness at the folly, I ruin a pair of splendid new trousers, nearly get shot, my secretary has left me and we *still* cannot recover your husband's valet?'

'We have not lost yet and Jacob is more than a valet in this family. We must ask Cousin William to help us again, but letters never seem to carry the right sense of urgency.'

'If it will be of any use I can bring forward my departure by a few days. It makes no difference if I put up at Brown's until my house is ready. I would be delighted to convey any messages to Mr McAllister.'

'Oh, Morna, would you? I don't want you to leave at all, and the children will be heart-broken, but I cannot have Rupert riding up to London, or even going post. The weather is still bitter and I'm afraid all this trouble has pulled him down considerably. I have not seen such rings under his eyes since his last attack. I'm not sure how much longer he can keep his health.'

'My dear girl, he is my brother. I agree he looks much shaken by this dreadful business, as are we all. Of course I will go to London and say all that is necessary to McAllister. I have every faith in your very clever cousin to find a cunning legal solution to our problem.'

Harriet, knowing William of old, was not entirely convinced and Rupert certainly did not want to leave matters to someone else.

'This is my affair, Ralph. You helped me enough when you asked Romero to – do what he did, at considerable sacrifice to yourself. I will not ask you to embroil yourself further; you have to make your way in society.'

He left so much unspoken.

'There is nothing more we can do except put Learoyd's confession into the hands of the Attorney General. William can do that for us and lend it any legal weight. I will travel up by the mail coach early tomorrow; I need only hand luggage.'

'Nonsense! I am just the man to explain things, if anyone proves sticky. I was there, you know, and was nearly murdered! If you go up to Town you are bound to say something cutting to the wrong person,' said Morna. 'Parcel up the confession and I will deliver it to McAllister. It is far better that I advise him of what's happened and that you stay here to keep an eye on the situation with Jacob. And on Frank West who, I think, is not to be trusted.' He rather liked the thrill of being on the fringes of an intrigue and was not sorry to have a reason to see Sebastian and London earlier than intended.

****

Morna took Learoyd's confession straight to William McAllister's chambers in Inner Temple. William had the tact not to ask how Rupert had acquired it, saying only: 'I assume no coercion was used in obtaining this document?'

'On the contrary, I myself was shot at by Dr Learoyd,' said Morna with some pride.

After kicking his heels in Whitehall for a week waiting for an appointment, William showed the confession to the Attorney General who blustered and hinted at the uncertainty of William's future career. William casually referred to his father whereupon the Attorney General modified his tone. Sir Hamish may have retired from government circles but he had been the *éminence grise* to Lord Liverpool's cabinet for many years and was privy to too many political secrets to risk upsetting the son.

'I must prosecute someone! Dammit, a magistrate was murdered! I have to set an example.' Sir Thomas Denman had held the post for barely two months and wanted to keep it.

'We could hold a fresh enquiry, sir. Walcot was not happy with the jury's verdict and recorded the fact at the original hearing.'

'You mean we could hold another inquest and return a finding of "misadventure"?'

'Better, I think, than blaming a mythical field-hand or leaving the matter unresolved.'

'What about this Archdeacon? Is he to get off scot-free? But we cannot have a scandal in the Church. If this ever reached the ears of the king I dread to think what would happen; there might be a constitutional crisis.'

'I understand that Dr Learoyd is suitably penitent and will be taking ship for Tasmania before the year is out. If one can believe his confession, and I'm inclined to do so, I am told that the death was partly accidental and happened in self-defence.'

The Attorney General was not concerned with the justice of the situation but his own predicament. 'Melbourne won't like it.' He rapped his fingers on the desk.

'I'm sure the Home Secretary has enough to occupy him, sir; there is no need to trouble him with this minor administrative error. He would not wish to face the Prime Minister if the truth came out.'

'What do you mean by that remark?'

'That an innocent man was charged and tried and possibly hanged when you and Lord Melbourne had been shown the confession of the real culprit. Lord Grey would not be pleased. I would advise keeping it between ourselves.'

Denham looked at McAllister's foxy face with misgiving. At length he said: 'You will arrange it?'

'Certainly, Sir Thomas. May I suggest that we hold the new inquest in Salisbury, away from Larkhill prejudices? Walcot is a sound man and can be trusted to round up a "suitable" jury within a few days.'

The news of the overturned verdict appeared in a discreet corner of the *Salisbury Journal* a week later. The London papers had long moved on to other scandals. Once more Larkhill was chattering with supposition. A verdict of accidental death was a great anti-climax; some were disappointed at the town being robbed of its notoriety. The original jurymen were openly indignant but secretly relieved; many had regretted their original verdict and the disturbances it had caused.

Those who had come to their senses said they knew all along that nice Mr Ombay would not have killed anyone; the Darvilles would not be supporting him if he had. He was only doing a "bit o' courting", so Violet in the Larkhill kitchen said, and now the poor boy was a cripple for life from that wicked man-trap. Sympathy swung in Jacob's favour.

Those who still murmured about Rupert's encounter with the gypsies and his quarrel with Horace West faced an audience of the respectable. It was acknowledged that while Mr Darville may be a little stiff, that was the aristocracy for you. Just because he refused to tip his hat to all and sundry it did not mean he was a killer. Unlike Frank West who was far too familiar with every hedgerow doxy and tramp.

It was agreed that young Mr West was behaving disgracefully; perpetually drunk, bringing all sorts of undesirables down from London. No decent servant would stay in the house.

His father had been much the same; it was no surprise that his poor lady had gone a bit queer in the head. Euphemia's sudden departure from Bourne Park was not to be wondered at. Mr Darville had been right to take a moral stand against such loose-living people.

Jacob came home to the manor. His short time in Salisbury jail had not been too arduous thanks to Darville influence. Rupert had paid for him to lodge with the warden of the jail. He returned to his valeting duties with much gratitude and the Darvilles agreed to his marriage with Delilah in the summer.

The day Jacob returned home, Rupert's knees buckled under him and the dreaded round of malarial agues and fever began. Harriet and Dr Makepeace spent some weeks nursing him back to health which tired Harriet more than she expected. This led to several female talks with Miss Humble and the revelation of the best news to aid Rupert's recovery.

Local gossip moved on, as Lady Durrington had predicted. A murderer on the loose was not good for business and the Cassandras in the Drover's Arms now turned their attention to Lydia Butterworth's new school for young ladies. Further up the High Street the patrons of the Three Crowns laid bets on who Larkhill's next parliamentary candidate would be.

Dr Makepeace was the only truly uneasy inhabitant but, as he had not spoken out at the first inquest and was not called for the second, he held his tongue, much to the relief of his wife.

****

Sometime later, when Clem was home from school late in the spring, Harriet found Rupert in the library of Quennell House. An ornate walking stick was propped against the arm of a chair. Rupert was rescuing more books to take to the manor but had paused in his task to stare pensively out of the window. Bright daffodils were nodding their heads in the stiff breeze. He turned as his wife came into the room wearing her driving cloak.

'Harriet? I did not know you were coming over today. What brings you here? You must not tire yourself.'

'I cannot trust you to limit your activities to anything sensible and Mrs Hobson had a crisis, which was no crisis at all. And I have some good news.'

Rupert turned back to the view and said slowly: 'What would you say if I pulled down Athena's Temple?'

'I would ask "Why?" It is a perfectly serviceable building and looks well on the hill. I thought you wished to convert it into an observatory when we eventually settle here.'

'Why would I pull it down? Because it is false. It pretends to be something it is not and that offends me.'

'But everyone knows it's not genuine. Goodness, there are hundreds of follies around the country giving great pleasure to their owners, or tenants. No one has so tender a conscience as to cavil at the fact they are not original.'

She went to stand by her husband as he looked out of the window. 'What's made you dissatisfied with the temple?' she asked gently.

'Do you think the children will be content in this house? They have grown up at the manor and regard that as their home. Am I wrong to want to bring you here?'

'They are all playing happily at hopscotch in the hall at this moment, can't you hear them? Henry has devised some fiendish new rules. Of course we'll be happy here and I cannot see Clem barring the children from Larkhill Manor when he comes into possession. But you have cleverly avoided my question about the temple. Why would you consider pulling it down? Does it hold such unhappy memories for you? Are you still thinking of Dr Learoyd?'

'No,' he answered slowly. 'But I find a folly somehow ridiculous and superfluous to my needs in this modern age.'

'I never thought that you would abandon your goddess.'

'Goddess?'

'Athena. The goddess of mathematics, wisdom, boldness and a hundred and one other things. But you may do whatever you wish, my dear, with your own property. I would only ask that you postpone any decision for a little while or I fear you may lose a prospective tenant.'

Rupert awoke from his reverie to look down at her in enquiry. She was in blooming health and had never looked lovelier.

'My good news,' continued Harriet 'is that I have had a letter from the Carters in Harrogate. They are taking the waters; such a splendid idea, we should try it ourselves. You remember them surely? It seems that now both girls are married and settled, Mr and Mrs Carter are hoping to find a permanent home in Wiltshire.'

She rustled in her reticule and drew out a folded sheet of notepaper. 'Mrs Carter hopes that Quennell House is vacant and that you will take them as tenants while they look for a house of their own.'

'The Carters? Yes, I remember them. Mr Carter is a sensible man. His son is an engineer of note.'

'Mrs Carter particularly looks forward to reviving her tea parties in Athena's Temple,' said Harriet half-quoting the letter. 'In fact that seems to be her prime motivation for returning to Larkhill.'

'Is it? How singular.'

'So you see, you cannot pull down the temple just yet or the Carters will not come.'

Epilogue

Larkhill was never quite the same after the Swing riots; too many of its men had disappeared into the hands of the law. Nation-wide, nineteen rioters were executed, over five hundred transported and more than six hundred imprisoned. The use of farm machinery slowly returned and the town moved forward into the Victorian Age, although the English never gave up rioting.

Delilah became Harriet's permanent nursery maid even though all the children were sent willingly to school after a carefree summer. Henry joined Young Clem as a weekly boarder in Salisbury and the three little girls enrolled in Miss Butterworth's Academy for Young Ladies in Larkhill as day pupils. Miss Humble gladly took on the role of housekeeper at the manor which relieved Harriet who found her hands full as the year went on. In the autumn, the Darvilles were blessed with another daughter, Ralphina Victoria, who was christened in St Saviour's church.

The earl was touched at the name and was a generous uncle and godfather when he visited. However, after three years indulging in the excitements of the capital he finally sold Castle Morna and most of its land to a South American mining millionaire. He took his fortune back to Naples accompanied by an even younger and more beautiful boy.

Rupert finished writing his book. He regretted the loss of the family property but could not blame his brother who insisted on sharing half the proceeds of the sale with him. Rupert made wise investments in the Great Western Railway and was no longer dependent on Harriet's money. What pleased Rupert even more was the gift of the restored Darville emeralds to Harriet. Ralph had gone to considerable trouble to find, buy them back and have them refurbished. Harriet salved her conscience by putting them away for Henry's future wife.

Bourne Park was sold. Frank West disappeared to London to drink and gamble away what money his father had left. He never spoke to his brother-in-law again. A few weeks before he was due to embark for Port Arthur, Dr Learoyd became one of the first victims of the Asiatic cholera that swept through England in the autumn of 1831. Letty continued to live with her mother in comfortable widowhood in Winchester.

George Durrington became the new Member of Parliament for Larkhill. He was quite shame-faced when confessing to his friend that he had accepted Lord Lydiard's nomination.

Rupert was delighted and Juliana even more so. Even after Larkhill was absorbed by the new Salisbury constituency a few years later, Juliana never failed to boast of her husband's former exalted position. For the short time that he held the seat, George was more than content to spend the parliamentary sittings in London among his naval cronies.

Mrs O'Leary did not go back to Ireland but found a situation as barmaid at the Drover's Arms. Rumour has it that Able Trottman has his eye on her.

The End

Printed in Great Britain
by Amazon